THE ROYAL DRAGONEERS

(THE DRAGONEERS SAGA BOOK ONE)

M. R. MATHIAS

2016 Modernized Format Edition
Created in the United States of America
Worldwide Rights

Edits and formatting by Dominion Editorial (Visit dominioneditorial.com)

ISBN: 1453887024
ISBN-13: 9781453887028

This is for Joel and Dee, two Dragoneers who didn't make it.

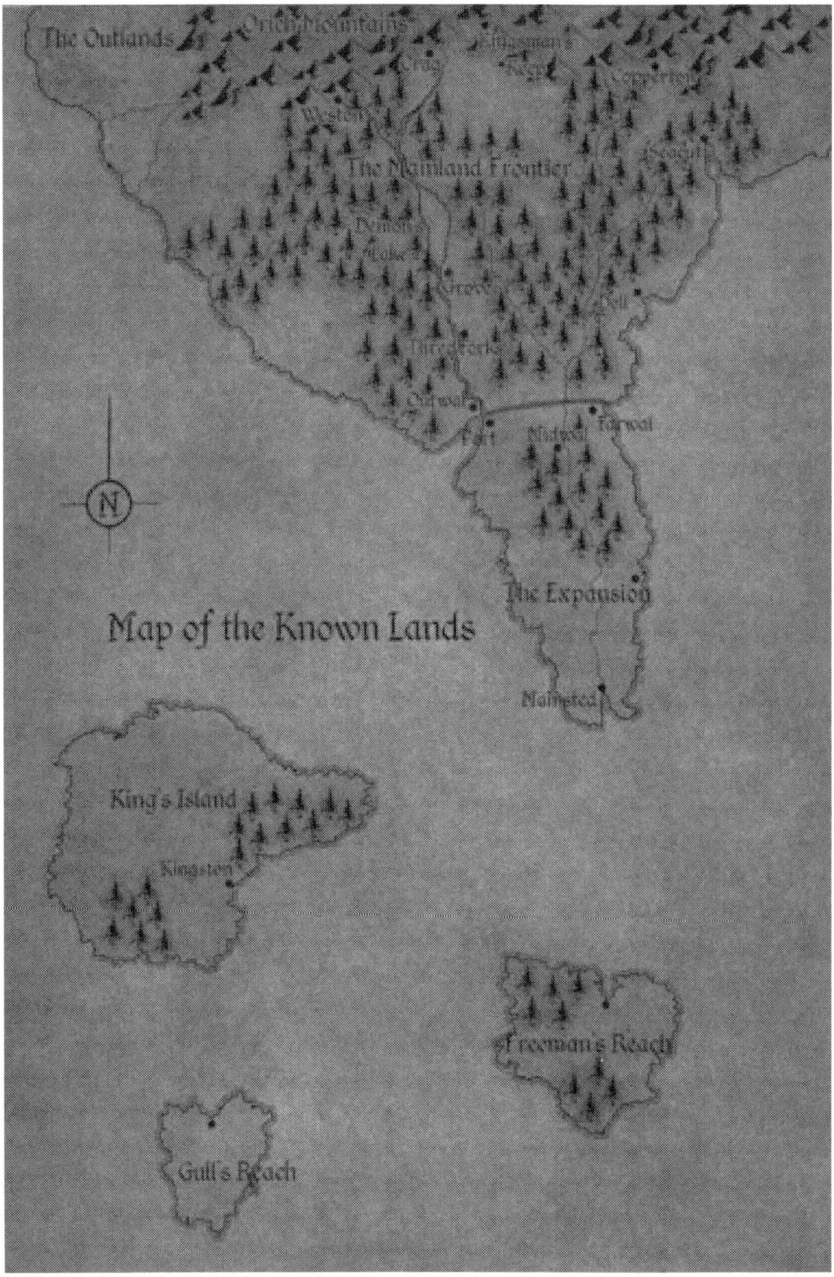
The Outlands
The Mainland Frontier
N
The Expansion
Map of the Known Lands
King's Island
Kingston
Freeman's Reach
Gull's Reach

PART I

THE FRONTIER

CHAPTER ONE

Jenka De Swasso peeked through the thick leathery undergrowth he was hiding in. The forested hills were lush and alive with late spring growth. The birds and other small creatures were busy making their symphony of life. It was a welcome cacophony, for Jenka was on the hunt, and it masked the noisy sound of his breathing.

Jenka was trying to see which way his prey was going to move. The ancient stag, once a beautiful and majestic creature, was now past its prime. One of its long, multi-forked antlers was broken into a sharp nub near the base. The other antler was heavy and looked to be weighing the weary creature's head to one side. All around its grayish-brown furred neck were scars from the numerous battles it had fought over the years, defending its harem from the younger bucks. A fresh gash, a dark trail of blood-matted fur leaking away from it, decorated the stag's shoulder area. Since there were no does moving about, Jenka figured this old king of the forest had lost his most recent battle, and his harem as well.

Jenka was sixteen years old, and he moved through the shadowy glades—between the towering pine trees and the ancient tangle limbed oaks—with the speed and dexterity of well-fit youth. He was dressed in rough spun and leather, brown and green, and when he stopped, still he blended into the forest like a bark-skinned lizard on a tree trunk. His face was well-sooted and the shoulder-length mop of dirty-blond hair on his head looked more like a tumbleweed than anything else.

Like any good hunter who aspired to be a King's Ranger, he was determined to get close to his prey, to get a good angle, and to make sure that his arrow went deep into the stag's vitals. A creature as undoubtedly experienced in surviving as this one could probably travel for a day or more with any lesser wound. Jenka knew that if he didn't make the right shot the creature would bolt away and not slow down. If that happened, it would end up getting dragged down by trolls or wolves long before he could catch up to it.

Jenka shivered with a mixture of excitement and sadness. If he could kill the animal, then he and his mother could eat good meat for the rest of the spring. He could also get a handful of well-needed coins for a shoulder haunch from the cooks at Kingsmen's Keep. It was a better death for the noble creature than to be stalked and shredded by hungry predators anyway, at least that was what Jenka told himself as he drew back on his bow to take aim.

The stag stopped in a small canopied glade carpeted in lush, green turf. The area was well illuminated; several slanting rays of dust-filled sunlight had managed to penetrate the leaves and branches overhead. The stag wearily bent its head down, pulled a mouthful of grass from the ground, and chewed. A pair of tiny, lemon-yellow butterflies fluttered away from the intrusion, their wings flashing like sparks as they flitted through one of the golden shafts of light.

Jenka had the stag perfectly sighted in. He was about to loose one of his hard-earned, steel-tipped arrows when the old animal looked up at him. Their eyes met and, for a fleeting moment, Jenka could feel the raw indignity the creature felt over having lost its herd to a younger male. The stag beckoned him, as if it wanted to meet its end, right there, right then. Jenka took a deep breath, resolved himself, and obliged the animal.

The arrow flew swift and true and struck the stag right behind its foreleg. Jenka squinted as the animal went bounding away. He saw that only the arrow's fletching was protruding from the stag's hide. It was a kill shot, and he knew it. The arrow itself would grind and shift inside the stag's guts as it fled through the forest, bringing death that much swifter.

The hunter's rush came surging into Jenka's blood then and, after marking the first crimson splashes of spilled life and the general direction that the stag had fled, he had to sit down and work to get his shaky breathing back under control.

Hopefully the animal would fall close; he would have to call for help as it was. It would take four grown men to haul the meat back to Crag after it had been quartered. Not for the first time today, Jenka wished his friend Grondy were there to help him. Normally Jenka and Grondy hunted as a team, but Grondy had recently been bitten by a rat while working in his Pap's barn. His hand was swollen to the size of a gourd melon. Jenka would have to track this kill himself, then run back to

Crag and round up some help before the sun set and the scavengers came out to feed.

The first step was finding where the stag went down. Jenka took a few deep breaths and tried to drown his excitement in the reality that there was still a lot of work left to do this day.

Groaning, he got back to his feet and set out to follow the blood trail. It wasn't hard to see; the splashes were large and frothy. Even the tinier drops were a bright scarlet that stood out starkly against the forest's myriad shades of brown and green. That the stag had been able to keep moving after losing so much blood amazed Jenka. It amazed him even more that the stag had fled upward into the deeper foothills instead of down towards the thicker growth around the valley stream. If the stag went too far into the hills, Jenka might have to give it up. Little gray goblins and bands of feral, rock-hurling trolls had ranged down from the higher reaches of the Orich Mountains as of late, and Jenka wanted no part of that. An ogre had been seen just three days ago by a well-respected woodsman from Kingsmen's Keep. There were also wolves and big tree-cats that hunted the area, but they were growing scarce as the troll sightings increased.

Jenka was an aspiring King's Ranger and knew he was already far enough up into the hills to warrant paying a little more attention. Heaving from exertion, he was none too pleased when he finally found the stag's broken body. It was lying at the bottom of a shallow, but steep, ravine. The creature had apparently staggered right over the edge and fallen into a heap at the bottom of the rain-washed gully.

Jenka had wasted far more precious daylight than he had wanted tracking the hearty animal. Now he had a choice: hurry back to Crag for help, or stand guard over his kill for the night. Jenka was torn.

Had he the energy left in him to run all the way back to the village he probably would have, but he was exhausted from the long, uphill trek. If he left immediately and had the luck of the gods on his side, the help he gathered still wouldn't make it back before full dark, not even if they returned by horseback. If he started looking now, however, Jenka was certain that he could round up enough deadfall to keep a fire blazing through the night. That would keep the chill of the higher elevation off of him, as well as keep the predators away. He wasn't all that keen on spending the night way up here in the hills, but he wasn't about to let the vermin have the meat of the once proud and mighty animal he had worked so hard to kill. Diligently, he went about rounding up sticks and branches and tossed them into a pile down by the stag's carcass.

While he searched for firewood, he let his mind drift. After pondering the shape of Delia the baker's daughter's breasts, and weighing that curiosity against the size of her father's well-muscled arms, he decided that he should worry about something else for the moment. That was when his mind wandered to the subject of ogres. More specifically, he thought about terrible old Crix Crux. Now he was glancing up every few heartbeats, scanning the area for the mythical, flesh-eating creature. Crix Crux was an ogre who was supposedly bold enough to venture down close to the villages built in the lower foothills around Kingsmen's Keep. He was responsible for the disappearance of at least six people that Jenka knew of, and probably dozens more from the other towns built along the base of the mountains.

Master Kember, Jenka's mentor, once told him that Crix Crux wasn't real, that the fabled old ogre just got the blame when someone went missing. Most of the time, he said being killed swiftly by a hungry ogre is a better death for the family to think about than the truth might be. Someone freezing to death because they fell asleep at their fire without building it up didn't make for good gossip. That, and the Crix Crux tale was good for keeping young boys from wandering too far away from the villages. Jenka laughed at himself. Crix Crux wasn't lurking in the thicket.

At least he hoped not.

At the last bit of daylight, Jenka climbed down into the gulch. He gutted the stag, dragged the pile of innards a good way down the gully, then hurried back to the carcass and used his tinderbox to start his fire.

Darkness slid over him like a tavern-wench's flattery while he struggled with his small, inadequate belt knife to cut himself a hunk of meat to roast. He tried not to think about all the wild and horrifying campfire tales he had heard over the years. It was no wives' tale that many a man had met his end in the Orich Mountains. Jenka knew all too well how treacherous and inhospitable these hills could be; his father had died up here. But if he ever wanted to be a King's Ranger he had to master his fear and learn to deal with the danger. Spending days at a time alone in the foothills was part of the Forester training he would someday have to take.

By the time he had his hunk of meat cooked, he was so scared that he had no appetite, and by the time he finished forcing the food down his throat, he was fighting to stay awake. Luckily, he remembered what Master Kember had said about Crix Crux, because it reminded him to throw some more wood on the fire before he fell asleep. The added illumination the new fuel lent the area allowed him to catch a brief glimpse of something gigantic moving about out in the shadows.

It might have been an overlarge tree-cat because its movements were sinuous and silent, but Jenka couldn't say for certain. A visceral knot of fear had clenched tight in his gut. He was far too terrified to think now, and he had to fight the base instinct he was feeling telling him, quite plainly, to flee. The slithery thing had amber eyes like windblown embers, and they danced with the fire's reflection. They hovered at a height close to his own, yet the thing had been moving hunched over on all four limbs like a bear or a wolf. Whatever it was, it was huge, and uncannily quiet. Reaching for his bow, Jenka swore that if it came any closer he would try to shaft it. He just hoped a mere arrow would be enough to deter the thing.

Eventually, the beast slid back into the darkness, leaving Jenka to wonder if he had really seen anything at all. Needless to say, he wasn't sleepy any more. He built the fire up even higher, and once again wished that Grondy, or Solman, or any of the other young hunters from Crag were there with him.

Jenka's mother was Crag's village kettle-witch, and she would be worried to death about him by now. Amelia De Swasso didn't have much coin, and a lot of people were a little afraid of her, but she had the respect of the other common folk. Nearly everyone in Crag had come to her over the years for a healing salve or a potion of one sort or another. Jenka knew that she would have Master Kember, Lemmy, and all the other hunters rousted out of bed before the sun was even in the sky. She might even send to Kingsmen's Keep for help from the King's Rangers. They wouldn't dare refuse her. Jenka's father had been a King's Ranger, and when Jenka was very young, his father had died in these hills saving the crown prince. A painted portrait of him hung in the keep's main hall alongside paintings of Captain Renny and Harold Waend.

All three had died on that terrible Yule day hunt, saving Prince Richard from the band of ferocious trolls that had attacked the group. Because of his father's sacrifice, everyone that knew Jenka went out of their way to look out for him. If it got out that he didn't come in during the night, it wouldn't surprise him if half of the village and a half dozen rangers came looking for him.

Jenka didn't let his guard down. He knew in his heart that the creature was still out there in the dark somewhere, lurking, waiting for him to fall asleep. He divided most of his remaining wood up into three even piles, until he felt certain that he would have fire until well after the sun came up. He lit one end of a remaining branch and tossed it down to the other end of the gully. He then took the wood that he hadn't put in his three piles and heaped it onto the flaming brand, so that he and the stag's carcass had a fire burning on each side of them.

Being that he was in a somewhat narrow gully surrounded by earthy ravine and fire, Jenka felt reasonably sure that he would survive the night. He sat to rest from his exertion and his exhausted body came crashing down from the rush of adrenaline he had been riding. He was just starting to relax when a sleek, scaly beast lurched down out of the darkened sky.

It was a dragon, Jenka realized, and he turned and bolted. He ran as fast as he could go down the gully into the darkness. He managed to grab up his bow as he went, but the primal urge to be away from the thing kept him from even considering using the weapon. He ran, and ran, and ran. Only after he stumbled over a tangle of exposed roots and went sprawling into some leafy undergrowth did his mad flight come to an end.

While he lay there heaving in breath, he considered what had just happened. He couldn't believe he had just seen a dragon, but he had. It was a small dragon, maybe fifteen paces from nose to tail, but he was certain of what it was. Master Kember had taken him and a few of the other boys out with the King's Rangers one afternoon to look at the carcass of a dragon that had crashed into a rocky prominence during a storm. It was considered an honor to be invited on such a trek, and Jenka had gone eagerly. The dark, reddish-gray scaled dragon had stretched forty paces from tail to nose and had a horned head the size of a barrel keg. Its teeth were the size of dagger blades and twice as sharp, and its fist-sized nostril holes were charred at the edges from where it breathed its noxious fumes. Master Kember had guessed its age at about five years, which made Jenka think that the dragon he had just seen was probably little more than a yearling. He decided that if he could master his fear, he might be able to sneak back and kill it. If he did, he could claim the long-standing bounty that King Blanchard paid for dragon heads, as well as bring himself to notice so that he could begin his Forester apprenticeship sooner.

Jenka crawled to his feet and hesitantly looked around. It was dark, but the trees up here in the hills weren't nearly as dense as they were in the lower forest. Enough starlight filtered through the open canopy for him to see. He started back the way he came, and when he neared the hungry young dragon, he dropped to his knees and crawled as quietly as he could manage, until he could plainly see the scaly thing feeding in the firelight.

It was amazing. Its scales glittered lime, emerald, and turquoise in the wavering light as it ripped huge chunks of bloody meat from Jenka's kill. Its long, snaking tail whisked around like a cat's as it raised its horned head high to chug down the morsel it had torn from the carcass.

Jenka decided that he couldn't kill it with his bow and arrow. He probably couldn't even wound the thing. Further consideration on the matter was rendered pointless when a heavy, head-sized chunk of stone suddenly crashed into the young dragon's side. It screeched out horribly and flung its head and body around just in time to claw a gash across the chest of a filthy, green-skinned, pink-mouthed troll as leapt down from the gully's edge into the firelight.

The troll fell into the smaller of Jenka's fires, sending a cloud of sparks swirling up into the air. Another troll bellowed from the darkness, and from another direction a second rock came flying in.

The dragon leapt upward and brought its leathery wings thumping down hard. It surged a few feet up, and then pumped its wings again. It was trying to get clear of a troll that was leaping up to grab at its hind legs. The dragon wasn't fast enough to get away.

Like a wriggling anchor weight, the troll began trying to pull the dragon out of the air. As hard as the young wyrm flapped its wings, it could do little more than lift the clinging troll a few feet from the ground.

Jenka wasn't sure why he did what he did next, but it was done. He loosed the arrow he had intended for the dragon at the dangling troll. The shaft struck true, and when the troll clutched at its back, it let go of the dragon and fell into a writhing heap. The dragon flapped madly up into the night, leaving Jenka dumbfounded and looking frightfully at not two, but three, big angry trolls.

He turned to run and actually made it about ten strides back down the gully before one of the eight-foot-tall trolls appeared from the darkness to block his way. It laid its doggish ears back and gave a feral snarl full of jagged, rotten teeth. Jenka whirled around to go back, but found another of the yellow-eyed trolls waiting for him. He started a mad, scrabbling climb up the side of the gulch but found little purchase there in the rocky, rain-scoured earth. He clawed and pulled with such terror and urgency that the ends of his fingers tore open and some of his fingernails ripped loose, but he couldn't get away. He was cornered.

More of the huge, well-muscled trolls were leaping down into the gully now. Their filthy, musky-scented bodies were silhouetted by the dancing flames of the fire and they threw long, menacing shadows before them as they came. Not knowing what else to do, and as scared as he had ever been in his life, Jenka put his back against the gully wall and turned to face the grizzly death that was closing in on him.

He saw that his bow was lying back where he had dropped it. His knife wasn't at his hip either. Beyond the flames, he saw the shredded remains of the stag's carcass. The dragon had torn half the meat away in only a few seconds. The trolls would have the rest of it, he figured. After they had him.

A fist-sized rock slammed into his chest, knocking all of the wind from his lungs. Other stones followed, and the primitive troll beasts soon went into a frenzied ritual of howling and savage fighting over feeding position. Luckily for Jenka, a well-thrown chunk of stone bashed into the side of his head and spared him from having to see himself being torn to pieces. All he could think of as he slipped into unconsciousness was that he would finally get to see his father, and he hoped his mother would never have to gaze upon what the trolls left of his body.

After that was nothing but blackness.

CHAPTER TWO

In the swimming world of liquid darkness where Jenka found himself, he felt like a tiny fish caught up in a powerful current. He had no memory of how he had gotten to wherever he was, or how long he had been there. There was a fleeting terror still lingering in the back of his mind, but he had no inkling of what the source of his fear might be. All he knew was he was tumbling helplessly through a vast, serene emptiness.

After some time, he opened his eyes and was shocked back into reality by the blood-dripping, horn-headed visage looming down over him. Slick, iron-hard scales sparkled like emeralds as they reflected in the fire's dancing light.

Like some curious, amber-eyed child, the young, green-scaled dragon leaned over Jenka's prone body, locked gazes with him, and then spoke.

"Thank you," it hissed in an unnaturally soft and slithery voice. "The trellkin almost had usss. They almost had usss, but we have besssted them."

Jenka's temples pounded and the world spun crazily with his effort to accept what was happening. His eyes closed for a moment, but he didn't let the dark current pull him back under just yet. "How are you speaking to me?" He asked the dragon. He didn't remember much of what happened, but here he was, somehow speaking to a wyrm that had ribbons of torn and bloody troll flesh dangling from its pink, finger-long teeth. It was incredible.

"I just am." The dragon responded, more into Jenka's mind than audibly. "I'm not supposssed to go near your sort. My mamra says that, though you are small and tasssty, you are a dangerous lot. She says that you like to kill our kind. But I wasss drawn to you. You saved me from the trellkin, ssso I saved you in turn. That makes us friendssss, doesss it not?"

"Friends then," Jenka agreed, thinking with perfect clarity that such a friendship could never be. King Blanchard hated dragons. Everyone in the kingdom hated them. The wyrms had been completely eradicated from the islands. Now, out here in the mainland frontier, when a herd was pilfered or a lair was found, the King's Rangers always went hunting and tried to find and destroy the creature responsible. Jenka figured that it would be that way until the entire frontier, the Orich Mountains, and even the Outlands were cleansed of the deadly creatures.

"My people are wary of your kind as well," Jenka said matter-of-factly. His head and side hurt terribly and it was anguishing to speak. "Make your lair deep in the mountains where men cannot go, and don't ever get caught by the King's Rangers, because they will try their best to kill you."

The dragon nodded his understanding with closely-knitted brow plates, and then snorted out two curling tendrils of acrid smoke from its nostrils. "Nor should you ever wander too far into the peaks. I have a feeling that we will sssee each other again. Thisss happening was no coincidence. I will be pleased when that time comes, but other dragons, the wild onesss, will feast on your flesh, ssso be wary."

"Do you have a name?" Jenka asked with a shiver at the thought of being eaten. "Mine is Jenka De Swasso."

"My name is impossible for you to sssay, but you can call me Jade. It isss the color the sunlight makesss when it reflectsss from my scal—"

A savage roar echoed through the night from a great distance away and caused the young green dragon to look up and give a call of its own.

"That isss my mamra calling," Jade explained. "If I don't go, ssshe will come looking. I must leave you, my friend, for both our sakesss." The dragon stepped away from Jenka and poised to leap into the air. Before he went, Jade gave Jenka a curious look. Yellow, jaundiced eyes flashed first to amber, then into cherry-red embers. Jenka felt the dragon's gaze tingling over his skin. Then he quickly sank back into the peaceful and painless current of liquid darkness from which he had just come.

* * *

"Jenka! Jenkaaaa! Where are you?" a familiar voice called over the angry chirping and indignant cawing of several feasting crows.

Jenka's face felt warm and slick. He tried to pull himself free of the clinging emptiness that still gripped his mind, but he couldn't quite get loose of its grasp. He felt something small and hairy crawling across his chest and a pair of fat, black flies kept buzzing around his nose. The air smelled coppery and sweet.

"Jenka! Jen—" The voice was closer now, and it suddenly stopped in a sharp, gasping intake of breath. "By the gods, man! Look at this!" The man paused a moment, then started calling out with a more vigorous urgency. "Over here! He's here, Lemmy, he's alive! It looks like he's killed a half a dozen trolls. Hurry man! Hurry it along!"

The excited voice belonged to Master Kember. He was a former King's Ranger who had taken a crippling injury to his thigh in a fall several years ago. He was now the village Crag's Head Huntsman and the unofficial mentor and Lesson Master to Jenka and a few of Crag's other miscreant boys.

Marwick Kember had known Jenka's father well. He'd been there when the trolls had gotten hold of him. Jenka thought that maybe Master Kember had pledged an oath to his father to watch over Jenka, or to protect him, or something of the sort, because Master Kember did both efficiently.

Jenka was glad he could register who was yelling for Lemmy. It meant that his mind was starting to work again. He only wished he could find the strength to respond, or at least to brush the little crawly thing from his chest. He hoped it wasn't a scorpion or a blood ant.

He tried to open his eyes and was rewarded with a searing pain that flashed from his eyeballs deep into his brain. It was bright outside—mid-day he guessed. He squinted and saw Master Kember back-sliding gingerly down into the gully. A fit of coughing overtook Jenka then, reminding him of the heavy stones that had smashed into his head and ribs. He rolled to his side and vomited. All of the exertion caused his head to pound with powerful surges of more sickening pain.

"Don't try to think, lad," Master Kember said as he knelt next to Jenka and went about inspecting his wounds. "Lay it back. Your head's been bashed in, and your arm bone looks bent." The look on the old huntsman's face graduated from attentive concern to pure pleasure after he saw that Jenka was in a survivable state. Looking around at the carnage the dragon had left behind, the old hunter shook his head in wonder. "How, by all the gods of devils and men, did you survive what happened here?" Then he looked directly into Jenka's bloodshot eyes. "What did happen here, Jenk?"

"It's a long story, sir," Jenka managed before another bout of heaving overtook him. When the debilitating fit subsided he said, "I think my cage is cracked."

A heavy clod of dirt came thumping down near the two of them, causing Jenka to reflexively curl up into a fetal ball. It wasn't another troll attack. It was only Lemmy trying to get Master Kember's attention. Lemmy was nine or ten years older than Jenka, and he was a mute. All of the women in Crag seemed to marvel over his wheat-golden hair and his easy manner. Though he seemed like a dunce a lot of the time, Jenka knew that he was as smart and able as they come.

"Lem, go find Solman and Rikky, and point them our way," Master Kember ordered. "I'll throw some green on them coals over there and make a smoker to mark the way. Then you take a steed and you ride back to Crag and figure a way to explain to Lady De Swasso that her young dragon is alive and well enough for wear. Let her know that we'll have him home by dark fall."

Jenka heard the words "young dragon" and most of the previous night's terror came flooding back into his brain; the stag he had killed, the trolls, and Jade. How he knew the dragon was called Jade he couldn't quite work out, because the conversation they'd had seemed more like a wishful fever-dream than any sort of reality, but the memory of those magical amber eyes was vivid enough.

After Lemmy grunted acknowledgment of his orders and loped off to carry them out, Master Kember stood and better took in the scene around him. Here was a troll torn completely in two, both halves ripped open where savage claws had gripped it. Down the gully was another troll that had no head and only one arm. Lying half-scorched in an exhausted fire was a troll that had been ripped open from shoulder to groin, and right beside that was another with one of Jenka's expertly fletched arrows buried deep in its back. Master Kember knew the Fletcher's work because he purchased the steel-tipped arrows himself down in Three Forks every fall. He awarded them to his young hunters when they achieved the goals he set for them. Jenka had earned quite a few of the good shafts. The decimated remains of a sizable stag lay shredded and strewn amid all the gore, and upon closer examination, Master Kember found another of Jenka's arrows. He walked around, shooing the noisy crows, and studied the scene a bit longer. Then he stopped altogether and cocked his head. He saw something glinting emerald in the sun. The retired ranger paced across the gulch, stooped and pulled the object from one of the troll's clawed hands. Looking closely at what he had found, he let out a long, low whistle.

"You, my young pupil, might be the luckiest boy in the entire kingdom," the old hunter started. "Killing that troll by yourself is certainly a feat of notability, but surviving the battle that took place after is simply amazing. Did you see it? Did you see the dragon that finished them?"

Jenka started to say yes, that he had even talked to the creature, but common sense bade him do otherwise. He didn't want everyone to think he had lost his mind, and he certainly didn't want a bunch of the King's Rangers up here trying to hunt Jade down and kill him. "I'm not sure what happened after I was hit in the head," he replied flatly. "I thought I was done for."

"You should be troll scat right this very minute, boy," Master Kember scolded. "What were you thinking, following that old stag all the way up into these hills? You should have ran back to Crag and found me or Lem."

"It was too late in the day," Jenka groaned as he slowly sat up and brushed the irritating bug out from under his shirt front. "I didn't want the tree-cats to have it. It just..." He leaned to the side and went into another bout of coughing. After he spit out a mouthful of mucus and blood, Master Kember grimaced.

"Lay back down, Jenk. Be still." The older man moved in to hover over Jenka and began feeling roughly along his sides. "Looks like you did crack your cage. Maybe a rib's poked a hole in your gizzard. You're gonna be a long while healing from this, but by the gods, boy, after killing a troll single-handedly, and surviving a dragon attack, you'll make Forester this year for certain. You'll be a King's Ranger before you know it!"

Before you could become a King's Ranger you had to be a Forester for two full years. Outside of performing a *rare feat of notability*—one that was worthy enough to find the king's ear—the only way to make Forester was to place in the archery competition or to kill the stag in the hunt at the annual Solstice Day festival on King's Island.

Jenka tried to smile. He had been training for both events most of his life, he had just never had the coin to get himself ship's passage across to King's Island. This year he had finally saved enough, but now he probably wouldn't need it. This was definitely a rare feat of notability, and since it involved a dragon, the king would most likely hear about it. Since Master Kember had helped save Prince Richard from the trolls the day Jenka's father died, the king would listen to anything Master Kember had to say.

Jenka decided right then and there that if he was going to keep a good part of what really happened here to himself, then he might as well lightly embellish the rest of the story to protect Jade. "I think I got the dragon in the brow," he wheezed. "The trolls tried to scavenge my kill. I tried to stop them, but the dragon came tearing through. It was as dark as the forest itself and fast as lightning, but I think I got lucky and got it in the eye. Tell the Rangers to look for a black-scaled wyrm with only one eye."

"That's my boy, Jenk." Master Kember praised as he used a kerchief and water from a canteen to wipe some of the gore from Jenka's face. "I bet you did get it in the eye. I bet that's why it fled, isn't it?"

"I don't know." Jenka coughed some more. "My head hurts, and I can't remember everything that happened. It's all jumbled up in my mind."

"Just rest, boy. Don't try to talk, or even think right now," Master Kember spoke soothingly. He saw that the wound on the side of Jenka's face was already healing, but he paid the unnatural phenomenon no mind. "We'll get some hands to haul you up out of this ditch, and a travois to drag you home so that your witchy mother can fill you full of her herbs and her horrible tasting potions and whatnot."

While they waited for help, Master Kember went over the scene again. He saw that something heavy had stepped on and smashed Jenka's long bow. He decided that maybe he would take the boy down to Three Forks and help him pick out a new one. He figured Jenka was growing and needed a heavier draw now anyway. He then decided that as soon as Jenka healed a little bit he would take him all the way to King's Island. There he would get an audience with King Blanchard and tell him firsthand of what happened here so that the gossipmongers didn't get the tale stretched out too far. A knot began to form in his gut telling him it might not be the right thing to do, that he had some heavy decision making to do soon. Jenka's father probably hadn't wanted his son to be a mere King's Ranger. It was a short-lived profession for most, but a well-paid one. Either way, it had always been Jenka's dream, and Master Kember was sure that Jenka's father would have wanted him to be happy. He would think on the matter and he and Jenka could talk about it later.

"Master Kember!" a distant voice shouted. Jenka figured it was Solman and probably Rikky too. Grondy wouldn't be with them because of his hand. Jenka knew Grondy would have tried to come look for him with the others, but his ma would have corralled him in the farm house, and then thumped him good for the effort. Jenka started to chuckle because he was certain that he was right. Grondy was probably locked in his room this very moment, rubbing the knots on his head and wondering if Jenka was all right.

Jenka was surprised that it didn't hurt when he laughed. He poked at his scalp where he had felt hot blood pulsing out of him the night before and was further surprised to feel nearly healed scar tissue where a fresh raw scab should be. His fingertips were healing, too. A vague memory of Jade's eyes flashing crimson and the tingling of his skin under that intense gaze made him wonder. Had Jade magicked him? His mother might know.

Master Kember heaped an armful of green, leafy foliage onto the ashy remains of Jenka's larger fire. Nothing happened at first, but slowly smoke started rising up and branches began to pop and crackle in the heat. Soon a billowing pillar of smoke was roiling up and out of the gulch, only to be sheared off by the wind when it rose above the treetops.

"Spotted!" Rikky's distant voice called out proudly. Of the small group of hunters that Master Kember looked over, he was the youngest. At thirteen summers old Rikky was probably going to end up being the best of them all.

Jenka and Grondy were born the same year and were the next youngest. Solman was the oldest student, but Lemmy was the oldest of the group save for Master Kember himself. Lemmy was more of an assistant than a pupil, though. He earned a wage, and he tracked as well as anyone in the whole frontier. Every once in a while, the King's Rangers would come over from the keep and ask Master Kember or Lemmy to help them with something or another. Unlike the village folk, the King's Rangers favored Lemmy for some reason. They treated him with the utmost respect, which had always piqued Jenka's curiosity. The King's Rangers had more or less accepted Lemmy as one of their own, which, in the past, had sometimes made Jenka a little jealous. Even though his father's picture hung in the keep's main hall, the Rangers were never partial like that to Jenka. They made sure that he and his mother were well fed, but they treated Jenka like any other village boy. He would have asked Lemmy about it, but it embarrassed him watching Lemmy struggle to convey a message without being able to speak.

Things got bad for Jenka for a while. Solman and Rikky were anything but gentle when they half hauled, half dragged him up out of the gully. The long, bumpy ride on the travois was even worse. Though he shouldn't have felt as confident about it as he did, he decided that he probably could have just ridden one of the horses, but the idea that his friends—and his mentor—might shun him for having been magicked by a dragon caused him to keep his returning strength and vigor to himself.

He felt his head wound again, and he was sure that he was feeling partially-healed scar tissue now. By the time they finally made it into Crag, Jenka was starting to think that the dragon really had done something to him. Jenka's wild, gray-haired mother came hurrying out into the street to greet her son, but was waved off by one of the young rangers gathering around his travois. Without a thought, she shouldered the King's Ranger who had waved her away to the side and, after kissing Jenka on the forehead, she poured a vial of foul-smelling liquid down his throat.

"You killed a half dozen trolls, then?" Captain Brody, the head of the King's Rangers, asked over the worried mother's shoulder.

Two of the other rangers were razzing the one she had just bullied aside, but stopped cold when they heard their captain's words.

"Here," Master Kember handed something that was green and shimmering to his former commander. "The boy said it was a black, but I found this. It was dark."

"Dragon scale." Captain Brody took it and gave Jenka a dubious look. He reached out and touched the pink scar under Jenka's blood-matted hairline and, after glancing down at the discarded vial of kettle-witch potion, he gave a short snort of disbelief. To Master Kember he said, "I'll send a message by swifter hawk to Commander Corda down in Three Forks. He'll get a message to King Blanchard that will be on the next boat to King's Island." Then in a more commanding and enthusiastic tone he said: "Digger, you and Balkir go round up the Rangers. We've got us another dragon to hunt!"

CHAPTER THREE

The King's Rangers combed the area around the carnage, but they never found Jade. They did find another dead troll over the ridge. There was a pinky-sized piece of broken dragon claw stuck in its wound. The young Ranger who had tried to hush Jenka's mother had it drilled and put on a leather thong for her as an apology. She scoffed at him, but didn't hesitate to put it in her pocket. It would fetch a pretty penny down in Three Forks in one of the hawker's lots.

Jenka played the wounded young boy as long as he could fake it, which was only about four days. He limped around and groaned a lot, but since the morning after they had dragged him home he had been feeling better than he ever had in his life. Because of his seemingly quick recovery, several of the rangers were buying potions from his mother now.

One day, Jenka came in from helping the baker chop down a bothersome tree and found the small table he and his mother shared laden with meat and savory smelling vegetables. He thought that she had just decided to splurge until she turned from her iron pot and started swatting at him and urging him out to the trough to get cleaned up for dinner. It turned out that they were going to have guests at their table this night.

It was only Master Kember and Lemmy who were going to dine with them, but they were as welcome in the modest, thatch-roofed hut as the king himself would have been. The old hunter had come to ask Amelia De Swasso's permission to take Jenka to Three Forks, and then on to King's Island, where they would spend a few weeks in an inn and attend the Solstice Festival, and hopefully get an audience with King Blanchard. He explained that Lemmy would be staying behind and would come by and take care of the heavy chores so she wouldn't be inconvenienced too much by Jenka's absence. He told her that Solman and Rikky were going with the group to compete in the contests. "We will be travelling in a well-armed group. It will be a safe and informative journey for Jenka, I assure you," Master Kember finally finished.

"I'll let him go, Marwick Kember," Jenka's mother said harshly. "But don't you tell me them roads is safe and all that. I know better. Don't even try to pull the wool over my eyes or I'll shrivel your stones with a hex. Them trolls are getting riled up `bout something, and there'll be sneak-thieves and Outland bandits betwixt Three Forks and Outwal, and pirates once you're out of the harbor at Port. I was born out on Freemans Reach and spent my middling years on King's Island brewin' potions for a Witch of Hazeltine. Any fool who thinks a journey across the frontier is going to be safe will pay their price. Now you tell that handy dimwit of yours to keep me stocked in cut wood, meat, and bear scat while Jenka's away, or when you return I'll…"

And so it went until the table was cleared. Master Kember was happy to be on his way. He wasn't used to being scolded and harped at and it showed plainly that his patience was worn completely through.

During dinner, Lemmy seemed to fade into his own shadow and did a good job of staying unnoticed, but within minutes of the serving dishes being removed from the table, he had the horses ready to go.

To Jenka, the prospect of the journey was more exciting than anything he could have ever imagined. The group was to leave at the end of the week on horses the King's Rangers would provide. An escort made up of two green Foresters and one seasoned old Ranger named Herald, who Master Kember always spoke highly of, would ride with them to Three Forks. That would take about four days. From there they would hire a wagon and travel for another day with an armed caravan until they were on the other side of the Great Wall that separated Port and Mainsted from the wild, mainland frontier. In Port, they would board a ship and sail to King's Island. Then there was the audience with the king, and the Solstice Festival to look forward to. It was all Jenka could do to keep still. His only regret was that Grondy wouldn't get to go with them.

The morning before the group was planning to leave, Jenka walked out to his best friend's farm to tell him goodbye. Grondy's hand was healing nicely, but his father needed him on the farm. They had gotten a contract to grow hay and corn for some ranchers down in Three Forks. Grondy's destiny, it turned out, wasn't with the King's Rangers. It was behind an ox and a thresher in one of the foothill's golden valleys. Jenka didn't want to taunt his friend with what he would be missing, so he held back with his description of the coming journey. Even so, Grondy confessed that he wanted to go more than anything. It was a sad parting, and Jenka spent a few long moments after he got down the lane from the growing farm studying the trees and wiping the dust from his eyes.

Later that afternoon, a group of King's Rangers came riding into Crag all bloody and raving about a kill. "We got that dragon!" they bragged. "Felled him way back in Calf Horn Valley."

They had come to fetch Master Kember and Lemmy, but when they stopped by Jenka's hut to purchase some healing potions from his mother, they drew Jenka into it, too. He was lucky that Master Kember waved him over and handed him the reins of the horse intended for Lemmy. Lemmy was nowhere to be seen, and Jenka was too worried that the rangers had just killed Jade to care about anything else. He mounted the offered animal and followed Master Kember and the rangers out of Crag and up into the hills. They rode until dark, then the rangers lit torches for them to see by, and they rode some more. Jenka figured they were already deeper into the foothills than he had ever been before.

The group came out from under the sparse trees and topped a ridge overlooking an open, star-lit valley. Off to one side of the open space, along what appeared to be a washed-out stream bed, there was a cluster of softly glowing yellow flowers. The petals were bigger than any Jenka had ever seen before, almost as big as bed sheets. It would have been quite beautiful had there not been the long, broken-winged body of a small dragon lying sprawled across the earth nearby.

Jenka's heart was thudding in his chest and the lump in his throat was the size of a gourd melon. The dragon was the right size to be Jade, but Jenka wasn't close enough yet to be able to tell for certain. As they drew nearer, the dragon's scales began to shimmer a deep, greenish color. Jenka's chest clenched with sadness, but then Captain Brody stepped up out of nowhere and quickly said, "Hurry! Close your eyes until after the flash."

"Whimzatta," a faint girlish voice spoke with a tongue-tangling inflection. Suddenly, a sphere of stark, white light the size of a man's head hovered in the air a dozen feet above the dragon's twisted corpse. The air became full of humming, popping static and took on the clean smell of the sky right after a lightning storm. Several of the rangers shied away from the orb as if it were contagious. The dainty, hooded figure underneath the magical globe seemed to think that was funny.

This was the first time Jenka had ever seen anyone use High Magic, and it was a little bit disconcerting. He had never seen one of the secretive druids that the rangers sometimes spoke of either. The Order of Dou supposedly had a monastery or a temple somewhere deep in the mountains. Some folks said they were elvish, but Jenka wasn't sure he believed that. Due to their common interest of the forest, the druids sometimes helped the rangers, but they had no sworn allegiance to King Blanchard or the kingdom.

Jenka cringed when he saw a pale, tattoo-lined feminine face peering out from under the hood directly at him. The druida's gaze cut right through him, and he felt his scalp tingling as if his hair were standing on end.

"Is that the one?" Master Kember asked. He put his hand on Jenka's shoulder, breaking the spell he had fallen under. "It's still got both of its eyes."

Under the bright magical light, Jenka saw that the dead dragon's scales were the color of a deep, blackish-blue bruise, not green. He knew instantly that it wasn't Jade. He was surprised at how relieved he felt. He hadn't expected to be so worried about a creature that he had only spoken to once. Sure they had saved each other's lives, but the truth of it was they were supposed to be natural enemies. Nevertheless, he was glad that it wasn't his friend lying dead in the glade.

"Maybe I missed?" he shrugged. "It's almost black."

The druida's magical light suddenly disappeared. In the momentary blindness everyone experienced while their eyes adjusted to the darkness, she moved impossibly fast and slid up close to Jenka's side.

"Liar," she almost purred the word into his ear, causing his blood to tingle with both fear and arousal at the same time. Her breath smelled of cinnamon and ginger, and she radiated a soft inviting heat like a woodstove.

"Master Kember, I would like a word with our young troll-slayer if you please." She gave a respectful head bow to punctuate her request.

Master Kember's expression showed the unease he felt at being this close to the eerie—yet exotically beautiful—tattooed girl. On the islands, and in Port and Mainsted, the practice of the arcane was more commonplace. There were witches and charm-makers on every corner, but out here in the frontier it was rare, and sometimes shunned. Jenka's mother used magic of a sort, and he saw how people were afraid of her for it, but it was nothing like the High Magic that this druida had just been using. Master Kember gave Jenka's shoulder a compassionate squeeze and hurried away, leaving Jenka and the druida alone.

"It's all right, Jenka De Swasso.," Her voice was sweet and liquid, and it dripped into Jenka's ears and flowed into him like honey. She looked surprisingly young; barely a woman. She had four thin, blue-green lines running diagonally across the bridge of her nose. There was an intricately-decorated circle on her right cheek, a similar square on her left, and on her forehead was a silvery triangle that pointed down at the tip of her nose, giving her brow a permanently sinister look. A few tendrils of snow white hair trailed out of her hood. Her eyes, though...Her eyes were pools of sparkling lavender that were so deep a person could drown in them.

"My name is Zahrellion, but you can call me Zah," she said. "Why did you lie about the dragon?"

Jenka was answering before he could stop himself. "Because Jade saved me from a certain death at the hands of the trolls. I can never forget that."

"Jade? You know its name? You spoke with this wyrm?"

"Yes I did, and I don't care if you believe me or not. Just don't tell—"

She cut him off. "Oh, I believe you, Jenka." Her eyes grew wide with a girlish excitement that she deftly quelled the second the emotion showed. Looking around to make sure no one was listening in on their conversation, she hooked her arm in Jenka's and led him away from the dragon carcass. "I've talked to a dragon too, way up in the icy peaks. They choose to aid people every now and then when things come to a head. A time like that is at hand. Crystal told me that something evil has awakened in the hills. Most likely, you and Jade will meet again." Her brows narrowed as the direction of the conversation took a sour turn. "We have a common enemy, dragons and men. The trolls don't like the humans, and we are spreading and populating the frontier like field mice. King Blanchard won't make the move, but he has planned it all out for his son. When Prince Richard takes the throne, the kingdom seat will shift to Mainsted, here on the mainland, and once that happens, there will be no hope for the trollkin."

The word trollkin was a slang term that included the little, gray-skinned goblins, the larger, black-skinned orc, and of course the trolls themselves. After hearing Jade call the trolls trellkin, he decided that maybe it wasn't a slang term after all. Ogres, Jenka had deduced, were another sort of creature altogether.

"They are starting to figure this out," Zahrellion continued. "Already they've been forced into the higher reaches where the ogres and dragons reign. Soon there will be nowhere left for them to go. The dragons, on the other hand, can always nest out of man's reach. Only a very few of the most foolish wyrms get their selves killed. Those are usually the mudged, like this one. There are hundreds of dragons in the deep of the mountains, Jenka. Some of the wyrms are older than you can imagine."

Jenka stopped her and shook his head to clear it. He had lost her words in the feel of her dainty hand on his bicep, in the warmth of her smile, and in the conviction of her voice.

"I'm telling you that we have to find a way to make King Blanchard or Prince Richard understand."

Her voice showed that she was becoming agitated, if not a little angry.

"Understand what?" Jenka asked stupidly.

She jerked her hand away, let out an exasperated girlish huff, and clenched her fists at her sides. "That the dragons want to help us when the trolls start their war! They're in the hills gathering and planning as we speak."

"War?" Jenka didn't understand. "Is it the Dragons or the Trolls who are in the hills planning right now?" Jenka had no idea what she was talking about. He was entranced by her very existence though, and couldn't get his mind to focus on anything other than her beauty.

She stared at him for a few long moments. "You're daft," she finally said. Her eyes were brimming over with tears of disappointment as she turned and stalked away.

Jenka stood there, slack-jawed, staring at the darkness until Master Kember came over and started speaking to him. "Fargin women'll twist your thinker till it pops."

"What?" Jenka asked.

"Never mind, boy. What did she say to you?"

"That the trolls are gonna start a war with us. That the dragons want to help us prevail, and that

King Blanchard has to know about it so that we don't keep killing wyrms." Jenka couldn't believe he had retained all of that, but ever since the beautiful druida had stalked away, Jenka had been thinking more clearly.

"That's nonsense." Master Kember shook his head with disgust. "Fargin trolls can't fight with any sort of form or muster. They end up fighting each other. By the hells, they'll stop fighting to feed on the dead while you're cutting them down. I've seen it. You didn't tell her we were going to King's Island, did you?"

"No, sir," Jenka answered. "Is the kingdom seat really going to move to Mainsted when Prince Richard takes the throne? I mean, I sort of understand the expansion and all, but where did we come from before the Dogma wrecked on Gull's Reach? No one ever talks about that much."

"That's a good question." The old hunter nodded. "There's an age-old saying about it. It goes like this: Don't worry about how you got here. You are here, and if you want to survive you have to keep doing everything that needs getting done."

"What does that mean?" Jenka shrugged.

"It means that only a few historians even care where we came from, boy. A few dozen people survived a shipwreck that washed up on Gull's Reach. From that meager beginning, we populated all three islands and set up the strongholds on the mainland. Then we built that fargin wall to keep the wilderness out. Now we are trying to tame the land between the wall and the mountains so that we can grow more crops and build more cities and towns. We have achieved everything you know about. We're not going back. We've been here two hundred twenty some-odd years. We are going to settle this frontier, and the trolls and dragons can be damned if they oppose it." He let out a tired sigh and changed the subject. "We'll have to postpone our journey for one more day. It'll be dawn by the time we get back to Crag."

Jenka was only mildly disappointed by the news of the delay. He was busy pondering Zah's beauty and what she had told him. The ride home was wrought with anxiety and excitement. Several times he started to ask Master Kember a question but caught himself. The idea that Zah might be right, that the trolls would defend their homeland, couldn't be purged from his mind.

He fell asleep back in his mother's hut as the sun was just starting to paint the horizon, and he dreamed he was flying high in the sky on the back of an emerald-scaled dragon. They flew across the oceans, over mountains, deserts and plains, until they found the motherland. It was crowded and noisy, and a haze of filthy air hung over the people like a cloud. There were no forests or fields, and the river that turned slowly through it all was clogged and thick with muck. Even the sea around the land was black and shimmering with an oily sheen. There were factories, and shops, and buildings, and so many people that Jenka couldn't stand it.

Jenka wasn't befuddled with Zah's beauty when he woke up late the next day. He was contemplative and distant. He could imagine Crag a hundred years from now, all crowded and busy, and he wasn't sure if he liked the idea of it. He finally forced all the negativity from his mind, like he sometimes did when he was hunting, and was decidedly the better for it.

Beyond being as tired as he could remember, he was also beside himself with a giddy, childish glee. He was about to go on a grand adventure and, after being invited with the King's Rangers last night, he felt he would make Forester this year for sure. He had just decided that things couldn't possibly get any better, when he learned that beautiful

Zahrellion and another of the Druids of Dou were going to be traveling to King's Island with them. After hearing that news, Jenka spent the rest of the evening floating around as if he were on a cloud.

Master Kember was none too pleased about the unwanted additions to his group, but he kept his opinions mostly to himself. Captain Brody had asked him, and ordered the King's Ranger named Herald, to escort the druids as a personal favor. He also asked that Master Kember help them gain King Blanchard's ear. Master Kember didn't like it. He didn't like it at all, but he was willing to do it for the captain. Crippled or not, he was still a King's Ranger at heart.

Jenka said goodbye to his mother early in the morning, and promised to deliver a written message to her former employer on King's Island. Visiting a true Witch of Hazeltine wasn't one of the things Jenka had planned to do, but he loved his mother and couldn't possibly consider refusing her simple request. After those tears were dried, he went and found Solman and Rikky at the stables. They both had their long hair chopped at the shoulders like Jenka's, and they were doing what they could to help the two Foresters get the horses ready.

As the sun was coming up and losing its battle to light the sky, the group of nine travelers gathered outside the stable in a light, dreary drizzle. They all had their hoods pulled up high on their heads and their cloaks fastened tightly. Not even the inclement weather could dampen their spirits though, especially Jenka's. He had been assigned the pleasant duty of personal attendant to Zah and her older male companion for the journey.

"Starting a journey is always such a thrilling feeling," Master Kember said optimistically to his three students and the two young, uniformed Foresters. Jenka, Solman, and Rikky all cringed, expecting one of Master Kember's windy proclamations. They were saved from a lengthy discourse on the beginning of journeys by the grizzled old King's Ranger, Herald. He harrumphed loudly over Master Kember's voice, spat a wad of brown phlegm from a slit in his dark tangle-shrub of a beard, and snorted. "It's just the possibility that we might not ever make it back home that makes it thrilling, Marwick. Now let's get this cavalcade moving before the buzzards fly down and eat us where we sit."

With that, they started out of Crag moving south toward Three Forks.

CHAPTER FOUR

By midday, the late spring sun had burned the clouds away, and though the lightly rutted road was soft under the horses' hooves, there hadn't been enough precipitation to make it muddy. Birds fluttered about and called out merrily from the thinning copses of tangle oak and pine trees that dotted the roadway, and a light breeze kept the travelers from getting too warm. The chink and jingle of the tack and the occasional whinny of one of the well-mannered horses provided a constant and steady rhythm to their passing.

"I'm Zahrellion, but you can call me Zah." The white-haired, tattoo-faced druida said to the two young uniformed Foresters. When they didn't respond, she continued. "This is Linux." She indicated her fellow druid. "What are your names?"

Linux was tall and thin, with a cleanly shaven head and a dark, well-trimmed beard that came to a sharp point a few finger-widths below his chin. The tattoos that marked his pale face were very nearly the same as Zah's, save the triangle on his forehead wasn't silvery. It was a darker color, like deep stained mahogany.

"Mortin Wheatly from Copperton, ma'am," the bigger of the two Foresters eventually replied. He had short-cropped, carrot-red hair and looked like he had never missed a meal in his life. He was thick necked, thick armed, and looked as if he might be a little thick headed, too.

"They call me Stick," the other Forester said quickly, then heeled his horse away from the two druids. He was dark skinned and had short, straight hair as black as pitch that looked like a helmet on his head.

"They call him Stick because he's thin like a stick," Mortin explained for those who didn't get it.

Jenka, Solman and Rikky all introduced themselves, and soon a light conversation about the qualities of different types of field rations ensued. Mortin and Rikky both swore that dried venison was the best because you could boil it into a pot of greens and water to make a warm stew, as well as munch it dry when you were on the move. Zah agreed that dried meat was a good choice, but claimed that sea biscuits were better because they would keep for months and could be made with special herbs that revitalized a person's body faster. Her argument made even more sense when she threw in the fact that ship captains had been using sea biscuits, not jerked venison, as the crew's main staple for as long as anyone could remember.

"We en't eatin' neither of `em tonight," Herald, the King's Ranger, chimed in robustly. "Tonight we'll be pullin' pork till the stars come out. That's the only reason I like making this fargin trek." He was a big, gruff, unkempt man of a sizable girth. He didn't look like much, but there was no mistaking the ease at which he sat the saddle. And if you happened to make out the embroidered emblem on the breast of his filthy tunic, you'd know to beware, because the star of the King's Rangers was the unquestioned law of the frontier.

The hills smoothed out a bit as the day wore on, and the slow, rolling plains spread away ahead of them like plush, green waves frozen in time. Behind them, the mountains rose up, sharp and intimidating, but ahead of them the world was alive and full of the promise of spring. Multi-colored clusters of shrubbery and wildflowers sustained a plethora of busy insect life. This kept the scenery along the way from becoming mundane. As the sun sank low in the sky, they saw a thin trail of chimney smoke in the near distance. Herald repeated several times, for the sake of those who didn't know yet, that the smoke was from a lodging house and pig farm owned by a barrel keg of a bastard named Swinerd.

Jenka recognized the name and quickly put the big, scruffy man's face to it. Swinerd and his three sons often sold pigs in Crag, and sometimes stopped to purchase a liniment or a salve from Jenka's mother. Once, Swinerd had gotten into an argument with one of the King's Rangers and a brawl had ensued. Jenka remembered how excited the entire village had gotten over the conflict. Wagers had been made, and old Pete had opened a keg of stout for those who had the coin to buy a drink. Swinerd had pounded the poor ranger half to death, and Jenka didn't remember seeing either man back in Crag since.

As they neared the formidable and well-constructed looking log building, the smell of swine refuse, pungent and ripe, filled their nostrils to the point of gagging. The lodge was off the main road a short way, and beyond it was an even bigger, open-sided building. Under that gray tiled roof were rows of pens, each full of squealing piglets and loud, grunting sows. A young man, probably one of Swinerd's sons, looked up from his labors and saw the group approaching. He immediately took off running. A moment later, big old Swinerd was stalking across the turf from the lodge, trying to hold his big splitting axe high with one hand while fastening his cloak around his neck with the other. He couldn't quite manage it, and that only seemed to further agitate the intimidating-looking man.

The cloak was discarded after about ten paces. Swinerd's fierce scowl showed that he was no longer concerned with the garment. One of the sons was coming out behind his father and scooped it up as he came.

"You fat dirty bastard." Swinerd snarled and started charging. Herald cursed and then spurred his horse ahead while drawing his sleek long sword. He raised the blade up high and heeled his steed into a full charge at the other man. The two Foresters looked at Master Kember for instruction, but the old hunter intently watched the two men.

It was odd to look upon; two grizzled men charging at each other, one in drab gray and green ranger's garb, riding a well-trained horse. The other clad in rough spun and animal hides, running on his booted feet.

"Why in the world are they…?" Rikky started to ask, but his voice stopped flat when the two men simultaneously let out very similar, primal roars.

Jenka could do little else but watch, slack-jawed and confused, as the scene unfolded before his eyes. He wondered why Linux or Master Kember weren't doing anything other than watching, and decided that if they weren't worried, then he shouldn't be either.

Swinerd swung his axe and sent Herald's sword flying away in a twirling glimmer of polished steel. But big old Herald leapt from his horse like some obese tree-cat and tackled Swinerd by the collar. They went tumbling into a tangle of arms and legs that looked like it would have been fatal for a lesser man. The two men ended up lying in a cloud of dust, side by side, head to foot. After a short, but tense silence they began laughing hysterically like two rambunctious young boys. Realization hit Jenka then: Herald and Swinerd were brothers.

The old King's Ranger hadn't been exaggerating. They were fed enough roasted pork to fill a small battalion and they were welcomed as if they were the king's own retinue. The lodge's common room was clean and empty, save for one of the hands that labored for Swinerd. He was at a plank-wood table near the ale keg, hovering over a plate of food. The log walled, plank-floored space boasted a large, stone fireplace at one end and three shuttered windows on the wall facing away from the pig barn. Swinerd's wife was an excellent cook, and she was as nice as she was round. She hummed and sometimes sang the words to a trio of old folk songs as she floated about the table, keeping the tankards full of dark stout that had been brought there all the way from King's Island.

The younger men and boys listened closely as Swinerd recounted the tale of how he and his sons had very recently saved a group of herbalists from a pair of roaming trolls. The herbalists came this way from Port and Three Forks every spring to gather their wild growing wares. They had chanced upon the wrong berry patch this year, though. Swinerd and his sons had been letting the sows fatten in a thayzle-nut patch down by Demon's Lake a few weeks back and had been able to frighten the gangly beasts away before they killed anybody.

Zah suggested that those trolls could be scouts gathering tactical information for their coming attack. Three of the four men at the table, Master Kember, Herald, and Swinerd, shook their heads and agreed that was foolishness. They didn't have enough fingers and toes to count the number of trolls they had fought over the years. They spoke from experience, which had come at a grim price for a lot of men.

"Trolls don't reason," Herald insisted. "They can't think or plan beyond their instinct to hunt and eat. It's that simple. Wolves are ten times cleverer than trolls."

Linux never entered the conversation, but Jenka saw a look pass between him and Zah. After that, she held her tongue when she didn't agree with the men. Her face showed her displeasure, though. A light tension hummed through the air, save for when Swinerd's plump wife was there to smother it with her lovely musical voice.

It turned out that Swinerd was just a nickname, which seemed obvious to Jenka now. Their mother had named them Herald and Gerald, and Gerald had been selling pigs to the rangers up at Kingsmen's Keep just as long as Herald had been a ranger. Kaljatig was the name their father gave them both, and his long years of working the Great Wall gave it some weight. The Yule pig at the king's own table had come from Swinerd's farm the last seven years running and he was proud of it. Swinerd also sold his hogs to the good folk up in the other foothill villages, and two or three times a year he sent a herd down to Three Forks. The anger he had displayed at his older brother earlier was over just such a journey that had ended four days ago near Demon's Lake when road bandits got away with a score of his pigs. Herald had promised to come down with a few of the rangers and escort the herd safely to Three Forks, but the king's business had kept him from keeping his word. Swinerd's oldest son had gotten knifed trying to defend the herd. The boy had survived the chest wound and was out in the bunk house healing. Swinerd had just been venting his anger over the situation, and the animosity was almost already forgotten.

Zah offered to look at the boy's wounds, but Swinerd refused her as politely as his rough manner would allow. Herald tried to explain that it would be good for the boy, but there didn't seem to be any sway in his brother's superstitious stubbornness.

Solman, Rikky, Mort, and Stick were put up in the bunk house. Since Jenka had been assigned the position of personal attendant to the druids, he was assigned a room in the main house with

Linux. Linux had already politely requested that a hot bath be filled for him, and as soon as Jenka finished his meal, he went about getting the water heated and hauled.

Zah, being a young lady, was given her own quarters. Jenka had to haul a bath for her, too, but that chore he did happily. When the work was done, he was too tired to haul a bath for himself. Master Kember and Herald each got a private room, and though they were all the way at the other end of the hall, their thunderous snoring kept Jenka awake most of the night. It was during a lull in this nocturnal nasal symphony that Linux spoke to Jenka for the first time.

"You have a destiny, Jenka De Swasso," his voice was eerily deep and his tone somewhat grave. "Zahrellion does, too. What that destiny is, I am not certain, but the dragons seem to sense it. That's why they have approached you two. I think that your path leads somewhere other than to the King's Rangers. I believe that there are more of you, and I believe that your destiny is far greater than that. I also believe that the trolls are far more powerful than the King's Rangers believe, and this is troubling."

"Are you and Zah human?" Jenka asked the first question that came to mind. "Or are you elvish, like the village folk say?"

Linux chuckled. "That is not the correct question to ask, Jenka, but it's a good one." There was a flash as a small flare of sapphire druid's fire burst forth on the wick of the candle sitting on the table between the two beds. After a beat, the blue color burned from the flame, leaving a typical yellow glow. Linux grinned at Jenka's unease. "You should ask me if I have descendants that washed up on Gull's Reach after the Dogma was swallowed by the sea. Now that is the proper question."

Jenka looked at the strange man for a moment. The pointed beard made Linux' head look unnaturally long, and his eyes were a clear liquid blue that rivaled the depths of Zahrellion's lavender orbs. But other than that, and the tattoos, he looked perfectly human to Jenka. Jenka shrugged. "Well?"

"Yes, my ancestors were on the Dogma, and so were Zahrellion's, but neither of us are completely human. Nor are you. There were a handful of the elvish on the Dogma, and a few of the little folk, if it is to be believed. It's true that some of the members of our sect have a touch of high elvish in their blood, but it is thin in most of us. A few, though, are still more elvish than human. There are smatterings of high blood in a good portion of the kingdom's people, but if you tell anyone about it, I'll be forced to spell you into a tree-sloth or a mud busker."

Jenka met the strange druid's gaze and was relieved to see a wide, toothy grin spread across Linux' eerie, tattooed face. Jenka wasn't sure about how much of what he had just been told was true, but he didn't doubt any of it. He was quickly finding out that the foothills and forests around Crag and Kingsmen's Keep were only a tiny little piece of a gigantic world, full of far greater concerns than his meager hopes and desires.

"What are we supposed to do to convince King Blanchard that the dragons don't need to be killed? Ridding the Islands of the deadly wyrms had to be a long and bloody business. Master Kember says that it's a grim sort of work, but it has to be done. He says that killing dragons is part of our heritage, that by conquering the dragons and trolls we are displaying our dominance over the frontier, like the leader of a pack of wolves does over the others."

"Ah, eliminate the competing predator before it can eliminate you," Linux shrugged helplessly at the foolishness of it. "Men are not as primal as most species, but they are animals, Jenka. I'll not get into that argument with you, though. Zah seems to think that she has a plan. She hasn't told me what it is yet, but she is a clever, clever girl. She said that you were a dimwit," the suddenly juvenile-seeming druid chuckled. "I'll save you some trouble, Jenka: That means that she likes you."

* * *

Morning came far too swiftly for Jenka. Linux felt sorry for him, and saddled his and Zah's horses while Jenka and the other boys went through their morning exercise drills with the two Foresters.

The day was pleasant, and the first half of it went by fairly swiftly. Jenka spent most of his time turning over stones of thought deep within his skull, while enjoying the wide open carillon sky and the vigorous life that flourished in the world. Zahrellion's beauty, and the idea that she liked him, kept him wondering. The complexity of what she wanted him to believe, and how it affected his future, kept a brooding look on his face. But every now and then he would catch Zah giving him a curious look. After that, he would beam for a little while. Once he caught her staring at him from behind a fist-sized gourd nut she was sipping. She held his gaze when he caught her.

A little after midday, the road eased up next to the Strom River. The Strom came out of the Orich Mountains up near Crag, but it wound away to the west before turning its flow southward toward the sea again. A man with a strong arm could probably throw a stone all the way across it, but it ran swiftly and looked fairly deep. The rutted road would follow the river's general course the rest of the way to Port.

"We won't get to cross the Strom until we get almost to Three Forks," Mortin, the carrot-haired Forester, said to the other boys. "Tomorrow we'll pass by Demon's Lake. That's where Crix Crux used to hole up before the pilgrims and the Kingsmen ran him up into the hills."

"How do you know?" Rikky asked in disbelief. "If that's true, then Crix Crux has to be older than water."

Jenka and Stick both chuckled at the young hunter's sound reasoning.

"It's called Demon's Lake because the wind makes a deep groaning sound where it passes over the grottos, not because of the Crix Crux fable,"

Zah informed them. "When our ancestors first left the Islands and started settling here on the mainland they feared the place because of the sound and called it Demon's Lake."

"That's true, lass, about them howlin' caverns, but that en't why it's called Demon's Lake," Herald heeled his horse over and added to the history. "Way back when they was building the Great Wall, a 'fore any pilgrims ever dared to venture farther inland than the coastal strongholds, they came a 'hollering that a lake monster had slunked up out of the caves during the night and snatched a man and the cattle he was watering. After that, it went and killed and ate a dozen caravan men who had just filled the king's water wagons at the lake." He paused and spit a wad of phlegm off to the side. "A group of Kingsmen went down into them grottoes and found some cattle carcasses, and half a man's body, too. Then, after about half of them got roasted to ash, they realized that they had holed in on an old fire wyrm. They went back to the construction settlements, where the wall was going up, and got reinforcements with lances and crossbows. They came back to kill the savage red bastard, but by the time they returned it had killed most of the troop and fled for the peaks."

"If that tale is true, then those men got what they deserved," Zah said with a touch of defiant anger in her voice. "How would you feel if some strange creatures came and violated your home and tried to kill you?"

"How would you feel if you was one of them innocent farm folks that fire breathin' bastard was a' eatin', miss?" Herald's expression was a study in indignant righteousness. He spat another wad of dark phlegm. Then he spat his words. "I lost a fist full of friends and a few kin to them scaly fargin wyrms over the years. If you ever knew the truth of things, about how them dragons nearly killed off our first ancestors and ended us, then you'd have a different bit of reasonin' in your pretty skull." He huffed away some of his ire and glanced around at the group. "When the survivors of the Dogma first washed up on Gull's Reach, they had to fight the dragons just to get from the shore into the thickets. Learned druid or not, you haven't read all the books there is, miss. There's a bundle of journals wrote by them survivors. I read some of them back when I was stationed on King's Island." Herald's grizzly expression softened a bit as a fond memory intruded on his anger. "My betrothed was a scribe there. She'd been markin' copies of old manuscrifts to preserve them."

"They are called manuscripts." Zah snorted. "And I am sure it was hard those first years out on Gull's Reach, but we washed up in their land. We are the ones who…who…um…" She faltered and mumbled something else but no one heard what it was.

Everyone was suddenly sitting still in the saddle and holding their breath. Even the horses had seemingly frozen in place. All eyes, including Zahrellion's, were now staring at the dark, sinuous thing in the sky that had just completely eclipsed the sun as it passed over them.

It was a dragon, a big old red, and it looked back and down at them. Curls of dark smoke streaked out of its snout with its slow exhalation, and its scales glittered scarlet and ruby in the afternoon sun. It was an intimidating beast, and it was banking around for a closer look.

Jenka scanned around in a panic. There wasn't a tree or a sizable bush in sight. Besides the swiftly churning river, there was absolutely no place for them to run for cover. Solman and Mortin panicked and charged their willing horses away from the group. Master Kember just managed to catch Rikky by the saddle and stopped him from joining them.

"Stay together!" Linux and Herald both commanded at the same time. Herald added, "Mind your horses now! Don't let them get away from ya!"

Jenka pulled on his reins and his horse backed up close to Master Kember and Rikky. He looked around for his fleeing friends, and his heart dropped to the grassy turf. Solman and Mortin had almost made it over to the river, but Zahrellion was by herself, about halfway between them. A glance at the sky told Jenka that if the dragon wanted to kill her then she didn't have a chance. Then, to make matters even worse, Zah's horse reared up and tossed her from the saddle. It instantly rolled itself back to its hooves and tore off in a mad dash, away from the flying death that was now streaking down from the sky.

Before he could stop himself, Jenka found himself spurring his steed forward in a valiant gallop out to save her.

Behind him, Master Kember let out a long desperate, "Nooo!" But it was already too late.

CHAPTER FIVE

Jenka charged his horse towards Zah, which put him directly in the dragon's path. Over his thundering heart, he heard Master Kember screaming his name and the loud, low hissing the dragon made as it drew in the breath that would probably roast him to ashes.

In front of him, Zah rolled herself to her feet. She managed to give Jenka an irritated but appreciative snarl, then raised her chin defiantly at the closing wyrm.

Jenka was almost to her now. Her eyes were sparkling like chips of maroon-colored glass as she waved her hands around in quick, frantic gestures. Pink light seemed to trail from her fingertips, and it began to look as if she were writing in the sky. Jenka chanced a glance back, and his heart nearly stopped cold in his chest. The dragon's wagon-cart-sized, horned head was right there on them, and those slavering jaws were showing him a mouthful of terrible-looking teeth.

Jenka actually clenched his eyes shut and scrunched himself down into the saddle in anticipation of the crunching inferno that was about to end him.

"Jenka! Nooooo!" Master Kember yelled again, but it was too late.

As the dragon's jaws came snapping down at Jenka, Zah raised her hand and held her palm out, as if that might stop the streaking beast from having her next. With fierce determination, she called out a sharp, commanding word. A thundering blast of sparkling, yellow power pulsed forth from her open palm in an expanding wave that rippled outward through the fabric of the world.

Jenka felt the heat of the dragon's foul breath and could hear the horrifying roar that came along with it, but only until his guts were jolted. After that, everything was absolute silence, even as his horse stumbled and fell, throwing him headlong into the rough ground just beside Zah.

The dragon had pulled up at the very last moment and had managed to avoid the brunt of the druida's magical blow, but the concussion that pounded through the world, and the raw arcane power of Zah's spell, caused the creature to instinctually flee north towards the mountains as swiftly as its wings could carry it.

"By all the gods of devils and men, is it gone?" Master Kember asked, as he and Linux both spurred their shaky horses over to see about Jenka and Zah.

"It's not coming back," Linux said over his shoulder.

Herald, Rikky and Stick trotted over to where Mortin and Solman should have been. The old King's Ranger quickly took in the tracks and sign and concluded that both of the fools had let their horses charge right into the river. He figured they had been swept halfway to Demon's Lake by now, if they hadn't drowned.

Jenka was on his knees clutching his ears. Beside him, Zah was curled up into a fetal ball crying like a heartbroken little girl. Her tears were not from fear or sorrow, though. The expulsion of so much magic had emptied her, leaving her with none of her normal poise or self-confidence.

"It was probably a mudge, Zah. It might have had him, and you did what you had to do to save him," Linux spoke soothingly. "Don't judge yourself for it."

"That's not why I'm crying, Linux." She growled through her tears. "After King Blanchard hears of this he'll never...Oh, never mind. Just leave me alone and go see that I didn't just scramble what few wits Jenka has." He nodded, wondering at the strange emotions of women, and went to do as she'd asked.

"I can't see King Blanchard ever siding up with something like that," Herald said as he trotted up. He hadn't heard Zah talking to Linux, but his statement put a sharp exclamation point on her sorrow. He told them what he had found, and that Stick and Rikky were scouting down the river looking for signs of the other two. He didn't expect them to find much. He was impressed and a little intimidated by Zah's show of arcane power, but he felt that his argument with her had been proven completely. Still, when he spoke to her, he did so in a kind, grandfatherly sort of way.

"You see, miss, I just..." he started, but she stared fiercely up at him, and her severe look made him bite his tongue.

"You say that you have seen dozens of men killed by beasts like that one," She wiped at her tears as she spoke. "Well, all those men died because all of them, all of you people, from the king down to his mighty Rangers, are ignorant!"

"Now miss…You…Your…thinkin…somethin…"

"Naw! Naw! Naw!" she cut over his stammering. "You're the experienced King's Ranger, Herald. I'm just a stupid little girl! You've fought scores of trolls and a dozen or more wyrm. You have all that valuable experience, but your hate for the dragons and your lack of respect for the trolls has blinded you! You've never even come across a true High Dracus. Linux, explain to him what a Mudge is, and see if a bit of light starts to shine in that ranger's empty head!"

Linux looked up from where he was treating Jenka's bleeding ears and shrugged. He didn't think that these men, especially Herald, cared what a mudge was, but he was wrong.

"Tell us, then," Master Kember's expression and tone showed that he was actually willing to listen. He was speaking to Zah, though, not Linux. He wanted her to answer the question. "What is a mudge?"

Zah strode confidently, if a little weakly, over to Herald, who was still on his horse. She took the canteen from the horn of the Ranger's saddle as if she owned it. After taking a few long sips, she handed it up to him.

"A mudge is a dragon whose blood is so impure that it has lost its elemental conscience. They remain somewhat intelligent, but they are half-crazed. It's the black ones mainly, because they inbreed like rabbits, and they don't school their young very well. But the darker reds and blues can be mudge, too, especially when they mate with a black." Zah seemed to be regaining herself as she went on. "Those dragons are the ones you catch sampling the cattle and venturing close to your settlements. Think about it, when is the last time a King's Ranger, or anybody else, killed a silver, or sparkling blue? You haven't had any trouble from, much less even seen, a snow dragon up close in a century, but yet we know they are up there in the icy peaks because every now and again we see them in the sky. Think back on every wyrm you've ever encountered and you'll know it's true." She paused a moment, letting all of that sink in, then continued. "What the mudged strains of dragons have lost is still very strong in the purer High Dracus. There are living dragons up in those peaks that were considered old when the Dogma's survivors washed up on the islands. They have watched us, and they respect all that we have done for ourselves. They are highly intelligent creatures, so much smarter that we are, and they would rather the humans than the trolls and the mudge populate this land." Zah let out a sigh of relief, feeling that she had finally explained herself well.

"That's only because we taste better, lass," Herald deadpanned, which caused Master Kember to burst into laughter. Linux laughed, too, and thus the tension was broken. As much as Zah tried to hold onto her affronted expression, she couldn't help but break a smile with them.

Jenka missed the whole exchange. He couldn't hear a thing. The inside of his ears felt like they were crawling with stinging blood ants, and his eyes wouldn't stop watering. For a good, long while he was only able to sit up and sip water and look around at the blurry world.

The first words he actually heard came later, after the sun had set. After they had given up on finding Mortin and Solman, they built a camp around Jenka. They rounded up Jenka's and Zah's horses, and searched the marshy area for washed up wood, but there were no trees to provide the fuel for a fire. Herald grumbled as they munched on bread and sausages around an eerie blue-green inferno that Linux had spelled to life. The flames burned with a hiss, didn't flicker very much, and were so hot that everyone sat a good distance away from them. For Jenka, it was a very surreal feeling to be a part of such a scene, especially when you couldn't hear. He was feeling better and better with each passing hour. His ears had stopped burning, but they felt completely closed. Then all of a sudden, he yawned. His ears popped, and with a flood of relief, he heard Master Kember complaining to Herald.

"...fargin magic creeps my crotch. It's unnatural."

"Actually it *is* natural," Zah corrected softly from the opposite side of the fire.

"Things you can't see, powers that that can destroy like what you did today, aren't natural," he shot back.

"What of the wind, then?" Linux asked, looking at them all with open palms. "It can blow the thatch off of a house, but you can't see it. In the peaks, it can blow ice so hard that it'll skin your face raw. Is a twister evil? Is it natural?"

"Bah!" Master Kember gave up his argument and found his bed roll. "I'll take the last watch," was all he said as he went. It was obvious that he was upset and worried about the two young men who had been swept down the river.

"I'm going to give Jenka's ears a look-see," Zah told Linux, then went to her saddle pack to rummage for something.

"Keep watch till well past midnight, boys, then give Master Kember a shake," Herald rumbled to Stick and Rikky, who were at the far edge of the illuminated, blue area. Then he made to turn in for the night. "If there comes a problem, don't wake me," he added with a nod of grudging respect at Zah's back. "Wake that girl. Let her deal with it."

Jenka had to bite back a chuckle. He didn't want anyone to know that he could hear just yet. He needed to think long and hard about everything he was learning about the dragons, the trolls, and the ways of men. It was hard to imagine that, not so long ago, his life's entire focus had been narrowed down solely to his quest to become a Forester and then a King's Ranger. Now he wasn't sure what he wanted, or needed, to do.

Jenka looked up and smiled, as Zah eased up beside him. Her pale face shone blue in the magical fire's steady light, and the triangle on her forehead glittered faintly with the reflection. When she whispered, "How are you feeling?" he acted like he hadn't heard her.

Tenderly, she inspected his ears. Her fingers were soft and tickly on his neck, and he had to wiggle his shoulder when the sensation became too intense. He truly liked her touch. When she softly whispered to him, her warm breath found his skin and stirred his feelings on a whole other level.

"Thank you, Jenka De Swasso, for that chivalrous attempt to rescue me today. If you could hear me, I doubt I would be so bold with my heart, but the spark you have tendered in me is potent." Her lips were so close to his temple that she might as well have been kissing him. "I have a feeling that the emotion might someday grow into an inferno and consume me. I know beyond a doubter's shadow that I'm not the one for you. That is why I have to ignore my feelings. I must keep them to myself. There is too much at stake." With that, she kissed his forehead softly, like a loving sister might, then went and curled up in her blankets near where Linux was quietly meditating.

After a short, confusing while, Jenka rose and joined Rikky and Stick, where they were posted at the edge of the weird blue-green fire's light. "What happened to Solman and Mort?" he asked them quietly. "Where are they?"

"So you can hear again, then?" Rikky grinned with relief. "You're a dimbuss, Jenk. You almost got charred up. You're lucky Zah did that…that… that yellow thing."

Jenka feigned a sharp whack at the younger hunter. Rikky ducked playfully. "I asked where Solman and Mort were, not for your thoughts on my foolishness, boy." Jenka's imitation of Master Kember was spot-on, but he was paling as he hunkered down between the other two.

"They rode off into the Strom," Stick said, with a look at Jenka that, somehow, combined reverence with doubt and concern. "Are you all right? You don't know how close you came today." The odd light caused Stick's eyes to contrast drastically with his dark skin.

"It doesn't matter." Jenka sighed. He knew that Solman was an expert woodsman and would be able to take care of himself if he hadn't drowned. Mortin he wasn't so sure about. Either way, he was fading quickly. He felt as if he had to rest now, and his body was demanding that he do just that. He lay back and closed his eyes, and immediately fell asleep on the turf. Rikky covered him with a blanket, and Jenka didn't wake until nearly dawn when Master Kember started booting him in the side.

"If you're drilling with the others, then get your arse a moving, Jenk," the old man said with another nudge of his boot tip. "If not, then get your arse up and start saddling the horses!" Jenka didn't move. "Rikky done told me you could hear again, so quit testing me."

Jenka groaned and grabbed at his back. In actuality, he felt great. Whatever Jade had done to him back up in the foothills was having a lingering effect. All of his wounds, especially his ears, were healing unnaturally fast. He wasn't a slacker, and he had never tried to get out of doing his duty before, but he didn't feel like drilling with the others today. He wasn't sure if he still wanted to be a King's Ranger, so he gave Master Kember an apologetic grin and went about readying the horses.

They made it to Demon's Lake that afternoon. It was a massive natural reservoir surrounded by ancient, dangling willow trees, wild tangle-limbed oaks, and shrub and undergrowth hearty enough to survive beneath them. Like a wavering natural fortress wall, a thick band of chest-high grass hugged the shoreline elsewhere. Beyond that was nothing but chill, cobalt water reflecting the sinking, copper sun in its wavering ripples. The lake was so vast that it extended all the way into the western horizon.

While looking for signs of Solman and Mortin, they came across fresh troll tracks. Individual and paired troll tracks were not an uncommon sight around the lake, but these tracks had been left by a gang of trolls numbering almost half a score. They had Herald scratching his head and glancing at Zahrellion. He wasn't ready to admit it, but he was starting to think that she wasn't so foolish after all.

"Must have been a dozen or more of them goblinkin come through here yesterday," he concluded. "One of them is carrying a staff or a pike."

"It could be a spear butt, or just a stick, or something else," Master Kember put in.

"My instincts tell me it's a walking stick or a staff. Look how deep," he inserted his finger halfway into a perfectly round hole in the soft ground. "They're all that deep and evenly spaced, like someone is leaning on a walking stick heavily."

"A troll using a walking stick?" Master Kember raised a brow at the King's Ranger.

"Don't make sense, do it?" Herald replied, with another glance at Zah. He gave Jenka and Master

Kember a strange look; the look a man has just before he starts into something he doesn't really want to do, then led his horse over to Zah.

"These trolls that are supposed to attack us, how do they communicate? Do they actually speak, or are they like critters and get along with posture and noises and such?"

"I'm certain that they have a language all their own," Zah answered, with a look to Linux for help with the response. She didn't feel that she could trust these men to tell them the truth: that a dragon had told her some dark force had awakened to lead the goblinkin against the expanding kingdom of men.

"One of our peers has been trying to imitate the grunts and growls of trolls for over a decade now," Linux explained. "Trollkin, goblinkin, whatever you want to call them, are built differently than we are. He has had little success with it, because the troll's throat is so complex that we can't make most of the sounds they use, but he has learned by his long experience with them that they are communicating with sound. Why do you ask?"

"Well I'm pondering if a man might learn to get along with them, to help them plan and such?"

"That is a good question, isn't it?" Linux asked them both. "And if this person could communicate and organize the trolls, could he not do the same with the mudge?"

"If it was a druid or a mage, couldn't they spell the trolls into doing their bidding? My ma once spelled a man to build a garden for his wife and it worked," Jenka said.

All eyes turned to Jenka then. Zah let the corner of her mouth turn up a fraction, and Linux made weird shapes with his mouth as he thought the possibility over. Master Kember remembered when young Orvin Longgras had built that garden. He frowned and shook his head at the fact that Witch Magic had been involved.

"I don't know `bout all that," Herald said, matter-of-factly. "But I know we got to get to King's Island and let King Blanchard know there be dragons in the skies, and gangs of trolls wandering around the lake attacking berry pickers and herbalists. That's my duty."

"Well, we need to find them boys first," Master Kember reminded.

"Agreed," Herald nodded. "But after that, we need to make some haste, `cause my old Kingsman's skull en't as empty as the lass might think. She might be seeing things better than the rest of us have been, but I en't blind!"

Just then, from a great distance into the chest high swamp grass, Rikky let out a keening wail. Master Kember was off at a gallop and Jenka was right behind him. Before they had even gone twenty feet, Stick's frantic voice came calling from the same area, "Over here! Over here! One of `em's dead! Over here!"

CHAPTER SIX

Jenka had to fight the urge to vomit when he slogged into the high grass and saw what the two boys were hovering over. It was Solman who had met his end there, and young Rikky had found him. Solman's pale, mud-splattered body was wide open across the middle, and the cavity that should have held his innards had been picked clean by the early scavengers. His head was lying at an odd angle, and one of his arms was horribly twisted. A more substantial creature had worried away most of his face, but his pants and boots were completely recognizable. There was no mistake as to who it was. Master Kember was trying to urge them all away so that he and Herald could look at the sign before it was completely trampled, but it was no use. Rikky was fiercely clinging to Salmon's body and sobbing pitifully.

"It's all right, Kember!" Herald said, loud enough to stop him from pulling Ricky off of the corpse. Behind Herald, Zah looked down from her mount and gasped. She spurred her horse quickly away, and Linux, who had already dismounted, sloshed off to tend to her.

"'Tweren't no troll did that," the King's Ranger said harshly. "That be a sword slash, or I'm a pixie's pecker-head."

"Probably those bandits that got your nephew," Jenka said the first thing that came to his mind.

"I reckon it is," Herald let out a long, low sigh. "The other one is probably close. If not, he got away."

Master Kember was looking at Jenka, and would have commented on his quick reasoning, had he not been nearly overcome with his anger over the loss of one of the boys in his charge. He was fuming, and seriously considered stopping the journey to King's Island in order to hunt down the bandits that did this.

Finally, Stick got Rikky to move. Herald stepped in and looked the area over, shaking his head in sheer disgust the whole time. When he stepped away and moved over to Master Kember's side, Jenka eased closer to listen.

"It's them fargin bandits. I'm sure of it." He twisted his neck and cringed in his chin. "I'm thinking our boys walked up out of this swamp grass and startled `em."

"What makes you say that?" Linux asked curiously, startling them all. None of the experienced woodsmen had even sensed the druid coming up behind them.

"That's a sword slash, the kind you make when you're facing a foe and defending ground." Herald snorted deeply, then spat a wad of phlegm off to the side. He rolled his shoulders, trying to picture the scene in his mind. "If you were going to kill someone deliberate with a sword, you would just run `em through."

"Or open their neck," Jenka added out loud before he realized he had spoken.

"Just so," Herald gave a nod of grim respect to Jenka, and continued. "There's a problem here, though. That carrot-headed boy is probably a captive. If he came up out of the brush behind Solman, he'd have been able to yell out and keep from gettin' killed."

"I don't understand." Linux looked at them all with his slick, bald head cocked sideways.

Jenka answered, and felt comfortable doing so, which caught Zah's attention. He really wasn't as stupid as she had first thought. "Those bandits have to be weary of the frontier, just like we do. When Solman came out of the grass, the bandits probably thought he was a troll," explained Jenka. "Solman and Mortin, if they were still together, most likely thought that the fire hole over there was from our camp. I doubt they had any idea of how far ahead of us the current carried them."

"Mortin has been around here some," Stick chimed in. "He labored down at Midwal for a stretch. He told me that he rode a few times with the Walguard when they came through Three Forks to watch over the clay pit caravans. That's where he did his feat of notability, fighting bandits in them tangle woods over there."

"What's the clay pit?" Jenka asked. The Walguard he knew, they were the men who not only manned the Great Wall stretching all the way across the neck of the mainland continent, but they also rode guard for supply caravans that came out into the frontier to gather materials, such as lumber and stone, for the kingdom's continuous construction needs. Jenka knew that there was a sizable outpost in Three Forks, called simply Three Forks

Stronghold. It housed and sustained members of the Walguard, the King's Rangers, and several of the more civic divisions of King Blanchard's established command. Jenka, having never been very far out of Crag, had never heard of the clay pits.

"It's not far from here to the east," Stick explained. "It's a cliff face that's been dug out and down so that it looks like a pit now. They dig up this thick mud called clay. It's reddish brown, and can be molded into shapes and baked into..."

"I know what clay is," Jenka smirked a little more harshly than he intended to. "I've just never heard of the pits."

"If Mortin's been 'round here, and he got away, then that's where he'd go," Herald reasoned. "He's a Forester now, and the Kingsmen at the pit will take him in and hear his tale, but if he got caught by them fargin road thieves, then he might be in a heap."

"So we track `em down?" Master Kember asked, with more than a hint of vengeful eagerness in his voice.

"No. I track `em down, and there really ain't no tracking to it. They still got some of Swinerd's pigs with `em. I can find a pig in a corn field." Herald's tone made clear to the crippled hunter that he was speaking as a King's Ranger and a superior now. "Make camp, Master Kember, and post a double watch. And you," he paused to point at Stick. "You get them crossbows unpacked and loaded, Forester. Show Jenka and Rikky how to use 'em proper, but don't be a wastin' no bolts. Then all three a 'ya go up to higher ground and start diggin' Solman a hole. I want that done before dark fall." He turned back to Master Kember and gave him a sharp nod. "If I'm not back, leave in the morning as if naught was amiss. I'll try and get in close on them bastards tonight when the moon first starts up, and if I see our boy I'll come back and we'll go from there. If I don't see him, I'll come back and send Stick to the pit to look for him." He put his hand on Master Kember's shoulder. "I have a sworn duty to see them two druids to King's Island, Marwick, or we'd all go a-bandit hunting, I promise ya."

Master Kember looked as if he were biting the end of his tongue off. His face grew beet-red, and after he gave a short nod, he turned and stalked away.

Later, when the crossbows had been assembled, loaded and distributed, Jenka took a break from digging and handed Rikky the little field shovel they had been sharing. Stick was off gathering rocks to help cover the nearly-completed grave, and Linux and Zah were meditating, or praying, or whatever it was that druids did, over Solman's stiffening corpse.

Jenka wanted to swim out into the lake and just float away from it all so that he could have some time to gather his roiling thoughts, but he knew he couldn't do that. He had grown up with Solman, and though they were never really all that close, he wanted his friend to be buried well. Beyond that, he felt the indescribable urge to be out there with Herald, hunting the men who did this. He knew that Master Kember shared the sentiment, but Herald was a King's Ranger, and he had laid down the law. They had to follow it.

It was almost full dark when Master Kember placed the last stone. His face was streaked with tears, and so were Jenka and Zah's. Linux and Stick kept themselves a bit distant. They never had the chance to get close to Solman and neither felt that they had the right to intrude. Young Rikky just squatted near Solman's buried head and stared at the long pile of stones as if he were in a trance.

While searching for rocks, Stick had found enough washed-up wood and deadfall to start a normal blaze. Master Kember was thankful for it. The last thing he wanted was to spend another night beside that overly hot, hissing blue druid's fire.

Master Kember, Rikky, and Linux took the first watch, which was fine with Jenka. He quickly found his bed roll, buried his face in his cloak, and cried out a good bit of sorrowful emotion before he fell asleep. Zah kept an eye on him for a while, but her sadness got the best of her, and she too sobbed herself into slumber. Stick just stared blankly at the sky. He considered that it could have easily been him lying there dead in the mud until Master Kember gave him a shake and told him that it was time for the second watch. He woke up Zah, and then Jenka, and the three of them sat around the warm, cherry-red fire coals watching the night over each other's shoulders.

Morning came with no sign of Herald, and Master Kember didn't confuse his orders. He had the group moving quickly down the rutted road before the whole of the sun was even in the sky. They rode like that for nearly an hour when they came upon what was left of Mortin's horse lying just off the road. Mortin had a standard-issue Forester's saddle that Stick recognized immediately. The animal had been torn apart and half eaten, which master Kember informed them only trolls would do. Almost all other large carnivores, he told them, tried to finish their kill, or at least protect it so that they could finish it later. His assumption in this case was backed up when Jenka and the boys marked troll tracks coming and going all around the horse's putrid carcass.

"Let's get it moving again," Master Kember urged them. "Herald and Mort are probably waiting for us up the road..."

"Herald is right here a comin' out of the woods at ya! And if I'd have been a troll, I'd have you!"

"Not so fast," Jenka said, shaking the tip of the crossbow bolt he had nearly fired at the King's Ranger by mistake.

"You're lucky Jenka has a little more restraint than that bandit did," Linux observed.

"Aye...s'pose I am," he shivered. "But see here! We called it true," Herald walked over and patted Jenka's horse on the chest. "I heard them theivin' bastards last night talking `bout it. I got real close. Said the boy came stumbling into the dying pitfire light and startled the one who was supposed to be on watch. They was razzing him about it pretty bad."

The idea of those men joking about Solman's death irked Jenka deeply, but not nearly as much as it angered Rikky and Master Kember.

"Did you see Mortin?" Stick and Jenka almost asked over each other.

"Not a sign of him, and they didn't say a peep about him, so I'm guessing he'd be headed over to the clay pit, if he didn't drown."

"Are you going to send me after him?" Stick asked, as if he were eagerly up to the uncertain task of riding a half a day alone, in territory thick with bandits and trolls.

Herald waved the Forester's eagerness off and strode over to Master Kember, who was climbing down off of his horse to walk with him. Herald didn't seem to need privacy, though, and his words carried to everyone's ears.

"I'm giving you an option here, Marwick. You can take Rikky and Stick, here, and go to the clay pits and round up some more men and go collect some King's Justice, or I can send Stick over there to do the same. Either way, them bandits'll be getting their due." He gave Master Kember a solid pat on the back and started to say more, but Rikky spoke for the first time that day.

"I want to go with Stick," Rikky blurted out hotly. "I want to kill them bastards that got Sol, and since they're bandits, if we succeed, that'll be my feat of notability!"

"You'll do just what I tell you to, son," Master Kember said flatly.

Rikky had never known who his father was, and when he heard Master Kember call him *son* like that, he didn't dare argue with him.

"Take him, Marwick," Herald urged. "He needs to help put a close to this. Take `em both and go catch them sons of bitches. There ain't but five of `em, and scruffy as hell, and full of all that swine they rustled. You can catch up to us on the island. Tell you the truth, the four of us can probably make haste with all this behind us."

"Four?" Master Kember looked around and saw Jenka. He shook his head in the negative. "I told his mother that I'd get him where he was going, Herald. I can't leave it on you."

"I'm a fargin King's Ranger, Marwick," He pounded at the dingy pale blue star emblem that was embroidered on his vest's left breast. "Jenka is a witness to an incident involving a dragon and trolls. No, *two* incidents involving dragons after that fargin fire wyrm swooped out of the sky and nearly got him yesterday." He put his hands on his hips and glared at Master Kember.

"You don't know his mother," Master Kember said with a shake of his head. "She said she would shrivel my stones if I let him get hurt."

"No, sir," Jenka corrected. "She said she would shrivel your stones if you kept trying to pull the wool over her eyes about how safe this journey would be."

"See, that's not a concern, then," Herald actually grinned at Jenka, but when he turned back to Master Kember his tone and demeanor grew gravely serious. "I really don't like leaving Mortin's fate to one of these lads, Kember. They be green as spring grass, but this matter of mudges and trolls has to get to King Blanchard's ear, and quickly I'm thinking."

"I'll do it for Mortin then. That way I'm not abandoning Jenka for revenge,"

"However ya sell yourself on it, Marwick, just save that carrot-headed son of a bitch and round up them bandits. Kill `em if you have to, on my order. Meet us on King's Island as soon as you can. I'll be bunked in the west guard house; the one near the Golden Unicorn Inn and Tavern. The druids will be put up there, too."

"See ya, Jenk," Rikky said, with a surprising bit of cheer in his voice. "I'll get one for you!"

"Just don't get yourself killed, Rikky." Jenka reached over and shook the young hunter's hand. "I'll mention you to the king myself if I get the chance, I swear it." Jenka shook Stick's hand as well, but he got down off of his horse and gave Master Kember a heartfelt hug.

"Just be yourself when you're in front of King Blanchard," Master Kember told Jenka. "It's what he respects most. He is a good and just man, and he has always had a deep regard for what your father did for Prince Richard."

"I'll make you both proud," Jenka had tears streaming down his face again, but he didn't try to hide them because Master Kember's face was slick with them, too.

After Master Kember, Rikky, and Stick headed eastward from the lake toward the clay pit, Herald went back into the tangle of growth beneath the drooping willow trees and came back with not one, but two horses. One was his, of course, and the other had been Solman's. He mounted his steed and gave the other animal a long lead. He gave a short warning that they would be riding a little faster than they had been and then spurred off southward down the road. They rode at a steady clip until well after dark, but riding in the night didn't seem so dangerous now because every so often they passed a well-lit cluster of farm houses, or a cattle ranch that was set back off the ever-widening road. The whole time, the swiftly-moving river flowed alongside them to the right.

Jenka was sleeping in his saddle when they trotted into a cluster of enough buildings to be considered a town. The town was fast asleep, save for a single man sitting watch up on an elevated wooden platform tower. He waved down at Herald, and Herald called out that it was the King's Ranger's coming in. Herald led the group straight to a large barn-stable that was set back from the cobbled main thruway. He opened the rusty lock on the door with a key he pulled from a ring at his neck, and opened the gate wide enough that the rest of them rode the horses right in.

"This'll be the village called Grove," Herald told them. "Don't get `customed to it `cause we'll be leaving afore the sun gets in the sky. Fork some hay into a stall and get some rest. We'll be treated to some hot oats and jammed bread in just a few hours, but after that, we're off again. We'll make Three Forks Stronghold this time tomorrow. There we can rest a day, and get a hot bath and a good night's shut eye."

Jenka's spine was aching from the ride. He was sore in places that he didn't even know he had, and his mind was numb from contemplating the fate of men among the dragons and the trolls. Once he was off of his horse, he fell asleep before he even lay down.

Late the next night they arrived in Three Forks.

CHAPTER SEVEN

Crossing the planked wood bridge over the Strom River, then riding into Three Forks proper was a sight to behold, even in the middle of the night. Especially for Jenka, who had never been out of the foothills. He had never seen so many lanterns, barrel fires, and flaming brands in all his life. He figured that the magnitude of illumination alone kept the wilderness from closing in on the great frontier city. They had passed several groups of riders and a small wagon caravan on the road coming in, but not so many folk as to hint at the true population of Three Forks. The bridge and the main thoroughfare, a cobbled road wide enough for several wagon carts to pass each other abreast, was lined with fancy lantern poles, with the kingdom's spread-winged falcon carved high upon them. People wrapped in light cloaks and tall hats moved about under them, even at this late hour. The road was lined with one and two story buildings pressed together so closely that, in some places, they looked to be one giant, haphazardly-built structure. The only thing that really separated the dwellings and shops from each other was the garish paint combinations that each owner had chosen to decorate their street front.

Off the main road, surrounded by a sufficiently-illuminated, well-cultivated garden of low shrubbery and otherwise wide-open lawn, was the twenty-foot-tall, crenulated, block-and-mortar wall that surrounded Three Forks Stronghold. It was an impressive sight to look upon. Jenka thought he would feel perfectly safe behind those walls. When Herald told him that the Great Wall was twice as tall and three times as thick, Jenka wasn't sure he could believe it.

The group rode into a tunnel-like portal that sported a score of arrow-slits in its arched ceiling and wall faces. Men uniformed in heavy-but-functional, steel-plated armor, carrying crossbows or pikes, manned the barred iron gates at the other end of the tunnel. One of them recognized Herald. Immediately, the gate clanked noisily upward. In a haze of exhaustion, Jenka followed Linux and the Kingsman who led them from the gates to the stable, then into the main building. They turned a few corners in the candlelit, oak-paneled lower corridors, then went up a flight of wooden stairs to a lightly furnished room. There, Jenka fell into one of the goose down mattresses, and didn't wake until the sun was well into the sky.

* * *

The city of Three Forks looked that much more fantastic to Jenka in the bright, mid-morning sun. He had been sent out to fetch some things for Linux from the saddle packs, and was slowly making his way to where he thought the stables were. He went into a wooden door near the main gates and found himself being herded up an overly long stairway by two big, well-armed men that he didn't want to try and squeeze around. He stepped out ahead of them onto the wide, crenulated lane atop the wall, and was blasted with fresh cool air and warm sunlight. It was from that vantage point that Jenka was able to look out over the reasonably-populated clusters of humanity in the streets. Directly below him in the park-like garden, loud and colorful groups of people moved about intently. The men were mostly dressed in functional, but formal-looking, long jackets, or typical rough spun laborers' garments. But some of them wore colored robes in pearly, pastel shades of peach and aqua; colors that Jenka could have never imagined existed. Some wore furred cloaks, and others long, billowing capes. Almost all of the women wore wide, frilly, belled-out dresses, and tall top hats that resembled the chimney stack on the roof of old Master Tolman's forge. At least the cleaner looking ladies did. Some of the women wore plain, rough spun dresses and were trying to sell their wares, or themselves, to the people who would stop and give them a listen. One woman was dressed in almost nothing, revealing her heavy, well-shaped breasts, save for the nipples, and even they dimpled the slight bit of fabric covering them so that nothing was left to the imagination. Jenka's eyes were inadvertently following her, when a gruff man with the crimson shield of the Walguard embroidered on his armored vest clasped a meaty hand on his shoulder.

"What business do you have up here on the wall, boy?" the Walguard asked rhetorically. "I never seen you before. Who are you?"

"My name is Jenka De Swasso," he answered hesitantly. "I'm here with a King's Ranger named Herald. I'm supposed to be fetching some things from our saddle packs, but I got lost."

"Aye," the Walguard laughed. "You got lost in a place with a hawk's eye view of one of the most fascinating whores in all of Three Forks." He squeezed Jenka's shoulder in a brotherly manner. "The stables are back down those stairs and a few hundred paces down the wall, that way, at ground level." He pointed. "You'd best be getting along, Forester. I heard tell that old bastard Herald will nick your ear with his dagger if you dally too much. But if you want to take that gal for a romp later, you can find her at the Brew'n House Tavern." He laughed at Jenka's appalled expression. "Bring silver if you go, boy. That en't no copper cunny there."

Jenka was glad that he wasn't running an errand for Herald, and he was more than a little proud over the Walguard's assumption that he was an actual Forester. Even though he knew what a whore was, he had never actually considered paying for company. He knew he had dallied too much, though, so he hurried back down the stairs and ran all the way to the stables.

When he returned with the leather satchel Linux had requested, he was surprised to find Zahrellion waiting in their room. Her long, white hair was wet and heavy, causing it to hang in clumps around her pretty face. Her cheeks were rosy and pink from the scrubbing she had just given them. She looked fresh and lovely, and was dressed in clean, tan-and-gray robes.

Jenka imagined that, under her gown, she didn't quite have the curves that the naked street-walker he had just seen had, but she was shapely enough for his taste. He was far too shy and inexperienced to say anything about it, though. He and Dalia, the baker's daughter back in Crag, had spent many a night exploring each other, but they had never actually done the deed. Even having heard Zahrellion confess that he had stirred something inside her didn't give him enough courage to voice his attraction. He suddenly felt very self-conscious, and he began looking around the room nervously. He noticed, for the first time, that Linux was nowhere to be seen.

"He went downstairs to the bathhouse," she answered his question before he had a chance to ask it. "I think you should probably go have a soak, too, and have the launderer there wash your clothes. I can smell you from here."

"What are we going to do, Zah?" Jenka ignored her comment. "How are we going to convince King Blanchard about the mudged and the trolls?"

"So you're seeing the right side of things, then?" She cocked her head and met Jenka's gaze and was pleased with what she saw there. "We won't have to convince him about the trolls." Her tone grew serious. "I was going to wait until you were cleaned up to tell you this, but Linux has shared a dream with a member of our sect back at the temple. The trolls have already started coming down out of the mountains in earnest."

"How did he…" Jenka started to ask, but knew that he couldn't possibly understand any answer she might give beyond the obvious. "No. Where are they coming down? Crag? Is my mother safe?"

"Lemmy was left to watch over her, so I'm hoping that she is safe. We don't know yet what passes and valleys the trolls may be using." She sat down hard on Linux' bed, which was made. Jenka's woolen blanket was still a rumpled mess on his disheveled mattress, just as he had left it. After noticing this, Zah took the time to flutter it out and smooth the results a little bit.

"Thank you," Jenka smiled, despite the new knot of worry that had just bunched up in his gut. "So how are we going to get King Blanchard to rescind the bounty on dragon heads and take up sides with them against the trolls?"

"According to Linux, the trolls number in the thousands, and that alone will give the king reason to consider the alliance. I just hope none of the stupid mudge attack between now and the time we get our audience with him." She sat back on Linux' bed with a huff. "If that happens, he may never listen."

"My father died saving Prince Richard from a troll attack," Jenka said, with a little fire in his voice. "If I demand to be heard, I don't think he will refuse me."

"You'll end up in the dungeons with the ravers if you so much as speak out of line to your narrow-minded king."

"No. You're wrong about that." Jenka went on. "Master Kember, my father, and two other men waded right into a pack of trolls to save the crown prince, and right in front of King Blanchard's eyes. I don't see how he could ignore both of us."

"Well, Master Kember isn't here, and just because you get the king to listen to you doesn't mean he will care what we have to say." She forced a smile, despite herself. "Go to the bathhouses and have a soak, Jenka. By the time you're done we might know a good deal more. The Stronghold's Spell Master is preparing a potion for Linux that will allow him to have a more extended sharing of thoughts with our peer back at the temple. I'll make sure that he asks about Crag."

"Thank you." Jenka sighed, trying to ignore the growing worry over his mother. "I hope Jade is all right, and Mortin, too. I think we would be better-received if Master Kember was with us when we have our audience, though."

"I cannot disagree with you." Zah rose and, staying well clear of Jenka's filth, she eased around him and opened the door. "Go bathe, and clear your mind of it all for a little while. If things don't look too bad, then maybe later we can venture out into Three Forks and look around." With that, she left him, and after a few whiffs at his own armpits, Jenka headed immediately down to bathe.

The water was almost scalding hot, and the room thick with steam. The launderer took Jenka's garments and promised that they would be cleaned, dried, and repaired within the turn of a glass. Jenka had put a handful of the coppers he had been saving into a small drawstring pouch around his neck before he left Crag. He was glad for that because he was certain the service wasn't free.

The floor of the bathhouse was slick, wet wood planking, and the tubs were inset into the floor like little, semi-private pits. Even after he was in one of them, soaking and scrubbing with the provided horse brush and soap, Jenka couldn't tell if they were individual tubs, or if it was one big tub with a multi-holed floor built over it. Either way, it felt heavenly to have the stress and soreness of several hard days melted away from his flesh. He had no idea when he would get another chance to wash himself, so he took advantage. He took the time to scrub his hair, and even behind his ears, like his mother had done when he was little. Then he lay back and floated in the water, as if he were floating through the sky inside some hot, steamy cloud.

When he woke, he knew immediately that he had been asleep for some time, because the parts of his flesh that didn't feel boiled felt as if it they had been pickled. He found his clothes folded nicely in the provided changing room. Despite being a little cooked, he felt fresh and clean after he dressed. He hoped Linux gave them acceptable news, because he really wanted to go out into Three Forks with Zah and take in the sights.

His wish was granted. So far, the trolls were coming out of the mountains west of the Strom

River, out in the wilds, where few men had tried to settle. But there was bad news, too. Weston was a small community of herders and farmers out that way, and it was believed that the village had already been lost. Linux had learned that bands of trolls, some as large as fifty strong, were coming south. They were crossing the Strom River, where the reservoir backs up and floods the flatlands just north of Demon's Lake. That meant that Master Kember's group, as well as the men working the clay pits, were all in grave danger. It also meant that Crag, Kingsmen's Keep, Swinerd's farm, and the druids' deep, mountain temple were all about to be cut off from the kingdom.

Herald knew that his brother's hog farm would probably end up being a savaged feeding ground for the trolls, so he wasted no time hiring a crew of mercenaries to ride that way and help see his brother and his family south, or at least up to Kingsmen's Keep. Small groups of Walguard and King's Rangers alike were being sent north to investigate the claims Linux was making, all on Herald's word that Linux could be trusted. Herald had played in all his favors to get that much done. Commander Corda was sympathetic but practical, and refused to send the bulk of the troops stationed at Three Forks north without solid evidence that the trolls were attacking.

His proof came later in the evening. While Jenka, Zah, and Linux were making their way through the crowded streets of Three Forks, a trio of riders came charging into the town, hollering that the trolls had attacked their party on the river road.

* * *

Jenka, Zah and Linux had gone to a leather shop. Jenka, following Zah's advice, had purchased a new pair of well-tanned woodman's pants and a matching vest with hardened steel shoulder pieces sewn into it. It gave his torso a triangular look; the point coming together at his navel, the other two corners making his shoulders look more substantial and a bit wider than they really were. Linux had paid for the fine-but-functional garments and had given Jenka a few coppers for the work he had done as their attendant. Jenka tried to refuse, but Linux insisted. Zah had then dragged the two men through a fragrant chandler's hut, then to a material shop that sold lace and other exotic fabric brought in from the islands. Linux explained to Zah that the material would be much less expensive on King's Island, and that there would be more designs to choose from as well. This allowed Linux to lead them to an armory that had been recommended to him. On the way to the armory, they tried to decide if they wanted to dine at the Melodious Mermaid Tavern, where a lovely woman supposedly played a harp every night and sang all the great old ballads of land and sea, or if they were going to The Jester's Corner, where jugglers, fools, and mimes entertained the patrons in the evenings. Those were the only two choices in Three Forks for entertainment unless you wanted to see half-naked women dancing and doing tricks for coins. It was the frontier, after all, and there were far more men than women trying to settle it. Three Forks was where they all came to get rowdy.

The trio was just outside the armory's opened doorway, and Jenka was salivating at the prospect of purchasing himself a good new bow, when the men that had been attacked came riding through and ruined the afternoon.

"As bold as Kingsmen, and twice as fierce they were!" one of the men called out to the curious folk out on the busy street. "They killed Rodger Poston and Garred Wheatly dead, and they ate

Will Prestam's arm! We're going to tell the commander now."

"Half a score of them tree-tall bastards, maybe more, set on us like starved dogs on a hambone!" another one of the riders added as he trotted by Jenka and the druids. The men were making their way through town toward the Stronghold to make their official report, and now the gossipmongers were running rampant with exaggerated half-tales of coming doom at the hands of the trolls. A tangle of mild hysteria ensued in the street, causing Linux to lead his younger charges back toward the Stronghold gates.

What had begun as the makings of a promising evening in Three Forks had been turned into a chaotic mass of confusion. And if this new turn of events wasn't bad enough, a bright, jagged streak of lightning split the sky as it started to rain.

Linux' uncanny ability to move between people got his group through the crowd and directly behind the procession of men who had survived the recent attack. As they went through the gates and the rain started to fall, Linux led them in with the others, as if they were a part of that group, too. It was because of this that Jenka got to squeeze into the Stronghold's great gathering hall behind Zah, to listen to what the men actually had to report.

"Who speaks?" A stern voice asked. Jenka knew Commander Corda's voice, even though he couldn't see the herculean man. He was the reluctant commander that had spent his early afternoon hearing Herald and Zah's arguments, and quizzing Jenka about his two encounters with the wyrms.

"I'm Bandle Millson, Commander." One of the attacked men answered. "I haul wood and shale for Bartlet's Outfit with my wagon rig." The traumatized man gulped in a well-needed breath of air, then started into his tale. "We was set upon by a score or more of them trolls out near Westfork Bend. We was loading cut wood for Master Drail's forge and for the kitchens here at the Stronghold. They just came a loping up on us out of the lumber groves and started to bashing us with limbs and such. Me and Harner, over there," He pointed to one of his haggard-looking friends. "We runned off, `cause we en't fighting men, sir. We're just humble wagoneers. But that boy over there stood up to one of `em so we could get away and got his shoulder smashed for it. There was something in the sky over the trees, too, but I didn't see it that well. The boy did, though. He saw it good." The speaker indicated the other man that was with them. He was clutching his shoulder, exactly like he had been when they had ridden through town. He didn't look capable of speaking because his teeth were gnashed together as tight as a bear trap. "He was just a wanderin' down the river bank when we first seen him. He saved us. His wounds might just need a look-see. I mean, if you have a man."

In the brief silence that transpired, everyone in the hall looked at the boy who had been brave enough to attack a troll to save the wagon drivers. Jenka got a glimpse of him and his heart thundered with excitement. "I think that's Mortin." Jenka's voice carried into the silence.

Zah gasped with relief as she, too recognized the filthy, injured person.

The boy looked up, and Jenka was pretty sure that it was the lost Forester. Mortin's face—his entire body—was just far too dirty for his carrot-red hair to show.

"Mortin," Jenka yelled, and he started to worm his way through the crowded hall. When he got there, Linux was already wrapping his cloak around Mortin's shoulders. Herald had appeared from somewhere, and was now bulling his way toward them, too.

"Clear the hall," Herald called out over the rising din. Then up at the commander who had a heavy gavel raised to strike. "This be the Forester we told you about, Commander! I don't know how he got all way round to Westfork Bend, but this is the king's own business here! Clear the hall, man! Get your men riding as far north as they can. We got good folk living all the way up into the foothills! Them trolls be startin' a war!"

CHAPTER EIGHT

Mortin had been so badly traumatized that he couldn't properly communicate what had happened to him. He moaned and wailed, but nothing that made any sense came out of him. The haunted look in his eyes was pitiful. It caused more than one hardened frontier veteran to look away and wonder what could cause such a thing. Only after the Stronghold's Spell Master gave Mortin a potion did the Forester even begin to speak intelligible words. Jenka would have thought that the stuff was pure piss, were it not fizzing and bubbling in the glass vial it was delivered in. After Mortin drank it down, though, his tongue began to cooperate with his jumbled mind.

"I snaw the kling!" Mortin shouted, before he sobbed into Zah's shoulder. "My Swaww Da king!" He howled again through his tears, with his face buried in her shoulder like some terrified infant.

It was hard seeing the once strapping young man reduced to such a dismal state of mind.

"Yes, Mortin," Herald spoke soothingly in the now relatively cleared-out gathering hall. "We were all going to see the king. And the Solstice Festival, remember?"

"Nawww thad king!" he wailed out.

"This is pointless, sirs," the black-robed, dark-haired mage said sympathetically. His official name and title was Spell Master Vahlda. He looked to be nearing the age where gray starts to form in a man's beard, but there was no beard on his face to give proof to it. "Unless the druids know of other civilized means, I think we have extracted all we can from this man without becoming torturers."

"Did he just say, '*Not that king*?'" Jenka asked the group, ignoring the Spell Master. Before anyone could answer, Jenka eased up beside Mortin and put a friendly arm around his thick shoulders. "What king did you see?"

"Gawlin king!" Mortin looked up at Jenka and moaned into the suddenly silent room. "Gawlin king and his big blah dwaga."

"The Goblin King and his big black dragon?" Jenka repeated.

"Yeh," Mortin leaned away from Zah then. He put his forehead on the table and wrapped his arms around the exposed areas of his face, as if he were trying to hide it.

Jenka looked up to see a whole bunch of blank stares looking back at him.

"It's obvious that he is delirious," Commander Corda said, albeit with little conviction. "The trolls would never have a king." The commander was a mountain of a man, very fit, and looked like he could easily wield every foot of the long, two-handed sword that stuck up over his shoulder. His beard and mustache were short and well-trimmed, and his dark, thinning hair hung to his shoulders. He wore well-worn crossing leather shoulder armor over a traditional green Kingsman's tunic.

"He said Goblin King, not Troll King," Linux interjected. "The trolls are cousins to the orcs and the goblins, and all of our lore cites an incident in the early years of the mainland expansion regarding just such a being. I can't recall the event's specifics, but I believe it involved the initial battle for Tohold, what the kingdom now calls Mainsted Port."

"That's correct," the Spell Master put in, remembering the tedious lessons he had on the subject. "Several tribes of trolls rose up, behind a supposedly mighty leader, and attacked the first settlers there at Tohold repeatedly. They called the leader of those attacks the Goblin King because he was bigger and more fearsome than the other trolls, and he wore a spiked ivory crown, but that's just the embellishing of a story about some battle with violent, blood-lusting trolls. I doubt that the being described in that incident was anything other than an exceptionally fierce troll, or maybe an orc who got a hold of a bird's nest and put it on its head."

"What happened? How did the battle go?" Zah asked. Her eyes were alight with both curiosity and concern.

"Well, of course the trolls were beaten back, but after Captain Fashant toasted the victory at a celebratory feast, an old Hazeltine Witch supposedly stood up and spouted a portent, saying that in a hundred years the Goblin King would return, only this time he would command a dark horde, and with it he would exact his revenge on the trespassers who had so easily overwhelmed his kin the first time around."

"Has it been a hundred years?" Herald asked, half amazed that he was doing so.

"By the hells! I don't know, Ranger," the Spell Master conceded. "You're not buying into this shit are you? If there is a troll king out there, it's probably some exceptionally clever bastard trying to stir up the fire."

"Goblin King or not, the trolls are bringing war, sir," Zah said boldly, meeting the Spell Master's gaze. Then she cut her eyes up to the Stronghold's Commander. "There's nothing you can do to stop it. All you can do is prepare the people for it by calling them in to safety. Anything less would be irresponsible."

"Irresponsible?" Commander Corda ground his jaws and turned a deep shade of crimson, trying to restrain the contempt he felt at being spoken to in such a way by a mere girl. An earthworm of a vein seemed to be crawling down his forehead. "Irresponsible would be abandoning all those herds of cattle and sheep, all of those villages and towns that were built by the ancestors of the very people who won't want to leave them behind. Not to mention all those fields full of spring crops, and all of the other resources that the frontier provides! Do you think those uppity sons-of-bitches on the islands give a pixie's pecker-head how many men have to die to bring them furs and wheat? They take twelve shiploads of lumber and cut wood a month, and still want more. I don't think you understand Uh…" he hesitated awkwardly. "Um…Milady"

Zah's words evoked a memory of the dream Jenka had after Jade had spoken to him. The vision of the filthy, densely overpopulated city, and the haze-filled air, came to his mind. Three Forks wasn't even close to as bad as the city in his dream, but what of Port? Or Kingston, the kingdom's seat, or the original settlement out on Gull's Reach? Jenka had heard one of the people in town say that the whole of Gull's Reach was nothing but buildings and roads, that Landing Monument and the surrounding Salvation Forest was the last little bit of wilderness left on the island, and that barely more than a park. Mainsted was rumored to be just as overly populated.

"There will be no one left to harvest the crops if you do nothing. You just don't understand what is coming," Zah said in a more peaceable tone. "But what about Kingsmen's Keep? Will you leave those men to be surrounded and starved out by the goblinkin?"

"You're barking up the wrong tree uh…Lady, uh…Mistress, uh…Sister Zahrellion," Commander Corda sighed at his inability to find the proper title for the druida, and she didn't bother to help him. He ended up waving the formality off. "It's Duke Watlin's decision to send out that many troops, not mine. I'm the commander of Three Forks Stronghold, nothing else. I don't have real authority over the King's Rangers or the Walguard. Just a bunch of half-trained Kingsmen who are mostly little more than rotten, spoiled, second and third sons from the island's more notable families. The Duke is in Port. Or maybe Midwal, I'm not certain which. One thing is certain though: if he's on the mainland at all, the Duke is somewhere safe behind the wall.

"If what you say is true, there is no way he will be able to stay ignorant of the situation long. Midwal and Farwal will be reporting similar occurrences, if this is happening like you say." He reached back with his right hand and fondled the leather-wrapped hilt of his huge sword, as he contemplated something. "Herald, what is it that you would have me do beyond what has already been done? I've sent out nearly two hundred men to investigate and to try and drive back the trolls, and a good number of my personal attachment is out searching for Master Kember and those bandits that killed that boy you told me about. I don't know what more you want from me. I cannot leave Three Forks unprotected."

"I would ask that you send a few more of your smaller, stealthier brigades out to the foothill villages, and at least make the attempt to escort the people back to Outwal or Midwal."

"You mean you don't think the Stronghold here will stand? Are you serious?"

"If what them druids say be true, then I'm not so sure, Commander," Herald answered sincerely. "If what that mussed-up Forester over there is mumbling has merit, then maybe that Great Wall will be put to the test, too. A fargin dragon that could crumble this Stronghold like it was a clod of dirt swooped on us just north of the lake, Commander. That don't happen regularly, even up in the peaks. They've lost the fear of us."

"Coming from anybody else, that would sound ludicrous," the commander sat heavily across from where Zah and Mortin were sitting. "Coming from you, makes it just plain frightening to hear."

"If you send someone to Crag, have them see about my mother and Lemmy," Jenka said, showing that he had a concern in this. And that he had no proper respect for authority.

He got a hard stare from both Herald and Commander Corda for speaking out of turn, but he didn't let it change the resolve he was holding firmly in his expression.

"You already have orders, Herald," the commander stated, matter-of-factly. "I can send three veteran brigades north past the lake. That's it. That's one for Crag, and one for Kingsmen's Keep, and one for Copperton."

"Don't send no one to the Keep," Herald said flatly. "Them fargin Rangers could hold that place for a century if they had to. There be tunnels underneath it, and caverns full of stores. It's the foothill settlements that need men: Crag, Copperton, and Seacut. Weston is surely done for, being that the trolls are coming down out of the Orichs right on top of `em." He shook his head at the sickening idea of the little farming and herding village overrun by rampaging bands of trolls. "When your men leave Seacut, they can take the coast road south and pass through Bayton. The men coming back from Crag can pass through Dell."

Commander Corda finally gave in. "I'll probably lose this post for doing it, but you've convinced me, Herald. I'm putting down that you demanded this action in my report too. That way we can sit in the dungeons together."

"Come, Jenka," Zah whispered. She took his hand in hers and led them out of the gathering hall as discreetly as possible. Once they were clear of the closing door, she spoke urgently. "If Mortin really saw a Goblin King riding a big black, then we have to do something." Her lavender eyes looked distant and afraid, yet they were alive with self-confidence. "Can you call Jade?" she asked. The only thing stranger than the question was the fact that she looked completely serious as she asked it.

"Jade isn't even his real name," said Jenka. "He's barely a yearling. How would I call him?"

"I'll have to call Crystal, then," Zah looked around absently for the answer to a question that had formed in her head. "We'll have to leave Three Forks proper," she said to Jenka. "You can go ready two horses at the stable. We will be out of the city by sunset, and we can be back before midnight. Linux will cover for us with Herald and the commander."

"Herald isn't our enemy," Jenka stated, a bit of unease creeping into his demeanor. "And who is Crystal?"

"You'll see." She smiled a brilliant smile at him, and when her eyes met his, they twinkled scarlet.

A tingling of static rippled over Jenka's skin, and after that he had no desire to do anything other than go ready the horses for his and the lovely druida's evening trot.

* * *

Master Kember and Ricky saw the Goblin King.

They watched him from afar and stayed as still as stone, so as not to draw his attention. Notice was the last thing they wanted from him, or from the fearsome-looking, black-skinned wyrm that he rode. The horned-headed troll-beast was bigger than a normal troll. He wore a large, orange-red-colored tortoise shell over his chest, and another over his back as armor. There were shoulder-caps made of smaller, similarly-colored shells, and there were what appeared to be human thigh bones dangling around his waist. The bones were held together with wire and chain, and they formed a protective skirt. His body was thick and muscular like an ogre, and covered in dark, coarsely-bristled hide. He was still tall and lithe like a troll, and his otherwise-trollish head was horned, regally, with glossy, ivory antlers that strongly resembled flames, giving the appearance of wearing a great, thorny crown. The malformed thing exuded power and radiated hatred. It was an awesome creature to look upon, and both Rikky and Master Kember were trembling down to the marrow of their bones.

They had tracked the bandits that had killed Solman to a small cottage in a lightly-wooded valley. It was a good distance from the clay pits, but in the same general area. They were watching now from a rocky precipice above the tree line, as the Goblin King sat atop his dragon before the shake-roofed cottage. With a series of barking growls, the Goblin King ordered a pair of orc. They, in turn, called out orders, and a pack of trolls began to decimate the place. The dragon helped by belching forth a long, thick jet of flame that started the roof blazing. Men came running out with swords and crossbows, but they were quickly set upon.

Even though those murderous bandits had killed Solman, and had probably robbed a half a hundred caravans, Master Kember still felt sickened when the trolls bore down on them. Though they were bad men, they were still human. He wished greatly that the horses weren't so far away; they had left them about a mile back by a pond near an orchard. He didn't want to be where he was any longer.

Rikky, on the other hand, was urging the trolls silently on as they tore apart, and then fed on the flesh of the men who had killed Sol. He was concerned about the strange scale-less dragon, though. It was as big as the one that had swooped on Jenka and Zah, and Rikky wanted no part of it, nor of the evil thing riding it. Now that Sol's revenge was being dealt, he found that he really didn't care about sticking around. Still, he held strong and did as Master Kember ordered him to do. To Rikky, it wasn't about what he wanted any more, it was about pleasing the man who sometimes called him son.

A scouting troll saw them huddled there, peering raptly down at the scene. It eased up behind them with relative ease. It was as startled as Rikky was when he turned and saw it. Both of them screamed out instinctually, but it was Master Kember who took the blow from the heavy stone the big dog-eared beast had thrown. Rikky heard the sickening *crunch* of bone beside him, and turned away from the troll to see Master Kember's head cracked wide open like a grayish-yellow egg. The crippled old hunter's good leg began thumping hard in the dirt, as if it were trying to run somewhere on its own. But there was no light left in his eyes. A rage came over Rikky then. He loosed a bolt from the crossbow he was carrying, just before he threw it aside and charged. His dagger came out, as the troll grabbed at the fletching protruding from its chest. It couldn't defend itself when Rikky came slashing in, low at its groin and thighs. The troll bellowed out loudly to warn its pack mates, and Rikky heard the thumping of the dragon's huge wings as it took flight to investigate.

Rikky didn't hesitate. He ducked away from the mortally-wounded troll and started running for what little cover was available to him. He wanted to head toward the horses, but he was afraid that the dragon might see them from above and kill them before he could get there. He couldn't believe that Master Kember had died like that, and hot, salty tears were threatening to blur his vision because of it. It was surreal. But he knew what he had seen. The image would be burned in his head for however long he survived this madness, which at the moment seemed like it might only be minutes. He had seen a good deal of the stuff that was supposed to be filling Master Kember's gourd lying on the man's shoulder, and a pinkish-gray lump of what was left of his forehead dangling over his face by a piece of hairy skin. The whole crown of his skull had been smashed back into the boulder behind him.

Had he not been fleeing for his very life, Rikky would have been curled up, heaving vomit from his guts, but his instinct to flee and survive was driving him now, and there was no time for that.

Behind him, he heard something, most likely a troll, crashing through the sparsely-spread forest after him. He didn't turn back, and he didn't run toward the horses, but he ran. He ran as fast as his young legs could carry him through the denser copses, and he shot like a fleeing lizard across the revealing spaces that opened up between them. He heard trolls coming at him from the side, like they were trying to flank him, but he cut the other way and was just starting to think he had thrown them off when the dragon roared out above him.

Rikky looked up to see the Goblin King looking at him through the branches. The mighty black dragon was gliding around to make another pass. He tried to run left, but immediately changed direction when a troll came loping out of the trees ahead of him. He turned the other way and ran smack into a smaller, gray-skinned creature that had stepped out from behind the trees. It was a goblin, or maybe a young orc. Rikky had seen neither creature before so he couldn't say for certain. Whatever it was, its snarling mouth, full of needle-sharp teeth, was snapping at Rikky's crotch as its razor-sharp claws began tearing savagely into his arms and chest. Beyond the little creature that was determined to shred him to ribbons, Rikky saw two tall lanky trolls; one with its bright, pink tongue lolling out the side of its mouth as it came charging in at him. He tried to turn and flee the other way, but he fell hard to the ground. The wind was knocked from his heaving chest. He felt claws and teeth tearing into his legs and spine as the haze of oxygen deprivation began to cloud his brain. The last thing he remembered, before blackness completely engulfed him. was his body jerking and wracking, trying to gasp in one last breath of air.

CHAPTER NINE

Zahrellion led Jenka beyond the limits of the city at a brisk, steady trot. She had studied a map of where she intended to go and went about getting there with confidence. Jenka had no idea that she was as nervous as he was. They rode south and left the main road, moving west, riding out past most of the outlying ranches and huts on a rutted dirt track, similar to the one they had taken out of Crag.

At the moment, they were moving through a stretch of marshy, overgrown field that lay just north of the first of the three river forks that gave the town its name. The moon was a sliver of silver, low in the cobalt sky, and the stars were out in abundance. The earlier rain had freshened the cool air, but the precipitation had left the ground soggy and soft. It was slow going for the horses. They were also out in the open, and that had Jenka nervous. At least once, he thought he had seen part of the sky being eclipsed by something gigantic flying swiftly overhead.

Zah explained that a smaller bird or bat flying lower in the sky would have the same visual effect, and Jenka dubiously contemplated that concept while they rode.

About half a mile away, on a rise to the south, a caravan or a wagon-train was encamped by the river fork. The banter and song from the great distance, and the lights from their bonfires only served to make the area around their destination; the huge, whitish-gray up thrust of rock that Zah was leading them toward, seemed that much more dark and secluded. Which turned out to be a good thing, for it was no lump of rock that they were approaching. The thing was suddenly moving, causing Jenka to tremble with both awe and fear. Millions of shimmering scales reflected the starlight from the sky. It was like watching a slithering mound of diamonds shifting and worming on a black silk cloth. The slithery creature's scales were a pearlescent white, each the size of a small child's palm. The dragon was as big as a barn, and its great, toothy maw came looming in at Zahrellion so fast that Jenka's horse nearly threw him, as it tried to shake its bridle and flee.

"It's all right!" Zah called over the dragon's heavy intake of breath. Her own words came out of her mouth in a cloud of steam, for the dragon's breath was as frigid as the high mountain air. "This is Crystal. She is my friend. She is the one that told me of your bonding. That's the reason why I offered the King's Rangers my services the night the rangers killed that young mudge. It was so that I could meet you."

Whether it was just a natural sound that a dragon sometimes makes, or a reaction to the term *mudge*, Jenka couldn't say, but after Zah had spoken the word, Crystal hissed like a scalded cat and withdrew her head. She rose up high, fluttering her wings wide into a more dominant posturing. Her leathery wings were a shimmering grayish-white. Jenka could imagine them wrapped around her body, blending her perfectly into a snow-capped peak like some long-frozen stone.

Jenka's horse was trembling violently beneath him. He wasn't sure he would be able to keep it from bolting much longer. Nor was he sure he wanted to, because as beautiful as Crystal was, she could still snatch them both in a single bite.

"I see that you have mastered the Summoning," Crystal said, more into Zah and Jenka's mind than aloud. Her voice was low, but decidedly feminine, which went well with her big, glacial-blue, vertically-slitted eyes. "You must teach it to the boy. Not so long from now, his bondling will be ready to leave its nest and join us. But for now, it cannot."

"I will," Zah sighed to clear her mind, and tried to gather herself. Though she had spoken like this to Crystal several times, and had even ridden her once, being this close to the mighty creature still thrilled her to the core. She had to concentrate to keep from forgetting the questions she needed to ask. "Is there really a Goblin King riding around on a big black mudge?"

"Yessss," Crystal hissed. "It is the evil force I told you about before, but it is no goblinkin, and it is no mudged dracus that it rides either. It is the demon Gravelbone who has come, and the hellborn beast he commands is not a dragon, but a nightshade. They are weak now, but they are gaining strength with every bit of fear and anguish they instill. Gravelbone has returned for vengeance. He is not the only dark thing that has awakened, but for the time being he is the one who concerns us."

Crystal slithered down into a curled position, where her head came to rest on her foreclaws. "Gravelbone will lead the goblinkin and the mudge against you. The mountains are infested with the lesser of the vermin, and they number beyond count. Worse, they are simple-minded and easily riled into action. The goblin hordes, when they come, will charge, blindly and willingly, headlong into death, for Gravelbone. They will try to consume everything in their path that their bodies will digest. The orc think a little more, but are twice as terrible. They will fight with their kin against you. Without our help, man will not survive here." She flicked her purple tongue forth and tasted her surroundings. Her breath wafted across the humans like a gust of frigid air. "Thisss demon won't stop at the mainland, either. If he succeeds in driving you that far back, then he will attempt to vanquish your islands as well."

"You said, '*without our help,*'" Jenka asked the dragon cautiously. "Whose help, exactly?"

Zah was drawn toward Jenka's boldness. It was no easy thing to speak to a dragon. Jenka had done so directly. She weighed his question and judged it not too ignorant or offensive. She realized then that it was a very good question. She listened intently to Crystal for her answer.

"There should be five when the Time of Confliction is upon us, and five of you as well, but that terrible dilemma will never come to pass if we let Gravelbone keep his head. Here, in this land, at this time, there are only three High Dracus that have felt the calling. One of us is too infantile yet to be of much help. The other has bonded with the hope of your people's future, but the strength of that tie is tenuous at best. You will meet him very soon, but his drake has bade me not to expose his identity, and I know that that is for the best."

"Are we still supposed to try and get King Blanchard to unite with you? I don't understand." Zah looked a bit let down. "I thought that there were hundreds of you that were going to help us, dozens at least. King Blanchard will not make a pact with just three dragons, will he?"

"Ahh, my full-hearted girl! It isn't whether you succeed in convincing him to join us, but that you convince him that the possibility of peace between man and dragon exists. We are all pawns in a fairly grand design, and don't be surprised if you have to pay a price for your convictions. Remember what we have discussed before, yesssss? Faith, yesss? Trussst and faith in one another, and the hope that we can forge a peace for the future."

Jenka got the feeling that the glorious dragon was manipulating Zahrellion more than just a little bit. Sort of like how she sometimes manipulated him. The circumstances took on a new light, and doubt about Zah's assessment of the situation began to creep into Jenka's mind.

The dragon must have sensed Jenka's uncertainty, for it loomed its big head over and captured him in that deep, liquid-blue gaze. Veins of scarlet and gold pulsed and throbbed like lightning flashes in a tempest through the dragon's glacial orbs. They were as big around as pumpkins, and inside their depths, slitted pupils focused down to a sliver. Above the eyes, terrifying brow plates, as long as a man's arm, narrowed under milky, clear, icicle-like spiked horns. The big snow wyrm's breath was freezing cold, and Jenka began to shiver, as did his horse.

"Jade will wean himself soon, clever boy. Then you will have your hands full, I assure you. When time gifts you in abundance, which I think it soon will, do not waste it. Learn from Zahrellion, find your magic, and soon your bonding, and ours, will be completed."

Jenka's doubt evaporated, as visions of soaring through the skies riding Jade's sleek turquoise and emerald scaled back filled his mind's eye. Beside him, Zah, on Crystal, and another unidentifiable person riding a richly colored blue wyrm, banked and curved through the sky as they flew toward the shimmering, orange evening horizon. Ahead of them, Jenka saw the silhouette of an impossibly tall castle thrusting up out of the sharp mountain peaks. He knew that it was his future home that he was looking at, and that fact simply made the vision all the more compelling. When would this come to pass? He wondered to himself, *Is it really my future to live this?*

"Yessss, Jenka De Swasso," Crystal hissed out loud her response to the question Jenka had asked solely within his mind. She then rose to her haunches and leapt into the starry sky. She threw out her wings with a snap, and a few deep thumping wing beats later, she was gone.

* * *

Rikky felt the claws and teeth that had been tearing at him turn loose, and he half-crawled half-hopped as fast and far away from the little goblin as he could, which wasn't very far. His left leg felt horribly wrong. Suddenly, men were thundering in from everywhere on horseback with flaming brands held high. They were shooting arrows with bows and crossbows, and calling out to one another urgently. A few of them wore the blue star of the King's Rangers, others the red shield of the Walguard. Some sported the Kingsmen's spread-winged hawk. Rikky didn't care who they were. He was just glad they were there, and that he was no longer being torn apart. The wounds he had taken began to burn intensely. Afraid to look down at himself, he gauged the eyes of one of the Kingsmen as they rode past and looked at him. Not seeing any shock or disgust in the man's face, he chanced a glace and immediately wished that he hadn't. The lower portion of his left leg was virtually meatless, leaving his shin bone completely exposed. Shock overtook him then, and everything disappeared from his mind completely.

He woke after a while and opened his eyes to find that he was tied like a grain sack over some-one's horse. For a moment, there was no sensation other than the jarring and bouncing of the gal-loping animal, and the sound of terrified calls of hardened men tactfully fleeing from something. Then the pain came again. Everything went blood red in Rikky's mind, and it seemed like he might actually die from the raw agony he was feeling. An explosion of hot, sticky gore burst from his guts up through his throat, splattering down across the rump of the animal he was tied to. After that, unconsciousness mercifully took him under again.

Later, Rikky opened his eyes to find that it was morning. He was lying down under a wild-limbed oak tree beside a pair of curious looking Kingsmen.

"I think he's coming out of it," one of the two men said to the other.

"Ask him, then," the darker-haired man urged his companion. "Ask him if he seen it, too."

"Did you see it?" the other man asked stupidly. "Did you see the horn-headed troll on the dragon?"

"Aye, I did," Rikky rasped. "I'm gonna kill that bastard."

"Ha!" the darker-headed man laughed. "Kill that, will ya? I doubt you'll survive the night, boy. And even if ya do, there's no doubt you'll lose that leg." Then to his companion, "I told you we wasn't seeing things. Lets' try and keep him alive till we get back to Three Forks so that Commander Corda can hear his bit of the tale, too. He was one of the ones we was sent after, I think."

"Wasn't you riding with that crippled ranger? Kember?" the lighter-haired Kingsman asked.

"Aye," Rikky grunted. The pain was becoming too intense to bear, but he gritted it back and went on. "A troll bashed his head in. It snuck up on us while we was watching that big black Wyrm."

Rikky wanted to get to Three Forks badly. He had to tell Jenka about what had happened to Master Kember. He was fever-stricken, and he wanted to scream out in agony and cry until his tears ran dry over the loss of Master Kember, but he wouldn't show his emotion to these men he didn't know. He was afraid. He didn't have any kin save for his mother. He didn't want to lose his leg, and he wanted the pain that gripped his body like an ever-tightening vice to go away. But more than any of that, he wanted to survive. He had to survive. How else could he avenge Master Kember's death and kill the Goblin King?

CHAPTER TEN

By the time Zahrellion and Jenka made it back into Three Forks Stronghold, it was nearly time for the group to rise and prepare for the day's journey. No one had questioned their absence during the evening, save for Herald, who had readily believed the tale Linux had told him. Jenka had just shut his eyes when Herald tapped on the door to Linux' room to wake them.

Their destination, Outwal, sat just this side of the Great Wall. It would take every bit of the day to get there, but this part of their journey wasn't going to be made on horseback.

Though he was exhausted from his all-night adventure with Zah, the excitement and promise of the day's travel gave Jenka enough energy to get the carriage loaded. After that, he slept, his head bobbing in the corner of the once plush, but now dingy and overused, hard-topped buggy.

Herald was riding boltman up on the box with the driver, so Jenka had his legs stretched out to the side, taking up the entire width of the seat across from Zah and Linux. Zah was asleep for the first part of the trek as well, her tattoo-covered, but otherwise pleasant, face scrunched and slobbering in her bald-headed companion's lap.

They were awakened when the driver suddenly pulled the wagon to a halt. Herald spoke excitedly to a group of men outside. No one was alarmed. Though they were still outside the Great Wall, they were in the heart of civilization. There were ranches and clusters of homes, even larger dwellings, where multiple families lived all under one roof, all around them. Travelers and herders passed by constantly, and every few miles there was a well-manned Kingsmen's outpost, or a tavern room that served as the same. There was no danger of troll attacks or dragons here. There were bandits, but they would have little interest in a carriage full of people. They would be after cargo or coin, not common folk. Herald still insisted on riding guard and manning the crossbow, and this gave the passengers a little more comfort and confidence in their safety.

By the conversation outside, it sounded like a group of Herald's fellow King's Rangers were trying to sort the gossip and rumors they had been hearing from the truth. The stop was short, and the carriage was quickly jerked back into motion and picking up speed. Jenka couldn't sleep after that, and he gladly accepted a bread roll, stuffed with ham and cheese, that Linux produced from a basket at his feet.

After he ate, Jenka drank from a canteen, then began to think about what Zah's dragon had said, and what it had shown him in that vision. More vivid than a favorite memory, the scene had been so perfectly clear, as if he were actually living that moment. Crystal had said that the other dragon of the three had bonded with their future. *What does that mean?* Jenka wondered to himself as he looked out the small, dirty portal at the strange, progressing world outside.

They were continually passing amazing feats of human ingenuity and constructions beyond anything Jenka could have thought possible. There were mechanical plows, with dozens of steel-forged moving parts, working the fields, and an intricately-carved marble statue of Lady Herron—the firstborn of the realm—that stood a dozen feet tall. There were spiraling towers built at the corners of some of the prouder buildings, which were topped with roofs of hammered copper that shined like molten, golden spear heads in the sun. Flamboyantly-dressed jugglers entertained in an open pavilion on a busy intersection of roads, and a silver-haired man dressed in black robes blew flames from his mouth as if he were part fire drake. Some of the carriages and wagon carts they passed looked streamlined, and they were constructed and painted so cleverly that Jenka thought the gods themselves might have had a hand in their design.

As they neared Outwal proper, the congestion and proximity of the growing structures became so dense that it felt to Jenka as if they were passing down a long, high-walled corridor. The sun was leaving the sky, and the landscape ahead of them fell away towards the sea, giving only the slightest hint at the size of the protected peninsula that lay beyond the Great Wall. They had a hilltop view of the kingdom lands all the way south to Port, and the sea coast to which they clung. Jenka held the carriage door open rather than enjoy the sight through the grimy glass. On one side of the city called Port was the sea, but on the other was nothing but wide-open landscape that stretched east and south as far as the eye could see. The view shed some perspective on all the overcrowding, reminding Jenka that, crammed and busy as the cities were, there were still thousands upon thousands of miles of open land and forest out there that hadn't been touched.

Just then, Jenka caught his first sight of the formidable Great Wall, and he was taken aback. The stone block monstrosity rose up over forty feet above the ground and stretched its way across the land in a gentle arc until it disappeared into the eastern horizon. There were towers spaced every so often along its length, and men moved about between them on the wall top. The western end went right into the sea and ended a good distance out in the bay with the great octagonal tower of a light house. Beyond the light house, the fading, rose-colored sky looked to be brewing the makings of a summer storm.

* * *

Late the next morning, the sky looked ready to empty itself, but they were lucky and stayed ahead of the impending downpour. They came to the well-guarded gates of iron-banded wood that stood open, leading to the tunnel that would take them under the Great Wall. Jenka found that he was feeling claustrophobic, and more than a little afraid. Zah didn't like all the people and the lack of openness either. Linux promised that all the congestion would be forgotten soon when they were out beyond sight of land in a ship on the open sea.

Herald called out "Here we go!" and into the tunnel they went.

If the lantern-lit world under the gigantic man-made barrier weren't so intriguing, Jenka would have closed the curtains and huddled inside. He did close the door though, just to keep out the stale smell.

The wall, built in thousand-foot-long sections, was completely filled with tunnels, passageways, and wide-open rooms, explained Linux. At the end of each section was a tower that rose some distance above the top of the wall. From the tower tops and along the wall, the Walguard stood watch over the frontier, protecting the kingdom from intrusion. Linux told them there was supposedly a lane where a wagon could cross the entire peninsula inside the wall.

The idea that men had built such a fortification, Jenka decided, was a testament to their desire to survive. Again, it was hard for Jenka to imagine that, just a few hundred years ago, there had been only the Dogma's handful of survivors, washed up on the shore of Gull's Reach.

The inside of the tunnel was a world unto itself with trading houses, taverns, and guard barracks. There were huge, torch lit corridors, teeming with wagons, people, and animals, all moving to and fro with a purpose. Jenka marveled at it all. Against all the odds, humanity had exerted its dominance over nature's treachery and had flourished in this land, above ground and below.

Jenka was tired of the noise and hubbub all the people made as they got along through the seemingly-endless, smoky, and suffocating passage. He was tired of not seeing grass and trees and the open sky. The only life here that wasn't human were the rats, the skinny, yapping dogs that chased them, and the filthy carrion-bats that sometimes came sweeping by the window out of nowhere. Some of the people looked as haggard and worn down as Jenka felt, as if the world below was sucking the life right out of them. And the smells. Sometimes it was mouthwatering, like when they passed a busy bakery, or a spice gallery, or an open pot of stew. Sometimes the aroma was sickening and putrid, when they passed an open refuse pit or the rotting corpse of something dead in a darkened corner, but always an undertone of musky sweat and filth permeated everything they came across.

It was a longer tunnel than Jenka had imagined it could be. Jenka couldn't see the trolls ever getting past an obstacle such as the wall that rose above his head any more than he could imagine them rising up with the mudged strains of dracus to even attempt it. Then again, he could picture them working together, flying in swarms over the wall, rendering the boundary impotent. This sudden image caused Jenka to realize why their journey to King's Island was so important. Gravelbone didn't have to take the lands beyond the wall. He could drive man back behind the barrier and besiege the islands just by holding the frontier.

All of this, this civilized way of life, the luxuries and customs that men were growing used to in the long-tamed lands, all the wondrous contraptions, and all the resources used to build them were about to be threatened with extinction. Everyone who didn't get behind the wall might be slaughtered but that, Jenka decided, was only a small bit of the populace. It was the people of the islands, and on the mainland peninsula; the people who had no inkling of where their meat, fur, wood, and grain came from. The people who depended on the resources that came from the frontier that were really about to be put under siege. Jenka saw it all coming to pass, as plainly as he had seen himself soaring on the back of a dragon through the sky, toward an impossibly tall castle with Zah and another rider. None of it seemed real to him, yet the fact that it was really happening kept asserting itself into his mind. He was left in a state of confused enlightenment, deeply stained with the bleak and dismal truth of things. If they didn't intervene and stop the demon-troll called Gravelbone, then the fate of humanity on this land would take a drastic turn.

They emerged from the hot, loud tunnel into the kingdom proper, and Jenka saw the city of Port and the mighty sea again, this time from a much lower perspective. All coherent thought emptied from his ever-contemplative mind at the sight of the ocean. The vastness of the sea made him feel small. The realization that he, the dragons and the trolls, and this Gravelbone, might all just be unimportant parts of existence, assaulted his brain. Was humanity, or even life itself, that significant in the grand scheme of things? Wasn't humanity's survival directly related to nature's decline? Jenka didn't have the answers, only more questions. He was glad when they stopped, and when his head finally found the pillow that evening. He was tired of worrying, wondering, and thinking. He slept like a rock.

The morning's travel brought with it the smell of brine and the screaming of gulls. Port was as crowded and overbuilt as Outwal had been, but Port had the endless open sea to gaze upon, and the warm breeze to keep the foul air from lingering. Just as they were coming into the city, there was a stretch of road that Jenka found improbable beauty in. The green, hilly fields were exceptionally rocky, and the salty moisture kept the larger trees from growing, leaving a few miles of unmolested, open terrain between the road and the pounding sea shore. Birds spiraled and frolicked all about the area, and a rabbit went streaking from rock cluster to rock cluster before diving back into its hole. That stretch of wild land, because of its stubborn rockiness, had been left to its own devices, and that made Jenka smile.

A forest of ship masts with white and yellow sails decorated the harbor. Jenka had never known there were that many kinds and sizes of ships. He had only ever seen drawings of them Lemmy had made a long time ago. Some of the ships had four or five sets of sails, and others only a tall, wide triangle of canvas. Jenka could see how the wind carried them over the water, but not how they steered askew of the direction it was blowing. They intrigued him, and he watched out the glass the comings and goings of several different vessels as the buggy bounced them closer to the docks.

It was late afternoon when the carriage finally came to a halt near a dock house. It sported the spread-winged falcon of the realm on a huge banner rippling above the building. Above it was another banner, this one boasting the anchor and wheel of the King's Fleet. Jenka was glad to be out of the carriage because the last mile or so of the ride had been over a dock of planked wood, and his teeth were numb from the jarring of the iron wheels on the rough surface.

The earliest ship they could take, the *Serpentina*, was to leave Port with the late-evening tide, which gave the travelers just enough time to wash off the road grime and enjoy a hot meal in the King's Fleet Commons. The barracks' bathhouses were clean, and the launderer efficient, and in less than a turn of the glass, the men were sitting round a table laden with bowls of steaming clam stew and mugs of watered ale. Zah had chosen to use a private bathhouse rather than bathe in the presence of the men, and she had taken the carriage to do so.

On a podium in the common room, a pair of colorfully dressed musicians performed a sort of story song. It incorporated spoken dialogue over a plucking lute, but the men went quickly and often into a rambunctious chorus and everybody there, save Jenka and Linux, knew the words and joined in.

A uniformed man, clean-shaven, with three brass bars of rank pinned to his collar, slid up next to Herald and poured a thick dollop of liquid from a silver flask into the grizzly ranger's mug. After a short bit of conversation, he eased out the door, and Herald followed. Jenka ate his stew and drank deeply from his mug until the slight, but welcome, feel of the ale began to warm his blood. He listened to the performers and even picked up the words and joined in on a chorus or two, but in the back of his mind he was still thinking about demon-trolls and friendly dragons. He also began to wonder what was happening with Rikky, Stick, and Master Kember. Had they learned about how Mortin had lost his mind yet? Had they captured or killed those bandits? Did they ever make it to Three Forks?

His concerns evaporated into a cloud of lavender aroma that reached his nose as Zahrellion came around the table and slid onto the bench beside him. The triangle on her forehead glittered yellow gold as its silver surface reflected the lantern light, and her flowing white hair shimmered with an uncanny pearlescence. Her eyes sparkled scarlet, and her smile was slight yet wondrous. "It's going to be all right," she reassured absently. His grin of a response made her smile come to life, which lifted his heart in turn.

His long, brooding face had been worrying Zah since they had spoken with Crystal, but now a bit of sailor-song had seemingly broken his funk. She would have interrupted his carriage ride broodings sooner had there not been such a bright, constant gleam of intelligent reasoning shining in the depths of his eyes. She could tell that he was starting to see the subtle complexities of the situation, and she was also starting to feel that tingly simmer in her belly again. He wasn't the foolish boy she had first thought. Her mind screamed for her to wall the childish and foolhardy attraction in, to deny it, but she just didn't want to. Nor did she think she could resist temptation if it presented itself.

Luckily for both of them, a steamy, three-day shipboard romance was averted by fate. The two of them spent their entire first night at sea hugging the ship's rail, vomiting their guts out. The rest of the voyage was no better, for they were miserable with seasickness and couldn't keep anything they tried to consume in their bellies. By the time they were in sight of King's Island, Zah had no desire left to be Jenka's lover. The idea that her druidic gods were punishing her for her lack of resolve had taken strong root in her mind, and she never wanted to feel this ill again.

The sea swells were fifteen feet high, and rough, when the ship neared rocky cliffs thrust up out of the sea, so high you couldn't see the tops of them, but after they passed a certain point, the northern extension of the island dampened the ocean's flow, and the water smoothed off considerably. The Captain kept the cliffs to the right of the *Serpentina* as day slid into night, and when Jenka woke, the gull-infested cliffs were still there. Jenka fought to keep down the sea biscuit he had braved earlier, and stayed above to watch them put ashore. He was glad he did. At the royal harbor at Kingston, rising up around the turquoise sea was King Blanchard's glorious castle fortress of white marble. It was nothing short of amazing and bordered on miraculous to behold.

Jenka had to keep reminding himself to breathe as they approached.

* * *

Rikky didn't get to Three Forks conscious, but he got there. Jenka, Herald, and the druids had long since left, but once Rikky's identity was learned, he was taken immediately to a private chamber, where Spell Master Vahlda looked him over. The mage called for a field surgeon, and the two of them spent most of a night removing the leg and fighting the infection that had set in.

Rikky survived another night, but only because of the powerful potions that Master Vahlda had poured into him. He woke long enough the next day to tell them all what he had seen and what had happened to Master Kember. He never once thought that he would be believed, but to his surprise, nearly a score of men had reported seeing the big black dragon and its horned-headed rider.

Commander Corda listened to young Rikky's tale personally. He promised that Rikky's mother would receive his pension as if he had died a fully fledged Forester. He honored Rikky's request to have a scribe come and take down a message for him, and even offered a bird to fly it to its destination.

Rikky vowed never to forget the kindness and respect Commander Corda showed him while he was lying there staring into the face of death. Rikky was glad for the comfort the man's assurances gave him, but he had no intention of dying just yet. He was determined to live so that he could spend his days trying to kill the fargin Goblin King.

He was unconscious when the first reports of the massacre at the village called Grove came in. According to the riders, the whole place had been destroyed and most everyone killed and eaten by the trolls and goblins. Later in the night, when Rikky was wide awake and fighting back a fever, Swinerd's bunch came thundering into the Stronghold calling out about Crag.

Rikky's screams of anguish and sorrow were long and loud, and they left him exhausted. Before he collapsed back into unconsciousness, he managed to send a man to stop his message from flying. He now needed to add another passage. Along with his own mother and a good portion of the people of Crag, Jenka's mother and Lemmy the mute were believed to have been eaten alive by the horde of goblins that started pouring out of the mountains. It was only right that Jenka be told of his mother's probable fate, and Rikky kept himself conscious long enough to add the news to his missive before telling the man to let the bird fly for King's Island. After that, depression and sorrow took hold. The empty blackness of the place Rikky found himself slipping was welcome.

PART II

DUNGEONS AND DRAGONS

CHAPTER ELEVEN

If the Great Wall spoke of man's domination over the wilderness, then the city of Kingston spoke of man's aspirations at heavenly glory.

Seven white marble towers rose up out of a crenulated monstrosity of huge, rectangular buildings. The center tower was the tallest, easily reaching a thousand feet into the sky. The others were slightly shorter and fell equally in height and distance as they went outward from the center in a gentle, embracing arc. To Jenka, they looked like some colossal candelabra. The hulking constructions underneath the slim spires had been whimsically built, one atop the other, by three generations of royalty. The royal family had lived on the island since the kingdom seat had moved there from Gull's Reach eighty-five years earlier. All the other buildings of the city, also white marble, were generously decorated with high-rising entryways and balconies sporting columned balustrades. There were roaring lions or wild looking Gargoyles watching over from the corners of the structures and towering statues of the realm's heroes stood guard proudly in the plazas and parks. There were added-on balconies and arching elevated walkways spanning between the towers like spider webs. There were long multi-level wings with row upon row of arched windows and high-peaked tile roofs. There were wide-open gardens with eye-catching fountains that somehow spewed water high into the sky. And behind it all, the rocky gray island rose up and out, like some terraced stadium bowl designed by the gods to cradle the height of human achievement.

Every bit of exposed building face; every block, brick or stone in Kingston, save the roads and the roofs, was formed from the same silver-veined, white marble blocks. Amazingly, every single roof tile and all of the window shutters that Jenka could see were painted a rusty red; the exact color of the baked clay tiles that came from the clay pits back on the mainland. Even the new construction that Jenka could see—despite the canvas-draped scaffolding that had been built around it—was of the same unmistakable white marble.

There was a high-arched entryway connected to a port cache that reached boldly out into the sparkling harbor, and this is where the ship seemed to be going. A Deck Master was pounding a heavy drum, and six men at each side rowed the ship slowly to the steady booming tattoo. The harbor was busy elsewhere, with net haulers, sleek fancy passenger boats, and huge cargo ships that did nothing other than sail between Port and Mainsted Harbor. Near the royal entrance there were no other vessels about.

Two well-armed men in matching plated-leather armor and cloaks as blue as the ocean's depths stood watch from a raised platform. Two other men on the platform turned a crank that lowered a huge, rusty chain strung just above the waterline. When the Captain promised the customary round of rum to the crew to celebrate their safe passage from the mainland, the rowers began to pull that much harder. Once under the port cache they saw no more of Kingston's wonders. They went ashore over a mechanical long plank, which rotated out to meet the *Serpentina*. They were ushered, without refreshment, and with a bit of alarming urgency, through a maze of corridors and stairways into a lush, open bailey garden. Here, His Royal Highness,

King Blanchard, was in the process of holding court.

The courtyard was wide-open lawn, and the day was beautiful. If you could discount the three twelve-foot-tall walls and the towering building face keeping the space closed-off from the rest of the city, it almost felt like being in a forest glade. There was a raised patio lined with well-crafted marble falcons. The tops of their wings extended wide and acted as a level, waist-high rail, while their heads and bodies served as balustrades. Below them, a woven mesh of leafy vinery had overtaken the wall face, the snaking green tendrils resembling upward-licking flames. On the patio sat the king, in the largest of three high-backed thrones of hickory, inlayed with silver and gold. The thrones sat on a round scarlet carpet. On the carpet, a score of people, mostly garishly-dressed men, listened intently as the queen went about passing judgment on a matter that the king was supposed to be hearing.

King Blanchard was older than Jenka had imagined him to be. Jenka had always pictured a late middle-aged man: tall, fit, and powerful looking. At the very least, a regal-seeming man. King Blanchard was exactly the opposite. He looked like an ancient, bloated hog, complete with an upturned, piggish nose and heavy jowls. His cheeks were splotchy with veins, as smooth as a baby's rump and as round as the moon itself. His fleshy, layered chin lay over the golden chains he wore, and his steepled fingers were the size of overstuffed sausages. The jeweled crown on his head was too small, and it looked as if it might be painfully pinching the top of his balding pate.

Beside him to the right, sat a serious looking young man who slightly resembled the king, in the sense that he was dressed similarly and as regally as the ruler of the realm, and he was sitting in a raised seat before a group of subjects. Otherwise he looked nothing like King Blanchard. Jenka assumed, correctly, that this was Prince Richard. He was thin, tall, and dark-haired, and a few years older than Jenka. Jenka had been two and the Prince only a boy when the trolls had snatched him up. The look of disdain and contempt he held on his face as he looked out at the people before him was more than a little noticeable. It was the woman on the king's left, the blooming flower amidst the thorny shrubs, who Prince Richard took his looks after.

Queen Alvazina was strong-jawed and delicate looking at the same time. Her hair and eyes were dark under her silver crown, and the set of her brow showed that she was actually listening to what she was hearing. She looked able to have her way with either of the men who sat with her, and the ill-attired commoner speaking to her now seemed thankful for the sincerity of her attention. King Blanchard was half-dazed—drunk maybe—and might have been drooling. Prince Richard, to Jenka's immediate distaste, was now staring openly at Zahrellion and Linux, but mostly at Zah.

It was the queen who was actually holding court here, Jenka decided. When the man before her was finished, she granted his request with a smile. He was quickly ushered from the carpet, and the announcer called out for, "High Ranger Kaljatig, and the party under his escort," to come before the court for questioning.

It took Jenka a moment, and a sharp tug at the sleeve of his attractive, new wide-shouldered leather attire, for him to realize that High Ranger Kaljatig was actually Herald. He had heard the name when they were at Swinerd's farm but hadn't recalled it.

The petitioners and courtiers in attendance eased in closer, and more than one murmured a bit of speculation as to the nature of this unexpected questioning. Prince Richard seemed to be taking an active interest in the coming conversation as well, and even bothered to elbow his father into wakefulness so he wouldn't miss what was about to transpire.

Save for the two times he had been in the presence of the dragons, Jenka couldn't ever remember being as nervous as he was when he took his knee before the royal family. It didn't help that in the last three days he hadn't slept, and had only been able to keep down a single sea biscuit.

"Rise. What is this, Ranger?" King Blanchard asked Herald roughly, as if it had been Herald who had just woken him from his slumber.

"Your Majesty, I be First Ranger Herald Kaljatig. Commander Brody at Kingsmen's Keep ordered me to escort these two druids here to have audience." Herald sucked in a nervous breath and continued. "This boy," he indicated Jenka, "killed a troll and survived two encounters with the wyrms. He is Marwick Kember's pupil and has a tale worth tellin' as well." Herald gave Zah, and then Linux, a look nearing shame, then dropped his eyes. "He, and the druids, seem to think that the dragons want to help us in the battle."

"Battle?" the queen chimed in loudly. "What battle?"

The king grumbled and waved her off, "It's nothing but some overzealous trolls getting ideas in their feral heads. I received a bird from Commander Corda on the matter. He said that he had it under control, and that the clay pit caravans would be back to hauling in no time."

"It's more than some exited trolls…uh," Jenka couldn't believe he had spoken out like that to the king. He felt a wave of hot embarrassment flush through his body. What was he going to say; that a demon called Gravelbone was loose upon the land and a dragon had told him so? He was still half delirious from being seasick for so long and had very little color in his pasty face. Stammering, he tried to control the damage he might have done with his contempt. "Uh, Majesty, uh, forgive me for speaking out of turn." Jenka fell back to a knee humbly. "There were scores and scores of trolls coming down out of the mountains as we were leaving Three Forks Stronghold, and that was five days ago. Ask Herald," Jenka looked up at the King's Ranger pleadingly. "Commander Corda told us all that Weston had been completely taken, and my mother is stuck up in Crag."

The people gathered around the conversation gasped and exclaimed concern and horror, and a few of them walked quickly away, seeking to protect one mainland interest or another. The scribes who sat at a table behind the thrones were scribbling furiously, and the scratchy sound of their quills was constant amid the murmur.

"Is this true, Ranger?" Prince Richard asked. His curiosity now seemed genuine, and his ill expression had been replaced by one of sincere concern.

Herald was nodding in the affirmative and about to answer aloud when King Blanchard broke back into the conversation angrily, as if the last few statements had never been spoken. It was a tactful attempt to divert the conversation away from its present course, but the emotion behind the outburst was real enough. "Who are you, boy, that you speak to your liege with such familiarity? What is your name?"

"Jenka De Swasso, Highness. Son of King's Ranger Jericho De Swasso," Jenka stayed down on one knee as he proudly answered through his embarrassment.

"You're the boy?" this came excitedly from the queen. "Your father and Kember saved my Richard from the vermin. You and your companions will stay in the castle, in the royal guest apartments, and you will sit at my side during the tourney tomorrow. Tonight you must join us at the king's table. I want to hear all about you and your…your mother." She turned sharply to her husband. "You will send a battalion to Crag, won't you?"

"Two shiploads of Kingsmen were sent yesterday to help deal with the issue of the trolls harassing the clay pits and the lumberjacks," Prince Richard informed. "I'll send a bird with orders for a detachment to fetch Mother De Swasso and have her brought to Three Forks Stronghold, just as soon as I see Master Zofel."

The happiness in the queen's eyes, and the fact that Jenka's father had saved his son caused the king's anger to quell itself. Still, he scolded Jenka and the queen both with his brows and asked Herald another question. "Why haven't I gotten word from the mainland yet?"

"You're getting it now, Father," Prince Richard calmed. "A bird arrived a few hours ago, but Master Zofel is helping to ready the grounds for tomorrow's games." He turned to a man wearing fine leather armor who carried a long straight sword at his hip. His collar had a circular insignia that Jenka didn't recognize. "Squire Randle, find Master Zofel and have him bring the messages he has received in the last few days. Have him bring a cage full of eager swifters and a scribe to help him."

"Which messages should I tell him to bring, Highness?" the squire asked. "There are scores of them each day."

"Everything," the queen said sternly. "Bring every message that has been received in the last five days and bring them to the Main Hall's annex. We wouldn't want them blowing away out here." The queen gave this order, and the squire, having no intentions of questioning her as he had the Prince, strode purposefully away.

King Blanchard scowled and shook his jowls at his wife, then nodded thanks at his son for having handled her concern so deftly. He then looked at Herald directly. "You look like you need to say more, Ranger. Tell me all of it, man, but over a table board and a tankard. I know who you are. We have some of your brother's swine roasting in the pits for the morrow's feast. I don't know what's in that grain he feeds those pigs, but they're the best in all—"

"Your Highness, you don't seem to understand," Zahrellion stepped boldly up and interrupted the king. She didn't wait for him to respond to her interruption, and she shrugged off Linux' hand when he tried to keep her from continuing. "The trolls are coming." Her tone was urgent and pleading, but the expression came out angry, a little defiant even, and King Blanchard began to glow a deep shade of enraged scarlet around the neck and cheeks. "They are being led by a demon called Gravelbone, and they are bringing war to the mainland. They will fight the kingdom till the end. They do not want—"

"Silence, girl!" King Blanchard raised his bulky body forward as he yelled over her. The hickory throne groaned with distress beneath him. "Do you think I care what the trolls want or don't want? It is Duke Watlin's duty to deal with the mainland vermin. The trolls are not coming here to Kingston, I assure you." A chuckle was quickly stifled in the gathered crowd at this.

The king was enraged, and his round crimson face jiggled with his anger. Spittle flew from the corner of his mouth as he spoke. "You'll spend a while in the dungeons for that sort of insolence, miss. If it wasn't for what his father done, that boy right there would be going there with you." He shook an accusing finger at Jenka. "I'm the fargin king, am I not?"

"You are, Father. No one has forgotten," Prince Richard tactfully intervened. "Remember though, these druids are religious pioneers, come to warn us of what they have observed in the peaks." He glanced pleadingly at Zah to say no more, and then at Linux, telling him with his eyes to restrain her mouth. "Great-Grandfather granted the Order of Dou amnesty to pursue their strange arts, remember? The druids may lack manners and protocol, but I don't think that they have any intention of disrespecting you or the throne."

"Yes, Husband," the queen's criticizing voice held a tone that made the king cringe and scowl that much more. "They are to be our guests, and it sounds to me like you need to find out what is going on with all of this and direct your rage elsewhere. While you've been lost in your cups and foul couplings, things seem to have been going unattended."

"Shut up, woman, before I have the headsman shorten you a foot." The king waved away the heavily muscled guard that had eased up behind Zahrellion to arrest her. Jenka was thankful for it, because he didn't know what he would do if she let loose one of those powerful yellow blasts of magic here.

The king raged on, "And if things have been going unattended, then Duke Watlin might be the one who needs your scolding. Do what you will with these queerly-marked religious folk. I'll be in the annex, hearing the whole of my Ranger's tale. The boy will come, too. And Richard, I expect you to join us just as soon as you round up that lackey of a Message Master and set that bird to wing. Tell Commander Corda that we want a full report on the troll situation, especially up in the foothills. He is to report directly to Kingston now, directly to you. Duke Watlin just might need an appointment with the headsman. Have the Walguard search him out and ship him here. Now, this court is dismissed!" With that, the heavy king stood and stomped off into the white marble building, angrily waving away the attendants and any other who dared approach him as he went.

CHAPTER TWELVE

The annex was a high-ceilinged room, as big as a ranch house, connected to the much larger Royal Gathering Hall. The royal gathering hall was filled with row upon row of finely decorated plank tables, all ready and awaiting the guests who were to attend the morrow's feast. The annex had tables as well, but those four were plain, exposed pine without a cloth over them. It wasn't quite festival time in Kingston, but preliminary competitions in several events were being held to cull out some of the unworthy competitors before the upcoming Solstice Festival. Thus, the feast was prepared to commemorate the beginning of the season's games.

There was no fire in the well-used hearth, which was fine with Jenka. The air was sticky with humidity here, and he still wasn't feeling well. The heat would only have made it worse. He wished that he were outside in the open until trays of fruit, bread, and cheese arrived.

The tankards came next, kept full by a trio of well-rounded servant girls. The ale wasn't watered down at all; Jenka felt it warming his guts immediately. After two swigs he was spinning in the seat he had been given. He was next to Herald and across from the king. The two heavily-armed and armored King's Guard watching over their liege had eyed him suspiciously at first, but they were now listening raptly to Herald, as he spoke of things that seemed fantastic and unreal to the island-born men.

The king had asked Herald to start at the beginning, so Herald was getting into his side of the tale of Jenka and the trolls that Jade had killed. To Jenka's surprise, the over-plump king was acting less like a monarch and more like an ordinary man. He had changed out of his heavy, formal robes, and Jenka could see there had been a time when the man was fit. His arms, though the size of hams, didn't jiggle and shake like his chins and cheeks did. There was a thick layer of muscle underneath all that bulk. His crown had been removed, but a ring of peachy red skin had been indented, leaving a perfect line ringing around his skull.

Every so often, a nervous young man dressed in a pale blue robe and slippers came in and placed a satchel full of messages on the next table. Jenka figured he was the scribe helping the Message Master carry out the queen's order.

"How did you survive it, boy?" King Blanchard asked Jenka directly, causing him to flush with embarrassment again. He hadn't been listening to Herald, and he wasn't sure what exactly the king was referring to.

"He's been green at the gills since we left Port, Your Highness," Herald came to the rescue. "He throwed his guts up all the way across. Go on, Jenk, tell the king what happened from the start of it."

Jenka gulped down his unease, sipped deeply from his tankard, and went into an abbreviated version of his hunt for the stag and the mayhem that came after. The only portion he left out was the part about his conversation with Jade. He didn't mention it, but he didn't hide the fact that the dragon had returned to kill the trolls and save him. He threw in a few words about Rikky, just as he had promised he would do, but he doubted that the name even registered with the king. When he was up to the point where the red dragon had swooped on them, he paused and sipped deeply.

King Blanchard and his two King's Guards, as well as Herald, Prince Richard, and a man who was most likely Master Zofel, were all looking at him with a strange sort of reverence.

"Well. That is remarkable. But it's not a troll war now, is it? I'd like to hear Kember's side of it, too," the king said to Herald. "I trust that man's judgment till the end."

"Aye," Herald agreed with a nod and a raise of his tankard. "Marwick's a good `en, but he's after them bastards that killed his charge."

Jenka was feeling better now that he had eaten a few bites of fruit and some bread. He took in a deep breath and decided to plunge into what he now felt he had to do, no matter what the consequences were going to be for it.

"That was just the beginning. King Blanchard, Prince Richard," Jenka respectfully attracted their attention. "The Druida Zahrellion is right. The trolls are coming out of the hills in droves. Herald knows it, and so does Commander Corda. We spotted scores of tracks around the lake. They may have a leader now, and that makes them a little more dangerous because now they have a purpose. They figured out that if the kingdom seat moves to the mainland, then they will be driven deeper into the mountains, which brings up the other matter at hand." Since both the king and the Prince were listening intently, he decided to take advantage of the moment. "There are dragons, the druids call them mudged, that are feral like the trolls. They are the foolish ones we sometimes catch and kill. There are also other, purer strains of dracus, the whites, greens, and blues; the ones that we only see in the sky. They don't want the trolls forced back into the peaks into their territory. They—"

"This is ludicrous," King Blanchard cut in. "The dragons are dragons and the trolls are trolls. I'll take you down to the royal armory on the morrow, boy, and you can look upon the dragon head that sits down there. It once belonged to the wyrm who maimed my grandmother, Queen Marilla, right before these very eyes." He pointed two meaty fingers back at his chubby face. "That wyrm was as blue as the sky itself, and cunning. I saw the intelligence in its eyes. It would tell any tale that would get it what it wanted, I assure you. In the end, just like in the beginning out on Gull's Reach, it will be us or them. There's no sense putting off the confrontation. And *of* course the trolls don't want the kingdom seat to move, and as soon as they can breach our Great Wall they can have a say in the matter. But how, boy? How are they going to do it? How can you even begin to speculate what the trolls and dragons think? They are beasts, mighty beasts, but beasts nonetheless."

"The lass is a powerful mage, Highness, and as bold as they come," Herald said into the silence. His grim tone conveyed the seriousness of his words. "I en't no fool. There truly be something to all of this. I seen her blast ripples through the sky and damn near kill that big red wyrm that attacked her and Jenka by the lake. And I seen an awful lot of troll sign, just like the boy said. The girl thinks that the mudged wyrms are going to side up with the trolls. If they did that, then our Great Wall won't hold `em back long."

King Blanchard paled a few shades as the possibilities sank into his fleshy head.

"Has she spoken with a dragon? Have you?" Prince Richard looked at Jenka hard. He left the table where he had been helping the Message Master and the scribe sort through the unorganized satchels of missives, and moved to stand near his father's side. "How have you come to believe what it is you are telling your king?"

Jenka met the Prince's eyes, and a sudden dawning struck him then. The Prince was the future of the realm. He was the other person who had bonded with a dragon. Jenka gave the slightest twitches of his head, then acted dumb. "I'm not sure I understand what you mean, sir."

"Here! Here it is," Master Zofel exclaimed, more to the scribe beside him than anybody else. He was ignored until he let out a saddened sigh and said, "Oh, dear heavens, no."

Prince Richard held Jenka's gaze, while everyone else looked at Master Zofel for an explanation. Jenka gave the Prince a short, affirmative nod, and the relief that flooded into the future king was plainly visible. Both turned to face Master Zofel as he started to read the little scroll he had found.

"My liege," the message began. "The Stronghold gates have been opened for the people of the frontier, and as many men as can be spared have been sent out to call them in, but only until the enemy comes at us here. The trolls are organizing under some sort of Goblin King, who rides the back of a nasty black wyrm that he has put under his command. I would not believe these things myself had not eleven of my men been killed by the thing. There are other witnesses and other victims, too. Also other dragons have been seen in the skies here in Three Forks. They have been swooping on the herds left in the pastures. The trolls, along with packs of their smaller goblinkin, are ransacking the frontier villages and settlements. Weston has been decimated. I fear that the men you are shipping will not number nearly enough. There has been no word from Kingsmen's Keep, or Copperton, and that is not the worst of the news I bear.

"A man you respect, one the frontier's greatest men, Marwick Kember, was killed by a troll as he was tracking bandits."

"No," Jenka sobbed, as tears came filling up and over his eyes. He was so overcome with sorrow over the loss of Master Kember that he didn't even realize that nothing had been said about Crag.

The Message Master read on, but a little more sympathetically. "Kember's charge, one Rikky Camile, was maimed in the attack, but he survives. He witnessed this Goblin King as well. I granted him a boon for his service. He will be sending a message by swifter to his companion, one Jenka De Swasso, who I think you will find to be of interest. Your Ranger, the two druids I told you of in my last report, and the De Swasso boy, all left Three Forks three days ago, and have most likely been at sea for a day or more as this is takes the wing. It is possible that you will receive this before they arrive.

The ba…The bo…" Master Zofel harrumphed and then coughed back an emotional sob. He strode round the tables quickly, and completely ignoring the two guardsmen and the Prince, stooped over King Blanchard's shoulder and pointed out where he had stopped reading.

King Blanchard read to himself from where the other man had stopped. He let out a long, slow breath and then removed Master Zofel's hand from the parchment. After a very long pause, filled with naught but Jenka's quiet sniffling, he went on. "Crag's been taken, too." The king said, matter-of-factly. "No matter what you hear, Jenka, have faith that Commander Brody will honor your father's sacrifice. He is an honorable man, and he has sworn to do so, as did Kember. If it was possible, Brody got your mother to the Keep. I'm sure of it."

Jenka put his face down on the table and let out a long, slow, keening wail. The long week of travelling, and the last few days of sickened exhaustion had finally taken their toll. Jenka's emotions had combined into a torrent, and the restraining dam could hold them back no longer. He was sobbing unashamedly before the king and future-king of men. He felt hollow and ill, and the sobs that wracked his haggard body caused his stomach muscles to clench, but he didn't care. Master Kember, Solmon, and possibly his mother were all dead.

"Come, friend," Prince Richard put a hand on Jenka's elbow and gently helped him to his feet. "Master Zofel and Wilam here will escort you to your chambers in the guest apartments. At this point, it's clear that rest is the thing you need most. We have much more to discuss here, and it would be unfair to subject you to it all." He gently helped Jenka to his feet and handed him off to the Message Master. With a nod, one of the guardsmen held open a door for them.

Once they were gone, King Blanchard ordered one of his guards to go fetch the druids. "Do it with grace, Garner," he added as the man was exiting the annex. "I've already gotten off on the wrong foot with that girl." He turned to the other guard. "You can stand watch outside the door. When Garner returns, let the druids in. Then have him round up Admiral Wheetly and the master commander. Make sure that there are plenty of runners about the hall. We will have need of them. I fear this will be a long evening. Send to the harbor and have two, no, three ships immediately cleared for the transport of men and their gear to the mainland."

Jenka was in a daze, as he was led through the grand castle. Down long, carpeted corridors lined with tapestries and fancy brass lantern sconces they went, under arched openings and through halls lined with standing suits of polished armor. They passed people of all sorts, then went into a wide open, eight-sided rotunda with a ceiling made from stained glass that rose a hundred feet above their heads. They went up a wide, marble stairway that climbed in a segmented spiral around the inside of the wall. Finally, Master Zofel urged them across a landing, to a set of hand-carved, oaken doors, with the image of a giant falcon's head carved into them. The predator bird's beak came to a point just above the floor where the two doors met. The bird's intimidating eyes were set in a fierce stare, as if it were about to swoop out of the sky and snatch you. Small brass ring knockers accented the falcon's sharply focused pupils, but they didn't have to use them. The doors swung silently open as they neared. Jenka would have thought it magic had a servant man of middling years not scurried out of their way from behind the doorway.

There was another long, lushly decorated hall beyond the portal. It was lined with more sets of oaken double doors, all carved with falcons in various states of being. One door had a bird flying high over a well-detailed forest of skyward-reaching pines. Another had a falcon splashing into the water with claws extended. The head and tail of a fish could be made out behind the tiny, misshapen droplets of water that hadn't been left out of the pristine detail. Jenka was led to another door with the image of an ancient tree trunk that still sported a few of its heavier branches. High upon one of them a lone falcon was preening itself in the warm summer sun. The fact that Jenka could discern what the creature was doing and the weather of the scene on the carved wooden slab was a testament to the skill of the craftsman. Though he was feeling lost and miserable, and more afraid than he had ever felt in his life, Jenka couldn't help but marvel at the work.

Inside the immaculately furnished room was a tray of warm meat and bread, set beside a clay pitcher of water and a wash basin. The aroma of the offering found Jenka's nose, but he had no desire to eat. He went straight to the fancy, down-filled four poster bed and fell headlong into it. Master Zofel and the scribe were quickly forgotten as a fresh wave of despair caused Jenka to bury his head in the pillows and scream out. He didn't even hear the door close behind his escorts as they left him and, mercifully, he found a deep and dreamless slumber soon after they had gone.

CHAPTER THIRTEEN

At some point during the night, Jenka had awoken and disrobed. In the late morning, he was pulled from his dark slumber by a raucous cheer wafting up through an open window. He rose to find that he was naked save for his small cloths. There was a different tray of food on the table, as well as a small fold of paper with a handwritten note on it. He washed his face in the basin and ate half of a sugary pastry before the cause of the previous night's grief crept back into his mind. A tear slid down his cheek for Master Kember, but he held back the flow, hoping in his heart of hearts that his mother and Lemmy were locked up safely behind the impenetrable walls of Kingsmen's keep, and that little Rikky would find the strength to survive his crippled condition. He wondered about his best friend Grondy and his family back in Crag. Hopefully they had all gotten to Kingsmen's Keep safely. He refused to believe otherwise. After he forced down the rest of the sweet roll, he picked up the message. It read:

For the sake of propriety, you will be referred to as Sir Jenka De Swasso for the remainder of your stay. The attendant standing outside your door will retrieve for you anything you request, and when you are presentable, he will lead you to the terrace that overlooks the tourney grounds. We are all here enjoying the excitement of the joust, and would enjoy it even more if you would join us.

The message was signed by the queen herself, which astounded Jenka. He didn't really want to go, but he felt he had to. Master Kember would have wanted him to witness the events and to study the various techniques used in the different competitions. They had discussed as much as they were riding out of Crag. Solman and Rikky had been excited about the competitions, too, but they would never get to be a part of that now. Jenka suddenly realized how raw his sorrow was, and it was just too much for him to bear.

A lump the size of a fist formed in his throat and he choked back a sob. More tears fell then, as the uncontrollable sobbing took over. Jenka curled up on the floor into a fetal ball and began rocking to and fro. It was nearing the noon hour when he finally exited his room and asked the waiting man to take him to the terrace.

The cheering was coming in regular intervals now, and could be heard anywhere there was an open window. Jenka had gotten himself under control, and though he was filled to brimming with grief and worry, he was intrigued by the idea of seeing an actual joust. Master Kember had been training Jenka and the other hunters to track by sign and other practical woodsman necessities such as horsemanship, archery, and common herb lore for years. The group had never much concerned themselves with swords, spears, or jousting. There wasn't much need for fighting other men in the frontier. Jenka was curious as always, and a little eager, not only to see the remaining competitions, but to see Zah and to tell her that Prince Richard was the third of them. He also wanted to find out what had transpired in the annex after he had crumbled before them all. Surely King Blanchard had declared war on the trolls and was sending the might of the kingdom's army to bear down on the frontier.

The sound of the crowd's cheering suddenly grew very loud. They had come to an airy, three-sided room that opened onto an extended balcony. Jenka was still under the ceiling's shadow, but out in the bright sunlight, leaning against a fancy marble rail, a small group of finely-attired people were gathered, looking down at something that held them captivated. A score of people in all, counting servants and attendants, were there. Jenka's companions and the royal family, as well as a few highly ranked Kingsmen and their ladies, cheered and applauded happily. There were other noble folk, separated clearly from the common folk by their ornate jewelry and richly colored garments. They, too, were celebrating whatever had just happened down on the tiltyard.

Another cheer resounded, the sound coming from everywhere around Jenka. Zahrellion glanced back as she was clapping, and her beautiful smile beamed even brighter at him. For a heartbeat, she looked like some alien goddess from a bard's tale as the triangle tattoo on her forehead twinkled in the sun. Her smile briefly sagged into a line of grim sympathy, but only for a moment. Then she peeled herself away from the rail and hurried over to greet him.

She met him with a fierce hug and whispered up into his ear that she was sorry about Master

Kember. She held him for a moment, then reached up on tipped toes and kissed his cheek sweetly. "Your mother is surely in the Keep with Lem. He is more than half elvish, you know. He could move around the trolls without them even knowing he was there. You didn't know it, but he was once at the Druidom with Linux and me. He is strong. He has so much elvish blood flowing in him that he ages slower. He is nearly seventy years old, but looks like a boy. If he's looking after your mother, then she is safe, I promise you."

Jenka had to shake the surprise from his head so that he didn't forget what he was so excited about. If he didn't want to tell her about his realization so badly, he might have broken down again while she was hugging him. As it was, the information about Lemmy was so shocking, and yet obviously true, that he couldn't find any words at all. The Rangers had always treated Lemmy differently than anyone else, and Lemmy had never been a boy as Jenka and the others had. At least not that Jenka could remember. He couldn't remember quiet, golden-haired Lem ever being any different at all. He didn't want to get sidetracked, so he shook his head clear again and jumped right in.

"Prince Richard is our third!" Jenka exclaimed. "He is the future of the kingdom. That's why Crystal couldn't tell us who he was!"

Zah's eyes blinked a few times as the idea of it registered, then her mouth curled into a satisfied smile. "You're just in time to see him compete. He goes second, after the joust they will soon be announcing."

She took Jenka's hand in hers and led him toward the rail. As they approached, Herald and Linux both turned and gave Jenka a stiff nod. The queen saw him, too, and she stifled a smile into a compassionate, tight-lipped line. She gave a polite wave before tugging at her husband's sleeve and speaking. Her words were lost in the cheers, but Jenka thought he read her lips saying Jenka De Swasso as she nodded in his direction. King Blanchard didn't bother to turn and look at him, but he nodded once so that his wife would get out of his ear.

Jenka took the rail at Zah's side and had just started to take in the tourney grounds below when Prince Richard's man, Squire Roland, eased up behind him.

"The king would have a word, Sir Jenka," the squire said politely. "After that, Prince Richard would have you and Druida Zahrellion down on the field for a private word before he competes." His proper usage of her title pleased Zahrellion, but she didn't take her eyes from the tiltyard.

Jenka touched Zah's shoulder and she turned. "I heard him," she said flatly. All the joy and sadness of her previous expression was now replaced with frustrated ire. "Go see what that fool king wants. Then we will go see if the apple has fallen too close to the tree."

Jenka didn't even try to fathom what she was upset about. He soon found out.

"Ahh, Sir Jenka," King Blanchard welcomed him by waving off Jenka's bow and clamping a doughy hand on his shoulder. "Sit here," the king indicated the seat that the squire had been sitting in before.

Jenka sat.

"I don't know how much of this mudge business you believe, but I'm here to tell you that it is the truth." Jenka wondered why Zah had been so upset. It appeared that she had convinced the king of at least part of her theory. "Some dragons have intelligence and others don't," the king continued, while watching intently the impending crash of the jousters below. "Other dragons are so intelligent and powerful that they can win your mind and command you like a puppet."

The crowd held its breath, as the huge destriers thundered down the lane. The knight riding under the green stag's head banner took his foe's dampened coronal directly under the chin and went out of his saddle, heels over head. His competitor, a knight with the yellow rising sun on his banner, threw his lance off to the side, and he shook his gauntleted fist at the crowd in triumph. Most of the crowd cheered, but a certain contingent of people, all seemingly located in the same general section of tiered bleachers, threw red kerchiefs with pebbles tied in them down onto the lanes. Jenka thought that the fallen man's throat might have been crushed in the collision, but the people were cheering crazily.

"I will not rescind the bounty on dragon heads, but not for the reasons that hard-headed girl thinks." The king looked over at Jenka and held his gaze. Below, the man who had been unhorsed was still down, and a group of robed men and a distraught woman were all hurrying out into the yard to attend his injuries.

"She convinced me, Jenka," the king told him. "She convinced me that a dragon has gotten into her mind and altered her judgment." He held up a hand to forestall Jenka's comment. "I'll explain it to you, because I see that you are smitten with her, and I don't want your head bungled, too."

An attendant arrived with a tray of goblets and the king took two, handing one to Jenka. To be served anything by a king was no small honor, and the act wasn't lost on Jenka or any other aspiring noble in sight of the royal terrace. Once the attendant was gone, and both of them had sipped at the light, peachy-flavored drink, the king turned back to Jenka and went on quietly.

"If I rescind the bounty, then it is the mudged dragons who gain. These High Dracus, as she calls them, aren't the ones getting killed by men. They are supposedly mighty and clever and they live in the highest reaches of the peaks. How could we hurt them? Why would they care what our laws and bounties dictate? If they are so smart and powerful, then they really are beyond us, yet one of them wants me to stop killing the mudged. It makes no sense."

"I think that Zah has failed to explain why the dragons want the bounty gone," Jenka said. The steadiness of his voice conveyed a stability of emotion that Jenka knew he didn't really have at the moment. His grief and sorrow were just under the surface, festering again, waiting for a word or an action to help burst them free.

"Why?" the king asked, giving Jenka a look that said his opinion of him might suddenly gain a new, and not-so-elevated perspective after he gave his response.

"Your Highness, there is more I need tell you about the trolls. But about the dragons, there is this: As you know, some of them aren't as mudged as others. There will come a time when those dragons will have to choose a side. They might be the tide that turns the battle. They will be more likely to side with the High Dracus against the mudged and the trolls if they knew that the king of men has taken this step." Jenka didn't know how he had realized all of this, but he had. "They need to believe that, after the war, there will be at least the chance for an understanding to be reached between us. Otherwise, they could all just band together and annihilate us, then fight it out amongst themselves."

The king held his second chin with his hand and pondered the idea. Jenka took the moment and went on to tell him what he had been meaning to say the previous night.

"The Goblin King isn't going to have his hordes attack the wall," Jenka said flatly. "He will attempt to besiege us from beyond it."

The dubious look that came over the king's big, round face held much contempt, as well as a degree of mirth. Jenka was about to lose the favor he had somehow gained with his king if he didn't speak carefully here. "The islands are dependent on the resources of the frontier." Jenka opened his hands wide with open palms up, indicating that he wasn't certain of anything. "Once the Goblin King has forced us behind the wall, the way of life people here have come to enjoy will cease to exist. What will they do on Gull's Reach for firewood? How will the forges operate, and the kitchens? Captain Corda said that twelve shiploads of wood come from the frontier every month. That, and the clay pits, and the lake's water, and the iron and copper up in the mines will all be lost to you here."

The king's brows had narrowed as he began to see where Jenka was going with all of this. "We receive shiploads of lumber from South Port, and Mainsted Harbor, too. So do the other islands. What will he do once we are pinned, do you think?"

"That, I can't perceive," Jenka shrugged. "We must cut the trolls and goblins down and drive them away for good. We can't sit behind the wall and quietly wait for them to go away. We must take the initiative while we still can."

"You are your father's son, Jenka," King Blanchard said with a bit of pride. "Did you know that Jericho and I competed here once in the archery competition?"

Jenka didn't know it, but the idea of his parents being here reminded him that he had a message to deliver to the old Hazeltine Witch that his mother had once worked for. He would have to ask an attendant, or maybe Prince Richard, how to find her residence.

Down on the field, the man who had been injured was finally hauled away to the cheers and jeers of the people. This meant that Prince Richard's joust was coming up soon.

"I think we should cautiously open our arms to the High Dracus, Majesty. Make them show their loyalty to you by helping us defeat the Goblin King."

The king had that dubious look again, but he also showed some regard for the deep intelligence reflecting in Jenka's eyes. "Do you still want to be a Ranger like your father was?" the king asked suddenly.

Jenka took a deep sip of his peachy offering, and he shook his head in the negative. "I want to kill the Goblin King before he destroys everything I've ever known. I wasn't born on the Islands, Highness. I wasn't even born in your kingdom. I was born in those hills on the mainland under the peaks, just like the trolls and the dragons were, and that is my home as much as it is theirs. I will not let them take it from me." He paused to bite back a tear, then decided that his emotion was clouding his judgment.

"My son wishes to speak with you on matters of the mudged," the king said, seeing that the Prince's squire was getting fidgety. Already, the joust was being announced. "He has taken a queer interest in the dragons. Go with his squire, but when the competition is over this evening, we will meet again in the annex. My Commanders will be there to hear your thoughts. Together we will form a plan. I sent two more shiploads of men last night to fortify the wall and help the folks at Three Forks. Another ship is going up the eastern coast all the way into Seacut. They will free the people up at Kingsmen's Keep, and they will get your mother and the Rangers to safety." With that, the king turned back to the games and began clapping politely for the man who would be competing against his son.

The squire led Jenka and Zahrellion down a long, tight, spiraling stair, which opened into a segmented stable area. Men and horses stood patiently in various stages of armament, as squires, pages, and stablemen ran about, fretting frantically over the contestant they were assigned to attend. The crowd was roaring for their Prince, as he trotted his beautiful white destrier out into the sunlight. Jenka felt a bit of jealous awe at the sight of him.

Prince Richard wore a gleaming breastplate, lobstered gauntlets, and a polished steel helm with golden hawk wings sweeping back from the temple. All of the armor was chased with dark blue enamel work. He looked larger and more substantial than he had the night before, more warrior than Prince now. In the right light, the wings looked a bit like horns, and his faceguard lent his brows a sinister sharpness. The squire urged them over to a ground-level railing where they could watch the competition. The Prince spun his mount around and snarled at the crowd, adding to the terrifying effect of his helm. Jenka got the idea that the look was intentional and meant to strike fear in the Prince's competition.

Jenka's assessment was confirmed when the Prince trotted over near them and gave them a sincere, boyish grin. He cut his eyes at his squire before he lifted his visor, and the man stepped quietly off to retrieve the Prince's lance. "I am pleased that you, my fellow Dragoneers, are worthy of the duty that fate has given us. I had feared I would have to face the coming storm with children or fools at my side." The Prince's expression grew troubled. He glanced up at the terrace where his father and mother were watching with the kingdom's notables, and sighed. "I am sorry that I didn't meet you sooner, for your sake, Jenka, what I am about to do must be done. Do not interfere, Zahrellion. We will see each other again soon enough." With that, he spurred his mount over to his squire, snatched his lance up just under the vamplate, and raised it high to feed the frenzied crowd's excitement.

It was then that Jenka saw a tiny speck in the distant sky, streaking purposefully towards them just beneath the clouds. It was only a speck at the moment, but Jenka knew that it would grow larger as it came nearer. There was no question in his mind what it was. It was a dragon.

CHAPTER FOURTEEN

Rikky didn't know what to think. He was in so much pain that he hated trying to think at all. Worse, it was the lower leg and foot that wasn't even there any more; the part of him that had been eaten by that horrid little goblin, which was hurting him so badly. He had enough of his thigh left that he felt he could get a long peg-leg fitted, and he was hopeful, but he wouldn't even be able to breathe until the pain began to lessen. He longed to be fighting the trolls that were now harrying the people of the frontier into the Stronghold, or even fighting the pain of learning to walk again. He did not want to be fighting a ghostly pain that shouldn't even exist.

Outside the small closet-of-a-room he had been assigned next to the barracks in Three Forks Stronghold, Rikky could hear the frustration of the men. The trolls were pushing them in seemingly organized bunches now, they said. The Goblin King and his dragon had gained a couple of winged allies, and now other dragons swooped and harried everything they saw moving.

The Goblin King's horde had herded the people out of the frontier and behind the walls of the Stronghold. The gates were closed now, and a hundred or more people—some women and children—who hadn't been fast enough, had been torn apart and eaten within sight of the Walguard as they watched from atop the Stronghold's wall. There was nothing they could have done to save them except waste arrows trying to arc one out that far and get lucky. The city of Three Forks was aflame. Captain Corda admitted that they were about to be in a pinch. There were over four hundred people packed into the hold, a third of them women and children. The kitchens were thin for the harvest was coming up and the stocked staples hadn't been replenished since last year. There were only seventy-three trained Kingsmen and Walguard combined. The rest of them, sent out to the settlements and towns, hadn't returned.

Captain Corda said that they needed to be back behind the Great Wall. Three Forks would be completely cut off from the rest of the kingdom soon, and things weren't looking so good for making a break for it.

Rikky cursed the gods and mocked the Life Giver. He just wanted to stop hurting long enough so that he could wrap his mind around something other than agony, but it wasn't to be just yet. Pain engulfed him, and he fell back into the cool sea of oblivion that often saved him from losing his mind in the hurt.

When he opened his eyes again, Spell Master Vahlda was there, and so was Stick. Stick told him that he had made it back from the clay pits with the Kingsman and a few others. He looked like he had been raked across the chest by filthy claws a few days ago. Three long, festering scabs cut from his shoulder down to his ribs, and were oozing pus. His normally mahogany skin was pallid, and his eyes were sunken back into his skull. The Spell Master was working a healing spell, and Rikky clenched his jaws and shifted himself up so that he could better see. He had seen Master Vahlda do the very same thing on several other wounded men, and each time Rikky couldn't help but be drawn to watch the bewildering magic firsthand.

Stick sat on a cot with his hands high over his head. Master Vahlda was moving his open palm over the wound like he might do if he were scrubbing it with a rag. A warm, yellow glow radiated from beneath his hand, and a tangible static seemed to make the air around them hum, and crackle, and hiss. As the glowing power scrubbed over them, Stick's festered wounds were ever so slightly starting to lose their angry redness.

A slight drip of greenish yellow fluid started down the young man's chest, and he voiced his discomfort. Master Vahlda soothed him with unknowable words as he continued. The Spell Master's face was beaded with sweat, and his eyes began to sink into darkening sockets, but he didn't give up. Eventually Stick's long gashes faded into dark, ugly scar tissue, but the doing of the deed cost Master Vahlda a lot.

The act ended with the Spell Master pitching forward. Stick dropped from the cot he had been seated on to catch him. Master Vahlda was exhausted and incoherent, so Stick carefully laid him out on the cot across from Rikky.

"He'll recuperate," said Rikky. "You heard about Mortin?"

"Yeah," Stick rubbed and scratched at his scars curiously while looking curiously at the Spell Master. "They couldn't save the leg?"

"Nah, I was too slow getting here to keep it." Rikky heaved a frustrated sigh. "I'm gonna kill that fargin Goblin King, or I'll die trying. I swear it on Master Kember's soul."

"Them's heavy words, Rik. You en't seen how bad it is out there now."

"It doesn't matter," Rikky snorted, and pointed at his missing leg. "It's as bad as it gets right here. I might die, but that's not so bad. I'll die on my own terms, and that'll be trying to kill that fargin thing out there. Will you help me?"

"I will," Stick nodded. "I'm a made Forester though, so I still have to follow orders. But where I can help you, Rik, I will. What do you need?"

"I need a smith, or maybe a woodworker…or both, to come see me here." He winced. He was just a boy, and wasn't certain what he really needed. "I don't have hardly any coin, but I might be able to impose on Commander Corda for enough to get done what I need."

"A leg?" Stick moved over and pulled back the flattened sheet to see Rikky's stump.

The leg was gone from mid-thigh down, and a lot of the meat that should have been there had been eaten away so the grotesque limb was thinner and more scarred than it should have been. It hadn't had time to start healing at all. Stick swallowed hard, but started nodding hopefully. He could actually envision a sleeved piece sliding up onto the stump and maybe buckling diagonally across Rikky's chest and over his shoulder with leather straps. "I think you got enough to work with, but you need a lot more healing before you try to get around again."

"Na, Na, Na. It hurts like molten fire," Rikky clenched his jaws. "It can't hurt any worse than it does now, no matter what I do. I'm feeling the parts that en't there no more, nothing else. It's maddening. I'd rather not just lay here. Will you fetch me who I need? Will you talk to them craftsmen that came in from the frontier and help me?"

Stick looked down at his chest and shook his head affirmatively. "Should I get someone to tend to him while I go?" He indicated Spell Master Vahlda's peacefully sleeping form.

"Nah," Rikky answered with a nod of respect toward the mage. "He does this after almost every healing, and there have been way too many in the last few days. He needs the sleep."

"I'm off then," Stick told him. "I'll try and get someone over here that has an inkling of what you intend, but I got to hurry about it before I get new orders. Them trolls is closing on the Stronghold, and we might have to make a charge back to the Great Wall." He patted Rikky on the shoulder. "I'm sorry about Master Kember, I really am. And if we go retreatin' to the wall, I'll make sure you get there."

Rikky nodded his thanks, and though he didn't see Stick again, a man with a knotted string and a set of scribe tools came later that evening and started measuring and sketching ideas for Rikky to ponder.

Rikky added and took away from the design, and even grew a little excited about it, but the pain of his missing extremity never lessened. He began to savor the hurt, and used that pain to strengthen his resolve. He would get a peg-leg, and he would walk and ride again. He would suffer every single minute of it if he had to and, when the time came, he would kill that fargin Goblin King. "I will rise up and come for you," he told himself over and over again when the pain gripped him the most. Two days later, his peg-leg completed, the mantra of his revenge was scalded into his mind for good. "I will rise up and come for you."

When he tried his first step with the peg-leg, he fell face-first into the foot board and spent half the afternoon vomiting from the intensity of the pain, but he got up. "I will rise up and come for you," he told himself.

It would be no small feat to master the raw agony the device caused him, but he knew that he eventually would. It fit his stump well, and it would work, but when the call to evacuate the Stronghold finally came he still couldn't walk. He could do little more than cling to his wooden prosthesis with all he had as he was hauled like a sack of grain and tossed into a wagon with some other men. *I will rise up and come for you,* he kept saying in his head as two excited horses and a terrified driver started them out of the gates in the dark of night. It wasn't until they were being hounded by howling trolls, heavy rocks pelting the canvas, that he had his first doubts. "If I survive this flight, I will rise up and come for you," he amended with a snort of disgust at the idea of falling prey to the trolls again. "If I don't survive, I'll haunt this world for all eternity."

* * *

On King's Island, Prince Richard's armor sparkled like sapphires and polished silver in the midday sun. His horse snorted and pranced eagerly at their end of the long, divided jousting lane. At the far end, an ornery black steed carried a huge rider, plated in armor as dark as pitch. His horse's caparison was also black, and his banner sported a fat, blood-red spider.

Suddenly, the horn was blown, and both of the combatants spurred their eager destriers into a forward charge. The crowd cheered madly, waving their hands and urging on their favorite. Above them all, high in the sky, unseen yet by any there save for Jenka, was the approaching dragon. It grew in size as it came, and more swiftly now. Jenka caught a sapphire glint of reflection, then another. It was the blue from the vision Crystal had showed him. It was the mighty blue drake that had been flying towards that deep mountain castle with him and Zahrellion.

In the tiltyard, the two great masses of flesh and steel thundered toward each other. Jenka only spared them the briefest of glances because the dragon dove sharply and began corkscrewing its way down from the sky at an impossible speed.

Some in the crowd had spotted the wyrm, and the people began to scream and point up at the creature, even as Prince Richard and his foe met at full gallop. The Prince shrugged out of the way of his opponent's lance and twisted to deflect the blow even further. His lance burst into a shower of splintery shrapnel against the other knight's chest, sending the man out of his saddle. The man hit the ground hard, and rolled, then came up clutching at his shoulder.

When the prince turned to shake a victorious fist at the crowd he saw that the crowd was no longer concerned with the competition. They were looking up at the dragon. It was right there, swooping in, with its lower claws extended.

From the balcony, frantic orders were being called out. Kingsmen were running down the lanes between the tiered seats to defend the Prince of the realm. The Prince was out in the open, vulnerable, and his mother was hysterical. King Blanchard wasn't much better off. He had just been contemplating what Jenka had told him, giving it some weight, and now here was a sparkling blue dragon, come to attack them on right here on King's Island!

The dragon snatched Prince Richard off of his horse and was about to turn and flee, when someone threw a big spear from atop a nearby tower.

The screaming crowds trampled one another, each and every one of them overtaken by the dragon fear that the huge wyrms emanate naturally. Zah wasn't afraid. She threw her arm forth and sent an ear-shattering, directionally focused blast of crackling, yellow energy at the missile the Kingsman had launched. The streaking spear would have hit the dragon in its gullet, and could have hit the Prince had Zah not intervened, but instead it went flinging away like a single strand of straw blowing in a gale. Now, Kingsmen and city guard alike were all starting toward her, too. Jenka didn't know what to do, and he fell to the ground when the first of the Kingsmen threw him to the side to tackle Zah.

The dragon was lifting above the futilely fired arrows, and seemed to be crushing the prince in its claws. Jenka knew better though. The dragon was cupping its claws protectively to shield the Prince from the stray arrows and spears, but that's not how it looked.

Up and out of bow range the dragon lifted the prince, then into a long, wing-stroked flight out over rocky land to the north. From different places in the arena, King Blanchard and Jenka helplessly watched the beast fade into a speck and eventually disappear.

Zahrellion was yanked roughly to her feet. It took Jenka a moment to realize why. She had stopped the dragon from taking that spear. She had just thwarted King Blanchard's defenders. These men had come to arrest her, and probably him, too.

A Kingsman in a well-worn uniform started grabbing at him. Jenka pulled his arm free indignantly, and was saved from further conflict by Prince Richard's squire. Squire Roland pulled Jenka away from the confusion and nearly squeezed the breath out of him trying to restrain him when he saw the way Zah was being treated. Already, her face was swollen and bleeding, and she was being jerked around rather violently.

"You'll go to the dungeons, too, fool," the squire hissed into Jenka's ear. "You can't help her from the inside. Keep your head, man. Just keep your head."

A moment later, the squire led Jenka back to the annex. A few of the commanders had hurried there and were waiting nervously for their king. King Blanchard wasn't in the room yet, but he could be heard coming quickly that way. Curses and threats and even a sob or two wafted ahead of him.

A deep *whooshing* sound that pulled at Jenka's guts emitted from behind him. Linux stepped out of the blocked marble wall as if there were an open passageway, startling Jenka and the squire badly.

"I'll see you again, my friend," Linux whispered. "Take care of her, Jenka. I cannot stay, for I am more than just who I am. Rest assured that if the king doesn't set her loose soon, then the entire Druidom of Dou will come for her, and you, too, if the need be."

Jenka turned to respond, but the druid was gone. He had vanished into thin air, leaving Jenka and the squire, who had heard the whole conversation, gawking with wide opened mouths.

"Boy!" King Blanchard bellowed, as he came into the room ahead of a full retinue. Herald was with him, and he rushed over to Jenka with a mixture of anger and concern on his face.

"Make me believe that you had nothing to do with this madness, Jenka De Swasso," the king went on. "Make me believe it now!"

"That spear was going to hit the Prince, Your Highness," Jenka said quickly. "And Prince Richard isn't in any danger. I swear it."

"Fool," the squire said in a quick, angry hiss before the king could start in.

"How can you know what danger he is in if you are not involved?" the king reasoned angrily. "Take him to the dungeons, too!"

"Don't hurt him none!" Herald shouted loudly enough that even the king blanched back from the Ranger's intensity. "Nor the lass! Any man harms `em afore they be properly judged will feel my wrath!"

"Do as he says," King Blanchard conceded with a snarl. He then said directly to Herald, "Mind your station, Ranger, lest you go sit with `em. My son, your Prince, has been abducted, and those two have both been meddling with those intelligent dragons, and we both know it. They might have led them here. They could be unwilling conspirators. They could be spelled. You said so yourself. The girl is a mage. I'll not have the dragons learning from them what we are planning for the trolls."

The rough, callused hands of the overly-excited Kingsmen yanked and pulled Jenka out of the annex and down the corridor to a switch-backed stairway. Down they went, past landing after landing, and then down some more, until they came to an iron-barred door. Two scruffy, overweight men in filthy Kingsmen's uniforms sat behind it, wide-eyed and alert. The air was thick with the sickly sweet smell of rot. It was humid and stuffy. Jenka felt as if the walls were already closing in on him.

The guards looked as if they had recently been sleeping. By the sound of Zahrellion's sobs coming from behind one of the hammered steel doors, it was obvious that they had been awake for a short while at least.

The barred door came open, as one of the dungeon guards cranked on an iron wheel set into the wall. Jenka was pulled into the cell run and shoved with brutal force into a darkened rectangle. He went sprawling face first into a wet sludge of muck and hay. The sound of the steel door slamming shut behind him echoed loudly in his ears. The jangling and rattling of the cell being locked was loud and sent an icy shiver down his back. The silence that followed was deep and potent, only broken by an exceptionally loud wail coming from whatever cell Zah was in. A thin yellow line of light leaked under his cell's door from the torch ensconced on the wall outside. Other than that, there was nothing.

CHAPTER FIFTEEN

Rikky's pain was quantified by the rough jarring of the covered wagon. He wasn't the only one riding in the back of the dirty, plank-board vegetable hauler. There were four other injured men from Three Forks Stronghold, every single one of them as teary-eyed as a babe. The tears weren't from fear or pain. They were from the overpowering aroma of the half-rotted onions that hadn't been properly cleaned out of the wagon's bed before it was commandeered by Commander Corda. Rocks and heavier stones pelted the canvas. The wagon raced at breakneck speeds through the troll-infested copses that lay between Three Forks and the open southern trade roads. Only one rock had torn through the thin covering, which seemed miraculous to Rikky. The rock had hit him in the middle of his back. It was painful, but not nearly as much as the constant agony of his missing lower leg.

It was a terrifying ride. The driver kept the horses moving swiftly and had twice called back that the trolls had cleared out, only to begin cursing and praying like a madman when the stones came flying in again. The wounded passengers held on for dear life as the wagon careened and swayed and nearly tipped over. A few times they went airborne for a long, slow moment only to come slamming down as the wagon came back up to greet them. It was a wonder that any of them had survived this far.

The wagon began to slow, which was a relief at first, but then it became a worry.

"What's wrong?" a Walguard named Jess called out to the driver. Jess had been blinded when a troll's claw raked his face.

"Muaaaah," came a half moaned, half gurgled groan.

"Take a look, lad," Jess encouraged Rikky. "You're the only one seems well enough to do it. It don't feel like we're on the road no more."

Rikky looked at the other men. One was nearly cut in half, another's head was wrapped in dark, bloody cloth, and Jess had lost his eyes. The last man might have been dead, as he hadn't so much as moved since the wild ride had started. Jess had told Rikky earlier that the Goblin King had placed his palm on the man's head and he had lost all his sense.

Rikky sucked in a deep breath and pulled himself over to the flapping hole the rock had made when it had torn through the canvas and hit him. He had to pull and tear the material to get it open wide enough for his head to poke out and see.

He looked out, and was immediately slapped in the face with brittle, dead limbs. They scared him more than hurt him as they stung then broke away. He had seen enough to know that they were running really close to the trees and that the moon was mostly full and bright in the sky. He chanced another glance, and after wriggling an arm and a shoulder out, he got enough of an advantage to see how much trouble they were in.

"He's dead, or dying maybe," Rikky called out. The wagon swayed violently to one side. The horses had their own head and were still half panicked from the trolls. "We en't on the road no more, and we're…we're headed into the thicket. We're…We… We're gonna…Hold on!"

The wagon slung over onto two wheels then came back down hard. Rikky's body went tearing through the canvas as he was thrown in a hard, twisting tumble out into the undergrowth. There was the loud sound of cracking wood, and one of the horses screamed out horribly. Rikky screamed, too, from the agony of his initial impact, but he passed out completely before he even stopped his long, cartwheeling tumble.

Sometime later, when Rikky opened his eyes, he realized that his missing limb had stopped hurting. The rest of him hurt instead. He felt a few deep scratches and scrapes, but wasn't bleeding profusely from anywhere. He would probably be as stiff as a statue later. After enduring the other, more potent agony of his missing limb for so long, he decided he wasn't feeling that bad.

He looked around from a sitting position and realized it was just about dawn. The sun had already begun to pinken the eastern sky, and the moon had passed below the horizon for the night. He could see no sign of the wagon, but he didn't really expect to in the dark. It was surprising that it wasn't crashed right there beyond where he had flown out of it. He doubted that it could have gone far in the semi-thick shrubbery, knee high grass, and sparsely-treed terrain.

As the sun came up, he held himself still and listened for the others. He heard crickets and an irritated owl, then happily chirping morning gales and an insistent woodpecker. Something larger huffed as it went along, low in the brush, but he heard no men calling out or otherwise conversing. He thought he heard a horse whinnying, which gave him hope. If he could find one of the two horses he might find a way to get onto it and ride it. Finding a horse with one leg and no crutch was going to be the test.

As the sun came up, Rikky heard a repetitive, moaning call. He called back, but the response was the same moaning as before. It sounded a little like the wagon driver, but Rikky doubted that he had lived. He didn't think that the driver was alive when he had been thrown. He had seen the man lying with his head twisted at an impossible angle on the wagon box, his arms dangling limply near the spinning spoke wheel. That was just before the wagon had been jarred up onto its side and threw him.

Rikky struggled, crawling his way over to the nearest tree. It took some effort, but he got himself upright and standing on his good leg. Looking around, he could make out the rectangular silhouette of the wagon bed lying on its side, amidst a fairly distant jumble of shrubbery. Off to the right, a horse had its harness lines tangled and was snorting his frustration at not being able to get free. Rikky realized that what he had thought was an irritated owl hooting in the night had actually been the exhausted horse.

After scanning the immediate area as best as he could for anything he might be able to use as a crutch, Rikky realized he would have to crawl all the way to the horse. He knew it would be no easy task, but he set to it with tightly-clenched jaws and a heart full of hopeful determination. The ground was soft, but the shrubs were thick and sometimes thorny. It was an exceptionally bright morning. It was humid and steamy, as if it had rained the previous day. He was sweating and frustrated, and clouds of mosquitoes swarmed around him. He ignored them, knowing that there was nothing he could do about them. When he finally made it over to the frightened animal, the sun had climbed high into the sky, and he had several dozen itching, red welts on his arms and neck.

Luckily, the wooden crossbar of the wagon harness was attached to the leather lines that the horse had dragged and tangled. The horse was glad to see

Rikky. It visibly calmed when he started talking to it. It didn't have a regular riding bridle, but Master Kember had trained all of his boys in horsemanship. Rikky wouldn't need any saddlery. Rikky's problem was going to be getting up on the damn thing with only one leg. He decided not to attempt it yet. Instead, he went about cutting the tangled lines while leaving the horse hobbled enough so that it could graze and wander a bit but not get away.

He found that the harness bar was as tall as he was. It would have made for a poor staff had it not had a big, swiveled, iron eye-ring cinched into it at about elbow level. Rikky could get his whole hand in the ring up to his thumb and could hang his weight on it as he hop-stepped along. He carried the horse's line with him as he went. The animal cooperated and lazily moved along with him, grazing and snorting when he stopped to grimace away the pain or get his wind back. Once, one of the injured men howled out from inside, or beyond, the toppled wagon. His desperate voice startled the horse. It made to bolt, and would have yanked Rikky to the ground and dragged him had he not shouted out a sharp command and yanked hard on the line he had rigged to the animal.

His makeshift walking stick felt like it was made of solid iron. It was an awkward and somewhat painful process for him to move along, but he finally got to the wagon. It was on its side, and there was no one to be seen around it.

It was Jess who had been howling out for help. He was the only one who had survived the crash. He was as glad as the horse had been to hear Rikky coming, because he knew that without help he would never be able to make it to safety.

"Is that you, lad?" he asked as Rikky peered into the wagon.

"It is," replied Rikky. He started to ask Jess a question about how far they were from the Great Wall, but he was cut off when the horse tried to bolt away again. He had tied the lines to the wagon, and the wooden frame jerked hard as the horse's weight pulled the line tight. Luckily, it hadn't been able to gain much momentum and the leather strapping held.

Jess said, "Trolls!" just as one of the greenish-skinned beasts howled out loudly to its pack mates.

"Come on," Rikky urged. "We can outrun them if we get on the horse." He leaned his torso into the wagon and grabbed Jess' outstretched hand. Just as Jess stumbled out of the tilted bed the first rock came flying in and hit the wagon with a hard *crack*. This time, when the horse bolted, it snapped the line, leaving Rikky and Jess standing there helplessly.

First one troll, then another, showed themselves. Beyond them, more of the beasts grunted and howled. They had come for the easy meal the wagonload of dead and half-dead men would provide.

Rikky's instinct to run after the horse was quickly averted when his left foot didn't take that first step for him. He fell forward, dragging Jess down with him. It was a good thing, for that's when the rocks started flying at them in abundance.

* * *

Jenka couldn't stand being inside the dismal little stone cell. All he could hear were Zahrellion's sobs, and the fainter, more terrifying calls of someone who had been put down there long ago and forgotten. Worse still, was the feeling of ineptitude, the humiliating realization that he was completely and utterly powerless to help Zah, or the people of the frontier, or anybody, including himself. He couldn't even get himself some water to sip, but it wasn't for lack of trying. His throat was raw, and his voice nearly gone from yelling for it. He felt like less than a man. His dignity had long since left him, and now his pride was starting to slip from his grasp. He was about to start begging for the water when Zah let out another long sob filled with fear and confusion. It was just enough to keep Jenka from crossing that line. The indecency of it all gave him back some resolve. It was enough to stay his thirst for the moment, but there was no way to tell how long that would last.

It could have been hours, but it seemed more like days before somebody came and rattled open the eye-level slot to peer in at him. The scant torch-light filtering around the silhouetted head caused his eyes and head to ache, but when the visitor spoke, the voice was as welcome as any ever had been.

"Fargin hells!" Herald exclaimed angrily. "You! And you," he yelled to the dungeon guards. "This man, and the lady over there are to have fresh, clean water every hour, and three warm meals a day." He held up three fingers and wiggled them at the slovenly men. "I'll have the food brought to the dungeon gates from the main kitchen, not that bug-infested servant's hole. And if I find out that they aren't getting the meals I send, I'll come down here myself and cut you a new arsehole. Now get to fetching some good clean water and waste no time about it!"

"How long have we been down here?" Jenka had moved closer to the open slot and stood in the shadow, out of the yellow beam of moat-filled light penetrating his darkened box.

"Two days, lad," Herald sighed. "And a lot has happened."

"Can you have someone look at Zahrellion? She hasn't stopped moaning since we've been down here. I think she was injured by the men who arrested her."

"Fargin luggers," Herald cursed them. "I'll send the Spell Master down as soon as I can track him down. I'd have come sooner, lad, but the kingdom has gone mad with all of this. The trolls have set upon Three Forks and the folk cowering there are going to have to make an unprotected run for the wall. It's fargin madness. And here in the dungeon sits the two people that were trying to warn us all about it."

"Go check on Zah," Jenka rasped out the request. "She sounded like she was getting worse, and I'm concerned for her."

"Aye, lad, I will," Herald promised. "But only after I've seen you get a drink or two of clean water in you. I've done my duty to them druids. It's my duty to your da and Marwick that I'm trying to do now. If it weren't for the queen I'd never have gotten down here. She wants you let loose, but His Majesty is as thick-headed as a mountain ram. He thinks you two were tricked by the wyrms and led them here to take the Prince."

"The Prince is…"

"Not so loud, lad," Herald hushed. "I seen it as plain as day. He wasn't harmed none. That wyrm was protecting him, and I think that the three of you know more than you're letting on, but that discussion is for another day."

"I can wait," Jenka moved into the rectangular beam of light, and the sight of him caused Herald to lightly gasp. He was filthy and bruised, and his eyes were as red as blood. Worse, he was dehydrated, and his lips were beginning to crack and bleed. He had been seasick for days just before he was imprisoned, and his body was craving nutrition. "Go, Herald. She may be in bad shape. I'm not going anywhere."

"I'll go check on the druida, Jenka, but if that water isn't here soon, I'll start cutting pieces off of this fargin guard they left down here. I'm a First Ranger, and I can distribute the king's justice with impunity." He said it loud enough for the remaining dungeon guard to plainly hear.

He turned and strode out of Jenka's line of sight, and asked the now-nervous guard which cell Zahrellion was in. It was the one across from Jenka, and once the slot was open and Herald was peering in, Jenka felt a wave of relief wash over him. That changed when Herald turned around and looked back at Jenka. Zah's pitiful moan came from the opening, and Jenka heard it louder than before. It sounded raspy, as if fluid was gurgling in her throat. Herald looked in again, then spun back toward Jenka. The paled look on Herald's face was horrified.

The grizzled old Ranger looked more than a little worried by what he had seen. His eyes darted this way and that as he eased back over to Jenka's slot.

"What is it, Herald?" Jenka asked worriedly. "Is she all right? She sounds awful."

"I can't answer your question, lad." Herald looked more confused than anything now, and he spoke in a barely audible whisper. "I heard her, too, Jenka. Her voice came from in there, but she en't in that box. It's as empty as Solman's belly was when we found him."

"Magic?" Jenka asked, feeling the first bit of hope he had felt in days.

Herald just nodded, then went back and closed the slot on her door. As if to punctuate the strangeness of the situation, another eerie moan came from the empty cell.

CHAPTER SIXTEEN

"I'm right here."

Zahrellion's voice came from behind Jenka. He whirled to see a faint, ghostly image of her wavering right there in his cell. Reflexively, he took a step back and gasped. "Actually, I am lying at the foot of the door in my cell. I am projecting my image here," she corrected herself. Her voice echoed from some indefinite point that didn't quite correspond with the location of her image's mouth.

"Fargin magic creeps my crotch," Herald said, just as Master Kember had said a dozen times the night they had all been forced to camp around Linux' hissing druid fire.

"Are you all right?" Jenka asked worriedly. "You sound horrible." His initial shock had subsided, and his mind was starting to itch curiously.

"In spirit, I am strong, but my body needs attention, as well as food and water," Zahrellion's image answered.

"Mark my words, lass, the healer and healthy platters are a coming," Herald reassured nervously. His voice was muffled and reverberated through the heavy steel door. "I'm sorry, but it's all I can do at the moment. King Blanchard'll be leaving for the mainland soon with an unprecedented flotilla. Once he's gone, the queen'll soon have ya released to more civil detention."

"Once my body is healing, all Jenka and I will need is food and water," she replied confidently. "Prince Richard knows exactly where we ended up, and Crystal warned us that we would have some time on our hands soon. I think we shouldn't squander it. We won't be here nearly long enough, I fear." The last was said with a smirk directed at Jenka.

"Who is Crystal?" asked Herald, who now had his face pressed against the door so that he could better see into Jenka's cell. It was struggle for him to keep his head from blocking the light.

"Crystal is a dragon," Jenka explained weakly. He was tired of holding back the truth from Herald, so he let it all come out. "She's a mountain white that has bonded with Zahrellion. My bondmate is the green called Jade, that saved me from the trolls in the mountains. He hasn't weaned yet. Prince Richard has bonded with the blue you saw on the tiltyard."

"Well, that all be hard to get a hold of, but I'm a still listenin'," said Herald, in his crude way. "Tell me the whole of it, so I'm not stumbling around like a blind man out here."

Jenka told him the truth of what had happened during his first encounter with Jade and the trolls. Zahrellion told him about the midnight rendezvous with Crystal, and the two of them took turns explaining what they knew about the demon called Gravelbone, and the powerful hellborn nightshade that he rode.

Water came in clean buckets, and plates of meat, bread, and fruit followed. Zah had to break the spell she had cast upon herself and return to her body so that she could eat and drink. Herald had them open her cell door so that he could help her. He was appalled at the infected cuts and bruises on her arms and face, and he threatened that the queen would soon be down to inspect her prisoners. After that, the dungeon guards ran themselves ragged as every healer and potion-maker they could muster came by to attend her. While all this was happening, Jenka drank, ate, and dozed. There was plenty of food available now, and water would only be a shout away. Jenka remembered that he had unfinished business in Kingston, and just before Herald excused himself from the dungeons, Jenka called him over to his cell door.

"I appreciate you, Herald. Can you get into my things?"

"I can," the King's Ranger answered. "What do you need?"

"There is a bull-scrotum pouch in my shoulder pack with some copper coins and a silver piece in it. Also inside is a small, scrolled message that I was supposed to deliver to an old Hazeltine here on the island. I promised my mother. Can you take it to her? The street and number is written on the scroll, but I don't know my way around."

"Aye, I will," Herald spat a wad of phlegm on the floor and cringed. "But I'll not enjoy that strange sort of company. I'll place it in her hand, then move along,"

Jenka actually chuckled at Herald's foolish fear of magic. "Keep the coins for your trouble."

"Those coins won't solve my problems, lad," Herald grinned. "But I'll deduct a pint or two so as to get up my nerve to go see the fargin old witch for ya."

Later that evening, after most of the castle's healers and a couple of strange monks came to look in on them, after the guards had settled into their evening slumber, Zah's ghostly image appeared in Jenka's cell again, and she patiently gave him his first lesson in the arcane.

Eagerly, Jenka drank it all in.

* * *

Rikky and the blinded Walguard named Jess were in serious trouble. The trolls had surrounded the wagon they were huddled against, and were closing in. High overhead, a large, black dragon circled. The horse that Rikky had worked so hard to tether had long since run off. Even if they could find a way to call it back, both of them would never be able to mount it before the trolls got them. There weren't any weapons at hand, and there were three dead bodies' worth of scent to draw the hungry trolls closer. It didn't look good. Rikky almost wished that he was as blind as Jess so that he didn't have to watch the beasts coming to feast on his flesh again.

A flap of the wagon's canvas that Rikky had torn earlier fluttered in the breeze and grazed his head, causing him to spin around reflexively. He thought the trolls were on them from behind. Through the opening, he happened to see his long, wooden peg leg, lying just out of his reach inside the wagon with the dead men.

"I need you to reach back, Jess, through the hole in the canvas here," Rikky instructed quickly. The trolls were yards away now and a hurled rock thumped the wagon frame with a resounding *crack* that startled both of them. "That's it…no, the other way. You feel the shaft of my peg? It's made from a hardened spear shaft, you'll know the feel. Yes, there…now just give it a yank." He glanced about them nervously and knew it was too late. One of the coarse-haired, green-skinned beasts was bearing down on them.

The troll hunkered low and lumbered in at them, swinging a raking claw at Jess. Rikky pushed his new friend out of the way. The seasoned Walguard swung Rikky's crude peg leg hard on his way over and caught the troll squarely on the side of its snarling, doggish head. It wasn't much of a blow. It was a lucky shot, though, because it caused the lanky creature to stumble over them and into the torn canvas. Instead of continuing to attack them, the beast began feeding on the dead men piled in the tilted wagon bed.

The sound of ripping flesh and snarling delight sickened Rikky, but he held down his gorge. Two more trolls eased nearer, drawn by the sounds of their pack mate's feeding, yet wary of the two men. Several others were waiting cautiously in the thickets. Worse than that, the sleek, black-scaled dragon above was now swooping down to get its fill.

"Lay over flat," Rikky screamed at Jess, but it was too late. The dragon dropped out of the sky, coming toward them at breakneck speed. One of the trolls had to dive out of the way as the dragon, claws extended, threw out its wings to stall and hover right above the living humans. Its hind claw closed on Jess, and Rikky had no choice but to roll away. He grabbed his peg leg as he went, and fought back his terror-filled tears. Inside, he felt a bit cowardly for not dying right there with the blinded man. He expected the dragon to lift back up and fly away so that it could enjoy its human morsel elsewhere, but it never happened.

A roar as loud as any Rikky had ever heard resounded from somewhere beyond his vision. Suddenly, the black dragon was torn from the sky.

The other dragon passed with such speed and momentum that all Rikky saw was a blur of shining carillon.

Jess was jerked over roughly, and his shoulder was torn wide open, but he was alive. The trolls scattered, save for the one feeding inside the wagon bed. Rikky was in a daze of disbelief. It only worsened when he saw the shining blue dragon had a rider on its back wearing gleaming plate mail armor.

The huge, sapphire dragon threw the black mudge from its claws like it was so much fodder, then banked a sharp turn to blast a few of the fleeing trolls with its crackling, yellow breath. Rikky watched the black as it crashed awkwardly into the rough terrain and went for a bone-snapping tumble. His eyes found the blue as it came thumping down cautiously near them.

"Move away from the wagon!" the well-armored dragon rider called out.

"He's blind and wounded, man!" Rikky yelled. "And I've only one leg. There's a troll in there, too."

The huge blue dragon loomed its head down over Rikky and Jess, who was lying as still as a man could lie. Rikky might have thought him dead if his ruined eye sockets weren't rolling and twitching with his fear. The dragon pushed the wagon over onto its busted wheels, and then poked its head into the canvas like a snake investigating a rat hole. The dragon jerked quickly back, and a slosh of hot, thick, black blood splashed down on Rikky's filthy shirt front.

The rider patted the dragon on the back. The wyrm used its sinuous neck to sling the troll it had just crunched away to the side. "Get in the cart. We'll carry the whole thing to Midwal," the rider called down.

"Get in the cart?" Rikky asked back incredulously. "Are you mad?"

"Yes. Get in, and I'll have Royal carry you over to Midwal." If the rider had looked any less spectacular, Rikky might not have believed what he was hearing. Less than two minutes ago, he was about to be eaten by trolls a second time. But now, a dragon and its rider wanted to save him.

Remembering what he had overheard Jenka and Zah speaking about, Rikky decided that this was no mudged dragon. It was a deep sapphire blue, and its scales sparkled cleanly in the evening sun. Besides that, the rider's armor sported the kingdom's falcon on its breast. This was a kingdom man, Rikky was certain.

"Who are you?" Rikky asked, as he crawled over to Jess. "Can you tell me that?"

Prince Richard lifted his visor and gave Rikky a sympathetic grimace. "I'm the prince of the realm, Rikky, and Jenka De Swasso will be glad to know that you made it behind the wall to safety. He told my father about you, and then Commander Corda told us of your fate." Prince Richard forced a grin. "My father is stubborn, though, and I had to come on my own and hope that he brings the kingdom's might after me."

Rikky didn't say a word. He was stupefied by the fact that this man, his prince, knew exactly who he was. It was almost too much to believe.

"You are Rikky Camile, aren't you?"

"I am," Rikky finally said. He added a quick, "Milord," and hoped that he had spoken correctly.

"I'll take you to Midwal if you'll get in the wagon," Prince Richard urged. "Royal won't drop you, and we will fly smoothly. I am trying to get to Crag to help your families, and the King's Rangers who are holed up in the Keep, so I must hurry. I need you to spread the word that this dragon and I are not the enemy. We are going to try and get the people of the foothills to safety. Now get in."

"Let's do as he says, lad," Jess groaned. His shoulder was bleeding profusely, and he obviously needed the services of a stitcher and maybe a cleansing, too.

"Help me up, then," Rikky said. "I'll point the way if you help me over."

A few moments later, the ruined wagon cart lurched into the air in a manner that was anything but smooth. The dragon pushed his huge, leathery wings down, causing both Rikky and Jess to be forced into the floor of the bloody cart, then the dragon raised its wings and the cart dropped slightly out from under them. This happened a few dozen times, and Jess was heaving because of it, but eventually the dragon began to ride the wind, and the movement of the wagon became eerily calm.

It didn't take long for the Great Wall to come into view on the southern horizon. Rikky peered over the cart side through the now-tattered canvas. He marveled at the snaking structure as they drew nearer. Off to the far right, the glittering western horizon swallowed the coppery sun, and below them the world spread out in a sea of shadowy green, lightly-forested terrain. Rikky decided that, from this vantage, no one could possibly conceive that the world below had gone crazy with war. He had a million questions he wanted to ask Prince

Richard about Crag and about Jenka, Herald and the druids, but the wind whipped his unkempt hair wildly, and he could hardly hear himself when he tried to shout.

Jess grabbed at Rikky's good ankle and squeezed. Rikky looked down and noticed that the blinded man was paling dramatically. The old Walguard was bleeding out, and they were still a good distance away from the wall. Without even thinking about it, Rikky eased down and started moving his hand just over the wound as he had seen Master Vahlda do a dozen times or more. He spoke the strange words he had heard and then went into the humming rhythm that the Spell Master had used on the other wounded men. To his utter disbelief the same soft yellow glow began to emanate from his palm. Magic tingled through him and caused his hair to stand on end. The event didn't last long, but he held his concentration long enough for the makeshift magical healing to stanch the flow of blood from the gash. He collapsed, just as Master Vahlda often did. He didn't wake up, not even when Royal had to drop the wagon a dozen feet to the ground beyond the wall. Startled by the dragon, the Walguard were firing up at him and panicking like mad men.

CHAPTER SEVENTEEN

To understand magic, and to actually cast a spell, were obviously two separate things, for Jenka could grasp the concept of thoughts having actual weight and impacting the world uniquely, but he couldn't so much as make a spark when he tried to make simple fire. It wasn't that it was a complex spell; two sharp words and a flicking of the finger, but no matter how hard he tried, Jenka just couldn't manage it.

Zahrellion was so practiced in the arcane arts, that the insubstantial image she was projecting into Jenka's cell could cast the flame spell as if her real body were actually there. She could make the steel doors melt away if she wanted to, or blast them out of the walls, but she wouldn't. "I think things are going as planned," she told him. Then she added, "Don't forget to go through your Forester drills in the morning. We need to keep ourselves ready and fit. Prince Richard will let us know what to do, and when."

"Why is it so hard?" he asked her, a few days into his endeavor, still unable to produce a spark.

"It's a mindset, Jenka. It's a place other than reality, but almost exactly like it. You have to find the way into it. It's inside you. It will happen if you practice."

"I don't understand."

"Think on this question: you tell yourself what to do with your brain, but do you always do what your brain tells you to do?"

"No, uh…I, uh…"

"Yes!" Zah snapped sharply. It startled Jenka. He decided she was far, far, older than the little girl she appeared. She was more than just a little elvish, Jenka felt sure of it. Like Lemmy, she was slow aging, and she took every advantage of that gift.

"Even when you stop yourself from doing what your thought wanted you to do, it is still a thought that stops you," she was saying. "Your reasoning is what tells you an action is wrong or foolish. Your sense of pride and honor, or the lack of either, does not define what your gut reactions are, but your brain starts altering your instinctive reactions the instant they become substance." She forestalled his question with the palm of her hand. "For example: a man is startled by a troll in the forest. The gut reaction is fear and surprise. A coward runs, while a mad man charges. The question is what determines the choice. A soldier might not run because he is afraid of letting down his fellows, even if he is utterly terrified inside. A coward might lash out like a cornered beast."

She took a breath before she continued. "Imagine being a slave, or even in a strict military order such as the Walguard or the King's Rangers. Imagine having to do as someone ordered, and not being able to question that order. People do it all of the time. Imagine if a horribly intolerant, power lusting, half-primal predator was in charge of it all. Now imagine that predator; that corrupt Supreme Commander of that strict military order; that all-powerful slaver; the complete and utter master who controls everything you do, is really just you." She paused, giving Jenka's mind a moment to wrap around the idea.

He was silent for so long that she was about to withdraw back into her own body and leave him to his contemplation. But just before she did, Jenka looked up, spoke two words, then flicked out his finger hopefully.

To Zah's surprise, and to Jenka's mild disappointment, only the tiniest of a sparks flared to life on his fingertip. He heaved out a long, frustrated sigh, and grinned, despite himself. He had felt the tingle of power inside him, if only fleetingly. It was heavenly nectar in his blood. He quickly started working himself back into that deep, contemplative trance to find more of it.

Zah was pleased that he was starting to grasp the delicateness of the arcane. She went back into herself, drank deeply from her cup of water, and let her body rest so it could finish healing.

Jenka slowly slipped back into the deep, dreamlike daze. He soon found himself traipsing through a cold, foggy, forested valley. In his mind's eye, the towering pines and their blue and gray-needled cousins still held snow. One side of the valley was a rocky, frozen cliff face that thrust up into the hazy blue sky. The cliff was somehow buffering the wind, lessening its gusting force. Out away from the protected area, it was blowing ice and snow in torrents.

Perhaps the valley floor he was walking on had once been level with the land atop the cliff above. He considered this as he trudged along. Maybe the land had come apart and this half had sunk away, not the other way around.

The ground was mostly ice-covered dirt, with chunks of crumbled granite mountainside strewn about the scattered pines. In his humid and sticky cell, Jenka's breath came out in clouds, and his skin began to grow chill and goose-pimpled. A harsh, and somehow loving growl came from ahead of him, and the roiling fog parted, revealing the source of the sound.

It was a gigantic, emerald-scaled dragon, the biggest Jenka had ever seen. It was so huge that it radiated its own heat, causing the cool air to steam and condense into the misty cloud that surrounded it. Its iron-hard claws were covered in flies and gore, but the fact that they were as long as Jenka's legs wasn't lost on him. Its tail was thick, like an ancient tree trunk, and its slick-looking green scales were the size of shields. The giant dragon's eyes were milky and fading as it lay there, its gaze locked with its offspring. It was busy communicating with Jade.

Jenka peered closer at Jade's mother and saw that the massive dragon had been bleeding profusely for some time. She had been torn open across the underbelly and gnawed on in several places. She lay on a wallowed bed, formed of nothing but the decimated carcasses of the trolls she had killed defending herself. Her wounds were mortal, and she was busy spending the last bit of her existence imparting vast volumes of knowledge into her young hatchling as swiftly as she could manage.

Worry struck Jenka like a hammer blow. He darted through the pines toward the mound of troll bodies, knocking snow from the branches and sobbing as he went. He was worried for Jade. Worse, he was feeling Jade's powerful sorrow, feeling Jade's pain. There was a flaring inferno deep inside the infantile dragon, a fire burning of rage and hatred for the things that had attacked and killed his mother, but there was a longing, too. Jenka recognized the feeling, for he felt it inside of himself. He and Jade were drawn toward each other. They bonded.

Jenka didn't think trolls could have made the long deep gash across the dragon's underside. He figured that only another dragon could have done that, or perhaps the hellborn nightshade that Gravelbone rode.

The hulking, emerald dragon turned her gaze upon Jenka then, and held it there. For a moment, Jenka's mind went blank. Then a kaleidoscope of images began streaming through his mind's eye. Images of land formations, of vast open seas, geometric shapes and strange symbols etched in tablets made of stone. All of this impacted his brain in strobe-like fashion.

"Do not be afraid to turn loossse of it, Jenka," a deep, yet distinctly feminine voice hissed into his mind. "If it wasss meant to be yoursss it will find itsss way."

Jade readjusted the set of his wings and stepped into Jenka's line of sight, breaking the enchantment. They shared a look that spoke of untold sorrow. Jenka's mind felt hot and electric, and his perceptions were so keen and alien that he was almost lost in their intricacies. Something understood passed between the two of them, and after the huge emerald dragon said a few heartfelt words to Jade, the young dragon leapt into the sky and began winging his way south.

Jenka saw a tear form in the old dragon's eye. The amber liquid pooled, and then tumbled over a filmy, upraising, lower eyelid. Jenka watched it flow down hard-plated facial scales and then drip off of a ropy, finger-thick strand of beard tentacle. The golden liquid plopped down on the dragon's scaled forearm, and should have burst, but it didn't. It bounced, as if it had frozen on the way down. It then rolled over and fell. The piece of crystallized tear thumped and rattled among the troll carcasses like a dropped stone. Jenka realized that the tear wasn't liquid any more. A glimmer of reflection from it caught his eye, and for some strange reason he marked its location firmly in his mind.

Jenka didn't want to watch the mighty green wyrm slowly die, so he pulled his mind out of the entranced state he had fallen into. He was down deep, tangled in layer upon layer of finely woven thought strands, all submerged in something as thick as molasses. Like a man swimming to the surface from the depths of an amber lake, he slowly ripped free of the tapestry and rose up and almost out of his reverie.

He stopped himself just beneath the surface. He was in the other reality that Zah had been speaking of, and he knew it. He had to try and light the flame.

With eyes squeezed shut in full concentration, he spoke the two words and flicked his finger. He opened his eyes and was momentarily blinded by the flaring green flame that erupted from his fingertip. It took him the span of five full heartbeats to realize that the fire he had created was burning his flesh.

"I did it, Zah!" Jenka exclaimed, trying to shake the fire away from his burning finger. His voice was loud, and it echoed through the stony dungeon to her cell. "I made fire!"

Her smiling vision reappeared in his cell almost immediately.

"Jade is coming for me," Jenka went on to tell her. "They killed his mother. The Goblin King and his horde." He stopped to suck on his blistered finger for a moment. "My dragon needs me to temper his anger, or he will destroy himself seeking vengeance. This isn't about the kingdom of men or the trolls any more for me. This is about my bond-mate."

Zahrellion was dumbfounded, but she couldn't argue the reasoning, or the sentiment behind Jenka's sudden change of motivation. She felt as strongly for Crystal, and she somewhat understood. "I'll help you then. Crystal will help, too. I'll tell her to go look out for Jade."

"Where is Linux?" Jenka asked. "Can you communicate with him? I would ask his aid, too."

"I can try," she replied and disappeared back into her body.

* * *

After literally dropping Rikky and Jess, from tree-top level, behind the Great Wall near Midwal, and then having to dodge the worst of the arrows that had been loosed at them, Prince Richard and Royal were flying north on heavy wings. Their destination was Crag, and then Kingsmen's Keep. The big dragon was tiring and he needed to feed, but the trolls had scared most of the game deep into the forested hills. Troll meat would do, but Royal was content to be hungry and patient. He hoped to spot some stray cattle instead of actually having to eat the filthy trolls that he loved to kill so much.

Prince Richard was tired as well. He had been riding, straddled between two triangular spinal plates, his legs bowed wide, for two full days now. They hadn't rested at all after the long, excruciating flight over the sea from King's Island. They had swooped on Three Forks and spent a few hours fighting the trolls now running amok in the emptied Stronghold, but the battle was pointless. When they started away, Royal spotted the trolls converging on Rikky and Jess at the wagon. The sparkling blue dragon had gotten the scent of warm human flesh, and had conveyed that perception to the prince. Of course, Prince Richard dutifully went to rescue the survivors.

Before the sun fled and left them flying sluggishly through the chill moonlight, they had spotted band upon band of trolls, ranging southward through the fields and forests. There were packs of goblins, too, and even a few of the bigger, barrel-chested, pig-snouted orcs loping along with the hordes. It was a terrifying sight, and Prince Richard was starting to feel like the odds against them were a lot heavier than anyone could have expected.

The few other dragons they had seen in the sky had stayed well clear of Royal. He was a pure-blooded dragon. Not only was he far more cunning than any of them ever hoped to be, he radiated a potent life-force that warned them of his superiority. To the mudged strains of dracus, he reeked of power and magic. They were terrified of him.

The village of Grove was a rank, smoldering ruin; inhabited now, mainly, by buzzards and crows. Some cattle had settled down near a grassy tree line out by the Strom River. The prince gladly dismounted and let his bond-mate go hunt. Royal promised to bring back some fresh meat for Richard. Then, with a weary groan of exhaustion, the dragon leapt back into the sky to go find a meal.

Prince Richard was sniffing at a pail of water he had just pulled up from the well in the center of town, when he heard a snuffling noise. He whirled around and was startled by a huge troll. It was bloated and overstuffed from gorging on the abundance of rotting human flesh. It belched out long and slow, then hefted the half-eaten thigh it was holding as if it were a club. Richard took a long deep draught from the water pail and discarded it. He then drew his gleaming long sword from the scabbard at his hip and started forth. In the faint starlight and eerie crimson glow of the smoldering town, it looked like his blade was already covered in blood.

The troll bellowed and charged, brandishing the human limb high as it came. Richard went low, but at the last moment the troll did, too. The prince's sword only slightly sliced into the beast's thick hide. Richard caught the meaty part of the troll's grim weapon across the neck and went rolling away hard.

The lanky beast wasn't as overfilled as Richard had first thought, and it came at him hard and fast. Blow after thumping blow rained down around him as he rolled away as deftly as he could manage. He took a few pounding impacts, but his custom armor deflected their potency well enough. He finally rolled to his feet and spun low again, bringing his blade around in a wide, slicing, ankle-level arc. The troll hopped over it, but came down in an awkward ankle-snapping jumble. Prince Richard stumbled away backwards then. He was glad he did, for the blast of scorching dragon's breath that Royal bathed the troll in left nothing but an ashy lump, that soon crumbled into a pile of cherry embers.

The sound of several other creatures, be they troll, goblin, or orc, could be heard trampling and scurrying into the night, away from the blue dragon's rage. The thankful prince found his pail and drank some more. He found the chunk of bloody meat that Royal had brought for him, and after washing it in the water, found some wood and fanned a fire to life.

Royal curled up into a mountainous ball, letting his body rest and digest the scant meal he had eaten. After the prince ate some of his meat, he crawled up into the crook of the dragon's forearm and closed his eyes. He didn't open them until he was tumbled out of his slumber by Royal's sudden panicked movement.

The big blue dragon hissed out furiously at something, and when Prince Richard found what it was in the darkness, he wanted to crumble up into a fetal ball and sob.

The slick, black nightshade loomed over them. Its long, snaking body didn't have scales like a dragon, and its eyes glowed softly, like the dying coals of a campfire. It was similar in size and form to a dragon such as Royal, but instead of exuding strength and regal might it radiated hatred and fear. It was larger than anyone had described, nearly as big as Royal. Worse was the thing sitting confidently atop the nightshade like the grotesque ivory-antlered monarch it was. It was Gravelbone, the Goblin King. His stealthy hellborn mount had crept up on them while they were sleeping, and the evil demon was grinning a mouthful of yellowed fangs over the pleasure it was feeling over simplicity of the feat.

Instinctually, the prince reached for his sword, but as his long steel blade came ringing free he heard the demon laugh hysterically. The world flashed lavender then, and a nearly invisible fist of magical power the size of a barrel-keg hammered Prince Richard back against Royal's scaly side.

Royal roared out angrily.

Prince Richard thought he saw the nightshade take a cautious step back, but was blinded and deafened by the next series of concussions that erupted over and around him. The prince was knocked aside and unable to tell if the powerful magic concussions were coming from Royal or had been directed at his bond-mate. The next thing he knew, he was being jerked violently into the air by a huge claw. Richard knew immediately, by the less than gentle nature of the thing that had a hold of him, that it wasn't Royal. When the gripping claw squeezed him so tightly that he couldn't draw breath, there was no room left for doubt. The nightshade had gotten hold of him.

As Prince Richard slipped into a haze of oxygen-deprived darkness, he wasn't worried about himself at all. He was worried for Royal and the people up in Kingsmen's Keep that he had intended to save. Blackness soon engulfed his consciousness, but by then none of it seemed to matter any more.

CHAPTER EIGHTEEN

Jenka had paced back and forth in his musty little cell for what might have been an entire day now. He was anxious and irritable, and the fact that he had to turn around every three paces was compounding his frustration. He was so filthy that he felt like he had a layer of slime coating his skin, and his hair was an itchy, tangled, knotted mat. He was worried out of his mind for his bond-mate. Seeing Jade's mighty old mamra dying like that had touched him deeply. It made him fear for his own mother. There was nothing he could do to help any of them, though, and that made him feel even less substantial. Jade was probably frightened and sad, out there all alone amongst the mudged and the trolls. Jenka was reasonably certain that Lemmy and the King's Rangers had aided his mother, but Jade was another matter.

Jade was inexperienced and young, and the trolls and the mudged were many. There was no way for Jenka to know if the yearling dragon even had enough sense to feed and rest before he attempted to fly across the ocean from the mainland. It was a long journey over nothing but the open sea, and there was no doubt that Jade was going to try to make it. The young dragon had spoken into Jenka's mind when they had shared that look up in the frigid peaks. "I am coming for you." The hiss of the words reverberated in Jenka's skull even still.

Zahrellion hadn't been able to reach out to Linux, but one of the other members of her order, a druid named Frunien, was supposedly coming for her, and had told her so in her dreams. She had shared a dream with her dragon, too. Crystal was now searching the skies for Jade, and if Crystal could find him, then she would help him in any way she could.

Herald had returned to tell Jenka that he had delivered his mother's message to the old witch. Herald said that she hadn't been half as creepy as he had expected her to be, but that she hissed with extreme displeasure and shooed him away when she found out that Jenka was locked in the dungeons.

Jenka wanted to tell the King's Ranger that they were going to break out, but he didn't want to involve his friend in the treachery. He wanted to be honest with the man, but there would most likely be severe consequences for the escape, especially if King Blanchard was still on King's Island when it came time to abscond.

Jenka asked Herald if he had seen Linux, or if he had gotten any word from Rikky, or any news about Crag, but there had been only one bird from beyond the wall in the last few days. That missive had been an urgent plea for help from Commander Corda. He was about to abandon Three Forks Stronghold to the trolls. There had been several messages from Midwal and Eastwal, though. The frontier was apparently overrun with bands of angry vermin, and the skies filled with hungry feral dragons. The mudged pillaged at will on both sides of the Great Wall now, and a few people had reported that some of the trolls had taken to riding on their backs. The future seat of the kingdom, Mainsted, had been swooped upon several times already. There was still no word from Kingsmen's Keep, but Outwal, the overcrowded city just outside of the Great Wall, had been decimated. The last message from Port stated that there were at least a thousand human casualties in the battle to flee Outwal, most of them common folk.

It was more than Jenka could imagine, so he tried not to think about it. It wasn't to be, though. The concern over his friends and loved ones kept forcing itself into his thoughts, reminding him that he was as useless as wings on a rooted tree.

Jenka felt Jade's anguish, and more than a little of the dragon's desire to end this madness. He would have pounded his fist against the moldy dungeon wall had it not already been raw and sore from doing so earlier. He and Jade would relish exacting some well-deserved revenge on the Goblin King, but no matter how hard he tried, Jenka couldn't clear his mind enough to find that place where he could communicate with his dragon. There was just too much tension and worry.

Later, while Jenka was still brooding and pacing, a retinue of well-armed and oddly-robed men arrived at the dungeons. Herald had gotten it so that the head-high feeding slots in the cell doors stayed open, and Jenka watched in utter shock as the large, hooded men came and forcibly took Zah away. She screamed and sobbed and twisted and pulled, but she refrained from attempting to use magic against them. Then they put a hood over her head, and she went still.

It was long after the noisy ruckus had subsided and Zahrellion had been taken away that Jenka thought to ask someone who they were and where they had taken her.

"Back to the mainland with the flotilla, under the King's own guard," the jailor informed him.

"They was a wantin' to chop your top, but the queen, may the gods grace her forgiving soul, argued against it."

"Quit trying to scare him, Dink, or I'll knot your noggin," Herald growled as he came in. Straight to Jenka's cell door he went, shouldering the guard out of his way. "Sorry, boy," he apologized to Jenka. "We didn't see that one coming. Them druids sent a messenger to the king. The man walked right out of the thin air and told King Blanchard that if Zahrellion wasn't waiting for them when they physically arrived, then they were gonna blast the wall open for the trolls." He shook his head, and huffed out a very unsatisfying sigh. "Help the fargin trolls! Can you believe it?"

"It was a calculated bluff," said Jenka, remembering one of Master Kember's lessons. He too exhaled, long and slow. "My plan is ruined," he mumbled under his breath.

"What plan?" Herald asked, rather loudly, then cringed. "What plan?" he hissed the question again in a much quieter voice. "And what's a calfunatered bluff?"

"Calculated," Jenka corrected, before he turned and paced away from the cell door. He took three strides then had to turn and walk back. He did this twice before he spoke.

"We were going to escape, Zah and I. Our dragons are coming to the island as we speak, and her magic was our way out of here. Can you get word to her before they set sail?" Jenka pressed his grimy face against the door, and pleaded to the King's Ranger with his eyes. A whiff of Jenka's rancid scent hit Herald's face like a fog, causing him to look down and study the shine of his boots as he spoke.

"I'll try my best, lad. But keep your message simple, lest I get it all scrabbled up."

"Just tell her to keep the dragons away from Kingston until I can figure something out. Can you do that? Tell her that we will meet in the other place."

"I can remember that, but I've a got to get going `cause it's already nearin' high tide, and the flotilla is about to set sail. Don't go breaking out just yet. As soon as the king is gone, Her Majesty will try something. I'm sure of it."

"Thanks, Herald."

Though he forced a friendly grin, Jenka's spirit had deflated completely. He needed Zah's instruction. He enjoyed her company, and he had grown to depend on her. Now she was gone. It irked him that she hadn't just used her power to control the situation. Jenka knew that, if he could master even a fraction of the magic that Zah had, he certainly wouldn't be sitting here feeling as impotent and as helpless as a newborn babe. He was finding the few strands of hope that had been supporting him snapping away, and now he was falling. "I'll be here for a while, it seems," he finally said to Herald. "Go on, before it's too late."

Herald spat a wad of phlegm off to the side, gave a short nod, and then strode out of Jenka's range of sight. Two heartbeats hadn't passed before Jenka was pacing again. This time his stride was deliberate, and he could only take two strides before he had to spin around.

After a while, he grew dizzy and faint. When he lay down on his pallet, he quickly drifted away into a terrible, spiraling nightmare.

* * *

Royal did his best to pursue Gravelbone and the nightshade that had gotten hold of Prince Richard, but it wasn't enough. Royal had been injured by the slick-skinned, hellborn beast's searing magic. His heavy wing strokes seemed to be tearing at an open wound, near where his shoulder and wing muscles came together, in the center of his back. His bond-mate was being abducted, and he was less than pleased about it. When he was set upon by two mid-sized mudged dragons, and lost the Goblin King in the clouds, he quickly unleashed his fury. One of them, a deep-maroon colored mam, almost got him just above his wing joints near where he was already wounded. Royal twisted in flight to avoid the snapping jaws, rolling deftly over in the air. He drenched the startled mudge with his potent, liquid lightning breath. Any creature other than another dragon would have been charred to cinders by the heat of the stuff. As it was, the lesser dragon's wings were crisped to stiffness, and it went into a sharp, spiraling dive toward the fields below.

The other mudge flew away then, but it didn't go far. It stayed just out of range, waiting patiently for Royal to land. Royal knew it was there, and that the mudge would start calling in its mindless kin soon. He was determined to land in an easily defensible location, but what Royal really was hoping for was a chance to get hold of the beast before they landed, so that he could avoid another battle altogether. He was so busy searching below for an acceptable place to make his stand that he didn't see the other, larger dragon that had taken position high above him until it was almost too late.

When he sensed the other huge mudge, Royal immediately dove away and tried to start picking up speed. He spotted yet another dragon closing from the north, but it was too far away to be a concern as of yet. Royal decided that his only chance was to go on the offensive, and he started winging toward the mudge that had been shadowing him. The sudden realization that Royal was now targeting it caused it to falter. Trying to bank away, it gave Royal just the advantage that he needed.

From high above, the big crimson was swooping now, and when Royal lunged his head in at the smaller mudge, he made sure to be true with his bite. He couldn't afford to miss, because he would soon have to change course, and quickly. To his disappointment, the smaller mudge somehow shifted out of his mouth when he snapped it shut.

He had intended to snatch the smaller dragon up by the gruff and snap its neck, but it had twisted away. Luckily, Royal's toothy maw was as big as it was, because one of the mudge's wings got caught in it. Royal jerked around, violently ripping the delicate appendage away. The ruined beast, roaring, tumbled out of the sky. Royal altered his own course just in time to avoid the grasping claws of the red, as it came lumbering by like some flying mountain. It was old and powerful; not so mudged that it had lost its sense. But it was slow, and easily outmaneuvered. At least, that was what Royal was telling himself when the hulking wyrm suddenly twisted into an impossible corkscrew slither and managed to rake him with a razor-sharp claw.

It was a slight, yet debilitating, wound. Royal was winged, and he knew it. It was all he could do to maintain a straight course and try to slow himself down so that the unavoidable impact into the trees below wouldn't be the death of him.

The old red knew it had crippled Royal and was hoping that the crash would kill the sparkling blue so that it wouldn't have to risk his magic. There was one thing that the mudged dragons loved, and that was the fresh, clean flesh of a pure-blooded dragon. But they feared the magic of a high dracus. In the recent decades, the purebloods had grown scarce, but now it had one to feed on. This blue's flesh would satiate the red's vast hunger for weeks.

The red banked a slow turn and watched with a growl of disappointment as Royal threw out his wings, despite the gash that had split the fabric of one of them. Royal hit the tops of the towering pines and began laying them over as he came down. He managed to pull his wings in far enough that they didn't get snapped or twisted when he started his rolling, tree-snapping, tumble.

The landing wasn't pretty, but it wasn't fatal, which meant that the old red would have to fly down and finish it. It figured to do it while Royal was still stunned and recovering from his tree-flattening landing, so down it went into a graceful curling spiral.

Royal shook his head and tried to clear it. There was a broken stump puncturing up through the soft skin just in front of his hind leg. The pain was excruciating, and he couldn't find the grit to pull himself up off it. He noticed out of the corner of his eye that the red was easing down leisurely.

The old crimson dragon threw out its massive wings and dropped its thick hind legs to the ground. It then ran a few upright steps across the flattened trees before folding its wings along its bulk. Its upper body came down then, making it look more like some terrible overfed four-legged snake than a creature of the sky. It stalked like a wary feline along the edge of the newly-formed glade Royal's impact had created, its tail flitting and whipping around behind it. All the while, Royal could do nothing more than gasp and wince from the pain he was feeling. The unforgiving spike that held him from getting into a defensive posture was just too much.

The old red sensed that Royal was in no position to use his powerful magic, so it started moving in for the kill. It loped in and darted its head like a striking viper, with every intention of latching onto Royals neck to snap it, but Royal wasn't ready to die just yet. He forgot his pain. Using the grim knowledge that his bond-mate wouldn't survive without him as the fuel to fire his will, he twisted away, tearing the broken tree stump out of the earth as he went. Huge, yellowed teeth snapped shut just beside Royal's head, and Royal lashed out severely with his foreclaw. He caught the old red along the neck and it withdrew its snaky head just as quickly as it had darted it in. Realizing that the wound it had taken was nothing more than a deep scratch, the big crimson dragon raised itself up high and roared out its dominant anger.

Royal knew that he wouldn't be able to defend himself from the attack that was coming. He was just too wounded. The broken stump was still half inside the hole it had made, and every little movement caused him that much more pain. He had made his last stand and had failed. Now there was little he could do but grind it out, tooth and claw, with the hulking red. At least he would die fighting the filthy vermin that had been infesting the land. He wouldn't die easily. He would spend his last energy doing his best to return the wounds he received, but he knew he wouldn't prevail.

He wasn't able to avoid the mass of blood-red scales and frothing teeth when they came in at him this time. Hot sulfuric fire, the infernal blistering kind that only the reds can muster, swept across his head, singeing his lids. All he could do then was hope, and wait to feel the beast close and sink in his own fangs. When he felt the bulk of his body being chomped and tossed, like he was no more than a cub to a lion, even hope fled him.

CHAPTER NINETEEN

When Jenka fell dizzily onto his filthy woven sleeping mat, he went into a strange, tumbling slumber. The world grew thin around him. The air became insubstantial and hard to breathe. Eventually, everything stabilized, but he was no longer in his dungeon cell, at least his mind wasn't. He was suddenly surging up and forward through a misty cloud. After the sensation subsided, he drifted. He seemed to start falling, but only for a moment. Then he surged forward again, and he felt the cool air blasting at his face. He could hear the savage growling and snarling of two huge, battling predators, and then he could see them as the clouds swirled and parted away. He could smell things, too, but what information was contained in those strange and complex aromas, he had no idea.

A huge line of felled trees led up to a massive, red wyrm that was in the process of chomping on the neck of a wounded blue. The blue looked like the dragon that had taken Prince Richard from the tiltyard. It was that dragon, Jenka decided. It was Royal, and as if he had a second consciousness speaking to him, a familiar voice spoke excitedly in his head.

"It isss the Royal," Jade hissed. "You are with me, inside me. I needed you, ssso I ssummoned you."

"I'm what?" Jenka looked around and realized that he was seeing out of the young green dragon's amber eyes as if they were his own. Jade forced his wings downward, and they went surging up and forward again, toward the battle ahead.

"Where is the prince?" Jenka tried to turn his head and look around, but he found that he didn't actually have the ability to control his host's movement. Jade felt his intention, though, and quickly complied. The prince was nowhere to be seen, and Royal was floundering wildly. His long, snaky neck was clamped tight in the gigantic red dragon's jaws. The forest had been trampled, the trees laid over and broken as if they had crashed there. One of Royal's hind claws had stilled, but the other raked and scraped frantically at his attacker.

"Dive on him, Jade," Jenka commanded. "Get right in his face. Rake his eyes or blast them with your fire. That is one of our companions down there."

"Yesss," Jade hissed. "I've not mastered fire, but my mam gave me spellsss before she died." The young dragon threw his wings back and started streaking down. The force of the wind against Jenka was so strong that he couldn't even draw breath into his lungs. He began to suffocate and struggle, causing Jade some discomfort.

"Do not," Jade hissed into the ethereal of Jenka's mind. "You don't need air. You are only here in ssspirit. Your body isss still trapped back in that stone fortresss. Just lend me your confidence."

Jenka tried to relax himself, but it was next to impossible. The earth was right there coming up at him, and far too swiftly. Seeing out of a dragon's eyes was unsettling to say the least. When Jade blinked, his lower eyelids came up and over his eye like some filmy, amber-tinted veil. Jenka did manage to fight away the urge to draw breath. He didn't think that they would be able to save Royal. They were little more than a pesky insect compared to the ancient, red-scaled beast, and the mighty blue wyrm was no longer growling and struggling to defend itself. It was just twitching and jerking now under the bigger dragon's bite.

Jenka had to find Prince Richard. The prince was the future of the realm, and though Jenka was born out here in the frontier, he had been instilled with a sense of loyalty to the throne by all the men who had been around him as he was growing up. Finding the crown prince was his duty. Besides that, Prince Richard was the only one who could clear Jenka's name with King Blanchard. His desire to find the prince had deeper roots, as well. Prince Richard was one of them, one of the five that would face the storm that Crystal had spoken of and, as that idea struck him, a real sense of urgency gripped him. He started to mentally voice this dire concern when Jade turned an invisible corner in the sky and really started to dive.

Words as strange and powerful as anything Jenka had ever heard filled his mind, as Jade began casting the spell he was about to unleash. They were streaking downward insanely, directly at Royal and the big red, and after Jade spoke the particular word that completed his spell, the ancient red let go of Royal and turned toward them. Jenka felt the same thing that the other dragon had sensed. The feeling was similar to what he had felt when he had first used magic to make fire in his cell, but this powerful magic was raw, and magnified beyond imagining.

Jenka was consumed by the tingling electric energy, but he saw everything happen as if time itself had suddenly slowed to a crawl. The wagon-cart sized head, with its two yellowed horns and its bright, terrifying, yellow eyes came round at them. All the while, the beast sucked in a deep breath of air into its lungs. They seemed to be about crash into the thing, and Jenka reflexively tried to clench his eyes closed because the old wyrm was opening its huge bloody maw to blast them with its infernal fire.

Like some ever-widening cavern that they could probably fit completely inside, red-pink stained teeth bared themselves. Long, slitted pupils focused into a fine sliver of a line. Jenka found that he half-wished that he was safe back in his dungeon cell. Then, just as the ancient wyrm roared out and blasted a geyser of orange flame at them, Jade coughed hard and tweaked his wingtips slightly. A purple ball of roiling energy shot from Jades mouth like a wad of spit right down into ancient dragon's gullet and fizzled out. Like a ball swinging round a pole on a tether, Jade put them into a sharp, banking turn that the young dragon soon lost control of. Jade rolled over into a dizzying tumble. Once, then again, he flipped clumsily through the sky. It was all Jenka could do to keep from losing his mind. As they went skittering over the treetops like a poorly skipped stone, Jenka wondered why the spell Jade had cast, or whatever it was that he had done, had failed. Jenka tried once again to close his eyes. He had no desire to see the tree limbs tear his dragon's young body apart, but like before, Jade's eyes blinked amber, but wouldn't close.

Behind them, a blast erupted, so violent that it jarred the sky out of kilter. The massive concussion silenced the world completely. The force of energy that radiated outward, caught Jade from behind and pushed them. Like some struggling swimmer lifted by a surging wave, they rose above the dangerous trees, just long enough for the young wyrm to get his flight back under control. Jenka tried to turn and look back again, but Jade's long neck didn't comply. The dragon banked sharply around, and Jenka was immediately horrified by the amount of gore that he saw settling to the ground. He could taste sweet, coppery blood in the air, and the idea of it made him want to vomit. The hulking red's tail was still twitching lazily, but there was nothing left of its neck above the shoulder, save for the bits that had splattered out and painted the fallen forest crimson. Jenka soon felt the hunger that the flavor and scent kindled in Jade, and he, too, began lusting for dragon flesh.

"Look," Jenka spoke with is mind. "He's still alive, see? Spell him healed, like you did me when the trolls got me. You can feed after. We need Royal."

"I am weary, Jenka De Swassso," Jade hissed into Jenka's head. "I will try this, but then I must feed and rest. We should be away from here. The trellkin will come to feed, as will the mudged. There will be many of them."

"Aye," agreed Jenka. "But we have to help Royal get away, too. What did you…? How?" Jenka wasn't exactly sure how to phrase his question, but he tried. "What just happened? What did you do?"

"I cannot explain it," Jade replied. "It is complex." He came flapping down near Royal's wounded body like a giant, green-scaled duck, and landed awkwardly on the slick, blood-saturated trees that Royal's crash had laid over. Jenka saw for the first time how huge the red dragon had been. It was as big as the pig barns behind Swinerd's lodge.

Royal was fairly big as well, and he was grievously wounded.

When Jade eased cautiously up near the larger dragon, the limp blue wyrm let out a long, groaning hiss. "Gravelbone hasss him," Royal's voice was weak, but plainly audible. "Leave me. Leave me to my fate and go save the prince. The hellwyrm carried them toward the lake. The demon must not be allowed to hold him long. Tell his father, Jenka. Ask the king why my brother's head sits in his armory, why my dracar was even on that island in the first place." Royal's greenish-yellow eyes rolled upward, then, and Jade let out a long, sorrowful whine.

Something changed around Jenka, something substantial. He started falling backwards out of Jade's mind.

"Heal him, Jade," he shouted almost desperately. "Heal him, and then come for me!" The loud reverberation of his own voice echoing off of the stone walls of his dungeon cell was the only response he got.

* * *

Back in the dungeon, Jenka came at the steel door, pounding and screaming for the guards to immediately fetch Herald, or the queen, or even King Blanchard himself. He was frantic. He had to tell them what was happening.

"Shut your fargin grub-hole, boy!" the guard responded with an angry chuckle. "If you wake me up again, I'll see that your fast is broken with pissed oats and moldy bread."

"Come on, man," Jenka pleaded. "This is urgent business. Herald'll have your hide. I swear it. I know you don't understand it, but I had a dream about the prince. I know where he is, they have to know. He's in grave danger."

"Fall off, man," the guard grumbled. "That King's Ranger will be here soon enough. It's near dawn. The morning tide rolls out soon after, and since they ordered all the able-bodied men to the mainland, he'll be leavin' with `em. He's supposed to come around before they shove off!" The guard scooted his wooden stool back loudly, then came over and clanged an empty piss pot against Jenka's door for a few long moments. The sound was unbearably loud.

"Now you shove off, `cause if you don't let me sleep I'll just keep a banging." With that, the obstinate man slammed the little food slot and pinned it fast, leaving Jenka in total darkness.

Jenka dropped to the floor, lay on his back before his door, and started mule kicking it with everything he had. The sound was ear shattering, both inside his cell and out in the larger stone room where the guard was stationed. The guard grew angry and went into a rage of his own, hammering the outside of Jenka's door with the piss pot while Jenka kicked with all his might from the inside. They went on like that for quite a while, but Jenka started to tire. Then the piss pot pounding suddenly stopped and Jenka heard the guard speaking sharply to someone who had arrived.

"Who in all the fargin hells are you?" the now furious man asked, through clenched teeth. "What businesses do you have dow—" His voice stopped mid-word.

There was a bit of scuffling and the sound of rattling keys. The outer door to the cell block came open. Jenka had heard the sounds of the dungeon so many times now that he knew what every squeaking hinge or groaning bit of metal was connected to. A feminine snort, the sound of a disgusted old woman, came to his ears. There was a long, suspenseful moment of silence before Jenka started calling out that he needed to see the king or the queen immediately.

The piss pot clanged on the door again, but only three sharp raps. In the silence that followed, the slot was unpinned and thrown open. An old woman peeked a bloodshot eye into the cell, but her head blocked what little light managed to find the interior. She cursed herself then pulled herself back a bit so that she could see.

"Is that you, De Swasso?" she asked. "I suppose it is, with all that pounding."

"Who are you? I need to speak to the king or the queen immediately."

"No you don't," she snapped. "You need to shut your grub-hole like that fool guard said and listen to me." When Jenka held his tongue, she continued. "You're wormy, boy. I knew you would be when you was get."

"What?" Jenka asked incredulously. He didn't have time for this nonsense, and he started to say so. But when he got to the door to look out, he saw a look in her eyes that suggested that her words might have some merit. As hard as it was for Jenka to hold his mouth still, he did so.

"You was a wiggler when you was born. It's one of the few things I remember well," she said conversationally. "But that's neither here nor there. You know where it is, Jenka. I know you know. I have to have it. We'll need it when the Time of Confliction rolls round."

"What are you talking about, crone?" He had heard that phrase, "Time of Confliction" before, but at the moment, he couldn't remember where, nor did he care. "I need to see the king."

"Lisssten," she hissed. The way her "S" hung long made him think of Jade, and he bit his tongue yet again.

"I am an old woman. My name is Mysterian, and you should hold yourself still while I unfurl my mind or this could take all day."

Jenka recognized the name immediately. Had he not just witnessed a battle between dragons and their powerful High Magic in his mind's eye, he might have shied away from the old Hazeltine Witch who had trained his mother. Supposedly this woman was part elvish, like Lem and Zahrellion. Jenka's mother had told him that she was the oldest of the old, whatever that meant. Either way, he knew her reputation warranted his respect. He would give it to her, but only after she answered the most important question that came to his mind.

"Is she alive?" His face pressed so tightly against his door that it was painful. "Do you know anything about my mother?"

"Nay." She shook her head, sadly. "But as important as that seems it, too, is neither here nor there. What matters is whether you will do my bidding."

"What?"

"Listen, boy! I am old, and my mind wanders. Just sit still, and it will all work its way out of me."

Jenka let out a long, frustrated sigh and started pacing his cell. He felt as if he might burst into a thousand crawling pieces of worry. Prince Richard had been taken by Gravelbone, and Zah had been taken by her fellow druids, and this conversation was maddening. After a few moments, he went back to the slot and would have bumped the old witch in the head had the door not been there.

"I'll help you out of here and on your way if you'll go fetch that tear," she whispered.

"What tear?" Jenka was fed up. This made no sense at all.

"Husssh," she hissed. A spark of warning flashed in her eyes. It was a glinting hint at her own frustration, and it kept Jenka from voicing his annoyance. "If you'll swear to go get that mighty emerald dragon's tear, then I will let you out of here. We will use its vast power to kill the Goblin King, and his hellwyrm too, but when that deed is done, the tear is mine."

How she could have known that he had watched Jade's mamra cry that tear in a vision was beyond him, but her offer was one that he didn't think he could refuse. He didn't have any idea of the powerful magic contained in that little amber droplet. If he had, he might have thought better of giving his oath to turn it over to her. But at the moment, he didn't care what use she had for such a thing. If it could help him kill Gravelbone and the nightshade, then he would use it. If he succeeded in ridding the land of the demon and his wyrm, then giving the thing to the witch seemed only fair. Old witches often collected all sorts of odd substances. His mother had kept a jar of fresh bear scat by the teapot.

"I'll do it," Jenka nodded. "But I need a place to hide until my dragon gets here."

"Swear an oath," she demanded.

Jenka glared at her. His mother had taught him that an oath-breaker was the worst of things to be, and to be wary of giving his solemn word to anyone. After a long moment, he sighed. "I swear that I'll retrieve the mighty emerald's tear for you, Mysterian. I swear it by the name De Swasso."

It was a formal oath that he had heard his mother force several people to swear over the years, and it seemed to please Mysterian that he had worded it correctly.

She cackled out delightfully, as if the world that Jenka knew weren't hanging in the balance. "I knew you was wormy, De Swasso. I knew it since the day you was get!"

The rattling of keys resounded, and the heavy steel door creaked open, revealing the hunched old crone and the unconscious dungeon guard lying still on the filthy floor. The only thing more relieving than being free was the blast of relatively fresh air that wafted over him and filled his lungs with hope.

He didn't even notice the way the old witch cringed and fought to hold down her gorge at the smell of him.

PART III

HIGH MAGIC

CHAPTER TWENTY

Though she could have passed for a maiden of twelve and was as smart as an old crone, Zahrellion was only nineteen years old. She had lived at the Druidom since birth. One of her direct ancestors had helped found the Order of Dou, which was the little-used official name of the sect. He had been instrumental in getting King Ferdok to grant them amnesty from the kingdom and its laws so that they could research the powers of the arcane. Ideally, the sect wouldn't have had to build their temple up in the lower peaks, but the good folk of the kingdom would have been appalled at some of the things they had attempted with their unique forms of High Magic, so it was for the better all the way around.

Zahrellion's ancestor, one Grock Visium, had been a powerful practitioner of all things arcane. His specialty was item enchantment. He had spent the waking hours of his life studying, practicing, and creating ways to instill ordinary objects with power and purpose. One of the items he had created was known as the dampening hood. It was a velvety, drawstring bag, made to put over the heads of the rogue Outland pirates that were the terror of the seas back in the earlier days of the settling. Those bold and brazen outlaws, and a few of their women, often knew enough sea sorcery to cause trouble even after they were captured. The material that Grock Visium's dampening hood was made of had been enchanted so that it interfered with the brain activity and the voice of the person put under it. Without the ability to speak the proper words or think clearly, there could be no spell casting or walking the ethereal. It was a very effective way to transport a prisoner with the ability to muster the power of the arcane. It was a bitter irony when Zahrellion found herself staring at the inside of her great grandfather's device. Comparatively gentle hands led her down a long wooden dock to board a sea ship as if she were some old pirate's filthy ship witch.

The smell of brine was in the air, but it had a hard time reaching her nose. The gulls were calling out crazily around her and her escorts. Underneath the frantic, cawing tirade was the slow, but steady, repeating *whoosh* of the ocean's waves rolling past the wooden support columns, and the clomping of their boots on the plank-wood pier. Under the steamy hood, Zah was going mad with worry, and she was more than a little bit angry. After several days in the dungeons, she still hadn't been given an opportunity to bathe herself properly. Inside the hood, her breath was so vile that it was suffocating her. Frunien, the druid who had come for her, and the four Dourga attendants he had brought along to help escort her away from King's Island were all deaf to her pleadings. Frunien actually sympathized with her, but he wasn't about to remove the hood, at least not until they were well at sea.

They sat at harbor for far longer than anyone had expected. All the while, Zahrellion sobbed pitifully about her unclean state and her hunger. Truthfully, she was no bawling little girl. She was just trying to gain Frunien's sympathy by acting as one. Finally, the anchor chain was cranked up. Zah couldn't see them, but she could tell by the noise that there were quite a few ships setting sail together. A cacophony of rattling metal links, shouting sailors, and the pounding of oar drums filled the air, as they eased out of Kingston's harbor and made for the open sea. After that, Frunien's will broke quickly enough.

He ordered one of the Dourga to fetch a platter of fruit from the galley. The ship they had chartered was a fleet little sloop, and they were its only cargo. It was as plush as any in the Royal Line, and since its holds contained only ballast stones, Frunien had it stocked with fruit and a few other delicate staples. They weren't going to Port with the other ships, so it was going to be a fairly long journey. They were going east to skirt the entire mainland peninsula so that they could then head north and put in somewhere up in the Cut near the eastern foothills.

"Zahrellion, I'm going to remove the hood now. *Do not* do anything foolish." Her older peer explained that there was a copper tub filled with warm water and fresh robes waiting in a private chamber below. "Here comes a platter of fresh fruit as we speak." He started to fumble the drawstring loose, but hesitated. "Will you promise not to lash out?"

"I'll not do anything…" she started.

He made the mistake of assuming that she had finished speaking, for as he pulled the hood from her tangled, white rat-nest of hair he heard the rest of her words.

"...of the sort!"

She went straight to the Dourga who was bringing the fruit and greedily savaged not one, but two juicy, purple plums. The succulent liquid dripped off her chin and ran down her arms as she relished the slightly tart flavor of them. After she swallowed the fruit, she breathed deeply of the fresh salty air and took a moment to marvel at the small cloud of gulls that had followed them out to sea. Off behind them, like a cluster of floating geese, she saw the flotilla that was sailing to Port. She immediately understood why they were moving away from the other vessels. This ship was headed away from the confrontation, not toward it. Her anger washed over the relief she was feeling like some rogue tidal wave. She turned her attention on Frunien then, snatching the dampening hood from him to wipe her hands on it.

"I'll ask this only once," her eyes had suddenly grown fierce, and her tattooed brow dove into a sharp, angry V-shape. "Who ordered you to use my grandfather's hood on me?"

Frunien had backed up tightly against the ship's rail, and a few of the sailors who were up in the rigging laughed at him. They choked off their mirth when Zah gave them a quick glare. She wiped the plum juice from her face with the hood and then turned to face down her fellow druid again. As quick as a lightning strike, he was under the hood himself.

"No, Zah, please! No," he pleaded through the soft, suede material. His hands went up to his neck, but stopped several inches before they could grasp the drawstring. It was one of the qualities of the hood. It wouldn't be effective if the wearer could unfasten and remove it themselves. "Take it off, Zahrellion. I'm sorry. I'm so, so sorry."

"I don't hear you telling me who ordered you to do it, Frune. We are supposed to be an order of peers. We are sworn to preserve each other's dignity and act as brethren, to care for our fellow man with a loyalty only equaled by a mother's love for her own. Explain to me where this act is dignified or caring. I haven't bathed in more than a week, you fargin bastard!"

"I, uh…" the trembling man started, but stopped himself, because he almost toppled over the side of the swiftly moving ship. The sailors were laughing again, and riotously. One of the Dourga guards chuckled, too.

"Speak up, or you are going into the sea!" Zah threatened. Not even she knew if she was bluffing, and no one on board dared make a move to stop her.

“Linux told me to do it,” he sobbed then, as if he had just betrayed a dear friend. Zahrellion sensed the emotion, and it caused her temper to explode.

“You’re upset about breaking Linux’ trust, but not about putting me under that hood? You could have just told me to hold myself still.” She gave the three Dourga standing on the deck a glare that warned them to stay well clear of this business. “I could have blasted that cell apart at any time. I was already restraining myself.” She paused and put her hands on her hips. “You’ll not be getting out of that for a while, then,” she turned and challenged the entire crew of the ship with her grime-stained chin held high. Then she threatened to deliver her full wrath if any of them took it off. With that, she snatched the tray of fruit from the grinning Dourga and started down into the compartments where her bath was waiting.

As she lay there in the gray-tinged, lukewarm water, Zahrellion tried to reach out to Jenka with her mind. She spent several long hours floating on a deep cloud of concentration searching for him or Crystal. She found neither, and only stopped her efforts when the first waves of nausea started to flare through her belly. Whether it was because of her fatigue, or a lingering effect of the dampening hood, or the unsettling seasickness that was getting a hold of her again, she couldn't seem to find a way to reach either of them.

Before she toweled herself dry, she took the canteen of drinking water that had been left for her, stood in the copper tub and poured it slowly over her head and arms to cleanse her own wash water from her skin. If she was about to spend the next few days vomiting and miserable, she was determined to be clean while she suffered. After she put on the silver-trimmed black robe that had been provided, she found the bunk in the corner of the tiny room, crawled into it, and fell into the deepest of dreamless sleeps.

* * *

Prince Richard regained consciousness, and was nearly frightened back into oblivion by the large, cherubic monster sitting across from him, snarling hungrily. The last thing he remembered was watching Royal fighting fiercely to win free of the two mudged dragons harrying his pursuit. After that that he had been squeezed into unconsciousness.

It was an ogre sitting across from him, a hulking, deep-mountain beast, with olive-green skin and lower fangs that jutted up from its mandible on either side of its wide, flat nose. Its platter-sized feet were right there in front of Prince Richard, its bulbous toes the size of apples. It wasn't snarling any more, and Richard soon realized that it had been badly beaten. Mauled was the word that came to mind. It didn't look as fierce now as it first had. Now Richard couldn't decide if it was even alive. After glancing around the large, dank cavern he found himself in, he concluded that it was the wild, dancing shadows thrown from the green-tinted flames of the pit fire nearby that had made the thing appear to be snarling. An attempt to get himself up to his feet told him that he, too, was bound at wrist and ankle. This wasn't good.

He had no problem using the semi-sharp edge of his steel thigh plate to work the rope around his wrists apart. After that, the leg bindings came off as well. He stood, and with his back to the eerie, sea-green fire, peered into the depths. He could discern nothing, other than it was a deep, dark cavern that he was in. When he turned and started back toward the flames, he realized that he was in a cage of sorts. The cavern was a large scallop in the side of an otherwise consistent, tunnel-like shaft. The back of the scallop had been barred off to contain the ogre. The bars were formed out of bones, so long and thick that they could have only come from the skeletons of dragons. He hoped it wasn't Royal's bones. Some of them still had bits of gristle and meat at the ends, and the stuff that they had been lashed together with was black with gore and covered in flies. The bones were far enough apart that, even with his chest plate still on, Richard could turn sideways and fit through them. As he was starting to do just that, a long, curious groan emitted from behind him.

Prince Richard's initial instinct was to draw his long sword, but it was no longer at his hip. Instead, he hurried away from the hulking beast and squeezed through the bone bars as quickly as he could manage. It was from the outside of the dragon-bone cage that he looked back at the ogre. It was still sitting with its legs extended, but it was holding its arms out toward the prince, a pleading look on its bruised and swollen face. Its eyes were the size of cantaloupes and such a deep shade of blue that they appeared black. It was looking at him in a way that reminded him of the look the hunt master's pups used to give him when they wanted his attention.

Why he squeezed himself back into the cage, he didn't know. He removed his left gauntlet and used the edge of the protective steel plate as a blade. It wasn't as sharp as the plate that covered his thigh, but he wasn't about to get out of his leg armor to help free the ogre. The first bits of the heavy rope were starting to come apart when the thumping of heavy wings and a long, slow hiss came echoing down the tunnel at them. Prince Richard quickly lay back where he had been earlier and fumbled his gauntlet back into place. The ogre slumped back against the wall as well, and Richard sensed that the huge beast had suddenly grown afraid.

The blue-green flames flared brightly as the wind from the nightshade's wings blasted through the tunnel. Gravelbone was laughing deeply as he slid down from his hellwyrm's back, at least until he saw a bit of rope that Prince Richard had dropped outside the bounds of the ogre cage.

"Whaas diss?" Gravelbone's voice was a deep curious growl. "You gon run da blackness?"

Richard wasn't sure what the trollish looking demon was saying, but he was certain that it was talking to him. The tall, lanky, ivory-horned thing was stalking purposefully his way, seemingly amused that he had slipped his ropes. The rattling bones that made up his crude armor looked to be made of human thigh bones with a big orange-black tortoise shell for the breastplate. His shoulder plates were formed of smaller, similarly colored shells. Hanging from his hip was a wicked-looking blade that was as black as soot and so complexly saw-toothed that no sheath could hold it.

Gravelbone tweaked a latch and squeezed his way through an opening that the ogre could never have fit through, and he showed no fear of the huge, green creature, now cowering from his intrusion.

"Farga Crixn Cruxn yaa?" Gravelbone laughed spitefully at the crown prince's fear. "Lok tav tham," he held up a clawed hand and inspected it as he spoke another unintelligible series of phrases. Then his wild eyes went wide and flared the same orange-red shade of the tortoise shell armor that he wore. With an extending arm and an open mouth full of razor sharp teeth, he stalked the rest of the way over to Prince Richard and bent toward him. He reached out and palmed Prince Richard's forehead, his thumb pressing into one temple, the tip of his little finger into the other. His grip was mighty when he squeezed. It didn't surprise the Goblin King when the crown prince's hands came round and grabbed at his wrist, but it surprised Prince

Richard when a sickening glacial chill clenched his bones, and a terrifying vision flashed into his brain. What he saw shocked him to stillness, and the feel of Gravelbone's tainted High Magic, as it boiled the marrow inside his bones, nearly destroyed him.

"Thas Wha de cawl me Gravelbone," the Goblin King chuckled under his breath sinisterly.

In the eye of Prince Richard's mind he saw his dragon, Royal, being savaged by a gigantic, red-scaled mudge. The huge, crimson wyrm had the sparkling blue's neck in its jaws and was jerking its head back and forth. Worse, Royal's tail had fallen completely still.

A roar resounded from far too close to him, then, and the vision in Richard's head abruptly ceased. The ogre had worried his ropes free and had rolled up onto its knees. It swung a huge meaty fist and struck Gravelbone squarely in the temple, knocking him away from the prince. Gravelbone let out a shriek that ran up through the prince's ear canals and scalded the inside of his skull.

The nightshade's head darted in between the bone cage's bars, and then, with a snap of its slavering jaws, it chomped down on the ogre's arm with a sickening, wet crunch. The ogre slumped over and shuddered, while its bright scarlet lifeblood pumped out from exposed arteries. The blood looked black under the light of the strange green flames, as it flowed in a slick, glossy puddle across the cavern floor.

Luckily for Prince Richard, his presence was seemingly forgotten, at least for the moment.

CHAPTER TWENTY-ONE

"It's a relief to feel your presence, Jenka," Zahrellion said into his dreaming brain. She had been on the ship for two full days now, trying to reach out to him and Crystal with her mind. She had little success until Frunien started aiding her. The skittish druid had pledged his undying loyalty to her in exchange for removing the frightening dampening hood from his head. Together they pooled their magic, reached out farther and were able to search longer. They managed to communicate with Crystal yesterday, and now Zahrellion was intruding into one of Jenka's dreams.

"Why are you in my forest?" he asked her curiously. He wasn't thinking with his wakeful mind. He was in a dream state, and Zahrellion could only hope that he would retain, and later recall, the instructions she was about to give him. She was impressed with the depth of detail his mind projected into the lush greenery surrounding them. And when he eased up beside her ghostly form and slipped his arm around her, she warmed inside, though she couldn't actually feel his touch.

"It's not just your forest, Jenka," she smirked, but in a sweet, soothing voice.

Her stark white hair made her lavender eyes seem all the more alien, but the tattoos on her face and forehead weren't nearly as pronounced in this place that Jenka's mind had created. She was wearing rough spun, tied at the waist with cord, just like Daliah used to wear around Crag. "Is Daliah still alive?" He wondered aloud.

"I don't know. You have to listen to me," she told him. She forced away her curiosity at who Daliah might be. "Crystal is coming for you. She never found Jade. You have to find a way out of your cell before Solstice Day or she will harass Kingston's harbor until they set you free."

"The Hazeltine already helped me out," he mumbled absently. In his dream, he had been halfheartedly tracking an elk that looked more like an oversized version of one of the many table dogs the Rangers used to keep up at Kingsmen's Keep.

"What Hazeltine? Where are you now?" she asked with a touch of concern.

"I'm here with you. How could I be anywhere else?" He responded.

"It doesn't matter, love," she conceded. Even in the misty dream world they were in, the light press of his body against hers was distracting. "Either you will remember this conversation when you wake up or you won't," she finally said.

"That's true," Jenka commented. "Tell me what you must. I need to start what I have to finish so that I can get done what I've promised to do."

"Who have you promised what?" she was suddenly worried. The Witches of Hazeltine were notoriously tricky and not so honorable in most cases. "Jenka, what have you done?"

"Nothing, yet," he grinned like a schoolboy, his dirty-blond bangs hanging in his eyes.

"What happened? No…never mind." If she had been formed of actual substance, she might have pinched the bridge of her nose and sighed. "Never mind, just listen to me." Her voice grew stern and serious. If she could, she would have put her hands on his shoulders, so that she could hold him still and look into his eyes to make sure that the information was registering. "On Solstice Day, you have to get yourself up high on the northern ridge that rims around Kingston. You need to spend the whole day up there, high on the slope, meditating in your trance state, like I showed you. Crystal will find you, and you two can go look for Jade on the mainland."

"I need to talk to the king!" Jenka's dream-self started to remember thoughts from his wakeful consciousness. "I have to tell him about his son!" He was suddenly alarmed, and a little more aware of where he was and who he was talking to. "The Goblin King has Prince Richard," he told Zahrellion. "And the sparkling blue he bonded with was killed. I saw it all through Jade's eyes, but now I don't know where Jade's gone. He has to be hiding from the mudged dragons. The frontier is thick with them."

"You watched Royal get killed through Jade's eyes?" Zahrellion's surprise was only overshadowed by her sudden sadness. Glum sorrow, and her growing fatigue, crept up on her and latched hold, threatening to pull her from Jenka's dream.

"Aye," said Jenka worriedly. "Royal told me that the Goblin King's wyrm took him toward Demon's Lake. You told me that the lake was called Demon's Lake because of the wind blowing across the grottoes, but I think it's because that's where the nightshade has always made his lair. That's where the Goblin King took the crown prince. I'm sure of it."

Zahrellion started to fade. Her mind was already stretched thin, and this particular form of High Magic was exhausting. She needed to ask a thousand questions now, but couldn't manage to form a single one of them into words. She did what she needed to do most, which was just as important. She reminded Jenka to be up on the slope of the northern ridge on Solstice Day. After that, she faded out of his dream completely.

* * *

Jenka woke to the insistent, licking tongue of Mysterian's dog. It was a pitiful looking hound. He half remembered that he had been following a similar creature in his dream, but those images were already fading from his mind. The old Hazeltine seemed to have done well for herself, for the room she had put him up in was as big as the entire hut Jenka and his mother shared back home in the foothills. Thinking of Crag, and the forested valleys that surrounded it, put him in a stale mood.

He was terribly worried for his mother, for Jade, and for Prince Richard as well.

A glance at his surroundings reminded him that he was no longer impotent. He wasn't in the dungeon cell any more. He wanted to do something, but he needed to eat first. He had a bear's hunger gnawing at his belly, and he didn't want to go off half askew. He needed a plan.

With the frisky mutt in tow, he found Mysterian in her hot, tile-floored, sunlit kitchen. She was humming over a pot full of something that had an unsavory, alchemical smell to it. The dog went immediately to her side, sat on his haunches, and looked up at her expectantly. Jenka noticed for the first time that the dog had bald patches on its hind side.

"This en't no food, Slake. You remember what happened the last time you tasted my brew," she told the dog, as if he could understand her plainly. Then she looked at Jenka and forced a tired smile. "Keep inside, De Swasso. Stay away from the glass, too." A stern, serious look erased the friendly grin from her wrinkled old face. "There's a library upstairs if you know your letters. Find a thicker volume and hunker down. Those Kingsmen are out there in the city hunting for you, and we have a bit to talk about later." She left her wooden stirring stick swirling around the kettle on its own, and pulled a piece of bread from a loaf. She cut him some cheese from a slab as she spoke. "It won't be safe for you to move about Kingston. Just after we slipped the castle gates, they started rounding up the few men King Blanchard left behind and started searching homes in the seedier quarters of the city. Rumor has it that the queen has put a healthy bounty out on you because the cell guard told her you were raising a ruckus about knowing were that dragon took the prince."

"Aye," he nodded. "I do know where he's ended up, but it's not where his dragon took him. That wyrm is dead now, and the prince is in grave danger." As an afterthought, he asked, "How long is it until Solstice Day? How long was I in the dungeon?"

"The dragon that took the prince is dead?" She had paled considerably, but her face showed no emotion. "The day after morrow is the Day of Solstice." She cocked her head curiously and sniffled. "You just said, 'His dragon,' as if the creature belonged to the prince. What did you mean? How do you know these things? Just how wormy are you?"

Jenka had just taken a bite of the offered ham. He was chewing and couldn't answer her question. He was about to tell her that he knew these things the very same way he knew where the dragon's tear was, but he never had the chance.

Three booming knocks came at the door, and Jenka's heart suddenly threatened to burst out of his chest. The dog went berserk, growling and barking, its uncut nails clicking and clattering on the tiled floor, as it darted off to voice its displeasure at the front door. Before Jenka could even think, there was more pounding and some muted cursing to go along with it.

"Hold still," she ordered. "If you hear me start cackling like I'm crazy, then creep up them stairs and out the window at the end of the hall. The roofs will lead you to the end of the block. There's a hawker's lot down there, and you can blend in until they leave."

Jenka's heart raced, but he wasn't afraid. If he was taken in front of the queen, then he could explain that Prince Richard desperately needed help. He hoped that it wasn't already too late. Mysterian was about to open the door when he decided to go turn himself in, so that he could gain the queen's aid. But on his way to the door, he saw Herald duck in conspicuously and start toward him with a purpose. The grizzled, old King's Ranger looked as relieved as he did angry as he grabbed Jenka up into a great, crushing bear hug.

"Thank the gods of man and beast, boy," he beamed, but then his thick brows narrowed. "What's happened to the crown prince, boy? What was that guard rambling about to the queen?"

"You don't know how glad I am to see you, Herald," Jenka heaved a heavy sigh of relief as he pushed himself away from the man. "We have to do something, but I'm not sure what, just yet," Jenka said. "That same guard told me you were leaving on the flotilla with King Blanchard and the kingdom's host."

"Host?" Herald had to bite back a sarcastic laugh. "That was no host. It was a mess of boys and shopkeepers and such, but never mind that, boy." Herald looked as if he was stretched to his limits. "What of Prince Richard? That is where our duty lies."

Jenka noticed that Mysterian's ear was piqued to the conversation. He had just been about to tell her the whole of it, too, so this would save him an extra telling.

"You're not going to understand some of this, Herald, but here it goes," said Jenka. "I am bonded to the dragon called Jade. Zahrellion is bonded with the white wyrm called Crystal, and Prince Richard was bonded to the big blue that snatched him up at the preliminaries."

"You told me all this back in the dungeon," Herald interrupted. "But you just said the crown prince *was* bonded with the blue. What happened?"

"It was killed by a gigantic, red-scaled mudge," Jenka waved a hand in front of his face and sighed with frustration. "Just listen. All of that happened after Prince Richard was taken by Gravelbone and his nightshade. They took the prince to the grottoes by Demon's Lake. I'm sure of it."

"That demon has the crown prince?" Mysterian asked incredulously. "Why haven't you told me any of this?" Her tone was scolding, and more than a little angry, but moreover she seemed suddenly stricken. Her entire demeanor had changed.

"I was just about to tell you," he indicated Herald and shrugged. He wasn't sure why she suddenly seemed so concerned. Up until he had gone to sleep earlier, all she had talked about was the dragon's tear Jade's mother had cried.

"He's alive, though?" asked Herald.

"Aye," answered Jenka. "As far as I know, he is."

"What good would the crown prince do him dead, Ranger?" asked Mysterian weakly.

"I see your point," conceded Herald. "He's probably just a bartering token."

"That he is," Mysterian told them as she eased into the kitchen and took a seat at the table. "But not for no troll war or nothing of the sort. If the Goblin King noodles Richard's brain then we'll all be in a fix when he takes the throne, even more so when the Time of Confliction is upon us. That's what this is about. We Hazeltines were the ones who predicted Gravelbone's return, and if you know your history, then you'll know that it's true. It's been one hundred and forty-three years now since Shtaro portended that Gravelbone would return in one hundred. She was off by almost half a century. He is evil incarnate, and he will tamper with the crown prince's mind and barter him back for one concession or another, just like you suggested. Then, all the fargin demon has to do is wait for Richard to take the throne and start doing his bidding."

"How will we know?" Jenka asked dubiously.

"His dragon would have known," she replied. "It's a shame that he had to meet his end. Royal was magnificent."

"How did you know his name?" Jenka asked quickly. He hadn't told her the blue's name, and was suddenly very suspicious.

"Where do you think Prince Richard and Royal met and conversed, De Swasso, in the king's garden? I think not. Old Blanchard would have had Royal's head decorating the wall opposite the wyrm's twin. I helped them keep their secrets, so to speak."

"What is all of this?" Herald asked. "What are you two talking about? We have to do something."

"You have to go tell the queen, Herald," Jenka told him. "Have swifters on the wing as soon as possible. Have the men at Port form a battalion and send them up into the grottoes to get him."

"While you do that, Jenka and I will work a little magic here and see if we can't come up with something too," Mysterian told Herald. She had stood, and was now ushering him towards the door. "But don't you go snitching the boy's whereabouts to the notables or the queen."

"I'll not even respond to that, witch," Herald retorted. "My honor is unquestionable. I'm a fargin King's Ranger, and don't you forget it."

"You're the son of a pig farmer, and honor you may have, but wits you're short on. Mind your tongue. What if she orders you to tell her where he is? Will you follow that order? That's what I meant."

"I'll come back after the sun sets," Herald huffed. "In the meantime, I'll spread a rumor that the boy's holed up in the cobbles north of the harbor."

"In the cobbles? With the whores and the gutter-thieves?" Mysterian made a disgusted face at the King's Ranger.

"They won't look too hard for him there," he said, as she opened the door for him. "They searched that area first."

"Tell them I've headed south, Herald," Jenka said, not exactly sure why he had done so. "Trust me. I've something that needs doing on Solstice Day to the north of town. Keep them away from the ridge. That's where I'll be. While the people are trying to celebrate, I have to meet a friend."

Jenka was glad neither of them asked him who this friend was because he didn't think he knew the answer. He just knew that he had to be there.

CHAPTER TWENTY-TWO

As soon as the door closed behind Herald, Mysterian locked the deadbolt, took Jenka by the hand and pulled him toward the table in the kitchen. She sat heavily, and motioned for Jenka to do the same. She sighed as if the weight of the world were pressing in on her. When he started to ask a question, she shushed him with a reptilian hiss that made his skin crawl.

"Your world is about to change, and you need to sit still for it." She looked even older now and somehow defeated. "You're not who you think you are, and that's why Amelia sent you here. The note your mother sent was just a ruse to get you to my door."

"What are you saying?" Jenka's tone was sharp.

"I'm saying that Jericho De Swasso was not your real father." Her hand shot up to stall his protest. "Only the Witches of Hazeltine knew of your get.

Your mother is one of us, and one of the better of us, I assure you. You have no father, Jenka." She stopped herself and gave him an apologetic look. "The seed that quickened to life inside your mother was concocted and brewed, not spurted from a man's groin in a natural coupling."

"I don't understand, much less believe a word of what you're saying. If this is true, then why wouldn't she tell me? I never knew my father anyway, so there was no reason not to."

"Oh there are reasons, Jenka," Mysterian told him. "For one, Jericho De Swasso was a good and honorable man. He lived and died thinking you were his get, and his memory deserves no tarnishing. A divine sort of magic, like none ever seen before, had a hand in creating you. Just as some greater evil created that thing that calls itself Gravelbone. You must destroy him."

"So I'm a bastard. What does any of this, or that tear, have to do with saving the prince and the frontier? Why tell me now?"

"You have to kill Gravelbone, Jenka. There are no two ways about it. That abomination must die. If he doesn't, we cannot allow the crown prince to take the throne. He will soon be corrupted by that wicked thing, if he hasn't been already, and with

Royal no longer alive, we will have no way to prove otherwise. The council will order Richard's death and he will die. But if you destroy the abomination then Richard can be saved."

"The council? What council are you talking about?" Jenka was confused, and more than a little upset. Learning that the man who you thought was your father all your life really wasn't was not an easy thing to swallow. Learning that the seed that conceived you was a witch's brew was just plain disconcerting. Finding out that your mother may have been deceiving you all of your life was unforgivable, and the harshness of those sentiments began to boil inside of him.

"The Council of Three, Jenka. They are the ones who truly decide man's fate. They are the ones who rule from the shadows and make things happen. The Outland wizard, Vax Noffa; Linux of the Order of Dou, whom you've travelled with; and the eldest of us Hazeltine, who happens to be me for the moment, we make up the trio. You were destined to be our champion, but then that yearling dragon found you, and you bonded with him. None of us expected that to happen, yet it has. No one knows how truly powerful you will become, but we all know you will become powerful, and your actions will affect the whole of the realm. In truth, you are humanity's champion, Jenka. The Time of Confliction is swiftly approaching, and you and your fellow Dragoneers will have to defend us all when that time comes."

"Why is it that you need that dragon's tear so badly, then?" The question had formed on its own in Jenka's mouth.

The old witch's eyes narrowed, and she looked even older than she had just moments before. "I do not need it, Jenka, you do. I am old and foolish, and was thinking of using the tear's power to keep myself young, but that was before the prince and his eager wyrm went off trying to be heroes and got captured. In that crystallized droplet there is contained a wealth of knowledge and power. It was the power of the last known dragon's tear that finalized your conception, and it emptied itself of energy to bring you to life. Now there is another. I can sense it, but only you know where to find it. Only you."

"I think you've gone mad!" Jenka said hotly, as he pushed himself away from the table and started for the front of the house. "Only Jade knows where to find it. So I have to find Jade before I can make good on my oath. That is the truth. You'll not confound me, witch. I swore I would bring you that tear, but I'm going to find my bond-mate and the crown prince before I even attempt it."

"You'd be wiser to find Jade and the tear and then go after Richard," she told him. "With the power of the tear on your side you can make things happen. Without it, you're just pissing into the wind." She knew he wasn't listening to her.

"I'll do what I have to do, Mysterian, and I'll keep my oath, but to do it I have to find Jade," He spoke as he unlatched and opened the door. "I have to save Prince Richard from the Goblin King, too." With that, he snatched one of the cloaks from the post in the entry and disappeared into the sparsely crowded streets of Kingston.

* * *

Down in Gravelbone's expanding lair, Prince Richard was terrified. He had been forced to witness, from his cage, the execution and consumption of not only several men, women, and children that had been captured by the nightshade and the troll hordes, but also the decimation of any troll or goblin that had cowered in battle or failed in its given task. The orcs, it seemed, were intentionally spared Gravelbone's wrath, but only because they served him with a willing fervor and had a firm control over the trolls and the goblins. The ogres, Richard learned, were Gravelbone's enemy, just as the humans and the pure-blooded dragons were. Two of the hulking, green creatures had been herded into the cage, and then were reduced to mumbling idiocy by the Goblin King's horrific, palming grasp.

Richard stayed in the corner and out of sight, hoping to get the chance to slip away from the demon, but there were orc sentries posted throughout the main cavern area now, and bands of trolls constantly patrolled the long cave way that led up to the surface, not to mention the savage group of little goblins hiding down the end of the tunnel that led deeper into the earth.

The crown prince kept busy by sharpening a tin button he had gotten from the body of the ogre the nightshade had killed. It was the size of a large coin, and he thought that he might be able slice a jugular with it, if he got a lucky swipe in. It was nerve-wracking, repetitive work, because he figured that the freakish demon troll or his nightshade would hear the scraping and come finish him. He was trying, with little success, to block out the images of the two pleading children that had been eaten before his eyes yesterday. Gravelbone had let a small pack of goblins devour them right outside of the ogre cage where Richard was huddled. It was a sickening thing to be so helpless and afraid, especially when you were supposed to be the backbone of the land. He didn't think he would be able to live with himself after watching in a huddle of terror as the mother pleaded to him, the crown prince of the kingdom, to do something to save her children from those needle-sharp teeth.

Gravelbone had twisted the woman's head off and toyed with it for long hours after her blood had soaked into the rocky cavern floor.

The goblins were a little more than waist tall to a grown man, but they were deft and agile. Their skin was the color of damp ash. They blended into the shadows so well, that once, one of them had crept up on Richard and tried to take a bite out of him. Luckily, it had attracted the nightshade's attention, for the slick, black-skinned worm saved Richard from the goblin's teeth by snatching up the little bugger and crunching him. In the open, the goblins attacked like wolves or frenzied fish. A half-dozen of them could get on a man and eat him to the bone in a matter of minutes.

The orcs were every bit of ten feet tall, which was only a head taller than most of the trolls. They were bulky and heavy where the trolls were long and lithe. They had coarse, dark skin instead of bristled fur. The biggest difference between the two larger forms of goblinkin was that the orcs wore crude armor, and they carried the swords, axes, and other tools that had been collected from the villages they had sacked. All of them served Gravelbone dutifully, mostly out of fear, but many an orc relished the screams of the dying humans when the Goblin King gave them their nightly show. Richard was half expecting the evil, ivory-horned bastard to return any moment with fresh victims to torture him with.

Prince Richard held no false allusions as to what was happening. The demon was torturing him by killing the innocents. Gravelbone was showing his dominance over humanity one screaming murder at a time, and it was affecting Richard in ways he didn't understand. Richard had actually pleaded silently to the gods for the next victims to be men, not women or children. What bothered him most about this was the fact that he didn't pray for there to be no victims. It was as if that option had been removed from his mind completely.

Worst of all was that empty void in his soul where he used to feel Royal. The miraculous promise of hope that his bond-mate's very existence had given him had been extinguished. Hope had fled, and there wasn't much left to cling to.

"Pleeeeeaaaaaase!" a girl's voice howled from up the tunnel-like cave, causing a stir of excitement to rile the four orcs posted in the cavern. Somewhere, down the other end of the shaft, the skittering of goblin claws on the stone floor came to Richard's ears.

"Where are you taking me?" the girl cried out. The rough stone added an eerie reverberation to her futile calls. "Pleeeaaase! I want my mother, pleeease stop."

Madness was taking hold of Prince Richard's mind, and he didn't think that he could take it any more. He put his face in his hands so he didn't have to see her face when the Goblin King marched her into the chamber. He began rocking back and forth on the floor like an infant. It took the girl only a moment to realize that she had been led right into a big sticky brown mess of bones, insects, and gore. After that, her screams grew hysterical as the pack of goblins started for her.

"Looka yon," Gravelbone told the girl devilishly, as he held the hungry goblins at bay with a glare.

He pointed at Prince Richard. His voice carried easily to the crown prince's ears. "Yon Prins gon com save ya." The Goblin King started laughing manically, but the sound of his mirth didn't come close to drowning out the wet tearing sounds of the goblins when they started eating the girl where she stood.

* * *

Jenka sat on the rim of the cauldron-like ridge that cradled Kingston, looking down at the distant and nearly empty festival area. He had been sitting there most of the day trying to find his center and focus. He was half-tempted to stalk down to the tourney grounds, and win one of the competitions that had once seemed so important to him. If he weren't so confused and lost inside, he might have. At the moment, however, he had no desire to be a King's Ranger or to participate in anything that involved the kingdom. All he wanted to do was save the Prince, then go find his mother and ask her if what Mysterian had said was true.

By the look of things down on the competition grounds, there wasn't much happening. Some retired field Lord who had done some time out in the frontier was probably cleaning up the trophies, since every able-bodied man from all three islands had been called to duty, put on ships, and sent to Port to go fight the dragons and trolls.

Jenka gave a sarcastic chuckle. “What are you going to do when you get there, King Blanchard,” he asked himself out loud. He was up above the city, and no one could see him, much less hear him. “What would be the best thing for you to do with all of those men?”

An idea struck Jenka like a thunderbolt, but his excitement quelled as swiftly as it had surged. It didn’t matter if he came up with a perfect plan to swarm the grottoes and save the crown prince. His voice couldn’t be heard from the ridge above Kingston, and even if it could be heard, King Blanchard wouldn’t take the time to listen to him. “Would he?”

“He might,” a frigid and slithery feminine voice spoke from above him. Jenka whirled around to find Crystal there, her cold scales steaming lightly in the bright afternoon sun. Her huge head was looking almost straight down at him.

“Where did you come from?” Jenka asked, trying to get his thumping heart back into his chest.

"An egg," Crystal hissed out what might have been a dragon's laugh. "We are needed elsewhere, Jenka. Jade has gone missing and the Goblin King has taken over the frontier."

"Can you find Zahrellion?" Jenka asked hopefully. "Can you go get her and bring her back here?"

Another hissing laugh emitted from the dragon in a cloud of cold, steaming breath. "I can do much better than that, my friend," Crystal's voice was soft and inviting. She lowered her body and extended her long neck forward so that Jenka could use her forearm as a step to climb up onto her back.

"You want me to…?"

"Yessss," Crystal hissed again. "Trussst me Jenka. I can take you to Zahrellion. Then we can go find Jade and Prince Richard together."

Had Zahrellion not told him a little bit about the two times she had ridden on Crystal's back, Jenka might have declined, but the idea he'd just had for King Blanchard and the massive flotilla of ships was already evolving in his mind. With Zah beside him, he knew he wouldn't feel so inept. She could use High Magic, and something about her gave him the confidence he needed to succeed.

With more than a little electric excitement starting to tingle through his veins, he climbed up on the icy-white dragon's back and wiggled his arse between two of her triangular spinal plates. Before he knew what was happening, he was being jerked roughly forward. Once, then again, his head whipped backwards, but after that they were in the air, and King's Island was falling away below them.

Despite all of the uncertainty and fear he felt, Jenka was thrilled to the marrow of his bones by the sensation of flying on the dragon's back. For a long, long while he could do little else but enjoy the freedom and magnificence of the ride. But then the sun started to set behind them, and the prospect of flying in the darkness gave him reason for concern.

"I can see plainly in the night, Jenka," Crystal comforted into his head before he could even ask the question aloud. "There are many things we dragons can do that you don't know about."

"Just don't crash into the water, Crystal," Jenka thought back to her. "I never learned how to swim."

For some reason, the big white dragon thought that was funny.

CHAPTER TWENTY-THREE

A group of men, women, and children were holed up in a well-built stone keep just southwest of Del, on the mainland. The rider they had sent to Midwal had miraculously gotten through, and now Commander Charvin, the highest ranking member of military presently at the Midwal Gate, was organizing a party to ride out and try and rescue them. Rikky Camile volunteered to go, but had been turned away because of his missing leg. The commander noted his bravery. Rikky cursed the man, and then rolled back into one of the pavilions erected to keep the weather off the wounded refugees that had made it to safety.

Rikky had found a calling of sorts. His healing work wasn't nearly as refined as Master Vahlda's had been, but he could stop a man from bleeding out, or knit a broken bone back together if he had a solid nap between attempts.

He had told the commander, and anyone who would listen, that it had been the crown prince riding the blue dragon that had carried him and Jess over the wall to safety. They all listened, and a lot of them even believed his tale. Enough men had tried to loose arrows and spears at the sparkling blue that the event couldn't be denied, but the idea that it was King Blanchard's son riding on the wyrm was received skeptically.

Rikky's leg was still too raw for him to use his prosthesis, but a man that knew Jess knew another man who quickly built Rikky a chair with wagon's wheels attached to the side. With it, he wheeled himself around the encampment that had risen up around the Midwal gates. The league of open road that separated the city called Midwal from the Midwal Gate was now populated with the refugees from the frontier who were lucky enough to escape the hordes of trolls and goblins. Ricky spent his time helping Spell Master Gahry and the novice healers tend to the wounded among those folk, but he spent every other waking hour trying to walk with his wooden peg leg.

At the last moment, the apprentice healer who had volunteered to go with Commander Charvin's rescue party decided that he was more comfortable staying behind the Great Wall. The man had no reservation about showing his cowardice, and the commander was left in a pickle. The instant Rikky heard this, he wheeled himself out to the gates, where a steady rain had begun to fall on the waiting party.

"I'm no coward," he called out to the commander. "Are you?"

"No, boy," the commander answered with a look of respect that wasn't lost on any man there. "Get in a wagon, and keep track of your own chair. Can you ride if it comes to it?"

"Aye," Rikky nodded. "Can I go get my peg leg? I'll be walking with it before long, I assure you."

"I have no doubt you will." The commander nodded. "But I'll send a man to get it. We need to get you loaded up."

A few hours later, the rain was still coming steadily down. The scattered forest lining the road outside the gates provided little or no cover from the nasty storm, but the traveling was relatively safe because the trolls and dragons were hunkered down out of the weather.

Rikky felt terrible that he was getting to ride in a covered supply wagon. From underneath the dry canvas covering he could see some of the others struggling in the rain. They looked to be wet and miserable. The group was made up of three wagons, each carrying a driver and two other men. Each wagon had an equal share of the supplies, in case one of them got separated from the others. There were eight horsemen riding guard, and they appeared to be confident and capable men. Commander Charvin was one of them, looking every bit the part of a hardened veteran frontiersman. He wore the red shield of the Walguard proudly on his steel chest armor, and he carried a big, double-bladed battle axe. His men wore more functional chain mail armor and were armed with longbows, crossbows, and polished swords. The tunics they wore all bore the mark of the Walguard as well.

The idea was to travel through the night until the next day broke, then camp in the daylight. That way, they could make the old keep, where the refugees were trapped, as the sun was coming up the following day. If the ill weather held out, they could probably get the task done with little incident, but Rikky could tell by the clouds that the rain would soon blow over. After that, who knew what would happen.

The rain didn't stop that night, but as they were making the first camp, the clouds parted and the most perfect of days began. It was a slightly steamy, early summer morning and the birds and wildlife were enjoying it almost as much as the men were.

Rikky tried to sleep, but he couldn't. The day was just that wonderful. He sat in his wheeled chair watching a pair of scarlet butterflies flutter about a smattering of tiny turquoise flowers and reveled in the feel of the sun on his skin when the alarm was called. Someone had spotted a dragon in the sky and now men were screaming about trolls coming in fast from the north.

An archer that also served as the cook helped Rikky into his wagon and got him a crossbow, as well as a quarrel of bolts. Stones came flying in, and the sounds of chattering goblins could be heard. The wagon jerked forward, and Rikky was nearly tumbled out of the back over the wooden latch gate.

He caught his balance and fired a bolt at a troll that was about to pull one of the Walguard from his horse. The man stabbed the troll in the collar with his sword and yanked the blade out in a gush of black blood. He gave Rikky a nod, but Rikky was busy fighting to reload his weapon and didn't see him.

After he got the crossbow reloaded, he grabbed his wooden leg and strapped it on. It was no easy task in the bouncing, swaying wagon, but he managed it. He wasn't about to get stranded without it again. When he looked back out of the wagon, he saw a horse and man getting pulled down by a swarm of little, ash-colored goblins, as another man spurred his mount just out of their reach. Arrows were flying back at the attackers as the fleeing men and wagons pulled away. They seemed to be putting some distance between them, but then, a deep umber-colored dragon roared out just overhead, and blasted Rikky's wagon with its flaming breath. Rikky waited until the wagon slowed a bit, then jumped headlong out from under the flaming canvas. He tumbled in a half-controlled roll, then hobbled upright and started screaming from the pain that shot up through his stump. He bore the sickening agony and started hobbling alongside a rider-less horse that had escaped the goblins with only minor wounds. The Walguard rider he had saved earlier turned his mount and reined in beside Rikky, blocking the horse's escape. He loosed three arrows in rapid succession, keeping the pursuing goblins at bay, buying Rikky the time he needed to pull himself into the saddle. After that was a mad dash through the thickets, into a more densely canopied copse of forest. The one wagon that had broken away with Rikky and the Walguard rolled up into the trees, until it wedged itself stuck. Then the driver and the box man started coming after the two mounted men on foot. After a while the four of them settled in a cluster of tightly-rooted pine trees, and tried to gather their breath. It was then that Rikky felt something flare to life inside him, something powerful and inexplicable, like nothing else he had ever felt before in his life. The horse underneath him felt it, too, and it shivered with fear. Somewhere away from them, the sound of men being savaged by goblins and trolls resounded.

Behind Rikky, the Walguard sucked in a heavy breath. "There's another dragon," he whispered shakily. "It's as fargin silver as a sword, and it's right here." The roar that blasted from behind them caused Rikky's terrified horse to bolt. It carried him headfirst into a low-hanging limb. The blow knocked him out of the saddle and almost knocked him unconscious. When he squinted through the haze of his bludgeoned vision he saw that the Walguard and the other two wagoneers had fled. The silver-scaled wyrm came crashing into the clump of pine trees and loomed its big head over him, baring a full set of slathering, arm-long fangs. Rikky was drenched in fear. He could do little more than clench shut his eyes and hope that death was swift.

* * *

Prince Richard was dying inside, and he knew it. The horrors that Gravelbone forced him to witness were beyond vile. He had just been made to choose which of three men would get the swift death of the Goblin King's blade, and which two would feed the demon's personal little band of ever-hungry goblins.

After he cleaved the head from the man Richard had chosen, Gravelbone kicked it into the ogre cage where Richard was still huddled. The demon troll laughed manically when one of the stupefied green beasts started playing with it. Gravelbone and the nightshade had gone off then, back out to find more innocent people to bring back and kill for the crown prince.

What the ivory-horned bastard's ultimate goal was, Prince Richard had no idea, but if it was to drive him into madness, it was working. He had lost all sense of humanity. He even found himself sometimes anticipating the deadly displays. The idea of seeing the innocent people of the frontier butchered or eaten alive sickened him, yet he couldn't seem to keep from looking forward to the foul events. The fact that he could recognize his own disgusting enjoyment for what it was made it all the worse. He was about to succumb. But then, one night, he had a dream, and everything started to change.

He dreamt that he was flying with a young green dragon. It was Jenka's green; the yearling called Jade. He wasn't riding on a dragon's back. He was inside a dragon's consciousness. He caught a glimpse of his own bright-blue wing leather, and knew instantly that Royal was somehow still alive. Prince Richard was flying in spirit with his bond-mate. With this realization, pain struck him all along his long neck and behind his shoulder-blades where his wing joints were. It was a pain like nothing he had ever felt before, and the intensity of it threw him back into wakefulness just in time to hear Gravelbone and the nightshade returning again.

The Goblin King didn't have a human offering this time. It had two ogres. One of them was no bigger than a man, which meant that it was most likely still an adolescent. The other had heavy, hanging breasts, and was obviously the mother of the younger creature. The nightshade prodded them along with its fearsome-looking head, and by the way the two ogres were sobbing, Richard figured that the father had died trying to defend his family. The swath of shining, sticky blood that decorated the nightshade's chin and neck lent to that conclusion. Gravelbone immediately noticed the crown prince's interest in the new arrivals and started mumbling to himself proudly in his half-gibberish way.

"Wan Prins kom kiw dees wans," the Goblin King said to Prince Richard as he eased over toward the ogre cage. "Wan Prins kom kut em up, yeah!"

Richard swallowed hard. He had come to understand the Goblin King's deep voice and ramblings. "Want Prince to come kill these ones, want Prince to come cut them up," was what Richard heard. Although they were just ogres, he wasn't sure if he could do it, which was odd to him because he had already chosen the order of death for several of his fellow humans.

Those people were going to die no matter who you chose, he told himself. *These ogres are going to die whether it's you who kills them, or the orcs and goblins who do it. Or are they?*

The empty hole in his spirit was now filling with hope for Royal, and a newfound resolve was formed in his heart. He snorted and grinned crazily, and looked at Gravelbone with wild eyes, the same look he gave his opponents on the tilt yard just before a joust.

"I'll kill `em for you, you foul cretin," he said, as he mimicked the action of shooting with a bow and arrow. "I'll kill `em from right here."

Gravelbone laughed and barked out an order to one of the four orcs guarding the cage. "Jus wan aroo," the Goblin King added. "Jus giv `em wan."

The orc chuckled nervously, its dark, greasy face full of contempt. It poked the longbow and a single arrow down at Richard through the bone bars of the ogre cage and then backed quickly away, in case Richard decided to shoot him with the shaft.

Gravelbone thought this was funny and half threatened to feed the orc to the goblins if it didn't grow some spine.

"Wha wan?" the Goblin King asked excitedly. "Wha wah yoo gon kiw?"

Richard tested the draw on the finely-crafted bow and looked across the cavern at the trembling pair of ogre. Behind them, and half blocking the tunnel that led up to the surface, the nightshade curled up to rest and digest a meal it had recently eaten.

Prince Richard took careful aim at the mother ogre first. Then he shifted the direction of his aim over a fraction to the smaller creature. It had pleading, angry eyes, as if it would have willingly died fighting rather than be killed like this. When he was absolutely certain that the young ogre was looking back at him, he lowered his bow and pointed down the cavern the way they had come in.

"Whas dis?" the Goblin King asked angrily.

Before anything could stop him, Prince Richard brought the bow back up and aimed it at the mother ogre, but only until Gravelbone started chuckling victoriously. Richard loosed the arrow, but not at either of the green-skinned creatures. The arrow flew swiftly right past them and struck true, right into one of the nightshade's huge nostrils. When the hellborn wyrm rose up, roaring out its pain and anger, the Prince squeezed through the cage bars and charged the orc that had given him the bow. He threw the bow at it, and when it raised up its arms protectively, he sliced it with the big button he had sharpened. He cut across the open skin under the arm that the orc's crude armor didn't cover.

The other three orcs tackled him in a matter of seconds, but the two ogres had taken off running out of the cavern, and the nightshade's anguished thrashing was blocking any form of pursuit. A few of the hungry little goblins might have squeezed through, but if the two ogres couldn't fight their way out, it was no longer Richard's concern. He had done all he could for them, and now he had enough to worry about on his own. Gravelbone was charging over to clamp his palm on Richard's head and boil his marrow again.

Richard had never been so afraid in his life. He would rather die than feel that terrible pain again. He didn't have that option, and when the claw latched onto his forehead this time, the sensation was devastating.

CHAPTER TWENTY-FOUR

From a great distance across the sea, Zahrellion saw her dragon coming, and her heart leapt with joy because of it. Even in her elation, her mind started contemplating how she could get from the ship onto Crystal's back. There was no way the dragon could land on the ship, not without destroying the sails and the masts. Crystal was just too big. Her attention was averted from that subject when she noticed that her dragon had a rider. When Jenka shook his uneven blond bangs out of his face and squinted at the ship, he reminded her of a hero from some ancient tale. She noticed instantly that he was wearing the wide-shouldered leather armor she had picked out for him back in Three Forks. He looked good in it, and he looked comfortable riding on the dragon's shining back. As she worked to quell the warmth that was spreading inside her, she wondered why he hadn't gone directly after Jade.

Some of the men in the rigging saw the dragon, too. They started calling down warnings to the others.

Zah called out across the vessel as loud as she could, "If any man so much as thinks of firing an arrow or throwing a spear, I will blast them myself." A crackling orb of energy, pulsing pink and yellow, formed between her hands. She held it as if it were a ball she was about to hurl. The audible sound of several men gulping at the same time resounded over the waves.

"Stand down, men," the captain ordered from behind her. He had a long brass looking tube in his hand, and looked more than a little nervous. "There's a man riding that wyrm, and the lass here is full o'magic. I think, between the three of them and that other skittish druid, they could sink us if they wanted to. Not much a few pointed sticks is gonna do but rile `em up more."

"Aye, Cap'n," a man said.

"Aye," the others agreed.

"Thank you," Zah said. "I need to get on that dragon's back, Captain," she turned and smiled, and let the crackling orb extinguish in her hands.

The terrified look on the man's face was priceless. "Any suggestions?"

He stammered and harrumphed. To his credit, the roll and sway of the ship had no effect on his stature when it caused Zah to have to take a few steps to catch her balance. "Cargo boom," he said flatly. "We can swing you out and the beast, uh… the dragon, I mean, can get its neck right under, if its wings en't too wide."

"Which one?" She indicated the masts and the confusing mess of spars and crossbeams that the sails were rigged to.

"You're just gonna go, on a dragon? Just like that?" he asked incredulously.

Behind the captain, Frunien peeked up out of the companionway.

"I am," she insisted. "Now, please. The dragon has been flying for hours, and I'm sure that she would like to get herself over land so that she can rest her wings. The longer this takes, the more likely she will be to try and take rest on your ship, and I assure you, sir, she will not ask for permission to board."

"Linux will have my head," Frunien mumbled.

"Then come along," Zah snapped. "Crystal can carry three as easily as she can carry two."

"Crystal is her name?" Frunien was now watching the frosty white dragon ease in close to the ship. He could see Jenka sitting proudly on her back, and it astounded him. "No, Zahrellion," he shook his head in the negative. "You have a destiny, it seems. I'll not get in the way of it." With that, he turned and went back down into the belly of the ship.

The captain called out orders, and a series of ropes and pulleys were utilized to make a long wooden beam, able to swing out over the side of the ship, up high. Zah tied a short length of rope around the waist of her gray robes for a belt and fastened her cloak tightly. She then ascended the rigging as if she were born a sailor. In a matter of minutes, she was poised precariously out over the water, straddling the round beam of wood like some adventurous child on a tree limb. Crystal came swooping in, and as the two of them were really starting to feel each other's presence through their bond, Zah slipped upside down on the jib and extended her arms down. Crystal had to pull her wings in so that the left one didn't crash into the ship's rigging. She was coming in very fast because of this. At the last second, Jenka reached up and clasped Zah's dangling arms at the wrist and as Crystal came streaking past the ship, Zah let her legs go. She spun acrobatically into a straddled position behind Jenka on the dragon's back. It would have been a perfect feat had Jenka's arms not been nearly ripped from their sockets when Zah's weight, and the momentum of Crystal's flight, yanked them backwards.

As Crystal flew ahead of the ship and peeled away, winging north, the ship's crew gave a hearty cheer, followed by a long, loud sigh of relief.

* * *

Jade was sleepy. He had used all his energy trying to heal Royal so that they could fly away from the blood-soaked area where they had fought the hulking fire dragon. The spells he had cast, and the short swift flight had worn the young green dragon to exhaustion. They didn't make it far, but they had gotten away from the red dragon's gruesome carcass before the sun left the sky. They felt safe enough to land and rest in a small, starlit glade, surrounded by forest.

Royal fell into a fitful slumber as soon as he landed, leaving Jade to struggle to stay awake and keep watch for them. It didn't take long for something to come around. A pair of roaming trolls, on their way to investigate the coppery smelling carnage blowing on the wind, stepped out of the tree line and saw them. After hurling a couple of small rocks, they went loping away, most likely to get others.

Jade didn't wake Royal. The big blue needed rest and more healing magic. Jade's mother had instilled in him several spells of the restorative sort, but they were complex beyond Jade's reasoning; the young dragon wasn't capable of casting them yet. Beyond that, he had just cast the powerful spell that destroyed the huge red and then healed Royal well enough to get him in the air and flying. It was rare for a dragon of his age and type to be using such powerful High Magic, but desperation had filled him full of might, and he mustered the stuff from way down deep. It hadn't hurt that he had Jenka's strength with him to draw upon. His amber-tinted lower lids were now threatening to slide up. The exhaustion was getting the better of him.

For Jade, everything had a deep, urgent undertone. He had been on his way to save his bond-mate from the stone fortress he was trapped within. Jade needed Jenka, and Jenka desperately needed him. Thinking about these things kept him awake and alert enough to sense the presence of another dragon, as it cautiously approached them from above. Surprisingly, Jade could sense the aura of a pure-blooded dracus circling overhead. It was a welcome sensation.

The very same aura that terrified the mudged and worried the trolls and goblins filled other High Dracus with a sense of ease and comfort, save for the mating seasons, when it could cause terrible rage and jealousy among the drakes. This one was a mam, a female dragon, Jade was certain. And when it landed silently and came upon them, it made Jade nervous, but he wasn't afraid.

"Where are you taking me?" A human voice asked. A human boy's voice.

"Jenka?" Jade asked excitedly.

"Who was that?" Rikky asked back. "This is Rikky Camile. How do you know Jenka?"

With a loud *HISSSSSSSSSSSS*, Royal caused the mid-sized silver dragon that Rikky was riding to leap back and nearly toss him to the ground. Royal had felt Gravelbone's palm on his bond-mate's head, and had taken the wicked, tormenting abuse with him. Royal had a rage now, a rage that was boiling to life inside his slightly-healed body. Only because he knew the silver could help heal him more, did he restrain from lashing out at her.

After the quick display of dominance, Royal eased his reflexive temper back a notch and half-welcomed the silver to join them. It had come for the Confliction, from beyond the peaks, and had bonded with Rikky. Rikky was still in shock over the sudden happening. He had only half-believed the things he had heard Jenka and Zahrellion talking about. Now he had no doubt about them. He had sworn to kill the Goblin King, and Silva had agreed that it needed doing. Not because Rikky had sworn to it, but because Silva knew that it must be done before the Time of Confliction could begin. Rikky had no idea, nor did he care, what the Time of Confliction was all about. He wanted revenge on the thing that had caused Master Kember and Solmon's death, the thing that had destroyed Crag and the other foothill settlements, and the thing that killed all those countless, innocent people in Three Forks and Outwal for no good reason.

Royal was pleased to hear of their intention. His bond-mate was Gravelbone's prisoner, and was on the verge of death, or insanity, or both. Silva's help might be the tide that turned the tables on the Goblin King. Jade, speaking over Rikky's confused questions, told the other dragons that he still needed to go to King's Island to save Jenka from the stone fortress. Royal dismissed him as if he were a hatchling. As if Jade hadn't just saved him from the huge fire drake, and certain death at the hands of the scavenging vermin.

Jade didn't take the rejection very well, but he didn't let it distract him from what he intended to do. Since Silva was there to help Royal now, he had no reason to stay around. He didn't even say good-bye before he took wing and started flying south toward the sea. He would go to King's Island and get Jenka without the help of the others. If they didn't think they needed him, then he didn't need them. He needed Jenka though, and Jenka needed him. That's all that mattered to the young green as he flew south with all he had left in him.

The sun was breaking the horizon, and Jade was well out over the ocean when he realized that he hadn't rested and was still weak from all of the spell casting. He had no idea how much further he had to fly, but he was already faltering from exhaustion. Panic overtook him, and he turned around to go back to the mainland so that he could rest and eat before again attempting to make the long flight over the ocean.

He soon found that he had no idea where he was, or which way he was going. The panic was starting to debilitate him considerably. He wasn't able to make full wing strokes, and the ones he was capable of making were weak and shaky at best. The sun was high overhead so he couldn't tell which direction was what. Worse, there was no land in sight. He was losing altitude and would soon crash into the sea.

It happened then, and terror overwhelmed him. His left wing failed. It pulled reflexively in against his body. The other wing wouldn't close because it had cramped hard, and the muscle was knotted and pulling awkwardly. Like some tumbling leaf, Jade went fluttering into a spin and splashed into the slow-rolling, cobalt sea.

* * *

Silva cast several complex healing spells on Royal, and the two of them slept while Rikky sat high on Silva's bulk, watching through the daylight hours. It was after the sun had left the sky, and Rikky had gone to sleep, that a band of trolls, led by two larger orc commanders, attacked them.

Rikky had been so close to Silva's healing magic that it had affected him, too. His wounded stump no longer pained him, and he slid off of Silva's back with ease. He hunkered down in the woods while the two dragons had their way with the attackers. Silva's breath was a fountain of fiery liquid that lit up the night and consumed any creature that got in the path. Royal was still weary and wounded, but his fierceness was a terrible thing to behold. He darted forth and used a swiping claw to rip open two trolls and snatched another into his mouth with a sickening crunch.

The orcs ordered the trolls to charge forth, but some of them blanched and Silva roasted them in their tracks. It looked as if the battle was over, that the two High Dracus had prevailed, when a mudge and the hellborn nightshade came streaking past. They sent gouts of their own wicked breath spraying down on Royal and Silva. The Goblin King, with his crown of ivory antlers, laughed manically and threw something down at Royal. It was Prince Richard's falcon-winged helmet, and seeing it sent Royal into an uncontrollable rage.

When Silva blasted the mudge from the sky with a hot, lavender pulse of magical energy, the nightshade came to a hover just out of their reach.

Seething, Royal forgot his half-healed wounds and leapt into the air after it, but Silva held fast.

"Come, Rikky," she hissed. "We must pursue."

"I think it's a trap," Rikky shouted as he limped over to the lowered dragon. The few remaining trolls and the two orcs were staying well clear now. "It wanted Royal to follow! It's a trap."

"Royal knowsss thiss, but he doesssn't care. He will die trying to sssave his bond-mate as I would die to sssave you. That isss why we won't rush in," Silva hissed, after Rikky wedged himself in between two of her spinal plates. "Rushing in is for the drakes. Hopefully that fool wyrm doesn't get himself killed before we get there, but either way, the trap should already be sprung by the time we arrive."

CHAPTER TWENTY-FIVE

Jenka was as tired as he had ever been in his life. Riding on the white dragon's sleek, undulating, and ever-chilly back had taken its toll on his body. If he could have felt Zahrellion's warmth behind him it might have been better, but she couldn't get close because there was a triangular spinal plate between them. When they made landfall on the mainland peninsula's rocky bluffs, somewhere between Port and Mainsted, Jenka had never felt so relieved. When he slid stiffly off Crystal's back and tried to walk off the soreness, he decided that he had probably never felt that much pain, either.

Zah wasn't much better. She only had to ride halfway across the ocean, and she had ridden on Crystal's back before, but her muscles hadn't gotten used to the awkward, wide-straddled positioning yet. Jenka absently hoped that Jade's scaly body wouldn't be so cold when he grew big enough to be ridden. The chill of Crystal's body was unpleasant after a while.

Zah started a fire with her druidic magic, while Crystal left them to go hunt. The white dragon had been flying now for nearly a week with only the shortest of stops to rest and feed. Jenka hoped she found an easy meal, for she needed and deserved all the rest she could get. Jenka had stuffed his pockets with meat pies, purchased on King's Island before he had gone up on the ridge. What he hadn't eaten had fallen apart in his pockets. He offered Zah some of the crumbled stuff as he shook it out onto a flat stone.

She laughed girlishly, and for a moment Jenka forgot that she was elvish and probably three times his age. Her smile warmed him and he let it, but deep inside the idea of her age bothered him. She took a bit of the crust from the stone and nibbled at it. It irked him that nothing in his life was as it seemed; he wasn't Jericho De Swasso's son, Zahrellion wasn't a beautiful young girl, and the kingdom's fate was supposedly decided by a trio of representatives from different High Magic-wielding factions, not King Blanchard, as he had always believed.

Linux from the Order of Dou; Mysterian, the Hazeltine witch, who had brewed his seed in a kettle pot; and Vax whatever-his-name-was, the wizard from the Outlands, were the ones who decided it all. He chuckled out loud but kept his thoughts to himself. *If they are so powerful, then why do they need me to be their champion?* He asked himself. *Why me?*

When Crystal returned, she loomed her head down from high and laid a strip of fresh, raw meat across the stone Jenka had been using for a table. Then she curled into a tail-to-nose ball. Jenka put the meat on a makeshift spit and let it roast over the hissing blue flames while Zah got reacquainted with her dragon. By the time the meat was finished cooking, Zahrellion was fast asleep. Jenka ate half of it and left the rest close enough to the fire to keep the insects off.

He went to sleep and dreamed of frantic wing-strokes and cramping limbs. He splashed down into the sea and felt a terror so deep and primal that it threatened to drive him mad. He was floating in the ocean, rising and falling on the surface, as titanic swells lifted and dropped him at will. The persistent feeling that some huge predator was circling in the water underneath him prevailed. It was dark, and there was lightning in the distant sky. A terrible storm was rolling in, and he knew that if he didn't get out of the water and fly before the storm reached him he would surely drown.

As hard as Jenka tried to wake from the dream, he could not. He was stuck there inside his dragon's mind, trying desperately to swim up out of the water and get airborne. It just wouldn't work, and Jade was only succeeding in exhausting himself.

In Jenka's dream, daylight came around again, and at least he could tell the direction the current was taking him. He was being pushed eastward, away from either of the nearest land masses. His hope for survival was fading as fatigue took over.

When he reached the peak of the swells that were lifting him, he could see the storm he had seen the night before, still inching closer and closer to him. It was a black wall of roiling clouds, thick with flashes of wicked-looking lightning. Halfheartedly, he tried swimming away from it. He wasn't certain why he bothered, for there was no way he could outmaneuver the approaching weather. Nightfall was approaching again in his dreamland, and the terror was taking a firmer grip on his soul, when Zahrellion woke him with her soft, sweet voice.

"What is it, Jenka?" she asked. "What has you tossing and turning so?"

"It's Jade." He sat up as he spoke, the cobwebs falling from his mind like shaken droplets of water. "He's crashed into the sea and we have to find him before the storm swallows him up."

"Oh no," Zahrellion gasped, as she looked out across the ocean they had just crossed. The sky that had just been blue and sunlit was growing dark and nasty. To punctuate the situation, lightning crackled nearby, and the following thunder was ear shattering.

"Where's Crystal?" Jenka yelled in a panic over the rumbling. "Wasn't she just here?"

Zahrellion turned to see that her dragon was gone from where it had just been lying only moments ago. Turning, she scanned the edge of the storm and was just fast enough to see Crystal's stark white tail disappearing off into the roiling blackness. Then the rain started coming down in sheets, and the wind whipped into a torrent.

* * *

The only thing Herald hated more than traveling on the little ship was traveling on the little ship with the witchy old crone. Mysterian had gone into a tranced state and was sitting in the bow. She was using her witchcraft to call forth the near-perfect gust of wind that was pushing the creaking craft across the sea at uncanny speed. Like Herald, the small crew of fishermen was terrified, but they did their jobs and kept the boat sliding gracefully over the deep, rolling waves, if at an unnatural pace. It was clear that the boat wasn't made for the open sea, but nevertheless they were away from King's Island, beyond the point of no return now, and they were successfully outrunning the dark wall of clouds that had formed behind them.

When Herald told Her Majesty, Queen Alvazina, that Prince Richard was now a prisoner of the Goblin King, she had gone wild with rage. Not at Herald, but at her husband for being so hard-headed about the dragons and trolls. She was on a ship sailing toward Port before Herald even knew what happened. When he rushed back to Mysterian's residence to tell them about it, Jenka had gone. Herald remembered Jenka saying that he had to meet a friend north of town on Solstice Day. He had been lower on the ridge that afternoon. He had seen Jenka climb onto the back of the icy white dragon with his own eyes, and after he regained his composure, he went and told Mysterian what he had seen.

"Good for him, then," she'd replied. "We best get to chartering our own passage, Ranger. We'll be needed on the mainland before it's all over with."

Just like that, Herald was whisked aboard the net-hauling, single-sailed boat, and they were off. After a few hours of less-than-smooth sailing, Mysterian heaved a heavy sigh and knelt at the front of the craft. She began chanting and humming, and slowly but surely, a wind found the tall triangular sail and had been pushing them northward ever since.

The second day passed and they were closing in on the third night when she suddenly gasped out in horror, or maybe pain. The wind went still, and she slumped over. She moaned out loudly for Herald, and like some terrified child about to be scolded, he went forth, feeling the more pronounced roll of the boat on the huge swells. Without the strong, steady wind to keep the craft pressed into the water, it seemed to be on the verge of floundering.

"Northeast on the compass, Herald," Mysterian said weakly. "Row us yourself if you have to, but take us northeast, and have a man up in the nest searching the water. He's not far, and he needs us."

"What? Who?" Herald waited only a heartbeat before he decided that the answer didn't really matter. "Bah," he growled, as he turned and stumbled over to the man who seemed to be in charge of the disorderly craft. "Row us northeast, and put a man up high. There's something out there."

"What is it?" a man asked from behind the unsure Captain. "There's a storm about to run right up our arses."

"Ask the witch," Herald said flatly. "I'm a King's Ranger, and you're being ordered to row this tub northeast until the witch says otherwise. If you don't like it, then swim!"

Herald couldn't believe that one of the men actually looked at the sea as if he were about to jump over the rail. The sea rose up under them, the boat lifted unnaturally high as it floated over the huge swell. Then they went sliding back into the gulf between the waves. Rowing the boat seemed a futile effort to the crew, but they did it. Behind them, the storm wall slowly gained on them. They could only hope to please the witch so that she would call back her wind and save them from the tempest.

After the oars were locked in, and two men at each side were rowing, Mysterian called Herald to the bow again. She had turned so that she was sitting on her backside instead of kneeling. Her head was lolling over to one side with fatigue, but her eyes were open.

"It's Jenka's dragon. It's out there floating in the sea. Don't let these fools harm it. I can feel its terror. It's not dead, but it's frightened for its life."

Herald gulped hard. "His dragon? The yearling green he calls Jade?"

"Yesss," she answered. "Now let me rest while you find him."

It struck Herald odd that he actually felt a deep concern for the creature he had only heard about. In fact, he felt in his heart that it was his duty to his young friend Jenka to do everything he could to save the wyrm. He was a little unsettled about the idea, but he started speaking to the fishermen as if they were a group of young Foresters in training.

"Were searching for green, men. Scaly green dragon's hide," he waited for the murmurs to die down before continuing. "It'll get darker `n dark soon, so light them lanterns. It's not a big evil beast, son," he reassured one of the men. "It be a youngin', and we're going to save it or the witch will call forth a wind that'll blow this tub straight to the bottom of the sea."

Herald had added the last because the hesitant men had stopped rowing themselves toward a dragon. He couldn't blame them. What sane man would row himself towards a dragon? The times had turned anything but sane, though, and Herald had learned from nature itself that if you didn't adapt to the circumstances then you didn't survive. When Mysterian started cackling out crazily from the bow, the oars started to move again. Herald had to bite back a nervous chuckle that she would do such a thing to intentionally scare them.

The last bit of velvety orange was leaving the horizon when the man up high yelled out, "Dragon ahead!"

Jade was floating easily, but was afraid to his core because he was lost and alone, and didn't know what to do. The impact with the water had been quite severe, but his cramps had long since left him. He had eaten a few curious fish that had come too close, and he felt that he could probably fly again if he could get out of the water to get airborne. But he couldn't, and he was afraid.

His young wings needed two steps of momentum to take flight from solid ground. He had long since given up hope of trying to get into the air from the sea. Several times he had tried to dive and then swim up towards the surface. He just wasn't strong enough to get clear of the water. When he heard the man's voice echoing across the waves, he thrashed around, trying to see where the sound had come from. The noise of the splash he made was substantial, and several of the fishermen started praying out loud.

Mysterian crawled to the rail and pulled herself to her feet. She could feel the ozonic wrath of the sea-god Nepton in the form of the violent storm chasing them. She waited until a swell passed, and she could see the dragon clearly in the lantern light. In a voice as shaky as Jade felt, but with an unmistakable draconian accent, she spoke: "Terazal ephallenx. Friendsss of Jenka De Swassso we are. I felt your fear, Jahderialxellin. We have come to help you."

Like a swimming snake, Jade slithered over to the ship and slid his slightly-horned head up over the rail. She had spoken his true name as correctly as a human tongue could manage it, and it intrigued him. He blinked his melon-sized amber orbs, then flicked his long, forked tongue out at the fishermen counterbalancing his weight as they cowered against the far side of the craft.

He had never been able to just leap into the air like the mature dragons could, but he thought that after the storm blew over he could try. He knew he could slither up into the ship. As small as it was, it was still twice as big as he. If he could eat a meal and rest for a few hours he could try to leap into the air from the ship. Even if he failed to take flight, he could swim alongside the boat until they led him to land. He wasn't lost any more. He felt reasonably certain that these friends of Jenka De Swasso that could speak his draconian name held him no ill will, so he decided to trust them.

Jade gave Herald a long, tentative look, then turned to Mysterian. "Thank you, ssswitch," he finally hissed. Mysterian had no idea how the perceptive young wyrm could know that she was a witch. Jade slithered his bulk over the side of the boat and curled his wet, scaly body around the mast pole, forcing the craft to ride dangerously low, but steadier in the water. It was Mysterian's turn to be afraid then, not because of Jade, but because the storm had caught up with them, and Nepton's rage was potent.

CHAPTER TWENTY-SIX

Prince Richard wasn't sure if he was alive or not. If so, he wasn't sure he wanted to be. He felt a thousand years old, as if his skin had been fired in grease until crisp, and his bones felt like...well...they felt like gravel. The very fiber of his being had been scorched with Gravelbone's evil taint. Richard's vision was a milky, cloudy haze that revealed only a faint shadow world. His mind was mostly a jumble of incoherent ramblings, but every so often a coherent thought would manifest itself and linger.

He could tell that there were more orcs in the main cavern by all the noise they made. A few of the big, green-skinned ogres had been enslaved into doing the Goblin King's bidding, as well. All of them had heavy iron tools. Richard could tell by the sound the metal made as it clanged and dragged on the cavern floor. The vermin were excited and restless. There was a pungent plant smell in the air. Something was about to happen, and he was sure it was bad. He had felt Royal absorbing the demon's insane magic with him. He had felt his bond-mate's rage, and he knew that the sparkling blue was coming. He knew it was a trap, and he knew that Royal knew. If he could have mustered enough gumption to do more than stare blithering at the floor, he might have tried something crazy again. Anything to give his dragon an edge, but it wasn't to be. Already, he had forgotten what he was thinking about and was wondering what that clanging metal was again.

His attention refocused when he heard the nightshade's vile shriek. It came swooping into the cavern calling out some preordained signal. Prince Richard heard his dragon then. Royal was right behind the scale-less black wyrm. Royal landed before he entered the cavern, and when he came loping in, a half dozen orcs erupted into a hacking rage at his sides. They swung picks, axes, and scythes with heavy, penetrating blows. Royal let loose a terrible blast of prismatic energy that sent the nightshade flinging back against the cavern's stony side. Then he roasted more than half of the orcs that had been closing around him.

His neck was decimated by the bladed weapons, but he didn't retreat. "Come, my friend, and fly with me," Royal spoke to Prince Richard with his mind. "The demon didn't kill us, and now we are stronger for the sssuffering."

Royal thrashed and squirmed, and had all but ended the hacking vermin on either side of him, but the nightshade was regaining its wits and Royal hadn't forgotten that the Goblin King was around there somewhere, too.

"Come, my prince," the dragon coaxed and projected. "Come straight to my voice."

The nightshade was coiling to strike when Royal saw the dragon-bone cage where his bond-mate was being held. Royal spoke something in Ogrish and two of the enslaved creatures turned on the orcs and the nightshade as it struck. The other ogre went for Prince Richard.

Richard didn't see the blue-scaled tail that almost removed his head as it bashed away the bars of his cage, nor did he see his blood-soaked, raging dragon set into the hellborn nightshade. He did feel the grip of a large hand as it covered most of his forearm, and he felt himself being pulled into a cooler, quieter place where there weren't even any milky shadows to see by.

"Grunx druih vhagen cruxa?" the ogre asked. Prince Richard was too afraid to respond to the garbled voice, but he couldn't remember why. He had no idea what the thing had said anyway.

Behind them, a deep and primal roar resounded. It was followed by another terrible screech. The ogre pulled the crown prince deeper into the darkened cavern and loped at a pace that, for Richard, was a steady run. They moved like that for a very long time.

In the main cavern, Royal and the nightshade were in a wild tangle of tooth, tail and claw. The two ogres still helped the blue wyrm when they could, but there remained several orcs and a few trolls to contend with. One of the ogres called something out, and Royal shifted around in his grasp of the slippery nightshade to respond. Royal agreed, in the brutish ogre tongue, that the Goblin King would be on them soon. With all the strength his lungs could muster, he sprayed the wicked black wyrm with his liquid lightning breath. While the Nightshade writhed and squirmed, trying to get the sticky dragon's spume from its flesh, the two ogres charged up and out of the cavern. Royal backed defensively down the tunnel the other Ogre had led the Prince down. If it was all he could do, he would guarantee that nothing followed after his bond-mate. He was bleeding profusely about the head and neck and would die soon. It didn't matter. Royal calculated that getting around a dead dragon in a tunnel was probably just as hard as getting around a live one.

The two fleeing ogres were not who Gravelbone expected to see tearing up out of his lair where he was waiting in ambush. When he unleashed the devastating blast of dark crimson power he had intended for the big blue wyrm, he was more than a little disappointed. The two ogres were destroyed instantly, just as Royal would have been if he had come that way. The Goblin King let out a roar of anger, but then turned to find a wild-eyed silver dragon and an even wider-eyed boy flying down the cavern at him. His jaundiced yellow eyes grew scarlet and the makings of a spell began forming on his snarling visage.

Silva was no fool, and she was small enough that she thought she could corkscrew herself around and go back the way they had come. The demon had to duck a shower of flying stalactites that Silva broke from the ceiling with her whipping tail as she attempted her turn. Gravelbone lost concentration, which saved them from the spell he had been about to unleash. When the sleek silver dragon executed the maneuver, she didn't forget to leave the Goblin King a present similar to the one Jade had given the ancient red that had nearly killed Royal. The blast from her explosive spell sent her and Rikky tumbling up out of the cavern shaft wildly. Luckily, the lake was there, and Silva managed to twist them in that direction, for if they hadn't splashed down into the freezing clear water, their bones would have surely been broken to splinters on the ground.

Echoing up out of the grottoes, the Goblin King's raging voice could be heard for miles.

Silva gathered herself and wondered why Rikky was now laughing hysterically. When she asked him what was so funny, he replied, "I can't help it. Every time I start to swim toward the shore I go in a circle."

* * *

Jade slept until the heart of the storm was upon them. When he woke, he yawned and spread his wings wide. They caught air and started pushing the craft steadily ahead through the downpour. Already, his weight had saved them from being tossed around like a leaf in a raging stream. It was hard to tell where the sea ended and the rain began, for everything was soaking wet. The men all had to bail water, Herald too. It was either that or sink, so they bailed with all they had. Mysterian helped direct the churning wind where she could, but she was too tired to be much help.

Where the humans were afraid for their lives, afraid of Nepton's rage, Jade was elated by the experience. It was a terrific feeling, the hot lightning filling the air with sweet static, and the feel of the powerful gusts of wind on his wings. As for the rain, it was better having the wet stuff fall on him continuously than being trapped in the sea waiting to drown.

Jade knew that up above the storm clouds was fresh, wide open sky. He could have lifted out of the boat on a swell and flown away several times now, but he could tell that the boat wouldn't last without his weight to keep it pressed into the waves as they rolled crazily beneath them. He didn't want any harm to come to these friends of Jenka, who had saved him from the sea. He wanted to help them through the storm.

The witch had told him that Jenka had come back to the mainland looking for him. It made Jade feel the bond that much stronger. As he hugged the mast pole, he let his mind wander and saw Jenka, all wet and bedraggled, huddled against a beautiful, tattoo-faced girl. They were in the lee of a boulder before a hissing, blue-flamed fire. Jade knew the girl from Jenka's dreams. She was the rider of the ice dragon. She was one of them.

Back in the moment came a high-pitched, keening call over the booming and rumbling of the storm. It was a sound that only Jade could hear. It was a call from another dragon. He returned the supersonic call as any pure dragon would. A moment later, the icy white wyrm was streaking down out of the roiling clouds, tendrils of vapor trailing from its chilly scales.

Herald gasped, and Mysterian looked up long enough to see the rare spectacle. The two dragons communicated somewhat telepathically, and soon Jade was using the tilt and pitch of his extended wings to guide the boat after Crystal. They began moving faster, for Crystal couldn't just hover in the violent wind. The boat was sluicing through the storm-ravaged waters so swiftly that the men had stopped bailing and had begun praying again. Herald just stood there watching the mist trail away from Crystal's wings, as the warm rain condensed near her cold scales. In all his years as a frontiersman and a King's Ranger, he had never seen anything so strange and amazing.

The storm was getting worse. Lightning, bright and jagged, leapt from the sea and lit up the sky below the clouds. The men all saw the land then. They were running east, parallel to a length of bluffs facing southward into the sea. They would have been washed into them soon and been bashed into pulp and splinters for the crabs to eat had the white dragon not guided them away from their previous course.

As it was, the man acting as the captain of the boat took up the tiller again and was helping Jade keep them from getting too close to the danger. He ordered his men to start bailing water again, and they complied. Their fear of the dragons had all but evaporated. The crew, with the hope of getting through the storm starting to seem like a realistic outcome, began working together to get the water out of the hull. It was in this manner that they rode the storm out. Hour after terrible hour they bailed and prayed and followed the white dragon through the tempest until finally they slid out of the darkness into a fresh, sunny afternoon full of calling gulls and gentle waves.

"Clear and blue!" a sailor called. Jade nearly flipped the boat when he leapt out of it and began winging his way after Crystal. He couldn't wait to be with Jenka again.

* * *

The king's flotilla of ships reached Port just ahead of the storm.

Linux had shaved his pointed beard and donned a mummer's wig with hair long enough to conceal the dark, walnut-colored triangle on his forehead. The other tattoos, he hid with the makeup from a theatrical kit he had stolen back in Kingston. He moved about the gaggle of young bravados that happened to be on the ship and cursed himself for his mistake. They tried his patience to the end. If any one of them ever came face to face with a troll they would shit themselves. They were fools, and there were other ships full of eager men just like them, all about to be led into a slaughter.

The king had been on this ship, one of the finer of the royal line, but he crossed a plank-way to another just before they left Kingston harbor. He then moved to a third ship and Linux had lost him. Linux had wanted to be on the ship that King Blanchard was on. He had a plan that would save them all a lot of trouble, would have saved them all a lot of trouble to begin with had he thought of it sooner.

Linux had no idea, nor did any man on any of the three dozen ships in the flotilla, that the crown prince was the Goblin King's captive. The rumor was just spreading across the rails now. Men shouted the state of things from the docks to the nearer ships, then from ship to ship as they heard them. The docks were swarming with people come to see their king bringing them aid. Often, cheers erupted for no real reason that Linux could discern.

"The trolls took Three Forks and Outwal," a man yelled.

"Killed three thousand women and children in the doing," added another.

"There be dragons in the skies everywhere now," a skittish man repeated what he had been told. "Just look to the north and sooner or later you'll see one."

"They say Prince Richard saved a man and was riding on a big blue dragon over by Midwal."

This caught Linux' attention.

"That was afore the Goblin King killed the wyrm and captured the boy!" a more authoritative voice called up, far below them from a row boat holding its position so that one of the many ships could maneuver into the crowded harbor. By the look of his clothes, Linux marked him as a local. "The commander at Midwal has gone missing, too," the man continued. "A whole battalion went out to try and free some holed up folks near Del, but they got eaten by them little goblins that are helpin' the trolls now. They said there was orcs, too. I heard `em with my own ears, calling the news out to the king's ship a short while ago. Commander Corda from Three Forks went out on the queen's command to retrieve the crown prince just two days ago as well, and I seen them dragons across the wall with my own eyes, too."

All of this was news to Linux, and it meant he had to get near King Blanchard and get him alone just as soon as he possibly could. He didn't have to worry about Commander Corda seeing him now, and that was a welcome relief, for what he was about to do was sheer treachery. He had to do what he intended before the king went charging off into the frontier with an army of ill-prepared boys. Linux knew he would regret it, but he saw no other choice.

"Which ship is the king's ship?" Linux asked loudly, but he eased back from the rail into obscurity when the man looked up for the asker.

Somewhere behind them, way out at sea, thunder rumbled long and low.

"That three mast'd cutter called Moonseye," the man looked out with his hand held over his eyes, trying to shield them from the drizzle that had started to fall. He didn't see who he was talking to, but he pointed out the ship that was easing into a dock ahead of the others. It was a good distance away, and the rain was now starting to fall in earnest.

Transporting oneself over water was always a risky business, but Linux felt that the risk, in this instance, was worth the gain. If he didn't do something, all of the men on these ships would soon be feeding the enemy. He didn't feel he had a choice. He only hoped that Zah and Jenka would be about to help Prince Richard, and that Mysterian and Vax Noffa wouldn't hold it against him when he removed King Blanchard from the equation. It was the wisest thing to do, he reasoned. And with that thought, he stepped from the deck of the ship he was on across half a mile of open harbor, right onto the deck of the Moonseye. He appeared directly in front of the wide-eyed king of the realm and began pushing him. He carried the big man right over the ship's rail into a tumbling fall, where they splashed hard in the warm, salty water.

Half a dozen men leaped in after them to protect their king, another half dozen dove in and surrounded the man who had attacked him. One of the rescuers had been wearing armor, and several men followed in to pull him up from the bottom before he drowned. They hesitated when they saw the tattoos on Linux' face, now clearly visible since the water had washed the makeup from his skin.

"Bah," King Blanchard bellowed, trying to shake off some of the hands that were grabbing at him. "I can swim, man! Back off! I want that man taken to shore and gagged! He's full o'High Magic. Bind him, gag him, and then put him in the strongest cell you have, and stay clear of it until I get there! But don't harm him none. Not even a boot tip! That's an order!"

Linux almost laughed at how easy it had been to do what he had just done. He only wished he had thought of it sooner.

PART IV

GRAVELBONE'S REVENGE

CHAPTER TWENTY-SEVEN

"The best way to describe it is a stalemate, Your Majesty," a nervous sergeant said as King Blanchard and his slightly confused retinue stood on the top of the Great Wall in the pouring rain. They were looking out at the smoldering ruins of Outwal. The precipitation had quelled most of the fires, leaving a steamy, smoking, ash-coated mess.

From somewhere deep in the wreckage, a troll brazenly barked out to its pack mates. As the man spoke, several other trolls returned the call. "If we go out and try to reclaim anything, they attack the gates. They've even managed to hurl burning timbers onto the wall top, and the trolls that have taken to riding the dragons are treacherous with the stones they hurl. If we just sit here and watch, they stay back from the wall and pillage what's left out there."

"Look there," a young man pointed at the sinuous form of a middling-sized mudge, lifting up out of the wreckage. It winged its way to another section of the decimated frontier city and started circling above the rubble.

"Archers be aware," the sergeant ordered. "If it comes near, protect the king."

"How long has Commander Corda and the men he handpicked been out there? And where might I find this dramatic missive my not-so-stable wife has sent," the king growled. The angry displeasure he felt after seeing the destruction firsthand was plain, but everyone around him thought that something was wrong; all the plans he had laid while crossing over from Kingston had suddenly been discarded like so much refuse. Something had changed his mind about why they had crossed the sea, or so it seemed.

"If it pleases," a well-attired man stepped forward and bowed. He was bald, save for a wispy strip of gray hair that ran around the back of his head over his ears. "I am Mayor Pandre, former mayor I suppose now, for Outwal is no more." He paused only to wipe the rain from his brow. "Over the course of this nightmare, I have assumed many duties, most of them far beyond my meager station, and it would be my honor to guide you to hospitable facilities where you can rest and review the missive in question, but also to acquaint you with some of the other problems we are facing. I'm certain that, in your wisdom, you could find better men to…" His voice faded as the king began speaking over him.

"If you are as good at running Outwal's affairs as you are at licking my boots, then we'd hate to lose your services, Mayor Pandre, was it?" the king jested dryly. The grim look on his round face didn't falter, even when a few of the men in the retinue chuckled under their breath.

The now crimson-faced mayor dropped his head and began leading the group along the Great Wall's wide, road-like top toward a stair landing. They went down to street level and crossed a wide lane into a fairly clean section of city. The building the mayor led them to was a small fortress of gray block marble. It had stood in that very place, looking out over the harbor and providing shelter from these once wild lands, long before the wall had gone up. It was the original Port Stronghold, and there were tunnels that led underneath the lane to tunnels that went into hatches in the wall. There was even an underground road that traversed the entire peninsula inside the wall.

The accommodations were perfect for Linux, who had used a terribly powerful spell to switch physicality with King Blanchard. Linux was in the king's huge, ungainly body, while good King Blanchard was trapped in a cell in his. Linux would soon go make certain that the man was well cared for. It was his body, after all. After the shock of it wore off, the king would accept the situation like the true warrior that he was on the inside. Linux had felt the sheer power of will the king had in him when the transfer took place. It had given him a new respect for the king.

He had no idea what to do with his newfound power. It wasn't the sort of power he was used to. This wasn't the call forth a prismatic blast or step through a stone wall sort of power that he was used to wielding. This was the march legions across the continent sort of power. He would have to walk in his dreams and try to find Mysterian and Vax Noffa before doing anything serious.

The only thing he would consider doing before conferring with them was organizing a battalion of frontiersmen to go aid Commander Corda. If Prince Richard was really being held in the grottoes around Demon's Lake, there would be hordes of trolls and goblins in the area. The commander would need all the help he could get. Saving the crown prince was paramount, not only to the kingdom, but to the coming Confliction. One of the five that would make the stand had to be of royal blood. The portent had specified it. If the crown prince died, or had his mind scrambled by Gravelbone's evil taint, then the whole world could end up in a rut.

Linux wished he hadn't sent Zahrellion off like he had. She would no-doubt be outraged when she found out that he was the one who had ordered Frunien to use the dampening hood, but she would understand the necessity of it. He could have used her, and her dragon, at the moment; reconnaissance was needed. For that, he either needed Zah and her wyrm, or maybe Lemmy, or the best of the King's Rangers who remained along the wall. Since two of those three options were impossible, he decided on the third.

"Mayor," King Blanchard asked. "Who is the acting commander in charge of the military here, at the moment?"

"Why, you are," the man beamed as if he had just given an unexpected compliment.

"No, no, no." The king shook his head. Linux was starting to enjoy this. "Say I wanted to give an order. Say I longed to have a man thrown in the dungeons with that crazed druid, because he thinks I want my fargin boots licked. Who, Mayor Pandre, would I give that order to?"

"Uh," the man was visibly shaken now, and he was stammering beyond recovery.

"That would be Commander Wiklan, Your Highness," said a uniformed man of the Walguard, who had been escorting the king's retinue since they had arrived.

"I've already found him and established the new chain of command, sir," this came from Prince Richard's squire, whom Linux had met at the tournament on King's Island. "The captains of the Walguard, the Kingsmen, and your Rangers will all be in Haven Hall in a few hours to take orders."

Linux couldn't remember the squire's name, so he avoided it. "Good. Could you take the mayor here and find a man to listen to his needs? He seems to have taken on more than he is capable of handling and wants to be relieved of some of the duty. Have a man stock Haven Hall with every known map of the area, and have the western end of our Great Wall's plans brought here to my chamber, especially the subterranean sections." Linux had studied some of the design plans that the Order of Dou had somehow procured. He figured they might come in handy.

"I want all the hunters and Foresters, the ones who have ranged around the lake specifically, to be rounded up for questioning as well." Linux continued from inside King Blanchard's body. "Oversee it. And be nice about it, please." Linux caught his own hiccup of character and harrumphed into a short cough. "Round `em up quickly and respectfully, or I'll name a headsman here and put him to work." Linux even shook his jowls and clenched his fist like the king sometimes did. "That King's Ranger, Herald, was on one of our ships, too, I think. Have him found and brought here as well." Linux looked around and saw that several of the men who he didn't know, but who had been following him around for that last hour, were now bustling about. He realized that he knew none of their names, and since some of these men were close to King Blanchard, there might eventually be a problem. He had to figure out a plan, but he wanted to confer with the real king first.

He found a plush divan in the semi-private room the mayor had led them to and fell into it. It was hard work moving all that bulk about. He waved off an offered goblet of ale, but remembered that

King Blanchard would never have turned down the mug. He took it, and then took a long pull of the stuff. He found it cold and bitter, but refreshing. "Someone find out if there has been any word from Kingsmen's Keep. We've all but forgotten about them. I want a tub of hot water ready so I can bathe before our war council officially begins. And someone find out where they took that druid! Make *certain* he isn't harmed! I think there might have been a misunderstanding. I'll be visiting him as soon as I've washed the sea from my arse, so have a page ready to take me to him."

The room had almost emptied. A lone man stood looking at the king curiously, a twinge of doubt or concern revealed itself, but it was a fleeting thing. Linux knew that Spell Master Vahlda could sense something arcane, but was unsure of what it was. The man was afraid to make a fool of himself by acting on a vague suspicion before his king.

"What is it, Master Vahlda?" Having the king call him by his name put the mage way off guard. "Why aren't you out there with Corda's brigade? Aren't you his man?"

Vahlda shook his head, realizing that Commander Corda reported to either the king or the crown prince by swifter most of the time, and had probably mentioned him before, which reminded him of why he was there.

"I've brought the queen's message, and there has been another swifter from her that you should read, Majesty." He bowed as he handed the king the two scrolls. "As for why I'm not with the commander, sir. Well," the mage stammered with nervousness. "Uh, Commander Corda wanted me to tell you personally that a man he trusts with his life saw your son riding on the back of that blue wyrm willingly, and that they were fighting with us against the other dragons, and the trolls. That's what they were doing when they were taken down by the Goblin King." He shrugged and looked at the floor, knowing that hearing about his son might disturb the king deeply. He gave it no thought when the king growled, "Go tell them to fetch me a bath, man! The sea-salt's done rubbed my fat arse raw."

Less than a turn of the glass later, Linux was looking at himself through an open barred door, in a bunker full of cells built into a chamber below the Great Wall. When the king saw himself looking in, his eyes went wide and his face raged crimson. He would have been cursing and raising a ruckus, but there was still a gag stuffed in his mouth.

His hands were still bound as well, which caused Linux to shake his head sadly. It was only justice, he decided. The man had imprisoned Zahrellion and Jenka for no good reason. Still he wanted the king to be aware, to at least have a say in what was about to transpire.

Linux motioned for the guard to open the cell door and dismissed the man.

"You've gone mad, druid. I'll have your head for this," Blanchard growled after Linux removed the gag.

"You already have my head, Majesty, and no one will do what you tell them to do because you're just the crazed druid who attacked the king."

"Those fargin men are gonna pay for the extra boots they put in my ribs," Blanchard barked.

"Listen, King Blanchard," Linux started calmly. "Your son, the De Swasso boy, and Zahrellion are all connected to the dragons in a way that's far beyond any that your mind can grasp." He held up a hand to forestall the king's rage. "Prince Richard is in grave danger, but not because the blue took him, but instead because the blue got killed and the Goblin King captured him. I'm here to try and save him and the kingdom from your rage."

"This fargin treachery will be sorted out soon enough," the king spat his words. "Master Trayga, and Old Wilmer, they won't be fooled by an imposter, and I—"

Linux shoved the gag back into the king's mouth and cringed at the muffled shouting. When it died down, he said, "When you accept the situation and calm down, I will get you some food, and a bath, and include you in everything I do, but I'll not have you out chasing dragons and getting all those boys you shipped over here killed because you are thickheaded and raging."

Linux hadn't taken off the king's bindings yet and made no effort to do so now. He did pause after he shut the cell door and spoke through the bars. "By the way, the queen is on her way here. She said that Jenka and Zahrellion are already on the mainland somewhere, looking for your son. They flew here on the back of Zah's dragon, I'm sure." He paused, letting that knowledge sink into the king's thick skull. "If they hadn't been locked in a cell in your dungeon, they might have been able to prevent all of this.

"If you try and remember why that blue wyrm attacked your Grama on the tiltyard that day so long ago, you'll start to see where your problem lies.

For now, you have an inkling of how that dragon felt in those chains."

Linux was leaving the cells, following the two Walguard, a page and King Blanchard's two personal guards, when a pair of dark-scaled mudge attacked the men on the wall-top nearby. One of the wyrms had a troll riding its back. It was pulling stones from a bag it had strapped across its shoulders. One of the rocks nearly hit Linux, and he had to refrain from instinctually blasting up at them with a spell. Instead, he ran King Blanchard's huge, jiggling bulk across the wide lane and went for cover in the old Port Stronghold, where the war council was waiting for him. Before Linux had a chance to catch his breath, a man barreled into the hall behind him and informed them that more dragons were swarming the length of the wall. They were now under a full attack.

CHAPTER TWENTY-EIGHT

The rain was still pouring down, and Crystal hadn't yet returned from the sea. She had been gone a day at least. It was hard to say, because the sun couldn't penetrate the gloomy clouds. Jenka was huddled close to Zahrellion near her sizzling, blue-green fire. Not even the downpour could quell the magical blaze. They were speculating on Gravelbone's weakness and worried about their dragons, and Prince Richard, too. They talked about everything except Jenka's true heritage. He didn't want anyone knowing that he was some sort of spell-born abnormality, created from a witch's brew. They also discussed what Jenka had promised Mysterian. Zahrellion didn't like it, but she had to admit that everything she had ever read about dragon tears confirmed what the old Hazeltine had told Jenka. Jenka hadn't decided if he would honor his oath to the witch before or after they went after Prince Richard. The way it sounded to him, he might need its power to help them set things right.

Finally, Zah felt a tingle in her heart, making her grin from ear to ear. She knew instinctually that the dragons were all right, and when she told Jenka, he squeezed her close into a hug. They were falling into each other's comfort, and it was almost pleasant, even in the miserable rain.

After a long pause in the conversation, Zahrellion turned to face him. She looked deeply into his hazel eyes. Then, without warning, an urge overcame her, and she leaned even closer and kissed him.

For a few heartbeats, Jenka kissed her back, but the idea that she was elvish—and old—interjected itself into his head and caused him to pull away.

"How do you manage to look so young, when you act like such an old woman?" he ventured foolishly.

"I'm only nineteen years old, you bastard!" she replied harshly.

Had she known that he had just learned that he really was a bastard, she might have used a different term, but maybe not. She was steaming. It seemed that every time she opened up her heart to him, he acted like a dunce.

After she called him a bastard, he moved away and sat mostly in the rain to avoid her. Luckily, their dragons came flapping down out of the night. Zah was happy to be near Crystal, but not nearly as pleased as Jenka was to see Jade again. Jade felt the same way about seeing Jenka, and he lay down with his head on his outstretched foreclaws near his bond-mate. The rain was forgotten as the two of them talked and enjoyed each other's company for the rest of the night. The feeling of the magical bond that had formed between them was inexplicably pure and wholesome. Jade told Jenka about saving the sparkling blue and his terrible adventure out over the sea. He also told him about Silva and Rikky Camile.

Excitedly, Jenka told Zahrellion about Rikky, and through her quelling anger she admitted her surprise. Then she lay back against her dragon's cool scales, tuned out the rain as best as she could, and went into a trance. She tried to find Rikky with her mind, and her dragon tried to find Silva, but the rain was just too distracting for either of them. They both began to get the rest that they desperately needed, drifting off into an ethereal dreamworld and falling fast asleep.

Jenka was elated at the idea that Rikky had bonded with a dragon. The news that Royal was still alive and working with Silva and Rikky at the grottoes, trying to help free Prince Richard was welcome, too. As soon as Crystal and Jade rested, they would all go that way as well.

Zah hadn't decided what she would do yet, nor had Jenka, but one thought kept recurring in Jenka's mind. It was about the one person he had known all of his years, the person who had raised him and loved him since birth, the one person he knew he could trust no matter the situation. It was the person who had sent him to Mysterian. His mother might have kept the truth from him about his father, but Jenka didn't doubt her love for him. He felt he had no choice but to trust the things Mysterian had told him.

Crystal was exhausted beyond imagining from her two cross-ocean flights. And after leading Mysterian's chartered fishing boat into a sheltered inlet and carrying Mysterian and Herald a score of miles, setting them down near the old Mainsted wall, she was even more so. Jenka went out of his way not to wake either of the females. He used the time to debate what he was going to do.

For a long time, Jenka was too distraught to sleep, but Jade's warm body was comfortable. Jenka fell into a slumber despite his worries. He slept like a babe, and when he woke to a warm sunny morning full of calling birds and clean sea air, he felt invigorated.

His mood grew even better when he saw Zahrellion sitting by the fire, sipping liquid from a gourd nut. She offered him one of the hard-shelled, fist-sized fruits and he jabbed a hole in it with her dagger. As he sipped the tart, tangy juice from the gourd, he thought about the fact that Zah was only nineteen years old. If that was true, then he wouldn't have minded the kiss last night. The idea that she was elvish and old seemed ridiculous now. He decided to apologize, but couldn't find the words just yet. Later in the day, the words did come to him, but it would be too late.

He was on Jade's back, holding on for dear life, as the young green dragon labored to fly with the weight of a passenger. The result was clumsy at best, and nothing short of dangerous for both of them.

They flew for half a day before they saw the Great Wall. They had passed over the western outskirts of Mainsted, too, and Jenka was amazed. Mainsted was massive when compared to the other cities he had seen. The outskirts stretched for miles and miles. The city itself was surrounded by its own circular protective wall. The harbor cut up into the heart of the metropolis like a knife thrust.

They flew high overhead past Mainsted. They would have just continued past the Great Wall towards Demon's Lake, which was on the way to the deep mountain valley where the dragon's tear lay, had Jenka not spotted a mudged dragon. It was carrying a troll and was harrying the men atop the seemingly endless wall. Jenka first thought that it was Gravelbone and his nightshade, but Jade and Crystal both said that it wasn't. They said they would be able to feel the taint of the demon and his hellborn wyrm. What they were seeing now was just a mudge with a troll atop its shoulders.

Since it was all Jade could do to stay airborne with Jenka on his back, Crystal and Zahrellion went diving after the creature. Jade spiraled down more slowly, and Jenka was thankful. When they saw the sheer number of trolls and goblins lurking out beyond the range of the wall's bowmen, Jenka realized he might have been wrong about something. It looked like the feral goblinkin were amassing to attack at Midwal's gate. Maybe Gravelbone wouldn't be content to wait it out, because this didn't look like the makings of a siege at all.

Away from the wall on the frontier side, big orc captains, and brigades of trolls and goblins were actually drilling with weapons and moving in somewhat organized formations. Jenka was about to scout westward down the length of the wall when a trio of smaller, dark-scaled wyrms came up, flapping madly out of the copse where they had been resting. Only one of them had a rider, but all three began winging toward Jade and Jenka. Jenka barely had time to notice the mounds of fresh dirt hidden out in the trees. There were piles and piles of fresh brown earth, but Jenka couldn't think about that at the moment. It was all he could do to hold on, and all Jade could do to stay in the sky, as they fled back towards Crystal and Zah with the three mudged on their tail.

The dragon that Crystal was chasing was fleet and agile. It stayed well away from the bigger white wyrm, but made the mistake of swooping too low and took a steel-tipped arrow in its flank. It roared angrily and tore off towards the troops of trolls and goblins on the ground.

Zahrellion came to Jenka's rescue. She let loose a primal display of her crackling, yellow druid magic. The blast not only startled the mudged dragons, it startled the men on the wall-top as well. Once she was certain that the mudged were fleeing, she had her big white wyrm lead them farther north, away from the wall.

Jenka felt a twinge of guilt for abandoning the men, but they had plenty of shelter inside the wall if it came to it. He was glad Crystal had gotten them away from the mudge, and he found tears streaking down his cheeks as he thought of all the terrible fates that could have befallen the people of Crag. He decided he would go to Kingsmen's Keep to see about them before he went after the tear. He couldn't even hope that Zah would make the trek with him. Not only was she still mad about his ignorant comment, but she felt that Prince Richard's situation warranted her attention, not the dragon's tear.

Jade felt Jenka's sorrow, and that only made Jenka feel worse, for the young green-scaled dragon had already lost his mamra to the nightshade. The hole left in Jade's heart was still deep and raw, and the young green wasn't very keen on the idea of going to where his mam's corpse lay rotting.

Jenka had just convinced Jade that the tear could help them, when he realized what those piles of dirt meant: The vermin were tunneling under the wall! He had Jade wing in close to Zah to tell her.

She nodded that she understood, and told him to go do what he was going to do. She said that she and Crystal would go back and warn the Walguard of the tunnels. Then they would try to find Rikky and Royal and see about freeing Prince Richard.

“I’ll see you in your dreams, Jenk,” she called over to him. “Be careful, and hurry. We will need you in the end. I’m sure of it.”

He wanted to tell her he was sorry for offending her but, “Aye, and you!” was all that came out of his mouth.

* * *

It was a full day and half of a night later that Linux finally found the solitude he needed to search the misty ethereal for advice. It was also the first chance he had gotten to rest. The goblins and trolls had been attacking the Port gates of the Great Wall the entire time. They hadn’t been successful by any standards, and they were easy to kill from the crenels atop the wall, but the mudged dragons and their daring troll riders were a menace. They were attacking along the entire length of the wall, in the city of Port, and out in the harbor as well. They had caused several dozen deaths, a few fires, and more than a little panicked mayhem.

Linux had been acting the king the whole time. The war council he called hadn't had the chance to gather, and after hearing a few dozen reports, and visiting the wall-top himself, he came up with what he thought was a reasonable plan to defend the population of Port from the mudge.

He commissioned several crews of men to build a trio of massive, mechanical, crossbow-like spear launchers. Until then, the few dragon guns the Walguard possessed would have to do. The dragon guns were heavy crossbows that didn't quite live up to their name, but they had a nasty sting if you could hit your target. They fired long, slightly-barbed, steel-tipped arrows and, after seeing them in action, Linux deduced that a bigger version, built on a rotating pedestal, would be quite the deterrent. He reasoned that if the Walguard could score just one kill, even the mudged would grow weary of the sky over the city.

Linux put Master Trayga in charge of the task, which got the nosey elder out of his hair. He had Sir Wilmer, the king's favorite advisor and friend, shadow Commander Wiklan of the Port Walguard, which he hoped would keep both men acting sharp. After that, he stuffed himself as he never had before, at a table Mayor Pandre had arranged. Then he retired to his private chamber with orders that he wasn't to be disturbed.

After casting a spell that dampened the senses to the world around the huge body he was in, he went searching in the dreamy ethereal. He found Mysterian first, for she was searching for him. Then the two of them reached out to their counterpart, the Outland wizard, Vax Noffa. He didn't respond to their call, but both Jenka and Zahrellion heard it in the back of their minds. So did Crystal, Jade, and Silva, though none of them knew exactly what they had heard.

"I've assumed the king's body, Mysterian," Linux told the old Hazeltine. "I'm not sure what I'm doing, but I didn't want him marching all these fools he brought to the mainland out into the demon's madness."

"Since Vax doesn't seem to care about these happenings," Mysterian replied, "I say you keep defending the wall. Your girl, Zahrellion, and her dragon are trying to save the prince," her voice faltered then, for she had spent many days watching over Prince Richard, and had gone far to keep the boy's meetings with the mighty blue dragon a secret. Now Royal was supposedly dead, and it hurt her heart because she knew that Gravelbone had long ago poisoned the crown prince's mind.

"Is it too late?" Linux asked. "Could Richard have kept himself sane for so long?"

"I'll not assume, Linux, but I fear the worst. I want to see him for myself before we go that far, so at this point it matters not what we think."

"I agree, for now," said Linux. "What are we going to do about King Blanchard? Where is Jenka? He is our man, is he not?"

"He is, and I hope he rises to the occasion," Mysterian responded. "Don't get yourself killed in Blanchard's body, or he will stay trapped in yours for the rest of your body's life." The last came with a heavy-hearted witch's cackle, but a cackle nonetheless. "I hope the queen's ship wasn't lost in that storm."

"By Dou," Linux cursed under his breath. "I won't be able to fool her when she arrives. What do you think I should do?"

In answer, Mysterian cackled again. "That is your mess, Linux, but I'll help when me and this hard-headed King's Ranger get ourselves somewhere."

Just then, Linux was jarred violently out of his reverie, as a man burst excitedly into his chamber.

"So sorry to wake you, Your Majesty." The man groveled. "Both the commander and your man, Sir Wilmer agreed that you had to see this for yourself. They ordered me to wake you."

Linux was thankful for the man's deep fear of offending his king. Linux would never have awoken in character as the king without the reminder. As it was, he had to search his spell-weary mind for why the man was treating him like a king. When it finally came back to him he began acting as King Blanchard would.

"You'd better be convincing me why my new headsman's axe shouldn't bust its maiden's head on your melon! Speak up while I dress. Tell me what you know!"

"There's a dragon hovering high above the wall, a silver wyrm with a rider. He ran off some of them other wyrms. He even braved our arrows and swooped close enough to call out his name. He says he has word on the prince. He says that that Ranger you've got men looking for knows him well. He—"

"Quit babbling and tell me his name before I have you flogged, man!" Linux barked as he pulled a huge cloak over the king's wide shoulders and fastened it.

"His name is Rikky Camile. He says that even you might have heard of him from—"

"Does he have only one leg?" Linux was astonished. Master Vahlda had told him that Rikky's wagon was one of the ones that never made it to the wall when they had evacuated Three Forks.

"Aye, only one leg, and a peg for the other!" The man seemed as surprised as he was relieved to find out that the king did actually know the dragon rider.

"I'm coming behind you, man. You tell Commander Wiklan that any man who fires on that silver wyrm or rider will be tossed off the wall to feed the goblins. And send a man to fetch Master Vahlda. There is no doubt that he will want to see this!"

"Yes, Majesty," the excited man said before he backed out of the door and tore away at a run.

CHAPTER TWENTY-NINE

When Zahrellion and Crystal returned to warn the men at the Midwal gates about the tunneling, she was just in time to see the earth burst open in the middle of a cluster of tents on the protected side of the barrier. Like ants boiling out of a disturbed hill, dozens of child-sized, gray-skinned goblins began pouring out of the tunnel. The hole was five or six paces wide, and getting bigger as the little beasts threw the dirt out and away and surged forth. A troll emerged among the goblins, then another. They crawled over their smaller kin and started after any human unlucky enough to be caught in the proximity.

Crystal dove of her own accord. Zah followed her dragon's intention and started speaking old and powerful words from memory. She knew immediately, as soon as the magic began to form into being, that Crystal was lending her strength to the destructive spell. The potency of the pure-blooded dragon's magic tingled through her body like lightning.

A score of the goblins broke from the main force, and they did their best to avoid all confrontation as they moved southward towards Midwal proper. It would only take them a few moments to reach the second largest city in the realm. Another day's ride south—two days on foot—was Mainsted, the largest city, and supposedly the future seat of the kingdom. What the little goblins would do when they got to Midwal and found the city guard's archers standing on the modest wall that ringed around the city, Zahrellion had no idea. She would have gone for those vermin first if the sky hadn't suddenly filled with dark-scaled, feral dragons.

Four, no six, of the nearly black-scaled mudge were swooping on the wall-top archers, keeping them from protecting the people below. At least three had trolls riding on their backs, throwing stones the size of fists and larger. Another dragon, a fiery red that still had some scarlet luster to its scales, was breathing wide swaths of terrible orange flames across the confused refugees as they fell out of their tents and scrambled for cover. All the while, more goblins, and now more trolls, continued to pour out of the hole.

From some distance, a battle horn sounded. Men from one of the many keeps that had been built in the area before the construction of the wall must have finally seen the attack and were sending men forth. A few dozen armored horsemen galloped out of an open gate, and a score of pike men marched after them. Another horn sounded from somewhere else, but Zah couldn't concern herself with any of it.

Crystal came, streaking toward the opening in the earth, and Zahrellion focused her attention on the knotted mass of seething goblinkin scrabbling up from it. Her fingers traced a pinkish lavender symbol in the air before her, and then she threw her hand forth pointing at the hole. The very world seemed to pull inward toward her fingertip before the magical energy released into a warbling yellow flow that went streaking into the enemy. Crystal cut a sharp veering turn away from the area and managed to spew a jet of her glacial breath over some of the goblins. Frozen in place, they slowly cracked to pieces.

With a gut vibrating *whooomp*! and a bright, violent, flashing concussion, dozens of gray goblin bodies and a few trolls flew out and away from the hole. Some were screaming in pain, others were in gruesome bloody pieces. More than half of the goblins in the mouth of the opening were limp and lifeless, their bones and guts pulped by Zah's powerful spell. When Crystal pulled around and cut an arc through the sky back towards the wall, Zah saw she had caused quite a bit of carnage, but had really only succeeded in widening the opening for the vermin.

More of the filthy trolls came out with the goblins now. Many of them were holding their heads, as if their ears had been ruptured by the blast, others had clubs or sling sacks full of throwing stones.

Zah saw an orc come growling out of the tunnel then. It began calling out orders in the strange language the goblinkin all shared. The vermin started forming a protective ring around the passage Zah had just widened for them.

Suddenly, Crystal lurched through the sky into a spinning horizontal spiral. She narrowly avoided a streaking mudge. Zah was dislodged from her position between spinal plates. She started to lift away from Crystal's chilly body and there was nothing she could do about it.

Crystal felt Zah slipping and at the last second curved back up into her bond-mate, forcing her body to press back into her seat. It caused the relatively large white dragon to take a swath of the similar sized scarlet fire drake's heat across her belly, which hurt her deeply. They went careening through the air, avoided a hurled stone the size of Zahrellion's head, and almost collided with one of the wall-top archer's barbed steel shafts in the air.

"Away!" Zah yelled to her wyrm. "Get away from them. We can come back around after you've gathered yourself."

"Yesss," Crystal hissed. Her wing strokes grew longer and pushed them through the air faster and faster. Zahrellion didn't think her dragon would recover from the scorching blast of fire so quickly, but Crystal went banking hard around just as soon as she was over the frontier and out of harm's way.

"Hold on," the dragon hissed and put forth even more effort into gaining not only speed but altitude as she went through her turn. By the time they were facing the wall again, they were well above the other dragons. Only the scarlet fire wyrm seemed to notice them. Crystal took advantage of her position and dove right down onto one of the black-scaled mudge. Like a hawk swooping on a rabbit, she latched onto the smaller dragon's back with both claws and snapped its spine. She pulled up just past the wall and tossed the screaming, writhing carcass into the hole, nearly clogging it.

"Good," Zah called over the rush of the wind. "I wonder where those little beasts are going into the shaft? We need to find the other end of the tunnel."

"Yesss," Crystal agreed. "But firssst thisss."

The agile white dragon changed their course and took them streaking low across the ground on the kingdom side of the wall. When they neared the hole in the ground she spat forth her frigid breath and froze half a score of the goblins and a pair of trolls into solidity. An orc popped up just then and took the blast full-force, but not before loosing a bolt from the crossbow in his arms. The missile flew straight at Crystal's head. Somehow she corkscrewed through the air around its trajectory. She started to hiss something back to her bond-mate, but she felt Zahrellion go limp on her back. She had to fight with all she had to keep her rider from falling to her death. It wasn't until she was well away again, and flying at a much slower clip, that she curled her long neck back and saw the fletching of the crossbow bolt jutting out of Zah's bloody chest.

She made for a clearing in the scattered forest outside of the wall, but it was occupied by an orc and his company of trolls. She flew farther into the frontier because going north toward the peaks was her instinct. She knew she couldn't fly as far as that. By the amount of blood showing through Zah's dark robes, Crystal could only hope that the girl would survive until she found them a safe place to land.

* * *

Rikky and Silva were having much the same problem with the mudge that Zah and Crystal had. The biggest difference between the attacks on the wall at the Port gates and the battle at Midwal was that the vermin hadn't been able to tunnel under the wall near the harbor where the bulk of the populace dwelled; the water table and the rocky terrain prevented it. The goblinkin came under a few miles east, out in the cover of some densely canopied forest. The goblins and several bands of trolls, all following the orders of their fierce-looking half-armored orc captains, were tearing through Port's streets now. They destroyed everything that happened into their path. The men that had come over from the islands were mustering and getting organized, but the defense of the common folk was going to come too late for many. Already the northeastern quarter of the city was soaked in blood, and half aflame.

The worst happened late the second evening of the battle. Gravelbone arrived on the back of his black-skinned hellborn wyrm. With him were several dozen mudged dragons. They swarmed the wall-tops, instantly killing any man who didn't go for cover inside the structure. They swooped hard on the men wielding the ineffective hand-held dragon guns. Some of the wyrms had troll riders that rained down heavy rocks from above. They killed the crew and destroyed one of the bigger swivel-mounted weapons that the king was having built. Luckily, King Blanchard had been wise enough to have one of the crews building inside a wagon builder's shed, and another in a lumber barn across town.

Rikky hadn't understood why the king had wanted him to stay instead of going after the crown prince until now. He and Silva were the only real defense Port had at the moment, and they weren't proving to be much. King Blanchard had told him, had ordered him, to protect the assembly of the big spear launchers that were being thrown together. He said that when they were done, Silva could become the fox and let the mudged hounds chase him right into the line of fire. Once they killed a few of the flying wyrms, the sky over Port would no doubt settle back down. All of that had been before the goblins tunneled the wall to the east of the city. Now chaos was running rampant. There was open warfare in the streets. The few score of actual trained soldiers who had crossed the ocean with their king were beginning to form ranks around the different sections of the city. Still there were more and more of the goblinkin running wild, killing and eating everything they could. It was madness.

Silva used her molten breath to reduce troll after troll into hard, disfigured lumps. Rikky felt helpless and vowed to retrieve a good longbow as soon as he had the chance, for he could have been shafting trolls all along if he had one. As it was, he had to watch on as man after man was pulled down into the fray below and eaten alive.

An orc with a strip of chainmail running diagonally across his huge chest was barking and chattering out orders. Beyond him, more of the wild trolls were loping into the closer confines of Port. From above, a rock came zipping into Rikky's head and nearly knocked him from Silva's back. The silver wyrm did an impossible aerial direction change, and the troll who threw the stone was tumbling to the earth while his dark, blue-scaled wyrm felt the crushing of Silva's teeth clamping down on its neck. Silva shook the wyrm until its neck snapped, then let it fall away. Rikky watched as it tumbled into the dusky shadows. He couldn't help but cringe when the wyrm's upper half hit the wall-top, causing the broken carcass to go spinning into the wide lane that spanned between the wall and Port proper.

Rikky clung to the spinal plate in front of him as Silva made a slow turn, trying to take in the battlefield which the Great Wall and the entire city of Port had become. Several of the ships in the harbor were aflame, sending huge, billowing pillars of smoke up into the night sky. Several parts of the city were burning, too. The trolls had stopped invading the city, and were building up their numbers in the forested outskirts east of Port, just like they had the night before. The trolls still ravaging the city were more than enough for the men to contend with. Rikky knew that by morning the kingdom's forces would be exhausted and there would be score upon score of fresh goblins and trolls coming up out of the hole all night long. The morrow would bring a slaughter, and Rikky didn't want that to happen.

He racked his brain and decided that Master Kember would have gone straight to the root of the problem. He decided that he should find a way to close up the tunnel. He would have loved to have Jenka or Solman there to give him advice, but Solman was dead, and he had no idea where Jenka was. Better yet, if he had that druida that had blasted the big red mudge after they left Swinerd's farm, she could probably blast it closed.

"Master Vahlda!" Rikky exclaimed out loud. Then to Silva he said, "Take us to our landing on the wall. I have an idea. Can you carry two people?"

"Yesss," Silva hissed in her soft, slithery voice. "For a while."

When they landed, the men gave the slick, gray-scaled dragon a wide berth. In the light of the torches and barrel fires burning atop the wall she looked more of a muted pewter color than silver, like clouds just before a terrible storm.

Rikky didn't want to dismount because it would be a pain to have to climb right back up. Mounting his dragon with a peg leg wasn't easy. He told a man to run and fetch Spell Master Vahlda. "And remind him to bring his cloak," he added when he was finished with the order.

Less than a turn of the glass later, the nervous Spell Master was climbing clumsily up to sit between the spinal plates ahead of Rikky. Rikky had remembered that Vahlda was much more than a just a healer. He was an accomplished practitioner of the arcane, or so he had once said. Rikky asked him if he could come look at the hole from above and see if he could use his magic to close it.

"I don't know, but I'm tired of watching young men die, so let's see what we can do," The middle-aged mage said in a wearily sarcastic tone. "I might never get another chance to ride a dragon."

Silva didn't even give the man time to settle before she leapt into the air and started winging her way east. Long hours of healing the injured and logging the dead into the book had taken a toll on Vahlda. He let his chin rest on his chest and kept his eyes closed as they went. Rikky was just glad that he was actually doing something besides riding around on Silva watching. Silva was intent on scanning the sky ahead of them for mudge. None of them noticed the sleek black hellwyrm with its ivory-antlered rider gliding high above them. It was silently pacing them, getting ready for the swoop and kill to come.

PART V

THE DRAGON'S TEAR

CHAPTER THIRTY

Jade had been flying for a day and most of a night and still hadn't reached the base of the cliff where the corpse of the mighty emerald dragon lay. Jenka would have stopped them earlier, nearer Kingsmen's Keep, to rest and find out what the situation was there, but the area was thick with vermin. It had been in the deep of the night when they passed over Crag as well, and he hadn't been able to tell much. Now dawn was approaching, and they were much farther north.

He looked around and breathed in deeply, trying clear the worry from his mind. The foothills were far behind them now, as was any sort of civilization. They were almost in the heart of the peaks, which meant the terrain was deathly steep in most places. Jenka could see snow on the sharp ridges ahead of them. The trees were all tall pines and firs, scattered about in random clumps.

The sun was just starting to break over the horizon, but the horizon was far below the level of the mountains, so the first light of the day was muted and indirect. Jenka's breath came out in clouds.

He wondered about Rikky. He hoped they had rescued Prince Richard, but he had doubts that they had. Mysterian had left the impression that after he had the tear he would have to take on the Goblin King himself. He had no idea what to do if it came to that. He couldn't even cast a simple fire spell consistently. He had no idea what the witch thought he could do with a tiny amber droplet.

They were planning on resting for a while after Jade hunted them a meal. There had been fewer and fewer mudge in the sky as the night wore on. They had all left the mountains to go fight with the Goblin King's horde. Neither of them felt that there was any sort of threat this high up.

"I resssted when I watched for the Royal, but it wasssn't much. He offended me," Jade told Jenka. "I was angry when I flew out over the sssea." Jade still seemed to be bitter over the way Royal had dismissed him.

"I'm glad that Herald and Mysterian found you."

"Yesss, we owe the witch," the weary dragon said. "I mussst feed now. Will you be all right here?"

Jade let Jenka off just below a ridge near a relatively flat extension of earth. Even in the cloak, the air was cold and the light breeze biting. A half dozen dark-needled sentinel trees protected one side of the space, but they did little to block the cold air.

"I can't believe you flew this far without rest, then tried to cross over the ocean to King's Island," Jenka mildly scolded Jade after they landed. "That wasn't very wise. I'll stay against this tree until you return from your hunt. Then I'll be the lookout while you rest your wings," Jenka assured. He put his aching arse against the trunk of an old pine and slid down it until he was sitting on the freezing ground. He scooted around a bit to get out of the breeze and hunched into the cloak he had lifted from the post inside Mysterian's door. By the time he was settled and comfortable, Jade was already gone.

There was less life up here in the altitudes than there was down in the valleys, but still Jenka could hear some birds calling out. He listened to them and wondered about his mother and the crown prince until he drifted off into a fitful, jittery slumber.

* * *

Jade circled over a nearby valley, searching for a sign of movement from some unlucky creature. Even though he was hungry, he wasn't feeling the urge of the hunt. He was thinking and paying little attention to the terrain he was searching. In his heart, he was hesitant about returning to where his mother's decomposing body lay. It had been one of his favorite places when he was just a hatchling, but he had no desire to see it now. He wouldn't know what to think when he saw what she had become. It pained him to even think about it, but he understood that Jenka needed the tear that his mamra had cried to pay for the freedom that the witch had granted. The witch had saved him from the sea as well, and he felt that helping Jenka pay the debt was important.

Jade had something similar to a fleeting memory, a thought that had been implanted in his head by his mother as she lay dying. He knew that the tear had power, and that it could be dangerous, but that was all he had retained from his mam's hurried lessons. He would brave his fear and take his bond-mate there, but he had to feed and rest first, and feeding required him to pay attention. A short while later, his vigilance was rewarded.

Like a rabbit startled out of its hiding place by an owl or a fox, a large, iron-gray colored mountain cat bolted from the shadows of some boulders. Jade's focus was immediately drawn to it. The animal was nearly half as big as Jade and would be no easy kill, but the young dragon had no doubt that he could eat most of it.

Using a technique he had watched his mother use a few times, he swooped in when the fleeing animal was traversing a steep rocky face. The first time he shot past the big cat at close proximity, the beast froze in place, but that wasn't the idea. The idea was to knock the cat from its footing so that it tumbled down and hopefully broke some bones.

The second attempt was successful. The terrified animal balked at a leap and skidded forward with its momentum. It went into a tumble, flailing down the face of rock, futilely scrabbling for a purchase that would never come. When it landed, it hit hard on its side. Before it could recover and limp away, Jade dropped out of the sky and tore into its flesh. He was hungry like he had never been before. By the time he had sated himself, he was covered in dark sticky blood, and heavy from his gorging. He flew until he found a stream, then drank and licked his scales clean. After that, he returned to the flat area under the ridge and found Jenka asleep against the tree.

Jade curled up close to his bond-mate, close enough to keep Jenka warm with the heat of his body. He didn't sleep at first. He kept watch for most of the morning, but as the sun rose over the tops of the sharp mountain peaks and shed its warm rays on them, the young dragon found that he couldn't keep his eyelids down. It wasn't long before he too drifted into slumber. There he found Jenka in the misty world of dreams, and together they flew toward a woman's singing voice. The sound was so sweet and harmonious that it filled them both with hope and pulled them deeper into the ethereal.

"Where are we?" Jenka asked. His voice was a hideous sound compared to the woman's song.

"Shhh," Jade hissed softly. "Lisssten."

"Break from it, Jade," Jenka warned. "I think it's a spell."

"But itsss ssso perfect," the young dragon responded slowly.

Jenka shook his dragon in the dream and Jade jerked suddenly into true wakefulness. Jenka woke, too. It was late in the day and warmer than it had been earlier, but still cold. They both stretched and yawned, but neither of them could forget the song and the beauty of the voice that had been singing it.

"Who was singing, do you think?" Jenka asked Jade as he ate a few bites of the frosty meat the dragon had brought him. It wasn't until he swallowed the second bite that he realized he was eating uncooked meat. He decided that he didn't want to know what sort of creature it had come from.

Jade hissed a little more sharply than he intended. The song was still echoing in his head, and it distracted his emotion from the growing unease that was filling him. He found that a pleasant thing. When he lowered himself to let Jenka mount his shoulders, he let out a long, hissing sigh. After he got his irritation under control, he answered. "I do not know whose voice it was, but it was coming from the other land of men."

"The other land of men? What do you mean?" Jenka's curiosity was piqued.

"Far towards the sunset, in the upper reaches, there are settlements of men much like the ones I have seen along the land barrier that you call the Great Wall."

For a long time after they were in the air, Jenka was thoughtful. Jade had to be talking about the

Outlands, but Jenka had never imagined that there were cities there. From the tales Master Kember and his mother had told him, he gathered that there was a large trading village and safe harbor mostly populated by kingdom defectors and pirates. It was supposedly somewhere up north, on the west coast of the mainland.

Jenka wondered if they too were being attacked by the goblinkin and the mudge.

Jade's sharp hiss caused Jenka's mind to abandon the strand of thought it had started down. Then the smell of rot hit his dull scenting nose and he understood the dragon's sickened response.

The smell was putrid and thick, even in the cold air, and Jenka knew what it was from. It pained his heart deeply for Jade to be doing this, but it had to be done. He had to keep his word to the witch. He vowed not to forget the dragon's deed. He would strive to make up for it with every fiber of his being.

Jenka saw that it wasn't only the giant emerald rotting away against the base of the cliff. There were dozens of troll carcasses, and more than a few orcs as well. From the air it looked like some huge, festering scab at the base of an otherwise healthy, cold gray mountain ledge. Living creatures, larger ones, had fed on all of the dead until the meat had turned, leaving a sickening mangle of buzzing insects and squawking birds hovering over what was left of the carcasses.

Jenka was amazed at how accurate his dream had been. He had witnessed the emerald's death and her tear falling while lying half-conscious in King Blanchard's dungeon. It was unnerving that he had done such a thing, and he could plainly feel Jade's sorrow. That fact that he could feel the tear calling out to him was even worse. It was unreal.

Jenka gently asked his bond-mate to land nearby. "This won't take long," he promised. "I know just where the tear fell. I can almost feel where it is."

"Yesss," Jade hissed in response, as he circled to find a place upwind of the gigantic mass of gore. "I don't want to be here long."

Jenka could feel Jade's anguish, and his heart went out to his draconian friend. He dismounted as soon as the young dragon landed, and batting away the bugs and buzzards, he went straight to the place he had marked in his mind. By the end of summer there would be nothing but a skeleton here, but now it was like walking in foul sticky mud. The smell grew sharp and threatened to dislodge his gorge as he traversed the nasty stuff.

When he made it to the long lump of festering scaled dragon arm where the amber drop had plopped and rolled over, he had to gather himself. Then he reached his arm down into the muck between the rotting limbs of two trolls that had met their end there. He felt around and was forced to reactively pull his hand out as something substantial crawled across his fingers. Trying to hold his breath was futile, and when he exhaled and inhaled again he nearly vomited. Looking at his distraught dragon pacing nervously across the way, he decided to get this over with. This time when he reached his hand down into the mess, he found what he thought was the tear. It felt like a small river stone in his hand.

His assumption was confirmed before he even had the chance to look at what he held. A slow, intoxicating tingle began to creep into his hand. It spread up his arm, and when it reached his shoulder he was suddenly overcome with a rush of magical power so intense that he nearly fell into the gore face first.

Through the bond they shared, Jade felt the power of the tear as well. He knew it would overwhelm Jenka, for he had been overwhelmed in much the same way when his mamra had been instilling her lessons into his mind as she lay dying. He leapt into flight and, with wing strokes strengthened by his emotion, he went to Jenka, grabbed him by the shoulders with his powerful claws and pulled him up and out of the horrific gore before he fell into it. Jade flew upwind and landed softly beyond sight of the grave. He immediately began to fret over his bond-mate. Jenka hadn't moved since he had stiffened and started to fall over. The tear was so powerful that even in Jenka's clenched hand, with Jenka unconscious, Jade could feel the intense magic coursing through the bond they shared. Jade hoped that it was a temporary sensation. If it wasn't, he feared that the both of them would be driven mad.

CHAPTER THIRTY-ONE

Zahrellion looked around and found herself lying in a dense thicket of thorny brambles directly under an ancient, tangle-limbed oak. She remembered the arrow slamming into her chest and looked down reflexively. The shaft no longer protruded from her body. The wound had been healed somewhat, but there was still a noticeable amount of bruising and pain. Crystal must have helped her, but the big white snow dragon was nowhere to be seen. It occurred to Zah that Jade would have blended in perfectly to the environment she was in. Crystal's glittering white scales would no doubt contrast starkly against all these shades of green and brown. Zah sat up to try and better take in her surroundings, but it wasn't easy. Crystal had chosen a place for her that looked next to impossible to penetrate.

It was mid-afternoon and unpleasantly warm. By the way her bloodstained robes crunched and crumbled in her grasp she figured she had been there a while, a day at least. A flicker of movement caught her eye and she saw a curious troll leaning down to sniff at the edge of the thorny bramble patch she was huddled in. It saw her wild tangle of hair and almost dismissed it as some sort of foliage, but when light reflected off of Zahrellion's lavender eyes, the creature's ears laid back and it snarled doggishly. Zah was in no mood for this madness so she stood, traced a symbol into the air, and called forth a sizzling yellow ball of her magic. The blast shot through the brambles, opening a wide lane, and completely obliterated the troll. Zah quickly realized her mistake. She could see dozens of the feral little goblins swarming around now, and at least a half dozen trolls. They had been moving through the forest toward the wall, but all of them were now converging on her.

She didn't panic. She started calling forth another spell, this one more potent. Her fingertip traced a streaking line of pink energy through the air before her while her tongue twisted around words older than the world itself. A crackling static began to hum around her as she focused the energy from everything near her into her casting. She started to speak the word that would release it all, but a log the size of a full grown man's arm bashed into her temple, sending her into total blackness. The orc that had crept up behind her started laughing at his achievement, but when the goblins and trolls looking on chattered their mirth over the incident, the huge commander barked out orders, sending the lesser goblinkin quickly back on their way to battle.

The orc wasn't about to share the glory of this capture with the others. Gravelbone had promised positions of great power to any who captured one of the Dragoneers. This orc was going to drag the white-haired sorceress directly to the Goblin King's lair and reap his reward.

* * *

Rikky and Silva were in trouble. He had openly vowed to kill the Goblin King when Master Kember had been bashed by the troll, but when he came face to face with the ivory-horned demon, his courage quickly turned to water. The Goblin King and his nightshade were on their tail now, and they weren't going away. Gravelbone was chasing them, had been chasing them since the night before. The demon was enraged that Ricky and Silva, with poor Master Vahlda's help, had closed the tunnel to Port. The Goblin King was leading them into a trap similar to the one he had laid for Royal in the grottoes, but both Rikky and Silva knew this. It was tragic that Master Vahlda had fallen to his death when the chase began. Had Rikky not been so terrified, he would have been raging at the loss.

The city was far behind them now. Since the wall was still to the south of them and the sun was sinking in the sky behind them, Rikky knew that they were moving east and north. It was amazing how Silva could maneuver through the air to avoid the occasional magical blast of crimson energy that the Goblin King sent forth. Rikky had spent most of the flight ducked down and clinging to the spinal plate before him. At times he had been slung, whipped, and tossed, but he had somehow managed to remain clinging to his bond-mate's back.

"We'll never lose him," Rikky yelled out, though his thoughts were plainly clear to Silva. He just couldn't break the habit of speaking.

"Yesss," Silva hissed back inaudibly. "He is leading usss, but I keep misdirecting the chase. I have sssomething in mind. Do you trussst me, Rikky Camile?"

Do I have a choice? Rikky's mind answered before he could stop it. "Yes, I trust you." He looked over his shoulder and was rewarded with an eye-searing view of the setting sun. The nightshade was nothing but a rapidly closing silhouette, and he could tell that the fargin Goblin King was preparing another blast of magical energy.

"Dive," he called out. Silva was diving even before Rikky completed the thought.

The warbling mass of destructive energy shot over them like a comet, and the Goblin King howled out his rage.

Below them, Rikky saw more troops of goblins and trolls. There was no telling how many tunnels had been dug under the wall. It had become clear that the early attacks on Port and Midwal had been but a diversion to occupy the kingdom's forces while huge numbers of the Goblin King's horde passed under the wall at less-guarded positions. Soon the outskirts of Mainsted would be overrun, Port and Mainsted proper soon after. The hold on the mainland that men had worked so hard to gain would soon be lost.

Rikky felt the tingling of Silva's magic and didn't dare disturb his dragon while she cast the spell she was calling forth. Or was it a spell? Rikky wasn't sure, because there was a pleading quality to Silva's tone. He did trust her. He trusted her with his life. He wished to live long enough to prove it to her. Already, the persistent nightshade was regaining the ground lost when they dove. By the loud, angry tone in Gravelbone's voice as he called forth some more of his evil magic, it was clear his spell would be much more potent this time.

"Hold on, Rikky," Silva said into her bond-mate's mind. She had finished casting her summoning spell. Hopefully, another pure-blooded dragon would hear it and come to her aid. If not, then she was certain that she would be overtaken by the foul hellborn wyrm dogging her tail. With a snarl, she summoned all the strength she could muster in an effort to continue avoiding going the way Gravelbone wanted to herd her. For now, it was all she could do.

* * *

Prince Richard's head was starting to clear, but only slightly. He couldn't understand why he was still with the huge ogre. They were moving through a cavern that was vaguely illuminated by softly glowing yellow moss, but he knew that he was fleeing the most terrifying ordeal he could have ever imagined. He and the big, olive-skinned creature had been walking for quite a while, several days at least. They had stopped and rested three times and once had eaten a meal of raw, sticky larva the ogre dug out of a crevice. How long they had been moving and how far they had gone, the crown prince couldn't say, for he had long since lost any sense of time.

They stopped after an insubstantial tumbling of loose rock could be heard from the way they had come. A terrible yet familiar growling erupted from that direction. A few seconds later, the rump and tail of the huge, blue-scaled dragon appeared, backing down the shaft toward them.

It was Royal, Richard knew, but he didn't even attempt to decipher the strange muffled conversation taking place between his dragon's rear end and the ogre. They travelled some more and came to an opening of cavern large enough for the dragon to turn around.

It was a sickening sight. Royal's long neck and shoulders had been savagely hacked and chopped at by the orcs in Gravelbone's lair. The whole length of his neck was gashed and festering. The dank cavern quickly took on the sickly sweet smell of infection. The big blue wyrm's eyes, once lively, were dim and distant. It was a wonder he was still alive.

The ogre spoke something to the wyrm. Royal responded, and the ogre hurriedly left them. It lumbered off into one of the two other shafts leading away from the cavern they were in.

The prince could hear dripping water and moved to investigate the sound.

"Stay close," Royal warned lovingly. "The ogre will return with others and lead you out of here soon." It was obvious that his life was fading.

Prince Richard found the trickle and took off his heavy steel chest armor and then his undershirt. He soaked the filthy garment in the water dripping down the wall, wrung it out a few times, then used it to clean the scales around Royal's wounds.

It wasn't much, but it was all the comfort he could offer. Richard had never gotten the hang of magic. Mysterian told him that some folk just didn't have the knack. He wished he had practiced more or tried harder, for he knew that a healing spell, even a minor one, could go far in keeping his brave and loyal bond-mate alive. He swam through the muddle that his mind had become. He found a raw emotion there, not quite hate, a loathing perhaps. It was a loathing for all that was supposed to be good and righteous. He had done no wrong that he could imagine, yet he had been tortured to the edge of insanity. Now the only true friend he had ever known was about to die because they had the honor to attempt to save another. The crown prince could find nothing good or fair about any of that.

"Find the good," Royal hissed weakly. "Even in the turmoil of rage you are lossst in, there will be good. Find it, Richard. Find it and hold onto it, for it is only that bit of goodnesss that can sssave usss in the end."

"NOOOOOOOO!" the crown prince howled as Royal heaved out his last breath. "You are the only good thing left in me!" Rage flashed through Prince Richard. Rage and hate, and an awful lust for vengeance began to boil. Royal felt his bond-mate as he fell into the empty blackness that was death, and knew he had failed. He fought back the tear with all he had left in him, but it wasn't enough. Royal loved Prince Richard dearly, and it pained him beyond measure to leave his rider and bond-mate in this pitiful state of anguish. Though he knew Richard had been deeply corrupted by Gravelbone's taint, he couldn't hold back the tear that had formed of its own accord. When it thumped to the ground at Prince Richard's feet, he picked it up and was instantly consumed with its power.

* * *

Crystal had heard Silva's frantic summoning and struggled between standing guard over her bond-mate and helping her fellow dragon. She had chosen to aid the dragon, for the silver wyrm and this Rikky Camile, the boy who had lost his leg, would aid her and Zahrellion in turn. Since she stood out like a broken wing in the forest, her presence was likely to draw the attention of the vermin to their location. Zah would reach out to her through the bond they shared when she woke from her healing slumber. Otherwise the dragon knew the girl was safe. Not even the hungriest of trolls would brave those thorny brambles to get at a meal. There was no way Crystal could have known that Zahrellion would wake and draw so much attention.

Ahead and below her, Crystal saw the silver dragon undulating through the air on tired, heavy wing strokes. Directly behind Silva, with the unending vigor that only the hellborn can muster, was the nightshade. On the black-skinned wyrm's back rode the foul Goblin King. Gravelbone looked as fierce as ever with his fanged maw open wide, and his crown of flaming antlers. None of them had sensed Crystal's presence yet, and she gained some more altitude while trying to keep it that way.

Suddenly, a streaking blast of cherry-red light shot from the Goblin King's hand like a ray. The sizzling line of energy sliced across the silver's back, blackening scales and charring flesh as it went. Rikky's peg leg touched the ray and a faint whiff of wood smoke was swept away with the wind.

Knowing that even Gravelbone would have to catch his breath after such a powerful display of dark magic, Crystal came streaking out of the sky at them. The nightshade sensed her just in time to avoid having its wing shredded by Crystal's lowered claws. The move caused Gravelbone to take a deep rip across his shoulder, as he was knocked from his seat. As he tumbled toward the ground, the nightshade immediately dove after him. The silver dragon banked around to see what was happening.

After seeing that she was no longer being pursued, Silva began winging away from the area as fast as her weary limbs could manage.

The nightshade caught Gravelbone in its grasp before he hit the earth and then started back eastward into the setting sun. Crystal flew to Silva's side and led them to where Zah was supposed to be sleeping. When they arrived, Zahrellion was gone, and the air was thick with the foul smell of vermin. She roared out savagely, but she could only blame herself. She had left Zah there in order to answer the other dragon's call. She said as much to the exhausted silver in the impossible draconian tongue, and without hesitation Silva swallowed her fatigue and leapt back into flight.

"Where are we going now?" Rikky asked. "You need rest."

"The orcs have taken Zahrellion," Silva hissed. "We must help find her, for it was to save us that the white one left her alone."

"Then let's get it done," Rikky agreed, knowing in his heart of hearts that all of them would be better off with Zahrellion safe and on their side.

It turned out that she wasn't that hard to find. The orc that had been dragging her through the starlit frontier had picked her up, and was now carrying her limp body over his shoulder as he fled. Crystal's roar warned him from continuing. Her glacial breath froze a whole swath of forest into solid ice before the creature. It dropped Zahrellion and tore away like a frightened child.

Crystal picked Zah up in her claw and found a clearing they could easily defend. When they were on the ground, Rikky slid off of Silva's back and hobbled to Zahrellion's side. He used all the healing strength he could muster on her, and was rewarded with a lazy smile from the beautiful, tattoo-faced girl.

"I always thought it would be Jenka who would come to my rescue," she said.

"Your dragon came to your rescue, Druida," Rikky told her flatly. He was still too young to have developed a real interest in girls, and he was as tired as he could ever remember being. "We need rest, Zah. The whole of the mainland is under attack and, as far as I can tell, we are the only ones left to defend it."

CHAPTER THIRTY-TWO

"I'm the fargin king, man!" King Blanchard bellowed from inside of Linux' body. He was still in the cell he had been in since they arrived in Port, and had managed to get the gag out of him mouth. "I'll have you flogged to death, man, I swear I will," he told the guard for the hundredth time.

"I seen King Blanchard speak once down in Mainsted. You sound just like the fat bastard," the guard laughed. "I'll give you that, you crazed dimbuss." The cell guard's grin disappeared so quickly he almost swallowed his own lips.

"Leave us," Linux spoke to the guard from inside King Blanchard's body as he came storming into the torch-lit cell house. His personal guards stayed outside the doors. "Leave the key and close the door behind you."

"Yes, Majesty," the man bowed and slipped a leather thong from his head. Dangling from the strand was a heavy brass key. The guard hurriedly backed out and shut the steel-banded oak door behind him.

"Your treachery knows no bounds, druid!" King Blanchard said hotly. No matter how hard he tried, he could not wrap his mind around the idea of speaking to his own huge body. "This is madness."

"It is madness, Highness," Linux conceded. "The wall has been breached between here and Midwal in a dozen places. No telling how bad it is beyond. Soon Mainsted proper will be under attack, if it's not already. We're about to lose the mainland entirely, and I need to know what you want me to do."

"What do you care what I want?" the true king growled. "Do what you will. You already have." His tone softened, but only long enough to ask a question. "What of my queen? Has her ship been found?"

"It has," Linux comforted. "It took severe damage in the storm, and was diverted to Mainsted, but I fear that by the time she gets there the goblins and trolls will be there pounding down that wall as well."

"What can we do?" King Blanchard asked, in a tone that let Linux know that he was willing to listen and cooperate. "Send her ship back to Kingston, on my order. I thought that the fargin dragons were going to help us. Did they abandon the cause?"

"That silver dragon and Rikky Camile, with Master Vahlda's help, closed the hole nearest Port, allowing me this time to confer with you, so they have done something, but he and that wyrm were last seen leading the Goblin King away from here, and that was a day ago. Master Vahlda wasn't with them. The white wyrm and Zahrellion were helping defend Midwal for a time, but according to the latest reports, they too have disappeared." Linux paused and rubbed the king's fleshy chin with the king's meaty hand. "I fear they have been taken down as the crown prince was. We might have to abandon the mainland, Highness, but you will have to give that order. I will not make such a decision on your behalf."

"You stole my fargin body, druid! Why not make the decision?" Linux watched as his own neck and face grew red with rage. "We cannot retreat from this land! We have fought for generations to tame it and I refuse to give it up now. We must march the men, all of them, to Mainsted and make a stand if we have to. We should have been marching already. How did it come to this? What of my Rangers up in the Keep, and your brethren up in the peaks in the Temple of Dou? Would you abandon them too?"

"Their fate is out of our hands. Wouldn't it be faster to sail round to Mainsted harbor and try to meet the Goblin King's horde there? Marching through territory they have already invaded seems futile."

"Yes," the real king nodded Linux' head enthusiastically. "A third of our force by land though, mounted pike men who are seasoned but dressed as pitiful men running away. It has to be men who can ride well and outrun pursuit if they have to. If the dragons get them then it's a wash, but if the fargin trolls think that is all of us left and that we are retreating, then we might even have a chance to surprise them at the old wall around Mainsted. We have to think about Midwal and Farwal, too. The troops from Midwal, even the citizens, can make it all the way here inside the wall itself, but that would take days. What word from Farwal and the eastern coast? Richard sent ships there before he was taken from the island."

"There has been nothing from Farwal," Linux heaved a heavy sigh. "No word at all." It would be no easy task to load the ships with men. The sky over the harbor was full of dragons, but the mudged were afraid to go too far out over the sea. Once the ships set sail, they might have a chance.

"When are you going to undo this?" King Blanchard was livid, as he indicated the current body he occupied. Linux almost asked him to calm down so that the heart in his true body didn't burst. He had never known his veins could bulge so drastically on his tattooed forehead, but he saw them doing so now.

"Only Mysterian the Hazeltine, or the Outland wizard Vax Noffa can undo what I've done to us," he dropped his head. "Sorry."

"Sorry?" King Blanchard bellowed. "You're fargin sorry?"

"Yes, I am sorry, Highness," Linux growled back in the king's huge daunting form. "I never intended for it to go this far. I only wanted to save the men out there you were about to march to their deaths."

"Bah," the king huffed and sat down on the padded mattress brought for his bunk. "I know I was rash, but my son…That fargin dragon…" He stopped and put Linux' face in Linux' hands. "Oh, poor Richard," he half sobbed. "This is all happening because I'm a fool. Has there been any word from Commander Corda's party? Any word at all?"

"None, Highness," Linux told him. "They have been gone far too long to have made it. I must order the ships loaded. I'll make sure that you're put in acceptable quarters for your sail."

"I'd rather travel with you," King Blanchard said honestly. "I feel that we should stay close and make sure that nothing happens to the other."

"Will you swear you won't try anything foolish?" Linux asked. "I will have you released into my custody if you give me your oath."

"I give you my oath, druid." King Blanchard pledged angrily. "Just keep me at your side and we will both be the better for it."

Linux thought for a moment and decided that with King Blanchard in his body and close to him he might even be able to use some of his druidic magic without drawing suspicion. "Come, then," he said as he opened the cell door. "If you can pretend to cast a spell then we can possibly clear the skies over the harbor. How do we get the men from Midwal to start coming this way?"

* * *

Prince Richard found himself in a sea of raw power. He used his rage and his anguish to focus the power of the tear Royal had shed for him. He didn't understand magic very well, so he called upon the gods themselves, and he asked the impossible. Somehow they heard him, and they granted him his wish by returning life to the great, sparkling blue dragon. But the gods, in their wisdom, put a condition on this resurrection. Royal's extended life would cost the power of the tear. He would only live until the tear's power was spent, and then he would have to return to death. Neither the confused blue drake that woke, angry and hungry from the blackness, nor the raging crown prince had any idea how long that would be. Prince Richard felt as if it might not be long enough, so he coaxed Royal into leading them out of the grottoes so that they could use what time they had left to find and destroy the foul demon that had caused all of this misery.

Little did Prince Richard know that Royal was now a soulless entity. The honor and intelligence the majestic blue dragon had displayed in life was gone. He might as well have been one of the mudged. Only an aggressive wyrm of undetermined might was there for Richard to command

and, for the moment at least, Royal was agreeable to follow the orders that were being given, but on a whim he could easily decide to act on his own.

* * *

Gravelbone was irate over losing the silver wyrm and the one-legged Dragoneer who rode her. Part of his plan for the decimation of Port had been ruined when the two had collapsed the tunnel on his horde. There had been several dozen orc commanders in that hole, and they had all been crushed by some wizardly concussion spell. The act enraged Gravelbone, and he resolved to rip the silver's wings from its body while his hellborn wyrm ate the one-legged boy. He had chased them for a day, and would have had them had that icy white dragon not taken him by surprise.

He let his rage and the pain of the wound from the stealthy ice wyrm simmer, while he let the nightshade rest a while. He had to return his focus to what he had planned for Mainsted. Once that was done, and the crown prince was on his way to the throne, then, and only then, would Gravelbone be done exacting his revenge on man. After that, his true task, the task of enslaving the haughty humans and making them his chattel, could begin in earnest.

Returning to the nightshade's lair, Gravelbone barked and growled orders to the orcs in charge of the enslaved ogres. They had been doing a poor job of clearing out the rubble from the destructive spell the silver wyrm had cast when it had tried to free the crown prince with Royal. Gravelbone wondered if it was the same spell that had collapsed the tunnel near Port.

He half wished that fool Dragoneer on the pesky silver had succeeded in freeing Prince Richard, because now he couldn't be certain where the prince was. There were a score of ways in and out of the grottoes, and the prince could have taken any one of them out. The big, sparkling blue would die from its wounds. There was no doubt of it. Gravelbone had the orcs rub their blades in larnax resin. Once in the bloodstream, the foul vegetable substance killed quickly and painfully. A few of his horde had died while poisoning the blades. Prince Richard, however, needed to reach the wall and safety. He had been corrupted; he was but a tool to be taken out of the box when needed. A most important tool, no doubt, for after King Blanchard met his end, the boy would be the king. The boy would lead his people up from the ashes of all of this horror, right into the chains of enslavement.

To crush all the hope out of man and to end the threat of the Dragoneers and their pointless Time of Confliction, Gravelbone had special plans for Mainsted. He would make it so that no man would ever want to set foot back in his land, and any of the would-be noble dragons that thought they were better than the other creatures of the kin could perish with them. He had found a poison, a scourge far more potent and debilitating than mere larnax resin. After it was dried and ground, it was light and powdery and the hellborn were immune to it. That meant that after the humans were pushed back into the city, the nightshade could carry a wagon cart full of the infectious stuff and drop it over Mainsted. All Gravelbone's hordes had to do was push the people of the realm towards the great frontier city, just as men had forced the trolls and goblins up into the mountains over the years.

A short time after the poison was dropped, the people would start going mad and grow leery of one another. Their skin would fester and crack, and they would seep pus and blood for weeks until they were nothing more than walking scabs. Some would carry the pestilence back to the islands, and a large portion of mankind would become infected. That's when Gravelbone would call on the prince. That is when mankind would be forced to kneel before him and grovel.

"Something comes," the nightshade hissed into the demon's psychotic reverie.

"Hav da pedalence bin arvested?" The Goblin King dismissed the nightshade's warning. If it was an enemy approaching, he would greet them violently and thank them for not making him give chase to end them. He was more concerned if the rare roots and caps that yielded his poison had been collected, boiled down, and dried into powder.

"Another day, masssster," the nightshade responded. "My hellborn kin and I are immune, but the ogre slaves are not. Is the satchel-cart ready?"

"Yan," Gravelbone chuckled. "No aw 'e hav to do is wait. Onz da people of da kingda are convergin on Mainsted dewa dra aw git aw dem an wax em wryth. Da prinz will do da ress fa as."

"Can we hunt Dragoneers while we wait?" the nightshade hissed eagerly.

"Yah," Gravelbone laughed his deep, sinister laugh. "Dat we ca do."

* * *

Prince Richard slunk down behind the eerily silent blue wyrm he had once been bonded to. They were just beyond the light of the blue-green inferno illuminating the nightshade's lair. He had been a prisoner in the grottoes long enough to understand what the Goblin King was saying and he was enraged by the idea that the demon thought him nothing more than a tool.

"Now, all we have to do is wait," Gravelbone had said. "Once the people of the kingdom are converging on Mainsted we can drop our gift on them and watch them writhe. The prince will do the rest for us."

Needless to say, Prince Richard stayed deathly quiet as he waited for the Goblin King and the nightshade to go hunt Dragoneers. He and Royal had a little hunting of their own to do.

CHAPTER THIRTY-THREE

Zahrellion woke Rikky with a nudge of her boot. She handed him a gourd nut that already had a hole poked in it, told him that the dragons would return from feeding soon, and then turned away while he took care of his morning ablutions. As he stood next to the trunk of a nearby tree and urinated, he took in the beauty of the moment.

It was the beginning of what would be a typical summer day. A few birds were calling out and insects were buzzing around a clustering bloom of little yellow flowers. Everything was green and lush. The air was cool, but wouldn't stay that way. They were far enough south to be free of the mountain chill.

It would be another perfect day, he knew, and for him that usually meant trouble. They had to fly back to Port and report to King Blanchard. The king needed to know just how bad the invasion had become. They would surely have to shed some blood before the sun went down. It was obvious to Rikky that Mainsted would be where the kingdom made its stand. Master Kember had always said that it's best to fight with your back against the wall. In this case the sea would act as that wall. He was certain that the king would need them to help protect the retreating men from aerial attacks. Even though Rikky and his dragon had been exhausted and in dire need of the rest the night had afforded them, Rikky felt a pang of guilt for not returning to Port sooner. He also felt terrible about the way that his friend Master Vahlda had died. Falling from a dragon into a swarm of angry goblins was a horrible fate. It had been awful to look upon. As he returned to the fire pit, sipping the tart juice from the gourd, he was overcome with grief and began to cry. Zah saw this and went to his side.

"It'll be all right, Rikky," she comforted.

Zah didn't like the idea of seeing King Blanchard. After all, he had put her in the dungeon for trying to keep a spear out of Royal, but she knew that sooner or later she would have to face him.

Rikky felt a tiny shimmer of hope then. Knowing that Zahrellion was on their side, and finding out that Jenka would soon be returning from the mountains to join them restored some of the confidence Gravelbone had stripped away from him. Rikky still wanted to kill the Goblin King, but he wasn't so brazen about it any more. He was just a kid. The foul demon radiated evil, and when Rikky had felt the intensity of it, it had scared him deeply. That fear caused a tendril of shame to take root. Oddly, crying like the adolescent boy that he truly was into Zahrellion's modest bosom caused some of the shame to melt away.

"Does it hurt?" Zah asked Rikky, indicating the stump that used to be his leg. She reflected that just few weeks ago he had been whole and hopeful. Now he was maimed and full of rage and fear.

Wiping a sniffle from under his nose with his filthy sleeve, he shook his head in the negative. "After it first happened, after the goblin ate my leg, I felt the part that was missing. That hurt bad." He stopped and wiped his face again. "Where do you get the gourd nuts every morning? You were sipping from one way back when we were starting out of Crag."

"There is a tree that I visit in my dreams. It is old and bears the nuts as fruit. I take one or two from its branches, and when I wake, they are with me. I don't really understand it, but it happens. Linux," the name tasted awful in her mouth as she said it. "He says that Dou has blessed me. I feel more like I've been cursed."

"Yeh," Rikky nodded, his guilt and sadness almost forgotten. "I know what you mean."

When their dragons returned, they all took to the air and flew back toward Port. It wasn't the journey Rikky expected it to be. They flew directly there and didn't have to duck or dodge any pursuers. There were very few trolls moving below, and even fewer mudged in the sky, but that only meant that the feral dragons and the two-legged vermin had moved beyond the wall, and were most likely moving toward Mainsted.

As they approached the landing area King Blanchard had set aside for them on the wall, they saw that there weren't many men out on the walltop. The few there were had the smaller dragon guns at their shoulders and aimed at the dragons until they recognized Silva and Rikky. After that there was some cheering, and a few more men came out and gathered on either side of the landing area. All of them were armed with bows and wearing glittery chainmail armor.

Crystal was nervous, but Zah calmed her and had her land next to Silva on the wall. The armored men all faced outward then, and every one of them put an arrow to the string and prepared to defend the dragons. There was a considerable amount of fidgeting, as most of the men were trembling in their boots.

"Our own personal guards?" Zah asked dubiously. "Has King Blanchard really started to see things so differently?"

"I have," both Linux and King Blanchard answered as they stepped out onto the wall-top from the landing.

As quick as a snake, Zahrellion slid off of Crystal's back, marched three long strides over to Linux and slapped him with all she had. The resounding *whack* caused several of the men to glance at them and cringe.

"What in all the fargin hells was that for, girl?" King Blanchard asked from inside Linux' body. Even though it was the druid's flesh she slapped, he felt the sting of it sharply.

Linux laughed heartily from inside King Blanchard's bulky form, but it was clear that Zah had already become suspicious. Linux would never respond in such a way.

It took her all of five seconds to figure out what Linux had done. Quickly, she went to the king and slapped him just as hard. This caused the real King Blanchard to burst Linux' body into laughter. It also caused a few of the king's retinue to draw steel.

Rikky was dumbfounded, but ready to stand at Zah's side. His dragon and the frigid white wyrm had gone on alert, too. Roiling clouds of cold steam flowed from Crystal's nostrils in warning. Half the men in the immediate area grew goose flesh as the chill wafted over them.

"Hold! Hold!" King Blanchard's mouth yelled, as he rubbed at his fleshy chin. "I had that coming, boys, and I'm man enough to take it. Now turn back around and hold your post. He glared at Zah. "Keep your tongue, Zahrellion. I had to have you hooded because we couldn't have you retaliating or trying to bust Jenka free."

"She is a crafty one," the real king said from Linux' body. "And I owe you an apology, miss, but I can't give it here."

"I'm in a mood now to be killing vermin!" Zah spat. "What would you have us do?" She ignored King Blanchard's form and looked at Linux' body knowing that it was really the king.

"We are sending the men to defend Mainsted via ships." Linux told her from the king's body, but she still ignored him and looked to the real King Blanchard for orders.

He harrumphed and nodded, then looked ashamedly at his feet. "Do as he says, girl. He's been running things a bit better than I might've."

"That wouldn't be hard," she retorted.

"There are men on horseback making the retreat from here," Linux told her. "We need another substantial group to retreat from Midwal as well, to divert attention from the folk that are trying to get inside the wall. We want the Goblin King and his horde to think that the bulk of our defenders are retreating in fear. Watch over both groups if you can. Defend them, but someone should first fly to Farwal and see if they are as bad off as we are. I'm having written orders prepared as we speak. In addition, sweep along the wall and make certain that everyone who can gets inside of it and starts this way. We might not have enough ships for them all, but we closed up the breach nearest here. With the help of your fellow druid, we've moved our big swivel guns to the wall-top. We can defend Port until more ships arrive from the islands."

"I'll go to Midwal after I clear the sky over the men leaving here," Zahrellion said, climbing purposefully back onto her dragon's neck. "They know of us at Midwal. Rikky, if you fly the wall all the way east you can pass the word to Midwal that I'm coming and deliver the orders to Farwal. Silva seems quick, where Crystal is slower and more savage. She can bring down the mudge with her breath, but she can't cover nearly as much ground as you can." Zah wasn't certain if this was true or not, but Crystal assured her that Silva was fast. Zahrellion wanted to vent her rage on the enemy, not carry messages. It didn't matter. Rikky was glad to take orders from someone he felt he could trust.

"I'm waiting on scribes, then," Rikky pointed out the obvious. "What if I come across Jenka? What do I tell him?"

"Tell him to do what he wants to do." Zahrellion's tone was sarcastic. "That's what he's good at." With that, Crystal poised to leap into the air. At the last second, Zah stopped her dragon and turned to Rikky. "I'll see you in the sky over Mainsted soon, I hope?"

Rikky gave a short salute of respect then nodded his head. "Soon," he assured her.

As he waited on the scribes to finish sealing the orders, he looked at Linux and the king and found it fascinating that they had switched bodies. It seemed obvious now, but it was impressive that Zahrellion had figured it out so easily. He wondered how long it had been so, and then he diverted his attention to Crystal's shrinking form winging away. He felt sorry for the mudged and the goblinkin that crossed her and Zah's path this day.

A short while later, he was streaking through the sky high above the wall. There were corpses scattered here and there, marked by the fluttering of buzzard wings, or the feeding scavengers who jostled for position on their prize. There were plenty of dead trolls and goblins, too, and it seemed that the varmints had no preference between the human and troll flesh. For some reason though, the carrion left the bodies of the little gray-skinned goblins alone.

It was nearly dark when Rikky and his dragon made Midwal. Silva had to dodge a few arrows and chase off a pair of smaller mudged that were feeding on the humans attempting to get inside the wall. Silva caught one with a claw and winged it to the ground. The other fled south towards Mainsted and would no doubt be returning with others. Rikky tossed down the bundle of written orders for Midwal, then called down that the white dragon and the druida would be there soon. Silva made one slow circle of the darkening sky to gain altitude and warn away the mudged. Rikky couldn't believe the amount of carnage around the tunnel mouth and outside the huge, banded-wood gates. There were piles of dead in some places. He wiped a tear from his eye, bit back his anger, then had Silva work her way eastward toward Farwal. He hoped that the vermin had stayed away from the less populated eastern part of the peninsula, but he doubted that was the case. The Farwal gate was a good distance away, and Rikky wanted to get there, pass on the orders he carried, and then go help Zah.

In the middle of the night, he was set upon by a large fire drake. Out of nowhere, a massive jet of dragon's fire shot across Silva's path. She avoided it, but narrowly. She pumped her wings in an undulating rhythm of quick, bursting strokes that gained them some distance, but it soon became clear that the big scarlet wyrm was on the hunt. No doubt Rikky and Silva were its intended prey.

They flew eastward as swiftly as Silva could carry them, the red casually dogging them as they went. Soon the watch fires of Farwal were ahead of them. When Rikky looked back the sky was empty. The red had somehow swept out away from them into the darkness. Rikky couldn't see it anywhere.

As they neared the eastern end of the wall, he discovered that the flames he was seeing weren't watch fires. Farwal was an empty, smoldering ruin. The massive gates stood open, one huge, banded-oak panel lying askew. Save for the structures that were still burning, it was mostly ash. The fire drake and the troop of trolls still rummaging around the destruction had picked the place clean.

Suddenly, flames were jetting out at them again, this time from directly overhead. Silva turned away from the searing heat, but only partially made it clear. The next thing Rikky knew, they were making a clumsy landing on the frontier side of the wall, with the huge scarlet beast flapping down right on top of them.

* * *

Zahrellion and Crystal had helped to see the pike men from Port on their way. Then she and Crystal came toward Midwal and made short work of a middling sized, black-scaled mudge that had decided to roost just south of the city. The men from the Walguard, and the few King's Rangers that were left alive at the Midwal Stronghold had spent all of the night and most of the morning escorting people into the wall. Several different groups of refugees and civilians had been hunkered down in one building or another out in the city. Most of the trolls and goblins had gone south, leaving behind clouds of carrion to pick clean the bones of all the foul-smelling dead. Zah saw no sense in sending the men who were under orders marching off into the rear of the enemy. Instead, she scouted the flatlands for the trolls and the goblin hordes, and found a route that Midwal's pike men might ride horses around the enemy. A pair of dragon-riding trolls found her in the sky on one such reconnaissance flight and decided that they wanted to try and take out the white-haired Dragoneer and gain Gravelbone's favor.

One of them hit the ground as a solid chunk of frozen flesh and cracked apart gruesomely. The other mudge lost its rider to Crystal's snatching jaws, but managed to gouge the white's long neck in the exchange. Blood streamed back in bright droplets and splashed Zah in the face. She ordered her icy dragon to land, and went about casting a healing on the wound. The act tired her, but not so much so that she couldn't continue guarding the sky over Midwal. In the late afternoon she flew west to check on the men who were retreating from Port.

What she found when she came upon the group sickened her and left a hollow place in her soul. These men's lives had been her responsibility. Even Crystal felt the wave of nauseous guilt flood through Zah as they took it in from above.

The hundred eighty men and their mounts were dead. They had been half eaten and mangled by a horde of vermin. Some of the vile little goblins were still feeding. In a rage, Crystal bathed the whole scene with her icy breath. Only a small mudge managed to lift out of her frigid spew. It attacked Zah's face with raking claws and snapping teeth, but the druida let loose a spell that sent the feral dragon flailing backwards through the sky, only to hit the ground in a bone-snapping crunch.

It was then that she noticed several other mudged dragons closing in from the south.

"If you're out chasing me, then you're not killing the good folk of Mainsted," she mumbled.

"They aren't chasing us, Zahrellion," Crystal informed her. "We're baiting them in so I can crush them."

"Good," Zah chuckled despite the knot of revulsion she was feeling. "I hate running. But we don't want this to happen to the men marching out of

Midwal. They are depending on us like these men were."

Something changed inside Zah as those words came out of her mouth. Any bit of girlishness or dreamy adolescence remaining in her had just been scoured from her being. Her demeanor grew as cold as Crystal's breath, and she bit down hard on the meat of her cheek just to feel the pain. "Lead them back toward the Midwal gate." Her voice was decisive. "We will kill them as we can along the way."

CHAPTER THIRTY-FOUR

Jenka swallowed back his bile and fought to contain the nausea he was feeling. It wasn't the sickly sort of nausea, it was the kind you get when you are overly excited, or after you've achieved something grand and are extremely nervous. Jenka was breathless and tingling all over. Everything around him looked crystal clear, as if the edges of his sight had been sharpened to perfection.

He could smell the ogre hiding over the next ridge. He could sense the immense fear it was feeling. He could hear the scrape of a hawk's claw as it gripped the bark of the tree where it perched. He could even hear the slithery sound that Jade's scales made as they moved and shifted over each other.

He stood and took in the deepest of breaths, relishing the feel of the chill mountain air expanding inside him. The turmoil in his belly began to quell and was replaced by a surging of energy that radiated into him from the dragon's tear he still held clutched in his hand. Jade could feel it, too, and Jenka could feel Jade.

Looking at the amber jewel sparkling in the afternoon sun, he realized he was in that other world Zahrellion had tried to describe to him. He was effortlessly there. Instead of being inside himself, he was everything outside himself. Everything. That is what it felt like.

On a whim, he called fire to his fingertip. He wasn't disappointed when a short jet of blue-green flame shot forth in a quick burst. He realized everything Zah had been trying to convey to him made perfect sense now. He had been a slave to his surroundings. Now he was the master. He needed to decide what to do next because Zahrellion and the survivors would need their help, and he still knew nothing about Crag or the keep.

As always, his mind went back to his mother, and he decided that that was what needed doing first. Hopefully she was holed up in the Keep with Lemmy and Grondy and the King's Rangers. But before he could start away, there was the matter of the ogre huddled over the ridge.

As he thought about asking Jade a question, the dragon spoke the answer into his mind. "Yesss."

"Crixun cruxun, vaghsil gherd?" Jade said quite loudly. There was a long silence, but finally the ogre responded to the greeting. It eased up to the ridge and peered over at them like some gigantic curious child. Its eyes were set deep into its overlarge skull, and its eyeballs were the size of duck eggs. A conversation ensued between the fur-bundled, olive-skinned thing and the young green dragon. Jenka couldn't understand any of it. Jade mostly listened, and when the ogre stopped talking, Jade repeated to Jenka what the surprisingly intelligent-seeming creature had said.

"Gravelbone isss going to ussse poison on the great mannisssh city beyond the barrier." Jade stopped and looked at Jenka, with alarm firing to light in his melon-sized amber orbs. "The nightss-shade is immune and will deliver the ssstuff. The ogre won't go passst the wall for fear of it, but they will fight the trellkin with us on this ssside of the barrier. Thisss one's kin wasss enslaved by Gravelbone's orcsss. He says that the poissson is terrible and fassst."

"Tell them to go to the grottoes, the caverns by the lake," Jenka commanded with confidence. The creature seemed to be looking for instruction, and was showing a strange sort of reverence with its humble posture. Jenka wasn't certain how he knew this to be true, but he did. "With Gravelbone and his black wyrm worrying over Mainsted, the ogres might be able to clear out some of the trellkin that are concentrated in that area." He paused as Jade translated his wishes. Then, in the silence that followed, he had an idea. "Ask if they can send a few of their number to Kingsmen's Keep. The folk there, if there are any still alive, will need an escort east to the town called Seacut to meet the ship that Prince Richard sent there. Tell them we will go to Kingsmen's Keep directly, and ensure that the trellkin are few in the area when they arrive."

After Jade repeated Jenka's request in Ogrish, the ogre agreed to do these things. It loped off and could be heard calling out strangely to the others of his kind that were watching the ridge from below. Jade lowered his neck for Jenka to mount him. Jenka was surprised and a little alarmed that he had only sensed the one ogre. There were several moving about below their position now.

"Are you rested?" Jenka asked his bond-mate, though he could plainly feel the power of the tear coursing through the link they shared.

"Yesss," Jade hissed, as he formed a step with his foreclaw.

He knew that Jade was feeling as crisp and alive as he was. Even after he shoved the tear into the little drawstring coin pouch he wore around his neck they could feel its power inside them.

As soon as Jenka was mounted between Jade's small spinal plates, the yearling dragon took a single stride and leapt smoothly into the air. "Where is this Keep you continually worry about?" Jade asked. "You hope your mamra is there?"

"Yesss," Jenka responded in his mind. His slurred "S" reminded him so much of Mysterian that he had a chill. A disturbing thought occurred to him. He would have to give the tear to her when this was done. After feeling its raw power course through his body he wasn't sure if he would be able to. He definitely didn't want to, but he had given his oath and, according to his mother, that was the measure of a man.

By mid-afternoon, Jade was soaring out of the Orich peaks and gliding down over the foothills. The area was still thick with trolls and goblins, but the mudged could feel Jade and were nowhere to be seen. The young green dragon radiated power like the sun radiates heat. It was the tear's power that lent the sensation its potency, but the mudged couldn't tell the difference, which left the sky clear for Jenka and Jade.

Jenka saw a golden flutter of what he thought was hair moving in the shadows a good mile from the keep. Lemmy was trying to creep along a tree line, probably trying to get a message out, or just scout the area. He was a good enough Forester to move undetected among the vermin. Oddly the mute hunter looked up into the sky at them and used his hand over his eyes to shield his gaze from the warm afternoon sun.

"Who comes?" a soft male voice asked into Jenka and Jade's minds. "Who, young dracos, do you carry?"

"What?" Jenka blurted out loud. Then in his mind he replied to the question Lem had asked Jade. "Lemmy, you can talk?"

"Jenka?" Lem didn't sound as surprised as Jenka thought he should have, but then again Lemmy the mute wasn't a simple young hunter. He was an old elvish druid, who apparently could speak to dragons with his mind.

"Yes, it's Jenka, and Jade is my bond-mate," Jenka told him. "What are you doing out here amongst the vermin. They are as thick as gnats."

"And twice as pesky," Lem jested in response. "Someone has to find us a route out of here. There are forty-three people holed up in the keep, and three of them are Druids of Dou from the temple. There are too many people for my taste. I'd rather take my chances out here in the fresh air."

"There's a ship coming into the cut. It's probably already there. A handful of ogres are coming to help escort you to it. The men on the ship won't welcome the ogres, so be careful. How is my mother? Did Grondy and his family make it?"

Even over the great distance between land and sky, the silence that followed Jenka's question was palpable. Jenka's heart fell into his stomach and turned into an icy cold knot. Tears were welling into his eyes, and even Jade drew in a long slow sympathetic breath of air. "Both?"

"Your mother was wounded in the battle in Crag. Grondy died getting her here," Lemmy's voice was soft; a deep foreign sound. Jenka had never heard it before, and it didn't go well with the young-looking man. Talking to him at all lent a surreal feeling to the miserable conversation.

"I was carrying the two younger girls and only managed to save one of them," Lemmy was speaking about Grondy's two younger sisters. "Grondy's father went down bashing trolls like a warrior. Captain Brody braved the goblin hordes to aid us. Your mother passed a few days later in her sleep. The claw wound across her back had grown infected, and she refused to make a potion for herself."

"Go back to Kingsmen's Keep, Lem," Jenka's voice was commanding. "Ready the others to make the trek to Seacut. You'll not want to be around these woods tonight. And if you are, stay still, because everything that moves between here and that ship is dead."

As the sun left the sky, Jenka and jade hunted. Savagely.

Like some terrible monster from the old tales, Jade and Jenka unleashed the wrath of their anger and sorrow. With the help of the tear, Jade found his fire. Both of them could see well in the dim starlight. Jenka found that he could send hot warbling blasts of amber substance streaking down into the hiding vermin. The blasts were not nearly as potent as Zahrellion's magic, but they were deadly, and served his purpose well.

Long after the sun left the sky, Jade circled above the area between Kingsmen's Keep and Seacut. He dove swiftly and destroyed anything that they saw move. Troll and goblin alike met their end in droves. When morning came, the Dragoneer and his young wyrm ranged up and down the east coast until they found the ship that Prince Richard had sent.

The men on the deck of the three-masted galleon cowered at first. They later cheered when they saw that the green dragon had a rider and was diligently eliminating the band of savage orcs that had been stalking the shore and the ruins that had once been the substantial fishing village called Seacut. When the shore was clear, Jenka and Jade hovered over the vessel. Jenka called down and told them to expect Commander Brody and the folk from the keep. He told them to sail directly to King's Island, that there would be war and devastation in Mainsted. It was obvious that the people who had been holed up in the keep for the last few weeks would need attention, not more trouble.

They left the foothills then. Jade carried them directly to Midwal, where Jenka was struck dumb by the amount of carnage he found around the gates and the huge hole the vermin had dug. He felt hot tears of regret streaming down his cheeks. Had he and Jade not dallied in the peaks or spent so long killing trolls around the keep they might have prevented much of this.

"Please be you, please be you, please be you," an exited young voice sounded in Jenka's mind from out of nowhere.

"It's the silver," Jade informed.

Jenka looked up to see Rikky clinging like mad to the back of an undulating silver dragon as it came streaking above the wall-top toward them. It looked like a strange fish trying to swim through the sky, and it was fast. Behind the silver was a big scarlet fire drake, and it looked to be all the silver could do to stay ahead of its unpredictable jets of flaming breath.

Thinking as a cohesive unit, Jenka and Jade shifted their glide out of the approaching dragon's way. They poised to strike the red as it went past them, but the huge dragon anticipated their move and came directly at where they ended up. Its maw narrowly missed Jade's wing when it snapped down and then it was past them, or so Jenka assumed.

Like a whipping tree branch, the scarlet wyrm's tail caught Jenka squarely in the chest. Not only did all the air get pummeled out of his lungs, but he was swept clear of Jade's back and tumbling toward a mass of dead vermin just inside the Great Wall.

A claw caught Jenka and he felt it grip tightly into his chest and shoulder. He squirmed and twisted and felt the sharp painful grip on him begin to sink into his flesh. He caught a glimpse of the nightshade's black leathery hide over him and then saw Gravelbone's terrifying, antlered head glance at him and laugh. The Goblin King's wyrm had hold of him, and there was nothing he could do about it

Just then, the strangest of things happened. Rikky and Silva had changed direction and they came around swiftly in front of the nightshade. The big scarlet dragon was right on Silva's tail and it crossed directly into the nightshade's path of flight. The fire drake and Gravelbone's hellborn wyrm impacted violently in the air. Dropped, Jenka fell away from an opened claw and the only thing he could think to do was clutch at the tear dangling around his neck as he went. He held the pouch tightly as the hard stone wall-top quickly rose up to meet him. Then he impacted into it, and everything went black.

CHAPTER THIRTY-FIVE

Jenka opened his eyes to see Rikky leaned over him performing a healing. This shocked Jenka greatly for he was still woozy from his ordeal and had no idea that the young hunter had started using magic. The long silence after Jenka opened his eyes, and the blank expression on his face, made Rikky worry that Jenka might have cracked his skull. Eventually, a sad smile formed on Jenka's face. The brief, brotherly hug they shared was diluted by a few heartfelt tears. Jenka told Rikky about Crag. Rikky's mother was safe with Lemmy and the King's Rangers, but Grondy and several other people that they had grown up with had met their end. Rikky said a silent prayer to the gods for sparing his ma, then sniffled away his sorrow, and explained what transpired after Jenka nearly busted through the wall-top as if he were made of stone.

"The red and the nightshade collided. Then the red turned on the Goblin King savagely." He forced a grin as he spoke, because the sight had been fascinating. "I think it wasn't as mudged as the others. It still has some sense, and some magic about it. It's been chasing us since yesterday."

Jenka looked around. The dragons were poised defensively on the wall on either side of them. Jade wasn't doing a very good job of watching out because he was worried about his dragoneer. "Is it gone?"

"Yesss, you fractured this stone, Jenka," Jade responded into Jenka's mind. Rikky and Silva both heard the green dragon's voice as it carried across the ethereal.

It is only paver stones laid over planked joists," Rikky explained. "The rock was only this thick." He indicated the edge of a broken stone to the curious green wyrm. The stone was as thick as a man's wrist. "The springing of the boards under them must have cushioned his impact. It looks like the pavers gave away easily enough."

Silva hissed. "Your Dour is unnaturally ssstrong, hatchling. You hardened your dragoneer with it." She was speaking to Jade, and their conversation faded from the minds of their dragoneers as it continued.

“What do you mean, ‘hardened him’?’” Rikky asked his dragon, but she didn’t hear.

“What is Dour?” Jenka asked. “Are we Dragoneers?”

“It seems so.” Rikky struggled to stand, and Jenka saw for the first time the scorched wooden peg that was now his friend’s leg. “I think Dour is dragon magic. You know the druids of Dou?”

Jenka thought about Zah and Linux, and an extreme sense of urgency began to rise inside him. “They didn’t even shoe it,” he commented on the wooden leg’s lack of a cap as he got to his feet. “We have to go help Zahrellion. We have to stop the Goblin King. He has something terrible in the works.” Jenka went to Jade’s side and nudged his bond-mate with his mind. “That red was chasing you because the impure strains of dracus, even the un-mudged ones, have a strong repulsion for the High Magic the pure-blooded dragons radiate,” Jenka explained. The tear was not only full of raw dragon magic, it contained a wealth of knowledge as well. “The vermin feel it, too, but it causes aggression. Gravelbone agitates that aggression in them. If we can end him, then the trellkin will lose the initiative that has been driving them at us."

"You called them 'trellkin,'" Rikky commented, as he stroked Silva's scales to get her attention.

"That's what Jade calls them."

"Jade," Rikky nodded his approval at the young green dragon, then climbed onto Silva's back and settled in. "This is Silva," Rikky told him. The pewter-colored dragon nodded its head respectfully at Jenka. Its eyes were as gray as ash and slitted by fang-shaped pupils of a luminous orange. Silva leapt into the air from her seated position, which caused Jade to try and do the same. He had to take a step, but only one. If he hadn't had a rider on his back he could have done it, at least that's what he told himself.

A few hours later, Silva hissed out curiously. She told them that she could hear Zahrellion calling out to them. The amount of concentration it took to focus on her voice couldn't be attained while riding the dragons through the sky. After Jenka and Rikky dismounted, the dragons guarded over them again while they sat comfortably on the ground and found some focus. Once they established some concentration they could hear what Silva was hearing. Not only could they hear Zahrellion, but they could hear Mysterian the Hazeltine, and Linux as well.

"The ogre told me that Gravelbone intends to drop some sort of poison on Mainsted," Jenka informed them all as if he were in command. The power of the tear not only filled him with knowledge and power, but it filled him with confidence as well. "Only the hellborn are immune to the stuff, so the nightshade will have to carry it."

"It has to be our main objective," added Rikky.

"Herald here says that Mainsted's wall is as stout as the Great Wall is and impossible to tunnel under. That's where we are." This came from Mysterian. "The trolls are thick outside the city, and several hundred refugees are trapped out there. Duke Watson crawled out from under his mistress's sheets and relieved Commander Hawlkin. Then he immediately ordered the gates closed. He didn't care that people were still out there."

"The soldiers I was escorting from Midwal joined the refugees," Zahrellion said quickly. "We are having a time of it though. Oooh wait," she had to duck a stone hurled by a troll riding a cobalt dragon's back. "They are in some woods on a rise west of the city, and we could use some help. There are mudged everywhere in the sky and they are carrying trolls in what…baskets? Wait…Oh, Dou no, It's the Goblin King and…"

Her voice suddenly fell off. A heartbeat later Mysterian cut in over Linux as he started to speak. "They are sounding the bells. The bigger mudged are coming over the wall and setting trolls down in the streets. I can see them out my window."

"Tell Herald to put a blade in Duke Watson's chest," Linux said coldly. "That's a direct order from the King. He is here beside me. Put Commander Hawlkin back in charge, or have Herald take command. Did Hawlkin get the swifters we sent and start building the dragon guns?"

"There are two of the contraptions in the square, but the mudged are dropping trolls and goblins down into the lanes, and the men have abandoned them."

"Zahrellion, if you can hear us, we are on our way," Jenka said.

"Have Herald find a way to man those guns," Linux commanded. "There are five shiploads of men due there any time. We are half a day behind them. Use the guns to keep the sky over the harbor clear."

"Tell the gunners not to shoot at us," added Rikky. Then his breath caught.

"What in the hells?" Jenka mumbled, as the sun's rays were eclipsed by something large flying over them.

"It isss the Royal," Jade's voice joined the conversation. "Something isss wrong. It didn't notice us."

"Prince Richard was riding him," Jenka exclaimed. "I would recognize that armor anywhere."

"Be wary of him!" Linux warned. "He has been tainted."

"Silence, you foolish druid!" Mysterian shouted with her mind. Her witchy magic added to the potency of her voice and it sent tingling chills up Jenka's spine. "Hurry, Jenka, bring me the dragon's tear. You gave me your oath."

"Richard has surely been corrupted, witch, you have no…" As with the dragons' earlier conversation, Mysterian and Linux' argument faded out of everyone else's mind.

"Go help Zah and those people," Jenka told Rikky, as Silva poised to leap into flight. "I'm going after the nightshade."

A few days ago, Rikky would have argued about that, but after feeling the intensity of the hate and fear the Goblin King radiated, he was happy to give Jenka the honor.

Jade took two steps then leapt into the air behind the silver. "Can you catch up with the Royal?" Jenka asked Jade.

"No, but they can," his bond-mate replied.

Already Silva was undulating into a swift streaking sprint through the air ahead of them. Jade sighed and circled slowly to gain altitude. He could barely carry Jenka, much less go streaking through the air like a bolt fired from a crossbow. If they wanted speed, they had to get high in the sky and then dive. Once they were moving fast Jade could sustain the speed, but he couldn't power them into it. His young wings just weren't big enough yet.

By the time Jade was high enough to start into a momentum-building dive, Silva was closing on Royal and the mudge-filled skies of Mainsted. It was late afternoon, and there were few clouds, but it might as well have been dusk as gray as the sky was. Rikky surveyed the scene as they approached.

The thirty-foot-tall, roughly-circular block wall was protecting the structures behind it fairly well, but everything that had been built outside of the barrier was destroyed. Pillars of thick, dark smoke rose up around the up thrusting city. The score of towers inside the wall were mostly built for decoration, not defense, but the towers nearest the wall had been converted and were now manned with archers. Deadly volleys of arrows went streaking through the smoke-hazed sky. The wyrms were as thick as crows on a fresh corpse, and the larger ones were toting what looked like crudely-built wagon cart baskets full of goblins and trolls. One wyrm stood out among the others, the black-skinned nightshade. Everything in the sky stayed clear of it, even the mudged. Rikky avoided it, too, and searched the sky for Crystal's white scales. When Silva finally spotted her off to the west of the city, Rikky saw that she was way above the whole mess and entangled in a tooth-and-claw aerial battle with a dark blue wyrm. Both were falling toward the ground in a writhing tumble.

Rikky felt Silva start sucking in a deep breath as she banked her route toward Crystal. He had learned from several close encounters that he had to watch all around them for mudged swooping in, and for stones thrown from the trolls that rode them. With Silva focusing her concentration on what she was doing, he had to watch her back. If not, they could get torn wide open, bashed by rocks, or separated in the air. The last wasn't so bad for Silva, but for him it would be fatal. He wished, not for the first time, that he had a bow and a quiver.

Royal was out there over the city as well, and the big sparkling blue was snapping and gnashing at the smaller mudged as if they were pesky insects, at least until the huge scarlet fire drake that had collided with the nightshade came upon him. After that, Rikky lost them, for Silva was banking toward Crystal and the cobalt wyrm that was locked in mortal combat with her.

A streaming gout of hot liquid spewed forth from Silva's maw and coated the cobalt dragon's wing. Silva's hind claw ripped open the unsuspecting wyrm's back as she shot past it. The dark blue mudge turned loose of Crystal then and, just before they crashed into the ground, the frigid white dragon got air under her wings, lifting herself and her rider above the treetops. The cobalt didn't fare as well. Its wing was ruined and it slammed into the forest hard, impaling itself on a half a dozen tall pines. Rikky saw the people Zah was fighting to protect. Several had been crushed by the falling wyrm. Others were scrambling about the forested area trying to pull the survivors back into the cover and quiet them.

At that moment, a roar filled the sky from back over the city. It was the scarlet drake blasting Royal with a massive jet of flame. Royal disregarded the scalding attack and latched his big jaws onto the bigger dragon's neck. A moment later, the red was falling from the sky limply. It crashed into the formidable-looking ancient wall that had protected Mainsted for a nearly a century before the Great Wall had been built. The carcass crumbled an entire section of the barrier on impact. Goblins and trolls swarmed into the city over the dead wyrm.

From somewhere in the area, Gravelbone laughed out manically. His deep, crusty voice traveled through the ethereal clearly and resounded with both malice and confidence. Oddly the nightshade carried the Goblin King to the northeast then, away from Mainsted.

Using all the concentration he could muster, Rikky reached out and told Jenka this.

"He is probably going for the poison." Jenka replied. "I'm almost to Mainsted. Jade and I will try to meet them to the east."

"You bring me that tear, Jenka De Swasso!" Mysterian's voice was sharp and actually stung Jenka's mind with its inflection. "You have no idea how to use its power, and I do. Now bring it to me as you promised, before all is lost."

"I'll go after the Goblin King," Rikky said.

"I'll do it!" Jenka yelled both aloud and into the ethereal. "The witch can wait!"

"Don't be a fool, Jenka," Mysterian scolded. "Your mother would be ashamed!"

That did it for Jenka. He had to keep his word. He couldn't just stain the memory of his mam. He just couldn't do it.

"You better find some stairs, witch," he barked. "I'll drop it to you as soon as I find you, but after that—"

"Just bring me the tear, Jenka," Mysterian seemed eager now, as if she couldn't wait to have the thing. "Remember who sent you my way, boy. Don't you ever forget it!"

"Bah," Jenka cursed, as he willed Jade to veer back south toward Mainsted.

"I'll stop the bastard," Rikky said. "I'm already closing on them. I will—"

A scream, long and terrible, resounded through the ethereal, then cut off abruptly. It had been Rikky screaming, there was no doubt.

"Oh, Rikky, no." Jenka heard Zah sob.

When Jenka tried to ask Zah what happened, he got no response, no response at all. He scanned the sky, but couldn't find any of them. He did see the smudges of smoke lifting up from Mainsted ahead of him.

Such was the clench of his jaw as he and Jade navigated the busy sky over Mainsted that he nearly shattered his molars. It was no easy task the keep clear of all the swarming mudged. They were like gnats around a night lantern. Jenka saw Mysterian atop an old castle-like structure, huffing for breath and clutching at her chest. She had just run up several flights of stairs to get to the top of a wide, flat rooftop to meet them. Jade landed, and the old structure creaked under the weight of him, but it held.

Below, out in a park-like square of lawn, amid the city's more formal-looking structures, Jenka saw Herald and a score of well-armed men fighting to get to one of the dragon guns that had been built. They were holding their own, but making little progress. There were as many goblins and trolls as soldiers on the lawn.

Jenka felt as if he couldn't trust the old Hazeltine Witch. He definitely didn't want to. Every instinct he had told him that letting go of the tear was the most foolish thing he could do. He was about to have Jade lift back into the air, but a deep feminine voice repeated something he had heard before into his mind, and it stopped his dragon cold.

"Do not be afraid to turn loossse of it, Jenka." It was the voice of Jade's mam, and hearing it caused the young green dragon to hiss with sorrow. "If it wasss meant to be yoursss it will find itsss way back to you."

Jenka yanked the leather bag from his neck and threw it at the witch, and was suddenly filled with the horrible absence of the magic. It had been sustaining him and Jade. The void it left filled quickly with despair. Jenka almost fell from Jade's back, but after a moment he gathered himself. He found he wasn't going to die of want for the thing. Still, he longed to feel the tear's wonderful power again. Jade's anger and sadness was a tangible thing as well. After Mysterian darted over and grabbed up Jenka's pouch, she wisely backed away from the wyrm.

"Lead the nightshade here, Jenka," Mysterian cackled joyously, as the tear's power filled her. Jenka could see the years melting away from her visage. It was disturbing. An attractive woman of middling years stood where a matronly hag had just been. "Poison or no poison, lead the hellwyrm to me. I will use the tear to its full effect, and then we will see where we stand." She turned and started away, but stopped. Looking back over her shoulder with her eyes rolling from the rush of the tear's vast power, she added, "Go help that foolish King's Ranger get control of those blasted spear launchers before you go. He's going to get himself killed."

CHAPTER THIRTY-SIX

Rikky had nearly been knocked from Silva's back by a powerful blast of magic that some half-mudged wyrm had mustered up. The hair was scorched from his head and brows, and his flesh was slightly blistered, but he was still clinging to the silver dragon's back, and they were still chasing Gravelbone. The dragon that had blasted them was almost immediately bathed in Crystal's frigid breath and had ended up pounding into the earth like so much stone. Eventually, Zah and Crystal turned back, and let Rikky go after the hellwyrm alone. The king had ordered her to protect those pike men. She had let half of them or more needlessly perish already. She wasn't about to abandon the rest of them, especially since the common folk that had been locked out of the city were huddled with them.

It was all Silva could do to stay close to the tireless hellborn wyrm. Only when the black thing had left Mainsted far behind and then slowed and started into a circling dive did Rikky wish that he and his bond-mate weren't alone. The nightshade saw them and started back toward them, but Gravelbone told it no.

"Gons geh da petulenz, ooh ard. Na go," he ordered, and the nightshade went.

Down and down into a dark, shadowy valley it circled. Then it swooped across the dusk lit plain until it came upon a clustering of orcs and ogres working around several open fire-pits. The ogres were being whipped and forced to do some sort of shoveling work. Huge sheets of hammered steel spread out between the fires. On them were shriveling lumps of some sort of vegetable matter. A huge, high-sided wagon cart that had been turned into a basket was being filled with the powdery stuff. Rikky figured it was the poison Jenka had told them about.

He had Silva bank away from the area. In the fading light of the evening they happened to see a trench filled with dozens of ogre-sized bodies, each and every one of them still writhing and groaning. They were covered in bleeding black scabs from head to foot. It was disgusting, and the idea of it set off a deep primal fear inside Rikky. His instinct told him to flee this place, but he couldn't. His anger at the foul demon responsible for this was overwhelming. If he died keeping that poison away from the people at Midwal, then so be it. It was a death he could live with.

The nightshade circled back around and went into a slow hover out away from the fire pits. Gravelbone slid deftly from his wyrm and landed in perfect stride, then moved away into the darkness. The nightshade gathered up some speed, came around again, and latched onto the nearly full basket of powdery poison by its crude iron handle. It then started back toward Mainsted, seeming to ignore Rikky and Silva as they started after it. Rikky saw, or rather heard, the roar of a mid-sized fire drake as it swooped in at them from the side. He saw that Gravelbone was riding it and realized his mistake. Only Silva's agile wings saved them from being roasted in flames, and now instead of being able to chase down and attack the nightshade, Silva had to avoid the crimson-scaled wyrm and its ivory-horned rider.

* * *

Jade dove into the park where Herald battled to win control of the big swivel-mounted dragon guns. Jade tried to use his fire, and was surprised that, even without the tear's power coursing through him, he could do so. The jet of emerald flame cleared the way and soon big grizzled Herald was shouting out orders and spears were flying up at the mudged from the newly-built weapons.

Jenka reached out to Prince Richard with his mind, but there was no response. "They have usss closssed out," Jade informed him, as he left the area around the dragon guns and started winging them in the direction that Rikky and the Goblin King had gone. "Voicing in the ethereal is done at one's discretion. You can close my voice out if you wanted to. I cannot find the Royal's voice either."

Jenka found the big blue wyrm in the sky with his eyes, then lost him as he was forced to cling to Jade's back for his life. The young dragon did his best to outrun a dark, jungle-green-colored mudge that had singled them out. It took them a while, well into darkness, to lose their pursuer, but they managed it. Jenka decided it didn't matter if the crown prince knew about the poison. If he and Jade couldn't stop it from getting here, then it would be too late anyway. What Mysterian had meant when she had said, “Poison or no, lead the nightshade into the city,” confounded him. He would do as she wished, but only as a last resort. If he could down the nightshade out in the frontier, he had every intention of doing so.

Far behind Jenka and Jade, Royal’s bright yellow blasts of liquid lightning breath lit up the night. His thunderous roars sent terror through the mudged, but the smaller dragons weren’t running from him as they once had. Royal wasn’t alive, and the repulsion he had once emanated was no longer there. The mudged attacked the sparkling blue in groups of two and three, using one another to keep him distracted. Royal would attack and taunt them in turn. Then he would lead them over the city where Herald’s crew of dragon gunners would try to put a spear in them.

The dragon gun worked several times. Half a dozen mudged had gone crashing into the cobbles with spears jutting out of their guts. As the night wore on, the draw of the weapon lost its strength, and the missiles were now only doing minor damage to the dragons, if any. Herald left some men there to man the weapon, but he took the rest of them with him to protect the ships that Linux had told the witch about. The ships would be arriving soon, most likely with the morning tide, and the way things were, he didn't think the mudged would allow them up into the narrow harbor channel unless he did something to contain their attention.

Herald and his small troop began rolling the other dragon gun toward the harbor side of the city.

Like a great pie with only a small slice removed from it, Midwal wrapped around the sliver of ocean protectively. The trolls and goblins couldn't get to the docks from outside the barrier, at least not in sizable groups. The breach the huge scarlet dragon had made with its crash was on the other side of the city, and several inner walls that had once separated the slums from the working class, and the nobles from the merchants, still stood in their way. As a result, the big mudged dragons hauling goblins and trolls in the baskets were starting to concentrate on the harbor area now. It was against a sizable band of vermin that Herald and his five man troop found themselves as they rolled the second dragon gun down an otherwise-deserted lane toward the harbor.

From an open window above, a woman's scream fell away. Another voice called down a redundant warning to Herald's men. After that, the skittering of the goblins filled the air like a swarm of locusts.

Like a tight gorge during a downpour, the goblins came surging at them.

Things were looking grim. Herald swung his sword with all the might he had in him. His men were no slouches either, but without the other dragon gun operating to help keep the sky clear, the mudged were dropping goblins into the city by the basketful now. There were just too many of them, and the swarm of little gray skinned, toothy beasts had surrounded them, leaving Herald and his three remaining men no choice other than to stand with their backs to the dragon gun and fight to the end. Right before their eyes, one of their fallen comrades was devoured in a ripping, bloody frenzy. Cold, lifeless eyes, as gray as the skin on the toothy, child-sized monsters that bore them, glared hungrily. The other soldiers, the ones who had already fallen, were but stains in the cobbles now.

Using his gauntleted fist, one of Herald's men stepped over and punched a flying stone from its course. It would have bashed the side of Herald's head in had he not done it. Despite the armor he wore, the man broke his hand in the process. Now the goblins ringed round them focused on him, as he could no longer properly wield his sword.

Herald spun around and quickly stabbed one of the vermin, then turned back and took another, but it wasn't enough. His burly size was great in a brawl, but he didn't have the wind to hold out much longer. Like beetles converging on a decomposing carcass, the little beasts closed in to finish them.

As he was going down, Herald could hear the women and children from inside the shops and dwellings along the lane, screaming out in terror as the unrestrained goblins burst in after them. The first set of teeth found Herald's flesh then, and another, and he couldn't help but scream out himself.

* * *

"Where are you?" Linux called into Zahrellion's mind from afar. "Zah, can you hear me?"

"Not purposefully," she shot back. She was as tired as tired gets, and still doing all she could to protect the troop of pike men she had escorted and the sizable group of refugees the cowardly Duke had locked out in the frontier. It was no easy task, especially when the sky was full of hungry, mudged dragons and the ground was littered with bands of goblins and trolls. “Why did you soul-step into King Blanchard’s body? Have you gone mad?”

“Never mind that, Zahrellion,” Linux’ voice sounded urgent. “I am speaking as your superior in the Order of Dou. I am commanding you this. Blast the prince from the sky. He has been tainted by Gravelbone’s dark power. He is a threat to us all.”

“I’ll do no such thing, Master Linux,” she responded a little more confidently than she felt. He outranked her in the Order of Dou, and by not following his orders she could be punished severely by the other elders of the sect. She decided he had gone mad, and they would see it as plainly as she did. She honestly feared for him. One of the side-effects of soul-stepping was a loss of mental integrity. The simple fact that Linux had asked her to assassinate the crown prince proved that he had been affected.

“There is something wrong with the Royal,” Crystal informed her. “The prince, too, but I know not what it is.”

“See, Zah,” Linux said. “Listen to your dragon. They have been corrupted, they will be on our side till the end of this, but after everything settles, the demon’s influence will show itself. I swear it.”

"Then come kill him yourself," Zah said angrily. "You had that hood put over my head. Then you attacked and took over the king. The king, Linux. You have gone mad."

"Bah," Linux cursed, in a manner that was more King Blanchard's than his own. The king was in the next compartment sleeping. He couldn't allow him to know that he was ordering the crown prince's death. Switched bodies or not, Rigalt Blanchard would kill him if he learned of it. Their ship had just set sail from Port that morning and they would reach Midwal on the next evening's tide. A lot of people, mainly women and children stayed back near Port, inside the wall, but every able-bodied man had been given a sword and been put on a ship. Most of the ships he and King Blanchard sent were entering Mainsted harbor already, and he had to think about the threat to them as well.

"All right then. Help Herald hold the sky over the harbor. There are shiploads of men sailing in, and they will need protection from the mudged. I've seen firsthand what those feral dragons can do. They destroyed a third of the ships in Port. Protect those men from the fire breathers."

"What about the men, women, and children that I'm already protecting? Do I just abandon them?" Her voice had grown angry now. She'd had enough. She closed out her one-time mentor's voice and gained some altitude so that she might be able to circle out over the knife-shaped thrust of harbor jutting up into Mainsted. It was too dark to see much, but what she saw was disheartening to say the least.

Mainsted, like Three Forks, Outwal, and Midwal, had been decimated. Unchecked fires were burning everywhere, inside the city walls and out. Mudged flapped and fluttered about the towers and the lesser buildings, picking off the people forced out into the open. Royal was still there in the sky, chasing mudged and snapping at them when he could. He seemed thrilled to be killing them, and the tone of his savage roars carried a hint of the bloodlust that he was feeling. It scared Zah a little bit, for she could feel something was wrong there, too. It wasn't her place to judge it though. Prince Richard was a Dragoneer, just like her, Jenka, and Rikky. That fact seemed to outweigh her status as a Druid of Dou. Either way, the harbor needed to be protected for the men on those ships were desperately needed in the streets.

She had no idea how to protect the harbor and the group of people huddled in the forest below her at the same time. If she could reach Prince Richard, then maybe he could help her.

She tried and tried, but found no response in the ethereal other than Mysterian's giddy voice, babbling the words of a spell. When the witch finished her casting, an area near the knife-tip of water exploded into a humming green dome of pastel lime-colored energy. Several blocks were encompassed in the bright glow. The mudged that contacted the magical field fell dead instantly, and the other wyrms in the sky moved clear.

"I have the harbor, girl," the Hazeltine Witch said harshly, as if holding her massive shield spell was taxing her body greatly. Zahrellion had no idea that it was the dragon's tear Jenka had retrieved that powered the great protective zone. "Leave the sparkling blue and Prince Richard to me, but if you see the nightshade in the sky lead it to the harbor and call on me. I will be listening."

Zahrellion didn't know if Mysterian's instruction had merit or not. She was glad the witch had the harbor though, for now she could defend the forest from the mudge now fleeing the city from the humming green shield. A band of trolls had closed in on her pike men while she was conversing. She had Crystal swoop on them and send them scattering. The men on the ground did the rest and closed on the surprised beasts with their spears. This allowed Zah to go ward off another threat. She could see the strength of Mysterian's magic already fading, and wondered if it would hold till morning. Then a rock nearly smashed her off Crystal's back and she began to wonder if *she* would make it that long. She couldn't even remember the last time she had rested, and her dragon had been flying the entire time. It came as no surprise when Crystal suggested they land near the forest so that she could rest her wings for a time. Zahrellion didn't think it was wise, but she didn't dare refuse her brave dragon.

Just after they landed, Zah looked back at Mainsted in the distance and saw a huge explosion of yellow sparks and fire. In the sudden flash of light, she was awestruck by the sheer number of mudged still in the sky. They were wary of Mysterian's shield, but they were there and they were getting their fill of flesh to eat. Any spark of hope she might have been holding out was extinguished in that flash. The situation seemed hopeless. There was no way they could survive the night, much less hold the sky until the ships docked. And what would happen when the boats were emptied of men? They would just be more food for the feral wyrms to feast upon.

CHAPTER THIRTY-SEVEN

Jenka saw the nightshade coming, low in the distance, and urged Jade to meet it in the sky. Not far behind the black-skinned hellwyrm, the sky was pink with the coming dawn, and the silhouettes of not one, but two other dragons could be seen. Mainsted was a good distance behind him. Jenka figured that, because he and Jade were soaring up in the higher reaches, they had the element of surprise.

Jenka wasn't sure where the courage was coming from, but it was there. As always, Jade could feel it, too. An unspoken decision, a commitment to the fatal deed they were carrying out, was made by each of them. Thinking as one, they carved into a sharp dive to attack the nightshade, though it was clear that it was carrying the wagon-sized basket of poison in its claws.

"We have to take it out," Jenka thought.

"Yesss," Jade hissed and began drawing in breath.

They dove into a wings-folded streak toward the hellborn wyrm. As soon as they were committed to their attack, Rikky spotted them streaking down from above and called out a harsh warning to stay clear. Rikky's voice echoed across the ethereal and caused the nightshade to cut sharply away and avoid Jade's trajectory altogether.

Jenka cursed aloud, for they could have ended the nightshade had Rikky not spoken out. They had been in a position to slam right into the beast. They could have torn it in two, or at least they could have broken its spine. Jenka couldn't be mad at his friend though. Rikky had only wanted him to avoid the poison.

The wyrm following Rikky and Silva moved away and started climbing. Silva went streaking past Jade, still following the nightshade, leaving Jenka stewing in his frustration. Jade gave out a roar that conveyed his rider's anger perfectly. They just couldn't catch up. Jade wasn't strong enough yet. They had to start climbing again, to gain altitude.

"Be wary of that red wyrm behind me," said Rikky breathlessly into the ethereal. "The Goblin

King is its rider and he is furious that his feeble scorcher can't match Silva's speed," Rikky's voice sounded confident, if a bit resigned, and more than a little determined.

Jenka understood that his young friend had made the same commitment to die getting the nightshade down that he had. It was a *coffin chore.* That is what Master Kember would have called it. Jericho De Swasso had performed a coffin chore when he had waded into that band of trolls to save Prince Richard all those years ago. Jenka huffed out angrily and lent his determination to his bond-mate as they struggled to climb back into the sky. He didn't have time to ponder who, or what, his father really was.

"Get the nightshade, Rikky," Jenka said under his breath. "We're coming as quickly as we can. Rest assured that we will finish it, if it needs finishing, when we get there."

* * *

The fading dome of lime-green luminescence protecting the tip of the harbor hadn't been spelled into existence to serve that task, but it was working. The ships from Port were rolling in with the tide, and even though the men were leery of the strange magical field, they were thankful for the fact that the vermin, winged and legged alike, were staying clear of it. From every part of the city, outside of the glow, people were trying desperately to get inside of its range of protection. Pandemonium reigned. The men on the ships had just come from a city swarmed with mudged, trollkin, and terrified people. They hadn't been expecting Mainsted to be as bad yet. There would be no defending the wall here. It would be a battle in the cobbles and then, most likely, a full retreat to the islands. There were at least five hundred people in the city for every ship in the bay, and even a retreat could only come about if they could keep the dragons from setting the vessels afire.

Mysterian had called forth the radiant shell to save the fool King's Ranger from his death. She had grown fond of Herald. The spell would have normally protected a ten stride dome of area, but the tear's power had magnified her casting, and the result was spectacular. Herald and two of his men had been saved, but barely. More importantly to Herald, the dragon gun had been saved. It had been hauled into place near the docks, so that when Mysterian's shield faded away it could be put to proper use.

Herald's body had been brutally munched on in places, and he had lost a barrelful of blood. Mysterian used every bit of concentration and Dour that she could muster, and had cast a healing to stave off his bleeding. Now some apprentice spell workers were tending to him and the other wounded men. It hadn't been easy casting one spell while maintaining another, but with the power of the dragon's tear fueling her, and an iron hard determination, she managed it.

The cowardly Duke, who had locked those people out of the city, had been found. He was now gagged, lying in the corner of the modest, semi-crowded, second story living quarters where Herald had been placed. Commander Hawlkin had gone off to start organizing the troops as they disembarked from the ships. Mysterian was still standing in the window from where she had cast her spell. She hadn't moved in hours. If she did, the shield would fail. Soon she would collapse from exhaustion, but she would hold out until she could hold out no more, or so she intended. Everything changed when she heard Zahrellion screaming out to her in the ethereal.

"It comes! The nightshade is approaching!" Zahrellion screamed with her mind. "Oh Dou, it has the stuff Jenka warned us about in a basket, and Rikky…Rikky's wyrm is right on its tail."

"How long till they are over the city?" Mysterian asked as she let the shield dissolve away. She didn't wait for an answer. "Where is De Swasso?" she asked quickly. She moved through the startled people who had been standing around her. In a voice that they could hear, she commanded, "The protection has passed. Make sure that there are men on the dragon gun to guard the harbor." She had to get to the rooftop.

In her mind she continued her conversation with Zahrellion, "If you don't see Jenka, then you must lead it here to me. Near the tip of the harbor, girl! Do as I say! And warn the other Dragoneers away."

"They are almost there, witch!" Zah returned. "It won't chase me. It doesn't even acknowledge the silver that's right on its tail!"

Zahrellion wasn't surprised that there was no response, but she was surprised when Gravelbone, on the back of a mid-sized, red-orange-scaled fire wyrm, dove on her from above and behind her field of vision. The next thing she knew, she was nearly jerked backwards off Crystal's back. The Goblin King's new mount hooked its claws into Crystal's hindquarter and opened her flesh. A jet of flames shot over Zah, but just as quickly, Crystal's head snaked around and a blast of glacial frost bit the fire wyrm severely. It flapped madly away, leaving Gravelbone cursing and calling forth the words of some dark spell.

A distinctive roar filled the sky then. Royal, with the steel-armored crown prince riding purposefully on his back, came out of nowhere and bathed the Goblin King and his red wyrm in a swath of sizzling, liquid lightning breath.

Gravelbone's spell erupted in an explosion of lavender static that radiated outward and rippled nearly everything that it passed over. Zahrellion recognized the effect of the demon's foul magic, and it made her gnash her teeth together in anticipation. She found herself tumbling with Crystal, Zah half-mounted between spinal plates. Then they impacted into the edge of the forest with a deep, lung-emptying concussion. The last thing Zah saw before she was flung limply off her stunned and possibly mortally-wounded dragon was a band of trolls charging at them through the undergrowth. After that, all she could see was the back of her eyelids as she fainted away from the pain.

* * *

Prince Richard urged Royal at Gravelbone's mount while they had the advantage, but a cold ember-red glare from the ivory-horned demon troll froze their courage before the sparkling blue could do any damage. Royal banked away and winged his way back toward the great circular wall encompassing the city. The power of the tear Royal had cried for him would fade soon, then Royal would really be dead. Richard could tell from the moment his bond-mate sucked in the first unnatural breath that it wasn't the same Royal he had grown to love. Then again, he wasn't the same Prince Richard either.

He decided they should go after the nightshade. The sun was well up in the sky and the harbor full of armed men now. If what Jenka had told the others was really true, then it wasn't carrying more goblins in that basket. Rikky's silver wyrm was only half the nightshade's size. The crown prince figured that, if he couldn't muster the courage to attack Gravelbone, then maybe they could at least save the people of Mainsted from the stuff the hellwyrm was carrying.

A glance back revealed that some of the pike men he had heard Zah talking about earlier were coming out of the forest to defend her and Crystal. He doubted either was alive. If they survived, the men would keep the trolls off of them for a time. Rikky and his swift-flying silver mount could return and check on her. He and Royal were beyond recovery, and he knew it. The sparkling blue was already dead, and he himself corrupted to the point of cowardice by the foul Goblin King. They would do the deed. They were already doomed, but they had to hurry.

Royal flew with all the strength his own dying tear could provide him which, at the moment was considerable. They gained on the other two wyrms, but not before the nightshade neared the wall. A quick scan of the sky showed that Gravelbone didn't want to be near his hellborn companion when the poison was dumped. He was circling wide on the slightly-wounded fire wyrm, watching and waiting.

It amazed Prince Richard that Rikky had survived after a troll had eaten his leg. The last time, the only time he had ever met the young hunter, was when Royal had carried Rikky's wagon and dropped it onto the kingdom side of Midwal. That was when Rikky's wound had been fresh. That was before Gravelbone had seeped into his marrow and tainted him. Had it not been for Royal's dying wish, for him to find the good in himself, he would have been lost to the demon completely. As it was, he wasn't fit to call himself a man, much less a future king of the realm. He could barely stand himself.

Ahead, he saw Rikky's silver dragon lunge and latch its jaws onto the nightshade's tail. He shouted out across the ethereal for Rikky to let it loose, but for some reason his voice couldn't be heard in that way. He would have voiced an opinion when Mysterian and Linux had started arguing about his current condition had he been able to. He would have agreed with the druid, he needed to die, but he wouldn't make anyone have to order his death. He would die saving the people he had been raised to rule.

Royal felt his rider's intention and responded unemotionally. The sparkling blue was closing fast on the now slower flying nightshade. It was almost over the wall, and Silva was back-flapping his sizable, pewter-colored wings, holding its tail, trying to keep it from getting the basket over the populace. The nightshade was struggling to keep itself moving forward while not dropping the basket of pestilence that it carried. Even the nightshade feared the wrath of Gravelbone if it failed in this task.

Prince Richard had Royal corkscrew behind, and then just over Rikky and Silva so that Royal slid over them like a streaking snake. Slithering through the sky at an impossible speed, it went between the hellwyrm's leathery black wings and came down, snapping his jaws tight on the base of the nightshade's skull.

"Flee!" the crown prince yelled as loud as he could at Rikky. The sparkling blue wyrm had startled Silva so badly that she had already let the nightshade's tail go. They backed up and away on panicked wing strokes and narrowly missed a stirred-up cloud of the poison as it was slung around and out of the basket. The stuff fell like a handful of dropped flour down into the edge of the city.

There had been no need to hear the prince's voice call out the warning to flee. A deep repulsion was radiating from the sparkling blue. Rikky hated it, it was vile. "It's flying dead," Silva told him, but didn't elaborate. Rikky hadn't felt so awful in his life. Not even the pain from his missing leg had hurt so badly. The big blue wyrm hadn't caused the feeling when he had crossed paths with Royal before. Now all he and Silva could do was try to get away from the tainted beast, and they couldn't do that fast enough.

From a good distance away, a direct, wire-straight line of crackling, blood-red energy shot forth from Gravelbone's open palm. Such was its potency that it was plainly visible in the early afternoon sun, but where the ray touched the smoke from the smoldering buildings was brightest. The sensation it caused when it passed briefly across the skin of Rikky's exposed arm could only be described as having the marrow of his bones boiled. Had he a lesser tolerance for pain he might have just fallen away from his dragon. As it was, Silva tried to avoid crashing into the partially-standing remains of a building just outside the wall. The ray of demon power had touched Silva, too, and she was having a hard time recovering. Silva could do nothing to keep Rikky seated, but he held on somehow. How Prince Richard and what was once Royal were able to take the torturous feeling was beyond Rikky. The beam of demon magic followed them, scorching into their skin almost continuously.

Silva tried to get some air between her and the ground so they could rejoin the fight, but when they got turned back around, the nightshade was winging away and Royal was roaring and trying to stay aloft with most of one of his wing membranes scorched away. The Goblin King's beam found Royal again and this time he went down, flailing into the cobbles at the edge of the city.

Rikky urged Silva to chase the nightshade again, but Royal came surging up out of the lane with nothing less than vengeance in his dead eyes. "Find Zahrellion!" Prince Richard yelled as they cut in front of Silva's path. "She's down!" His once polished steel armor had a black line across the front where Gravelbone's ray had slid across, and the redness of his eyes was visible across the distance. Prince Richard barely looked human any more.

Rikky didn't bother to respond. All he could see now was the crown prince's back and Royal's flittering tail. As he called out to Zahrellion in the ethereal, he realized the hellborn wyrm was low over the northern part of the city now. If it dropped the basket of poison it would impact and billow out in a roiling cloud that would probably engulf an entire quarter. Rikky knew that if the basket was dropped from a higher altitude the powdery stuff might corrupt a much larger area. Apparently the nightshade knew this, too, for it started circling up and around, leaving Royal and the crown prince struggling to gain on it.

A few moments later, Rikky realized that Zahrellion hadn't responded to his call yet. Reluctantly he started after her, at least until he heard Jenka reply in his mind.

"She and Crystal are downed to the northeast by a strand of forest," Jenka informed coldly. "Go and see if they need your healing magic or stay and help Prince Richard. One way or another, this will be done soon. I'm almost there."

Jenka was lying. The nightshade had responded to Rikky's ethereal call earlier so he figured the hell-wyrm could hear him now. Jenka and Jade were already high above them all, riding a powerful river of wind. Jenka was about to oblige Mysterian and force the nightshade down low when it passed near the tip of the harbor. He could only hope the old Hazeltine would take care of the rest. He had found faith, though. His mother had sent him to her, and Mysterian had the power of the great emerald dragon's tear filling her. Maybe it would be enough.

CHAPTER THIRTY-EIGHT

Far below Jenka and Jade, down in the streets of Mainsted, a battle raged in the cobbles. Trolls and goblins alike fought to get through the masses. From the outskirts of the city, Gravelbone was directing them toward the harbor. They would die when the poison came out of the sky, just like the humans would. Gravelbone didn't care. He just wanted man away from his land for he hated humanity. He had no concern about the cost in lives it took to achieve his goal. His confidence in his plans faltered when he saw the young green wyrm and its Dragoneer diving at his unsuspecting nightshade again. He tried to call out a warning to his wyrm across the ethereal, but he wasn't fast enough.

Just like before, Jenka and Jade started into a sharp dive at the hellwyrm. It was nearing the tip of the knife-shaped harbor, and Jenka knew that was where Mysterian would be. It was gaining altitude, and Jenka was going to try and drive it back down. He didn't dare crash into it here; the poison would go tumbling right into the heart of the city. Prince Richard and his big sparkling blue were coming at the nightshade too, but lower in the sky. Royal's wing looked damaged, but he was still flying with determination.

Like a hawk coming down on another bird; a far larger bird. Jade dropped in fast, snapping his wings out into a stall. He raked a claw across the startled hellwyrm's wide-open, cherry-red eyes before the beast knew what was happening. Then, like a striking snake, the young green shot his head out and bit down on the long bridge of the nightshade's snout. He didn't let go, not even when the hellwyrm snapped its head back and forth trying to sling them away. Jenka was slung away from Jade's back. He saw as he fell that the two dragons were falling, too. He hoped Mysterian was ready. Jade wasn't going to let go, and the nightshade couldn't fly with the young green latched onto its head. Jenka knew from experience that the only way to go was down. The dragon and the nightshade glided into a slow arc at first, but then went into a spin that had them corkscrewing downward almost as fast as Jenka was falling. Jenka looked up at them; he didn't want to see his death flying up to greet him. He was proud of Jade, and he was proud of himself. His death would be swift. When he hit the ground it would be over, and if Mysterian did whatever she was going to do, then the people in the city would be saved. Jenka fell far longer than he thought possible. When he couldn't take the suspense of when he would hit the earth any more, he squeezed his eyes shut and waited for the impact.

* * *

Royal stopped trying to gain altitude when he and his Dragoneer saw Jade dragging the nightshade out of the sky. They altered their course to meet it in the air. Prince Richard wished that he could warn Jade away, but his ethereal voice hadn't worked since Royal had died. Prince Richard saw Jenka falling, but he thought the swiftly approaching silver might just be fast enough to catch him. It was undulating through the sky like a dolphin swimming through the air. It would be a close thing, but he couldn't afford to worry about Jenka. He had to get that basket away from the city.

Already it was sloshing great puffs of its contents out into the air.

A loud, crackling sound drowned out everything, including the savage roars of the dragons. From a rooftop below, a great swath of sea-green energy shot upward and engulfed Jade and the nightshade. Amazingly, they disappeared from the sky completely. The basketful of poison fell away from claws no longer there to hold it, and Prince Richard urged Royal into a streaking swoop to try and grab it from the sky. It was slowly rolling over and about to dump its contents over the city. From across the ethereal Gravelbone laughed out giddily. He had been prepared for this contingency.

Mysterian screamed out miserably at the terrible mistake she had made. The spell that had sent the hellwyrm, and Jade, a dozen miles out over the sea hadn't worked on the poison or its basket. She had no idea why, other than the possibility that Gravelbone might have enchanted them for just that very reason. She was an old fool. She should have expected this. The demon was meticulous. It looked like Prince Richard and Royal were going to try and grab the stuff from the sky. That was a good thing for the people in the city, but the crown prince would surely get infected, for already there was a faint stream of powder tailing up as it was whipped around and out of the basket.

Mysterian saw Jenka then, and her heart fell. He was falling limply, about to crash into a rooftop a few streets over. Herald would be crushed if Jenka met his end out here. Just as quickly as her heart fell, it shot back up into her chest and hammered out in both amazement and sorrow.

The very same instant the silver dragon came streaking over the rooftops to try and save Jenka, a great cloud of poisoned powder splashed up out of the basket. Royal had caught the container, but he was flying right through a cloud of the poison and Prince Richard was in it with him. She couldn't tell if the silver wyrm had caught Jenka or not, but she knew that the mighty blue dragon and the boy she had come to love had both just been poisoned. They flew south toward the sea. She imagined that the crown prince knew he was doomed. He had sacrificed himself to save the people of Mainsted a horrible fate. Linux had been wrong; Gravelbone hadn't completely corrupted him.

Mysterian was blasted out of her sorrowful state by a searing pulse of Gravelbone's crimson magic. She flew across the rooftop and only stopped when her head slammed into the parapet. The Goblin

King was furious and had tried to kill her as an impulse, but now he was calling out to Royal with his dark magic. The undead wyrm couldn't help but respond. It was a creature of his domain now. So was Prince Richard, for that matter. He commanded them back over the city and grinned with delight, when he saw the sparkling blue start into a slow banking turn at the edge of the sea.

Royal was soon winging his way back out over the city, answering a call he couldn't refuse. Prince Richard yelled and pleaded with his dragon to stop. He felt the demon troll's call, too, but was determined not to succumb to the foul thing.

"You told me, Royal," the crown prince called at his dragon out loud. "Find what is good in me and use it! I did that. I brought you back for a time, and now we have the chance to thwart him. Find what is good in you Royal. Let us go out over the sea and die as heroes! It is the best revenge we can hope for."

"Revenge?" Royal's voice was weak, but Prince Richard could hear it in his head, like he had before Royal had died. "You, Richard are the only thing good left that I can find." Royal shook his head and started turning again. "Guide me where you will, Dragoneer. We will settle for revenge."

As Royal banked back out away from the city, Gravelbone roared out his anger. The mudged fire drake he was riding was quaking with fear of its rider. Exhausted and injured, it was moving sluggishly through the air. Gravelbone didn't care. He had felt the power of the bond between Prince Richard and his deceased dragon surge back into existence. It was just enough to break the strands of control he had placed over them. He was twice furious, and his rage swelled to unimaginable proportions, because the fool prince had flown right through the poison, and that meant that all of Gravelbone's planning had been for nothing. Prince Richard would never take the throne. The long days of torturing the boy's mind down in the nightshade's lair had been wasted.

Gravelbone spoke the words to a terrible spell. He would unleash his anger on the people below with his dark destructive magic. He would have his horde feasting on man flesh for months to come. He finished his casting but was halted from saying the word that would level half of Mainsted when a small, primal scream closed in on him. What he saw shocked him so badly that he didn't even try finish his casting, much less try to defend himself.

* * *

Jenka was about to crunch into the cobbled streets of Mainsted. Rikky and his dragon were racing in to save him. Silva had to dip down between buildings and turn sideways in the air to grab Jenka, but she got him. She kept swimming through the air furiously above the rooftops. Jenka couldn't tell what was happening, because he was clutched uncomfortably in Silva's grasp. The silver wyrm wasn't nearly as large as Royal or the nightshade, and had to hold him awkwardly with both claws. Jenka was thankful for the reprieve from death, and wasn't about to complain. He just wished he knew what had become of Jade. His dragon had vanished from the sky with the nightshade.

Jenka only got to see part of what transpired next, and the little he saw was spectacular.

Gravelbone roared up ahead and above them, oblivious to the silver dragon streaking across the rooftops from his blind side. He was focused on something in the distance. When Silva curved upward to ride right up the mudged red dragon's tail, Rikky let out a savage scream and leapt from Silva's back. With his peg-leg held out ahead of him like a spear, he smashed right into Gravelbone's back, impaling him. The red dragon was so startled by Silva's stealth that it bolted away, flipping both

Rikky and Gravelbone into a tumble. There would be no swooping dragon to save them, for they were barely above the rooftops and there wasn't nearly enough time to for Silva to turn.

Jenka was tossed and repositioned by Silva's claw. Then he was let loose to tumble across a gravelly rooftop where he skidded roughly to a halt. He stood and looked back, seeing Silva's tail dip down below the edge of the building. He half limped, half ran to the parapet and looked down to see the silver wyrm savagely tearing into Gravelbone's flesh. Rikky was lying a dozen paces away, his amputated leg jutting up like a small tree stump. His peg-leg had skewered the Goblin King through the chest, pinning it to the ground, making it all the easier for Silva to tear away huge strips of meat from the floundering demon. Silva wasn't interested in eating the meat, but in a matter of moments the foul Goblin King was reduced to nothing more than bloody scraps.

Jenka should have been relieved to see Rikky groan and try to sit up, but he didn't notice. All he could think about was Jade. With everything he had in him he called out to his bond-mate through the ethereal. There was no response for several long moments, but his dragon finally gurgled out a reply. Jade was floating in the sea again. His wing was injured and he was lost. Silva heard the young green and immediately leapt into the air to go find him. Rikky, taken aback that his dragon had left him, managed a foolish grin up at Jenka.

"What of Zah?" Jenka asked. The last he had seen, she and Crystal were lying still as stone north east of the city, ringed by the soldiers they had been ordered to protect.

"I didn't go. I hope she is alive," Rikky sat in the street looking at his one-booted foot for a moment. His whole hairless head was pink and slightly blistered, giving him an alien look. "I decided to stay and help you and Prince Richard. I had sworn to kill this bastard when Master Kember died." He indicated the bloody mess that Silva had made of the Goblin King's body. "I want those antlers," he told a soldier peeking out of a nearby doorway. Then back up to Jenka he continued, "I finally found the courage to do it. It wouldn't matter if I saved Zah and let Mainsted get poisoned anyway." He took a deep breath and decided that he had done well. He hoped Zah was all right. "Do you think Prince Richard and Royal were infected?"

"Undoubtedly," Jenka nodded. "Can you reach out to her? I'm too worried about Jade to concentrate."

"Aye," Rikky nodded and sat himself very still.

After a few moments he shook his head sadly. "Nothing."

"Ssshe isss just unconsciousssss," Crystal whispered out to them across the ethereal. "We will survive thisss."

Jenka and Rikky both let out a long sigh of relief at this.

Later, as the goblins and trolls were being beaten out of the city, Jenka looked up to see his dragon flapping awkwardly through the sky toward the building he was still sitting on top of. In the distance, behind him, was Silva. The silver dragon came from a slightly different direction and was carrying something in her grasp. The sky was relatively clear of mudged. Only a few of them were brave enough to linger. When they saw Jade and Silva in the sky they grew wise and disappeared. Jade landed on the parapet, crumbled some of the mortared stone in his claws, then loomed his head in and started licking Jenka's face as if he were a puppy. His long tail tattooed a rhythm of excitement on the roof, and Jenka couldn't help but enjoy the warm show of affection.

"I'm glad to see you, too," Jenka told his bondmate. "What happened to the nightshade?"

"It livesss," Jade hissed. "It tore my wing and then fled. I sssaw the Royal drop the basket as it glided into the sssea. I dove down to save the prince. He sat on my back and we floated. The poison has infected him. Silva pulled us out and helped me catch air."

"It's Prince Richard," someone yelled from the street below.

"The silver wyrm brought back the crown prin…dear gods, he has been stricken," another yelled. "Some of that goblin dust fell on some other folk and they're all scabbed up, too."

"Stand clear of them," an old woman's voice yelled commandingly. The amber glow of the dragon's tear in her hand gave her the authority she demanded.

Jenka knew it was Mysterian giving the orders, and he limped over to the parapet to look down at the scene.

A wet, limp body, legs still partially-clad in steel plate armor, was lying in the cobbled street. The body was bleeding freshly in places, which made Jenka wonder if Prince Richard was dead or alive. He tried to see if his chest was moving, but all he could tell was that some of the wounds were already starting to scab. Silva carried Rikky up to the rooftop of the building across the lane from the one that Jenka and Jade were on. They, too, looked down at the horrid fate the crown prince had met.

When Mysterian came upon Prince Richard's body she wailed pitifully and fell to her knees in anguish. She held the dragon's tear out, squeezed it in her fist and began casting a spell. This caused her hand to glow so brightly that it revealed the bones inside her hand. When she was done, a bright, lime-green, oval-shaped dome the size of a coffin had encapsulated Prince Richard's form. Then the not-so-old looking Hazeltine Witch fell over into a heap in the street.

The spectators who braved the open tried to close in on the scene, but Silva leaned out over the rooftop and let out a long, slow warning hiss. Prince Richard had died a Dragoneer. He had been one of them. Needless to say, no one came any closer, at least not until dusk, when a contingent of soldiers and a fancy carriage pulled by very tentative horses came rattling upon them.

Linux and King Blanchard came out of the carriage in a rush. Jenka, as well as every person in sight of the scene save Rikky, was surprised when it was the druid who ran to Mysterian's side and tried to grab a hold of the magically cocooned body. "My son," Linux sobbed. "Oh what has happened to you, my son."

Jenka was dumbfounded. He couldn't understand why King Blanchard was looking away as if he were ashamed to be witnessing such a scene.

CHAPTER THIRTY-NINE

Over the next few days, Jenka and the other two Dragoneers spent their time on their wyrms, driving loose bands of the trollkin out from behind the Great Wall. The ogres had congregated out in the frontier eagerly waiting for them. They made short work of the vermin when they came, especially the orcs.

For the Dragoneers, it was rewarding work, to say the least. The three of them worked as a cohesive team and, even though Zahrellion was plagued with debilitating headaches because of her crash, and Rikky had a blistered face and head, they made it safe for the people huddled inside the Great Wall to venture out and restart their lives.

Jenka had learned that Linux had soul-stepped into King Blanchard's body, forcing King Blanchard's essence to inhibit the druid. It wasn't easy to grasp at first, but after seeing them interact with other people, he couldn't deny that it was the truth. King Blanchard seemed passive and withdrawn, while Linux was gruff and rude and trying to drown himself in his cups. Mysterian had sworn him to secrecy about it, but Zahrellion had long since figured it out and had explained it to Rikky. The three of them discussed these things freely when they were out wrangling vermin.

Queen Alvazina's ship arrived. She'd had a time convincing the captain that if he took her back to King's Island, as the king had ordered, her wrath would be far worse than her husband's could ever be. The wise seaman did as she asked and they arrived the evening after the Goblin King had been killed. That was two days ago. The queen had been holed up in the candle-rich alter house where Mysterian had Prince Richard's cocooned body taken.

The king had invited the three Dragoneers to a private meeting in the hall where Prince Richard was being kept. It was to be followed by an open-door celebratory feast in Mainsted's Great Hall this evening. The survivors of the attack on Mainsted were feeling festive enough to forget their sorrow for a time. Jenka didn't like the idea of it, but he would go because Mysterian had asked him to attend. She told him that she had a gift for him. When he asked her about why she had started to look older again she told him, "Some things en't all they're cracked up to be."

Jenka visited Herald the afternoon of what people were starting to call the "Victory Day." The old King's Ranger had a laugh over the fact that Rikky had all the hair, even his eyebrows, burnt from his head. Jenka found it funny that there was a chunk missing from Herald's arse. Neither of them could muster a smile when the subject of Rikky's missing leg came up. Neither of them knew what had happened to Stick or Mortin.

"You really got your arse chewed," Jenka jested, but Herald only scowled at him and explained why Jenka had to attend the functions he thought were so inappropriate.

"The people need heroes, Jenka," Herald told him. "There will be a time of rebuilding now, a better time than before, because the bigger threats of the frontier are gone now." He scratched at his hip, causing Jenka to chuckle over the location of the wound again. "Bah! Listen to me, boy," the King's Ranger went on. "The wolves, the tree-cats, and the goblinkin will always be out there, but we've three Dragoneers to defend us from the wild now.

Don't you see? You, Rikky, and Zahrellion are the defenders of the kingdom now. What good is a King's Ranger when there are Royal Dragoneers about?"

Jenka didn't like it. "Mysterian says that the Time of Confliction is coming, whatever that is. That's why she has been in the books trying to find an antidote to the poison. She says we will need Prince Richard."

"So it's true then?" Herald asked. "Prince Richard is alive? They all have a different story."

"Aye," Jenka nodded. "He is in a stasis. He will not change for the better or the worse until she breaks the spell she put on him. She refused the queen when she wanted the magical cocoon removed. She said that for every poison there is a cure, and she vowed to find it before she would undo what she has done. She won't even undo what Linux did to the king."

"She refused the queen and the king?" Herald cringed. "That blasted witch has got stones." Mysterian had saved his life. He couldn't help but like her. The fact that she wasn't afraid of anyone made him like her even more. She was of his age, or so he guessed. He decided he might try to settle her, though he wasn't sure a witch could be settled.

"What's this gathering before the victory feast?" Herald asked. "I was told that they are going to carry my bed to the temple. You tell them bastards I don't want to be jostled about."

"I'll tell them, Herald, on my way down." Jenka patted the old King's Ranger on the shoulder and left him. He had to get cleaned up for the event, so he headed for the bathhouse. He would ask the launderer to find him some suitable attire. He didn't want to stand before the king and queen in the grime-stained field armor that Linux had bought him.

Jenka found a pair of loose-fitting, black leather pants and a balloon-sleeved white shirt as crisp as parchment lying where his things should have been. There was a velvety-black suede vest that fit over the shirt with the look of a uniform about it. Over the left breast was a strange tri-coiled dragon emblem. Reluctantly, Jenka put it on.

Out where the dragons had been allotted a place to laze in the park, Jenka found Rikky and Zahrellion. Both were wearing exactly the same thing as he. Zahrellion's stark white hair looked clean and well-brushed. Her lavender eyes were held low and she had a sad expression on her face. Rikky still had no hair left, and his head and face were as red as beet juice. He looked irritated and as unhappy about having to attend the formal function as Jenka was.

When Zah saw Jenka, her eyes lit up for a moment, but then her nose wrinkled up as if she wasn't sure she wanted to feel anything at the sight of him.

"They called me a Royal Dragoneer," Rikky said as if it had a nice ring to it.

"Dragoneers we are, but our loyalty can't settle on the kingdom alone," Zahrellion spoke, but with little certainty in her voice. "I mean, we have to face the Confliction, and we may have to do it without a true prince among us. What I've read leads me to believe we might have already lost."

"It isss true," Crystal hissed from beside her bond-mate. "There is supposed to be one with royal blood to lead us into the storm."

"Yesss," Jade agreed. "And another will join usss."

"What is this confliction you keep talking of?" Rikky asked, but before Zahrellion could answer, a very timid soldier came into the park and told them that the king and queen were waiting for them.

The Dragoneers assured their bond-mates that they would return. The dragons decided to go hunt in the fading light of dusk. As their riders were led away, they took to the air. From somewhere nearby, a raucous cheer resounded as the brightly colored wyrms flew north over the city toward the plains. The people seemed to love them. The dragons, Jenka decided, made the people feel safe, just as Herald had suggested.

The private hall that they were led to had been turned into a makeshift temple of sorts. An altar-like podium with the crown prince's magically-cocooned body was at the head of the room. At a long table, below the strange lime glowing coffin-like thing, sat King Blanchard, Linux, and Queen Alvazina. Prince Richard's squire, Roland, was there, as well as Mysterian and another robed man who had his hood pulled so low that his face couldn't be seen. Herald's bed was at the edge of the room under a shelf full of flickering candles, but the King's Ranger was fast asleep.

The Dragoneers were ushered in and seated at the foot of the table. After the servants served them goblets full of sweet honeyed wine, the room was cleared of staff, and the heavy-banded doors were closed and bolted. King Blanchard stood to speak, but Linux waved him down and took the floor. It was a strange scene, because the moment

Linux started speaking it was obvious that it was really the king who was behind the voice.

"My son needs you," he said humbly. "His only chance resides in you. The kingdom needs you as well."

"Please," Queen Alvazina stood. "Please listen to Mysterian. She has found the antidote that will cure Richard…"

"That might cure him," Mysterian cut in. "You may need Richard when the time comes, but he is not the only one of you who has royal blood flowing in his veins. Saving him is important. It is important to me, but we have another storm on the horizon, and just in case the pulp of the scarlet blood cap doesn't cure him we must prepare to face the storm of darkness without him."

"What do you mean," King Blanchard asked from Linux' body. Everyone in the room was looking at her expectantly, save the queen, who was looking at her husband in the druid's body to gauge his reaction.

"Jenka, I lied to you," Mysterian told him in front of everybody. "The seed that kindled you to life wasn't brewed in a kettle pot. The queen, a loyal sister of the Hazeltine, milked the king's seed and your mother was impregnated with it."

"What," Both Jenka and the king asked incredulously, causing Herald to startle awake.

"I'm no prince," Jenka almost shouted. He pointed at the glowing magical cocoon accusingly. "That is the prince. I am a Dragoneer."

Zah couldn't help but smile when he said it.

"Never mind that," Mysterian said harshly as the sound of trumpets could be heard coming from the main hall, where the feasters were gathered. "Squire Roland, give them their gifts. After they accept them we must go give hope to the masses."

"Wait, witch," Jenka started, but the heft of the long bundle Squire Roland handed him made him hold his tongue. The familiar and welcome feel of dragon magic was radiating from what he held. Without further hesitation, he stripped the leather sock cover from the heavy object and realized that it was a sword. Set into the sword's hilt was the tear that Jade's mamra had cried. It had returned to him, just as she told him it would. When he placed his hand on the hilt the rush of the emerald dragon's tear flowed into him again, and from across the ethereal he heard Jade hiss a pleasurable, "Yesss," as the young green dragon felt the power, too.

It was all Jenka could do to contain himself as Dour filled him to brimming, and it became clear to him what he and Jade would soon have to do. They would go after the blood caps that might save Prince Richard.

Rikky marveled at the well-crafted longbow in the sleeve he was handed. He seemed to have little concern with all of the talk of magic and antidotes. He had always been a hunter at heart, and the bow was as fine as any he had ever seen. The arrows were from Herald and were the specially-fletched shafts that Master Kember had used to give the boys when they accomplished one feat or another.

Zah received a staff that had emblems similar to the ones tattooed on her and Linux' head carved into it. She seemed to be feeling some sort of sensation similar to the feeling the tear caused in Jenka. Jenka saw how the hooded man studied her reaction from the depths of his hood. He wondered if the man was Vax Noffa, the great Outland wizard who supposedly decided the fates of men from the shadows with Linux and Mysterian.

"The people await their heroes." Mysterian urged them all away from the table.

Squire Roland stayed behind to tend to Herald, who was already questioning him about what he had slept through. The robed man said something to Mysterian and Linux in the ethereal, but none of the others could make out what it was. Then he disappeared altogether.

Mysterian ushered them all out of the hall, down a long corridor into the overcrowded great hall. There they were received with chants and cheers from the thousands of people crowded in to see them. After that they were introduced.

"I give you King Blanchard, Queen Alvazina, and the Royal Dragoneers," an announcer called out over the din. "Three cheers for the Royal Dragoneers!" he added. The cheers that followed were deafening and, although the celebration was tainted with the sorrow of loss that afflicted them all, it still was a celebration for the ages.

Keep reading for special bonus content:

COLD HEARTED SON OF A WITCH

CHAPTER ONE

Jade was winging with all the strength he could summon and Jenka De Swasso was urging him on. They were a half day's ride by horse outside the wall. They had been chasing stray goblins and trolls away from the road that led from Midwal to Three Forks all day, with Rikky and Silva. For some reason, Rikky and Silva were on the ground, and now Rikky was in trouble. An orc had hold of Silva's tail, and three trolls were hurling rocks and tree-limbs, trying to pummel Rikky from his seat. Jenka didn't know what he and Jade were going to do when they entered the fray, but if they didn't do something, by the looks of it, Rikky was done.

"Yusss," Jade huffed eagerly as he brought them down into a sharp stall over the small clearing full of trolls.

"The orc, Jenka," Rikky yelled from Silva's shoulders. A log came hurling up, end over end, and cracked him across the back. Silva snaked her long neck out and caught the troll's arm. There was an audible "Chomp!" A terrible scream erupted from the troll as the limb was ripped from its body.

Jenka sent Jade a mental command and the young green dragon whipped his tail out. The hard tip snapped with a powerful crack right across the orc's neck. It let go of Silva, but when the wyrm instinctively leapt away, Rikky's unconscious form tumbled from between her spinal plates and thumped awkwardly into the undergrowth.

Jenka saw the area where he went down, but couldn't see him. He urged Jade to land right on top of where he thought Rikky was. As soon as his dragon's claws were on the ground, Jenka was sliding off of his mount. He drew the sword Mysterian had given him. The hum of the power contained in the dragon's tear mounted in its hilt filled Jenka, sharpening his senses. He found Rikky in a crouch trying to string his bow and was amazed that he hadn't died from the impact of the log. A moment later he realized that Rikky was in a daze. The younger Dragoneer wasn't able to manage the weapon in his hands, and he was having trouble sitting up due to his missing leg.

"Rhaahhgg!"

Jenka looked up to see a troll holding a chunk of tree high over its head. The limb was big enough to crush him and Rikky both. Without much thought, Jenka thrust his sword at the thing. There was no resistance when the blade punctured the beast's guts and withdrew, but there was a sharp discharge of Dour magic. The troll died instantly. It started to fall toward them, but the raging orc came shouldering past, knocking it to the side. The orc caught Jenka, pummeling him with a bone-crunching fist to the side of the head.

Not far away, Silva was fighting the remaining two trolls. She wasn't a large dragon, but she was fast. The trellkin had wisely gotten on each side of her and were trying to use position to their advantage. One of them darted in, but she ignored him. Instead, the pewter-colored wyrm spun on the other troll and bathed it in a swath of molten liquid spray. The troll writhed as it crumbled into the brush, its bristly skin stiffening and burning as it went.

Jenka looked up to see the bottom of a claw-toed foot coming down at his face. Above the foot was the snarling visage of the gruesome orc. The flash of memory that passed before his eyes made him think this was the end, but then Jade's thin attempt at a ferocious roar filled his ears.

As the orc's huge foot crunched his nose, Jenka felt the creature's weight come off of his head. He rolled up to see that Rikky finally had his bow strung and Jade was floundering at the edge of the trees. Jade's claws were latched onto the orc's shoulders. Jenka would have laughed, but his dragon looked injured. Jade had snatched the orc from the ground like a hawk grabbing a mouse. Only Jade wasn't strong enough to carry such a load.

Rikky loosed an arrow at the orc. The creature was struggling to break free of Jade's determined claws and somehow managed to deflect the missile.

"Arghh," Rikky growled as he pulled another shaft. With a determined snarl on his face, he rolled across the ground sideways until he was at the orc's side. He loosed the next arrow into its ribs. Then he loosed another that hit it in the neck. The foul-smelling beast continued to struggle, but not for long.

Slowly the orc's strength faded and eventually Jade let go of its shoulders. Jade was wounded, but not terribly so. Silva and the remaining troll were nowhere to be seen.

"Why'd you land?" Jenka asked as he inspected the small rips in his dragon's wing skin. "This will be sore for a while Jade, especially after we fly back to Mainsted."

"Ssores nows," Jade hissed.

"I had to piss," Rikky shrugged. "Prop me against a tree, Jenk. I still gotta go."

Just then Silva came back, flapping down among them. The smears of dark blood at the edges of her maw left no reason to question where the other troll had ended up.

Rikky let Jenka pull him up to a standing position, then hung from his neck and hopped over to the edge of the tree line. "I can't just jump down and take a piss like you can," Rikky told him. "It's nearly impossible for me to climb back on Silva out here."

In Mainsted, Port, and Outwal, Rikky had wheeled chairs waiting, and long ramps to help him get mounted. King Blanchard himself had ordered them to be built.

Jenka looked away while Rikky relieved himself, but continued the conversation. "What are you going to do if you have to go while you're flying over the sea with Zah?"

"What's she gonna do if she has to go?" Rikky chuckled, but Jenka heard little mirth in the laugh. Rikky and Zahrellion were about to take a long flight over the sea to a little-known island where they could find the mushrooms Mysterian needed to save Prince Richard from Gravelbone's poison. Jenka wanted to lead the quest, but Jade was too young and small to carry him that far over water, and now the young green wyrm was wing-wounded. Jenka wasn't sure Jade would be able to carry him back to Mainsted, where the Dragoneers were all soon expected.

"It's something to think about," Jenka observed as he waited for his friend to finish his business. "You'll not be landing anywhere for three or four days."

"Three days flight to the encampment out on Fisherman's Island, then two more to the Island that Mysterian swears is there."

"If she says it's there, it is," Jenka said.

"Then why isn't it on any of the kingdom maps?"

After lacing his pants Rikky hopped back up to Jenka's side. Jenka helped him over to where Silva was inspecting Jade's wounded wings.

"If it were, then it wouldn't be a secret, would it?" Jenka joked. He was pleased to see that Silva had used her natural Dour to somewhat heal Jade's injuries. He helped Rikky climb back onto Silva's shoulders, and then mounted his own wyrm.

"Herald's going to skin us," Rikky said as he urged Silva to leap into the sky.

Jade took two bounding steps before lifting off after them. If we keep King Blanchard and Linux waiting, we won't have to worry about Herald's knife, Jenka said into the ethereal.

I wonder if Zah will be there, Rikky mused.

Jenka almost replied, I hope so, but caught himself. He'd promised Zah that he would keep their moonlit walks a private matter, but nevertheless he hoped she was back from Kingston.

As they passed low over the Midwal gate reconstruction, a few of the men cheered and waved. The two Dragoneers waved back, but kept a steady pace south toward Mainsted. When they passed over Midwal City, the towers sounded the alarm bells, but only until they saw the color of the wyrms and knew they weren't a pair of attacking mudged.

When the city was behind them, Jenka spoke to Rikky through the ethereal again. You should go on ahead and get ready. That way, only one of us gets in trouble.

Nah, nah, Rikky responded. I'll stay with you. It's my fault Jade's wing was torn. Besides, I'll not let you take the blame, not when we're late because you turned back to save my skin.

Master Kember would have been proud, Jenka said, knowing it to be true.

Further conversation ended when they both saw the glittery white scales of Zahrellion's wyrm, Crystal, soaring toward them. Crystal was quite a bit larger than Silva and Jade, but some day Jade would be double the frost dragon's size. Silva, on the other hand, was as big as she would ever be.

Jenka's heart lifted at the sight. Ever since he'd learned that Zah wasn't an Elvish crone, he'd been falling for her. It was only a mild letdown when they found she wasn't riding her dragon. Most likely she was getting ready for the private gathering they'd been ordered to attend. King Blanchard, still trapped in Linux's body after the druid soul-stepped into his, had given the command. Herald and Mysterian were attending, too.

Jenka already knew what was going to be said. The exclusive gathering was to finalize the plans for Zahrellion and Rikky's quest. It would be droll and tedious. Jenka knew he would spend the whole time wishing he were going so that he could save the Crown Prince from the terrible affliction that had him at death's door. Not to mention that if he were going instead of Rikky, he would have a lot more time alone with Zahrellion.

Ssshe huntsss, Jade's voice broke into Jenka's thoughts. It took him a moment to realize his dragon was referring to Crystal.

You can go hunt with her after you let me off in Mainsted, Jenka replied. He suddenly understood that he was going to be the only Dragoneer around while they were gone.

Nos, Jenkas, I will rest my wings and hunts later thiss night, Jade responded, but Jenka was only half listening. He was thinking about how to get Zahrellion alone after the gathering, and what he would tell her. He wanted to tell her a lot of things, but he never seemed to muster the words when the time was right. That, or the time was never right when the words were filling his mouth. Either way, he knew that she and Rikky would be leaving soon. He didn't want her to go without knowing how he felt about her.

"The King's Ranger caravan!" Rikky called out over the rushing wind. When Jenka's eyes found him, Rikky was pointing ahead to the not-so-distant brown smudge hovering over the ground that marked Mainsted. Another cloud could be seen in the near distance. A sizable train of a dozen wagons and a score of horses was moving north across the dusty road.

Rikky slapped at the stump of his missing leg, indicating that it would slow him down once he was on the ground, then he urged Silva to speed ahead. Silva was fast. Soon all Jenka could see was a crow-sized speck in the sky.

Jenka tried to clear his mind of Zah and her leaving, but couldn't manage it. For a long time he envisioned the two of them making a home in the foothills, far away from all the madness of the kingdom. Then he thought of Prince Richard lying cocooned in the stasis that was keeping him from death. He let out a sigh of frustrated resignation. Prince Richard had saved Mainsted, and Jenka had long sworn to save the prince in return. As Jade brought them down over the city, Jenka found that he wanted to go on the quest with Zahrellion and Rikky, now more than ever.

CHAPTER TWO

"I don't give a pixie's pecker-head," growled Herald. Normally disheveled, and covered in road grime, the old King's Ranger had just come from the bath house and looked as spiffy as Jenka had ever seen him. "You're going north to help what's left of the King's Rangers reestablish Crag and the keep. That girl can handle her own. And she'll have Rikky to help her."

It was clear to Jenka that Herald wasn't willing to listen. It was a futile argument anyway. The two of them were the only ones on time for the gathering and they were standing before the lightly glowing cocoon of magic that contained Prince Richard.

The Crown Prince lay peacefully, as if asleep, inside the currently green-colored magical field. He was afflicted with the Goblin King's poison, a terrible stuff that had maddened and then slowly corroded from the inside out anyone who'd breathed it. If the stasis failed before an antidote was concocted, he would surely die. Jenka knew Herald was right about what had to be done, but that didn't relieve the urge Jenka was feeling to just ignore common sense and keep his word by saving his fellow Dragoneer.

The Dragoneers' Lair, as the hall was now called, was an intensely morbid place. Queen Alvazina was often found there arguing with her husband or weeping over her son's body. Like Mysterian, she was a witch of the Hazeltine, and she fully understood the magnitude of the situation. She knew Richard's life hung in the balance, and that there was no certainty about the antidotal potion Mysterian hoped to brew. Her sorrow seemed to sap the hope out of some of the others, thus the hall was sometimes the quietest place in Mainsted.

Unlike everyone else, Jenka found inspiration in the Dragoneers' Lair. The hum of the magical field that was sustaining his peer was the same sort of power that filled him when he concentrated on his dragon tear or held his sword. To Jenka, the mere presence of Dour was hope incarnate. Without it, Richard would be dead. So would most of the people in the city. When the lair was empty, Jenka often meditated in the hall, working the calling spell Zahrellion had taught him, and practicing the Dourcraft he was learning from both Linux and Mysterian. Rikky didn't seem to find the place objectionable, and sometimes joined him. Rikky read texts about anatomy there, but spent most of his time studying with the healers when the dragons were resting.

Herald was wearing his official King's Ranger uniform, a new one to replace the filthy set with the hole in the rear. This outfit was too big for him. Jenka was wearing the armor vest emblazoned with the Dragoneer emblem that had been gifted to all of them by the Crown, and his favorite calfskin britches. Standing there, trying to remain calm, he was a confused well of conflicting emotion. The only thought that lessened his frustration was what Mysterian put into his head when she greeted him at the landing in the dragon bailey earlier.

"What if Zahrellion and Rikky fail?" the old gray-haired Hazeltine witch asked with a clever gleam in her eyes. "You swore to see it through, De Swasso. If they fetch my caps, then your word will stay true. Besides that, there are concerns beyond Prince Richard, as you know. The Confliction is drawing nearer. All of the Hazeltine can sense it.

It's like a pesky insect buzzing around inside my skull.

"Never mind that now, though. If Rikky and Zahrellion fail in their quest, then you and Jade will have to make an attempt. By staying behind, you are strengthening the commitment of your promise."

Jenka decided that maybe she'd spelled him, because her words almost made sense. She and Herald were of a mind—and a bed—as of late, and with Mysterian's hold over King Blanchard and Linux, Jenka didn't stand a chance of changing any of their minds.

The King's Rangers needed Jade's might, that was certain, and Lemmy was still up there in the foothills looking over the survivors at Kingsmen's Keep. Jenka wanted to see what was left of his home and visit his mother's grave, if she even had one yet. It was true that Zahrellion could handle herself, and if she and Rikky got into a fix, Silva could fly back as fast as lightning to get help.

Jenka shook his head. "So be it, Herald, but I'm not leaving to catch the caravan on the morrow. I'm staying here until Rikky and Zah set out. I can meet the rangers before they get to Demon's Lake."

"You were set upon by orcs just outside the wall today, lad. Are you mad?" The old ranger had lost a melon-sized chunk of his arse to a goblin's maw. Apparently the wound itched all the time, for he scratched at it constantly.

Over the weeks that had passed since the battle over Mainsted, he'd lost a lot of weight. He looked to have aged a handful of years in that span, too. His growl told Jenka that he was wrong.

"You'll be leaving on the morrow, boy. You can hurry the bastards from Midwal to Three Forks where they'll be safe for a few days. If you don't dink around you might make it back in time to see yer fellow Dragoneers off, but after that you'll be escorting us all the way to Kingsmen's Keep."

"You said us." Jenka felt a spark of hope. Traveling with Herald was seldom dull. "You're going too?"

"If I can shake that witch I am," he had to whisper the last few words because 'that witch' and the other two Dragoneers were quickly approaching.

Rikky's chair made a rhythmic creaking as he rolled himself across the tiled floor. The sound filled the sudden silence.

Even before she was in the light thrown by the ensconced torches on the blocked stone walls, Jenka could see Zah's lavender eyes. Her stark white hair hung in neat, wetly combed strands, the ends splaying over the shoulders of her emblazoned armor vest. The silver triangle tattooed on her forehead glowed amber with the reflection of the torch flames. The thin lines across the bridge of her nose and the square and circle designs on her cheeks were barely visible.

Jenka was so taken with her exotic beauty that he just stood there and looked at her until Mysterian whacked him on the shin with her cane. "I see you've not been pondering my reasoning," the old gray-haired witch cackled sarcastically. Then to Herald, she said, "I'd bet the makings of my most sought-after curse that King Blanchard tries to get me to undo him and Linux this night." She cackled again. "Sooner or later I'll do it, but it won't be today."

Just then a side door opened and Linux, in King Blanchard's bulky body, stepped into the lair. "It needs to be soon, witch," Linux said in the king's voice. "The way his Highness abuses my core, it won't be fit to inhabit before long."

"You should have thought about that before you soul-stepped him, then," she retorted.

Linux stopped and took a deep, calming breath before nodding a greeting to the others.

Jenka shivered, thinking what it must be like to be trapped in another man's body. It was even stranger being around King Blanchard. He was still the boisterous, often drunk, monarch of the realm. But more than just being trapped in the druid's body, it was clear he hated having to act the part of the druid in public. No one but the Dragoneers, and a handful of others, knew about the switch.

As if he'd been reading Jenka's thoughts, King Blanchard came bursting in through the main entry. "I don't care what you do with the man, dear. Just get it done." He was talking to Queen Alvazina as a husband speaks to his wife, but it was Linux's body having the conversation.

Jenka had to shake his head.

"Watch it," the queen scowled at her husband. He scowled back at her, then motioned for Herald to take a seat at the long, oak table board. The queen paused in front of her son's impotent form and sniffled a few times. But then, with a huff, she gathered herself and joined the table.

Jenka grinned knowingly when Zah eased past him. She smiled a smile that only he could see and he was lifted by it. Rikky looked up and rolled his eyes. King Blanchard spoke to Linux and Mysterian for a moment. A short, snapping argument of hissed whispers ensued, after which both men skulked to the table with their heads hung low. Herald chuckled. Jenka could have told them that Mysterian wasn't going to listen. She and the Outland wizard, Vax Noffa, were the only two people alive that could undo their predicament. She wasn't ready to do so yet, and it was said that finding a coin at the bottom of the sea was easier than finding Vax Noffa.

Zah smiled at Jenka brightly. She was patting the cushion, indicating that she wanted him to sit there beside her, instead of across the table where he normally sat. He took the place, and under the table squeezed her hand. She squeezed his back, but the sharpness of the gesture worried him. He didn't have time to question his concern because Linux was already tapping a long pointer on the map that had been unfurled before them. In the king's voice, but with a precise articulation that didn't belong to the huge body, the druid commanded the room's attention.

"You'll see that the destination island has been added to this map, here." Linux tapped a thumb-sized horseshoe-shaped blot of ink that was darker than the markings on the rest of the map. It was a long way east from Fisherman's Isle, which was a longer way south from Gull's Reach. "It has been written, by early explorers and ship captains, that the serpent who claims the bay of this atoll is a stupid creature. The last herb-gathering expedition succeeded by landing on the outer shore and then hiking overland to the island's interior. Then, on the cusp of morning, they combed the beaches and gathered the precious mushrooms we seek."

"Why don't we just buy some from them?" Rikky asked.

"That was sixty years ago, boy!" the king bellowed with Linux's not-so-heavy voice. "Listen."

Jenka couldn't tell if Rikky's expression was a smirk or a cringe. Zahrellion gave the boy a look that showed her distaste over his interruption. Rikky rolled his eyes and shrugged.

"Them folks were lucky," said Mysterian. "The witches say that the coral wyrm feeds at night, then it slithers across the beach polishing its scales on the sand." Herald nudged her with an elbow and made a face, but then shrugged at the others. "It leaves its scat just above the tide line," she continued. "That's where the mushrooms grow."

"You need mushrooms that grow in serpent refuse to save my son?" King Blanchard asked incredulously.

"Moonlit," his wife corrected. "Only the mushrooms that form under a full moon will be potent enough to pull the poison out of our Richard."

"So what we need only grows in moonlit serpent shit?" Rikky asked with a chuckle.

Zahrellion let go of Jenka's hand and grabbed Rikky by the ear. Jenka hadn't known about the coral serpent. He would have worried about it more if he weren't enjoying seeing Rikky squirm under Zah's sharp twist. He decided it wasn't a concern or more would have been said about it. He'd seen Zahrellion nearly blast a huge fire wyrm out of the sky with her druidic magic. He had no doubt she could handle a stupid, overgrown sea snake. Still, the added danger gave him more to think about than his emotions.

"If you have to stay any length of time on the island," Linux went on. "You should stay on the ocean side of the land. That coral beast destroyed an unprepared exploratory ship back when the Expansion first began. You might be able to see its remains out in the bay."

"Why would we have to stay?" Rikky asked.

"You have to harvest the caps under the light of a full moon," Mysterian repeated the queen's statement. "Zahrellion and I have been over it."

Rikky didn't like being dismissed that way, but since Mysterian was a real witch of the Hazeltine, he didn't dare argue. Jenka understood his young friend's concern. He also knew Rikky was far more capable than any of them gave him credit for. Rikky was the best of them as far as Jenka was concerned.

"The first caravan of King's Rangers left here this morning. They will be at Midwal soon and then continue out into the frontier. Jenka, you will be flying guard over them when they move beyond the barrier midday tomorrow. You will stay with them until they reach Three Forks, then you will return to escort Commander Herald's smaller party north from here."

"Commander Herald's party?" Mysterian asked. "What's this, Herald?"

"I'm needed at Kingsmen's Keep," he shrugged innocently.

"We will speak of this later," she scolded, but a tiny bit of hurt showed through her angry visage.

Not enough to keep her from turning her gaze on Rikky. "You'll keep your peg-leg on, Rikky Camille. I heard about what happened today."

Mysterian then turned and started in on Herald about his leaving. Jenka watched as Zahrellion demanded a whispered explanation from Rikky. Soon the map was rolled and the table loaded with honeyed pork and game hens. Before they began the meal, Queen Alvazina stood and thanked everyone for their commitment to saving the Crown Prince. She looked at Linux's body when she said, "…and I speak for my husband when I say that no matter the outcome of your quest, your efforts will never be forgotten."

Zahrellion asked Jenka to meet her later at the usual place, so his distaste over the way of things between the king and the druid was soon washed away with eager hope. Underneath that feeling, though, was the ache of knowing that he would have to spend a long while without either of his two companions.

After dinner most everyone excused themselves from the Lair. Rikky rolled over to Jenka's side. "I have to go work on the portable chair Linux devised for me."

"Will it roll in sand?" Jenka asked.

"Doubtful," Linux said as he joined them.

Jenka looked up at King Blanchard's face. "Herald said you needed to see me?"

"While you are in the foothills, would you find Lemmy and take him to the Temple of Dou? There are drawings that I saw in an old journal written by a woman who claimed to have befriended an orphaned dragon." Linux hated to lie to Jenka about the importance of that journal, but he saw no other option at the moment. Stuck in fat King Blanchard's body, he couldn't return to the temple himself. His vile brother Lanxe would make a mockery of him. "I remember one of them showed the makings of a clever riding saddle. I originally dismissed it as some raver's scratch, but now, after working with Rikky and Silva, I think that the design may have merit. I'll send a missive for Lem explaining where in the Librarium to find the volume, and what I want him to copy for us."

"I told Linux how you fell into the wall that one time," Rikky grinned.

Jenka laughed, remembering how Jade had saved him from that impact with Dour magic. "Sure, Linux, we need saddles. I have questions for Lemmy anyway. I'll do it."

"Am I not the fargin king? Isn't the proper response, 'I'll gladly do it, Your Majesty?' " Linux did a perfect imitation of King Blanchard's voice and manner to go along with the body he wore. This caused a laugh that lightened the mood.

Jenka used the awkward moment to excuse himself so that he could get ready to go meet Zahrellion.

CHAPTER THREE

Like the Dragoneers, the dragons were treated well in Mainsted. A large open area, once a park, had been dubbed the dragon bailey. It was set aside for the coming and going of dragons. There were three shifts of attendants to take care of the wyrms' every need. A whole troop of hunters worked to keep fresh meat available. But at night the area was devoid of people.

Out beyond the wavering light of the night fires, there was a pond with stone benches lined around its overgrown shore. Jenka found Zahrellion sitting at one of them. She was fidgeting and looked anxious. He was nervous too, and her manner only made him feel less sure of himself. The words of love and commitment he had been about to spill formed into a knot just behind his sternum.

As he stood there afraid to say what was on his mind, the sound of the cicadas and a low-groaning bullfrog's repetitious call filled the moonlit silence. To his surprise Zah saved him by stepping up and mashing her mouth against his. The kiss they shared was long and deep. Only after Jenka's hands cupped her body a little too eagerly did she push away. "No, Jenka." She wasn't harsh, but understanding. "When we get back, after Prince Richard is well, maybe then we can think about ourselves."

The fact that the Crown Prince had just been inserted into the moment sent a flash of jealousy through Jenka. He had to struggle to overcome it. "I'm not thinking about myself," he pulled her back to him and whispered into her neck.

She gave in to the feel of his hot mouth on that place behind her ear, but only for a moment. "Jenka, I love you," she said. "And I know you love me, but we are Royal Dragoneers."

Jenka was too stunned by her words to respond. Her tone had been almost sisterly when she spoke. It was enough that the elation of hearing her say she loved him was set aside for the moment.

"Sit." She patted the bench as she resumed her seat. "We are leaving on the morrow, just after you."

That statement registered in his mind. "What? You can't be. Why?"

"It is three days from Gull's Reach to Fisherman's Isle, not from here." She shrugged as if she might change it if she could. "If we start from Gull's Reach in the next few days we'll be able to make the island during the coming full moon. If we dally any longer we will have to wait until the next."

He let the bad news sink in and then the contained feelings over hearing her words burst forth. "You really love me?" He took her hands in his. Her liquid lavender eyes said she did.

She didn't answer with words. Instead she leaned into him and pressed her head against his. Jenka felt the shape of the tattoo on her forehead. It was like a triangular piece of ice. "Yes I do," she said, before giving him a quick brush of her lips. "Rikky and I will be back soon enough." And with that she hurried away.

Jenka heard her sniffle and could feel the wetness from the tears she'd cried on his cheek, but the strange icy feeling that was still chilling his dome was the sensation that kept him from going after her. His mind was numb, and now he was more confused than ever.

The memory of when he and Master Kember first met Zahrellion up in the Orich Mountains flashed through his mind. “Fargin women’ll twist your thinker till it pops,” the man had said.

Jenka couldn’t agree more.

* * *

Zahrellion was sick to her stomach. She’d just done something she didn’t want to do. Jenka loved her, and she knew she loved him too. She also knew that it could never be. They were Dragoneers, not villagers. They would never be able to share what lovers have. She’d intended to make that clearer this night, but instead she’d left him thinking that when she and Rikky returned, if they returned, she wanted the romance to continue. She could only hope that the time apart would distance his feelings. She had more than she could handle ahead of her.

Rikky was a responsibility she wasn’t sure she was ready for. His disability wasn’t really the issue, it was his age. Since the troop of men she was supposed to be guarding had been killed by the swarming goblin kin, she’d been overly committed to her duty as a Royal Dragoneer. But she was afraid to be responsible for others. That’s why she volunteered to continually fly messages from the mainland to the islands. She could do that alone. Saying that Crystal needed the flying time to get ready for the quest was no more than a pretense. Crystal could fly from Mainsted to the serpent's island with ease. She was taking Rikky because it was the king's order for her to do so, but she also knew that the plan was sound, and that resting on Fisherman's Isle was smart. It was also smart to have Rikky there to guard the sky while she was gathering the mushrooms they needed. Still, she would have rather been going it alone on the quest, especially after Rikky had brought up at dinner the embarrassing subject of relieving oneself while flying oversea on a dragon's back.

She forced Jenka out of her mind and let her cheeks dry in the cooling autumn air. There were things about the coral serpent that only she, Mysterian, and Linux had discussed. The creature's venom was supposed to be deadly poisonous. It was ejected through its long, spiraled horn. The captain's log of an early exploring vessel described seeing the long, eel-like creature leap skyward to great heights as it tried to spear low-flying sea dactyls in the bay. Zah planned on telling Rikky all of this after they were well on their way. She wanted to tell him now, but Herald and Linux had forbidden it.

The secrecy was to keep Jenka from going off like a half-cocked crossbow, as they all knew he would. If he found out how truly dangerous the creature was, Zahrellion knew Jenka would go as much to keep her from having to face the danger as he would to save the prince. He was selfless, and that's one of the reasons she loved him so much. Arghh! Stop it! She told herself.

Ssstops whatss? Crystal responded in her mind.

Nothing, to worry about, friend, Zahrellion answered. Rest yourself. Before the morrow breaks we leave on our quest.

Yessssss, Crystal hissed. The excited sound sent shivers down Zahrellion's spine. By the time she recovered, Jenka was far from her thoughts. She needed to check the packs and the rigging, as well as make sure Rikky's special equipment was ready. She also needed to rest, though she slept quite well when Crystal was flying, so it wasn't a priority. She decided that they wouldn't wait for dawn. If they left early enough, they could make Gull's Reach by midnight next. They could rest the dragons there and gain a day in their race against the coming full moon.

If she could have stood to be in the room with Linux, she might have gone and helped Rikky finish his rig. She decided to send a message runner instead. Linux was mad. The Order of Dou, she had learned, was less a devout sect and more a cruel bunch of experimenting scholars with few scruples. All of it irritated her. She still prayed to the essence of Dou, and her druidic magic still obeyed her when she commanded it. But she was a Royal Dragoneer now, and all of those ways had to be behind her. Just like her love for Jenka, she had to let it go.

* * *

Jenka didn't sleep well, but he was up at the crack of dawn eating gruel with Herald and the men who attended the dragons. Jenka was almost as hurt as he was angry at Zah. She and Rikky had left before dawn. He didn't even get the chance to say goodbye.

He was disappointed in Rikky. He imagined that the boy was so excited that he just forgot to tell him. Still, it hurt Jenka's feelings that they left the way they did. He had half a mind to go off after them, to tell them what he thought of their departure.

"They be gone, boy," Herald said in an understanding way. "Now that you ain't gotta come back to see 'em off, you can get them rangers all the way up to the keep straight through. When you know they're safe, come back to Three Forks and fly guard over my group."

"I have to take Lemmy to the druids' temple, and more importantly to me, I have to make sure my mother is resting properly." Jenka's emotion showed in his narrow-browed scowl. "I will try to do what you need, Herald, but I wasn't born in this kingdom. I don't owe it my service."

"Your father were to hear that he'd crack the—"

"My father is the king, or weren't you paying attention?" Jenka's words silenced the old ranger. Jenka shooed the other men out of the little kitchen. His expression made clear that they were not to speak of what they'd just heard.

"Jericho De Swasso wasn't my father, Herald," Jenka went on after they'd gone. Jenka didn't mean to be so harsh with him. Herald was a good man, and didn't deserve to be talked to in such a manner, but it was done. "If Prince Richard doesn't recover, then I am the Crown Prince. I don't want anything to do with it. I am a Dragoneer."

Jenka took another deep breath and exhaled some of his frustration. With a sarcastic smile he added, "Keep my lineage in mind as you order me about, old friend." With that he whirled off to find Jade so they could go escort the King's Ranger caravan across the frontier to Kingsmen's Keep.

Other titles by M. R. Mathias

The Dragoneer Saga
The First Dragoneer – Free
The Royal Dragoneers – Nominated, Locus Poll 2011
Cold Hearted Son of a Witch
The Confliction
The Emerald Rider
Rise of the Dragon King
Blood and Royalty – Winner, 2015 Readers Favorite Award,
and 2015 Kindle Book Award Semifinalist

The Legend of Vanx Malic
Book One – Through the Wildwood
Book Two – Dragon Isle
Foxwise (a short story) - Free
Book Three – Saint Elm's Deep
Book Four – That Frigid Fargin' Witch
Book Five – Trigon Daze
Book Six – Paragon Dracus
Book Seven – The Far Side of Creation
Book Eight – The Long Journey Home
Collection -To Kill a Witch – Books I-IV w/bonus content

Collection –The Legend Grows Stronger – Books V-VIII
Book Nine – The Tome of Arbor
Book Ten – A Gossamer Lens

And don't miss the huge International Bestselling epic:
The Wardstone Trilogy
Book One - The Sword and the Dragon
Book Two - Kings, Queens, Heroes, & Fools
Book Three - The Wizard & the Warlord

Short Stories:
Crimzon & Clover I - Orphaned Dragon, Lucky Girl
Crimzon & Clover II - The Tricky Wizard
Crimzon & Clover III - The Grog
Crimzon & Clover IV - The Wrath of Crimzon
Crimzon & Clover V - Killer of Giants

Crimzon & Clover Collection One (stories 1-5)

Crimzon & Clover VI – One Bad Bitch
Crimzon &Clover VII – The Fortune's Fortune
Master Zarvin's Action and Adventure Series #1
Dingo the Dragon Slayer

Master Zarvin's Action and Adventure Series #2
Oonzil the oathbreaker
Master Zarvin's Action and Adventure Series #3
The Greatest Quest

Crimzon and Clover I-X

ABOUT THE AUTHOR

There are few writers in the genre of fantasy that can equal the creative mind of M.R. Mathias – now acknowledged as a master in this genre of dragons and dwarves, and magic, and spells, and all aspects of fantasy.—Top 100, Hall of Fame, Vine Voice, Book Reviewer, Grady Harp

M. R. Mathias is the multiple award winning author of the huge, #1 Bestselling, epic, The Wardstone Trilogy, as well as the #1 Bestselling Dragoneer Saga, the #1 Bestselling The Legend of Vanx Malic fantasy adventure series, and the #1 Bestselling Crimzon & Clover Short Short Series.

You can find M. R. Mathias at DragonCon every year. Just look for the #Wardstone Dragon Car. Book signings, and booth appearances will be listed in advance, on the blog.

Use these series hashtags on twitter to find maps, cover art, sales, giveaways, book reviews, upcoming releases, and contest information:

#Wardstone – #DragoneerSaga – #VanxMalic – #MRMathias

To hear about new releases, sales and giveaways,
follow M. R. Mathias here:
www.mrmathias.com
or
@DahgMahn on Twitter and FaceBook

16248361R10350

Printed in Poland
by Amazon Fulfillment
Poland Sp. z o.o., Wrocław